The rebel earl did not stir.

Nothing broke the ominous silence as he continued to hold her with his powerful gaze, refusing to release her.

This was a declaration of war! There would be no more game playing, no more trifling and laughing at her expense. The gravity of the O'Carroll and his desperate-looking men told Regan that.

Regan was more frightened than she had ever been, but she would not leave Ireland. Wrapping her cloak more tightly about her, she cast Connor O'Carroll one last contemptuous look and set off swiftly towards Heaven's Gate.

As her foot pressed still harder into the side of her mare, the O'Carroll and his men preserved the formal, ritualistic silence of their sudden appearance. Her supposition had been true! War had been declared. The next time she saw the man, blood would be spilled. Regan knew it with a certainty.

Dear Reader,

This month we are happy to bring you *Rogue's Honor,* a new book from DeLoras Scott. Those of you who have followed DeLoras's career since her first book, *Bittersweet,* will be delighted by this tale of the Oklahoma land rush and of partners each with their own dark pasts.

With *Heaven's Gate,* the writing team of Erin Yorke has created the dramatic story of a wayward English countess and the renegade Irish lord who is determined to force her surrender.

Lindsay McKenna's *King of Swords* is a sequel to her January title, *Lord of Shadowhawk.* Abducted and held for ransom, Thorne Somerset learns to love the bitter soldier who holds her fate in his hands.

A fugitive Union officer and a troubled Rebel girl overcome seemingly insurmountable odds to find happiness in *The Prisoner.* Set at the close of the Civil War, this tender story is the first historical by popular contemporary author Cheryl Reavis.

Next month look for titles by Maura Seger, Julie Tetel, Lucy Elliot and Elizabeth August from Harlequin Historicals, and rediscover the romance of the past.

Sincerely,

The Editors

Heaven's Gate
Erin Yorke

Harlequin Books

TORONTO • NEW YORK • LONDON
AMSTERDAM • PARIS • SYDNEY • HAMBURG
STOCKHOLM • ATHENS • TOKYO • MILAN
MADRID • WARSAW • BUDAPEST • AUCKLAND

Harlequin Historicals first edition May 1992

ISBN 0-373-28724-0

HEAVEN'S GATE

Printed in the U.S.A.

Books by Erin Yorke

Harlequin Historicals

An American Beauty #58
Forever Defiant #94
Heaven's Gate #124

ERIN YORKE

is the pseudonym used by the writing team of Christine Healy and Susan Yansick. One half of the team is single, fancy-free and countrified, and the other is married, the mother of two sons and suburban, but they find that their differing lives and styles enrich their writing with a broader perspective.

For Kathy Krieg,
the aunt who gave me my first opportunity to tell
stories, and who still continues to listen today.

And for my father, Peter McGovern,
my brother, Francis McGovern,
and all those who eased their way, and, of course,
for George, who made my way so much easier.

Chapter One

The English court, 1567

"Leave? But you can't mean that!" Regan was so dismayed at the queen's directive that she neglected to guard her tongue in the royal presence, but the disapproving murmurs of the courtiers in attendance quickly recalled her to her senses.

Though her heart might be fractured at the possibility of being sent from the court of Elizabeth I, Regan Davies was no one's fool. Dropping gracefully into an obsequious curtsy, the young noblewoman hid her clenched fists and dampened palms in the folds of her elaborate skirt, raised her head ever so slightly and sought the sovereign's pardon.

"Please excuse my intemperate speech, your majesty, but I fear I did not hear you correctly."

"You may rise, child, though I'm afraid it will not improve your hearing," said Elizabeth tartly. Glancing at Sir Robert Dudley to measure his reaction to the girl's dismissal, the queen saw no special concern . . . but then, Robert was usually quite circumspect in his affairs. Returning her gaze to the comely eighteen-year-old now standing demurely before her, Elizabeth permitted herself a small smile of satisfaction. "Make no mistake, Lady Regan. You will depart the palace for Ireland on the morrow. I have spoken."

"If I have done anything that offends your majesty, please tell me, and I will correct it—" Regan prayed against all hope that this was not the case, but one couldn't really be certain. The queen had spies everywhere. Lord, let the woman know nothing, she implored silently...though she might suspect. Dudley seemed frightfully calm, reflected an increasingly distraught and irritated Regan; couldn't he show the least bit of emotion instead of chatting so nonchalantly with the musicians? It was all his fault that she was in this predicament!

"Now then, my dear girl, whatever might be on your mind?" baited Elizabeth, watching the blonde's color heighten at the question. "A lovely young woman of proper upbringing such as yourself could do nothing but bring beauty, charm, and refreshing whimsy to my court, and, undoubtedly when I am otherwise engaged, countless hours of amusement to my courtiers. I can't imagine that you would repay my kindness to your father by doing me ill... No, I merely wish to see that you receive what you deserve, Lady Regan—possession of those lands in Ireland I had promised to your father in recognition of his loyalty so many years ago."

"But I could never be truly happy unless I were here serving your majesty," assured Regan softly, somehow finding the courage to meet the queen's eyes. If she only sounded sincere enough, perchance...

"If your truest wish is to serve the Crown, then you will do so by assuming responsibility for your property in Ireland," Elizabeth stated firmly. "Should you refuse to do as I command, you will find your lodging and sustenance elsewhere. In either case, you will leave my court tomorrow."

"I know nothing of Ireland," protested the queen's ward.

"You are your father's only heir, Lady Regan, and *he* ·oked on the settlement of these lands as a unique oppor- ιnity to please his monarch and increase the influence of ιe Crown," said Elizabeth, gesturing to Dudley to rejoin ·r. "You are now being offered the possibility of restoring ιe wealth unjustly wrested from your family twenty-odd ·ars ago when Sir William spoke out on my mother's be- alf though all others condemned her. I should think that ·u would welcome the chance to fulfill your father's dream ιd one day return to this court triumphant as mistress of a vilized bastion of England amid that heathen island to the ·rth."

"Then I may return?" asked Regan breathlessly. Per- ιps things were not as bad as she feared. If she could come ιck in a few months, the leaving might be more easily tol- ated.

"Why, of course you may," assured the red-haired sov- ·eign. "As soon as the Davies' plantation is rightfully es- blished and the tenants properly quartered and pledged to ιe fealty of this court, we should be most happy to wel- ·me you back." Fortunately, considered the queen to her- ·lf, that would undoubtedly take years, given the tem- ·rament of her Irish subjects. "In the meantime, I've sent ·r your father's lieutenant, Gerard Langston. I am ar- ·nging for him to be your guardian away from court, and ·y exchequer will give him a purse, a small one, mind you, · assist in your resettlement."

"Thank you, your majesty," said Regan as she curtsied, ·xious now to be excused from the royal presence.

"I wish you Godspeed, my child. May your journey be uitful for you, and for England," offered Elizabeth gra- ·ously. "Sir Robert, come sit by me whilst the musicians lay. I am ready to be amused."

Having paced among the meticulously manicured paths f the palace gardens for over an hour before she realized that no one was apt to join her, Regan was in a rare mood indeed when she headed back indoors. As she threw open the door to her rooms, she muttered to herself, unable to decide whether she was more angry with Dudley or the queen.

"An unfair world this is! Just because *she* wants to be amused, the rest of us are expected to interrupt our plans and do *her* bidding. He was supposed to meet *me!* What gives her the right to order people around and change their whole lives just because *she* wants her way?"

"The fact that *she* is the sovereign ruler of England might have something to do with her presumption to authority," remarked a gravel-toned voice from the shadows of the dimly lit room. "I would have expected you to understand that."

"Now you sound just like Father, Gerard," snapped the cranky young woman as she shook her hair free from its protective restraint and ran her fingers through the long blond tresses, wishing she could rid herself of all life's restrictions so easily.

"And well I should, since I am the closest thing you have to family," chided Gerard Langston, thumping his empty cup down on the wooden table and reaching for the nearby bottle. "Suppose you tell me just what mischief you've been up to that I receive a royal summons to come at once and fetch you off to Ireland."

"I've done nothing untoward," protested Regan, fingering a miniature of Dudley that was always close to her heart regardless of where he chose to be. "Her majesty wants Father's land settled in her name, that's all."

"Were that the case, Regan, haste would not be such a priority that our universally frugal monarch would furnish you with a purse, no matter how meager. What have you done to anger her?"

"If I'd angered her majesty, would she be paying me to leave?"

"Mayhap. I know her not well enough to guess. What have you done of late?" pressed her late father's most trusted man.

"Nothing, really! Elizabeth doesn't like me because I'm younger and prettier than she ever was, that's all there is to the matter," sniffed the girl, moving behind the modesty screen and beginning to disrobe. Wasn't it bad enough that the queen had banished her and Dudley seemed to care not? Did she have to tolerate an old man's lectures, as well?

"Were that the case, Regan, you would have been packed off within a week of your arrival at court, not six months later," disputed her visitor dryly. "I might remind you, my dear lady, you're not too big to be turned over my knee if that's what it takes to hear the truth."

"You have threatened me with that since I was an infant."

"Aye, and the time you borrowed Lady Morgan's prize stallion for the afternoon, I made good on the threats, with your father's permission, of course . . . or have you forgotten?"

"I never regretted my actions for a minute, Gerard. That poor animal was never given a proper ride. He was pampered and fussed over, but never exercised to his limits. Gerard, you'll never know the joy we shared together, galloping over the fields, jumping streams, reaching higher and higher till . . . I mean, until you caught up with us, that is. Anyway, a person like Lady Morgan doesn't deserve such a splendid creature if she can't satisfy its needs," Regan finished defiantly, praying Gerard hadn't noticed that she'd been speaking of more than a horseback ride.

"Good Lord in heaven . . . that's it, isn't it?" All of a sudden, Gerard was around the screen, confronting a half-clad Regan as she stood blushing before him. Wearing only her farthingale and bodice, she shivered when she saw the outrage in her guardian's eyes. "You bloody fool, you bedded one of Elizabeth's dandies, didn't you?'' he demanded angrily, looking almost as though he might strike her.

"No, it wasn't like that. He cares for me, I know he does. Ever since I came to court, he's been kind to me, including me in outings, engaging me in conversation, seeking me out as a dance partner, even bringing me marchpane or sweetmeats—"

"And yours were the sweetest meats he'd ever had, I'll warrant,'' Sir William Davies' friend snorted in disgust. "Heaven protect us from innocent maidens! Child, didn't anyone teach you better than to fall for every popinjay's attentions?''

"He's not a popinjay, and he loves me!''

"Yes, and I'm the son of Henry VIII!'' mocked Gerard, more angry at himself for not anticipating the dangers of Elizabeth's court when he urged William to permit his daughter to attend the queen. "Has no one ever explained the ways of men to you?''

"Just exactly whom did you have in mind Gerard? Father? Hardly! He enjoyed the favors of any female within arm's reach when it suited him. And you?'' Regan had had enough grief for one day and would no longer hold her peace; it was her heart speaking its loneliness now, and each word cut like a dagger through Gerard's indignation. "You never so much as recognized that I belonged to the fairer sex, with your teaching me to hunt and shoot like a man. Tell me now, who's to blame?''

The man before her looked shaken as she waited for his reply, but he made none. Instead he opened his arms as though to enfold her in his embrace, but Regan was not ready to be comforted and moved farther away from him.

"Elizabeth said I was to be my father's heir and be accorded the privileges of a male. Then what's so wrong with my taking a lover...except that the man in question belongs to her?'' Fury coursing through Regan's veins heightened her color and her eyes sparked a bewitching green, visibly demonstrating to Gerard just how beautiful and how clearly vulnerable his charge was. He doubted any man could protect Regan from her headstrong impulses, least of all a man as tradition bound as he was.

Shaking his head at the injustice of it, Gerard vowed to do his best to keep his friend's daughter safe from her own desires and Elizabeth's power. The only way he could hope to do so was to convince her to follow the dictates of the queen; even if he had to be a bit devious to do so, such was the only course open to him.

"I swear on my life that I don't know what I've done to deserve the grievances the Lord has assigned me in this world. I could be living with my widowed sister and her five young ones. Instead I'm saddled with the likes of you and your father! Why?" Striding away from Regan, he returned to the comfort of his mug and took a long swallow while he waited for her to follow him. Moments later, she stood before him, clothed in a wrapper.

"My father was a good friend to you, Gerard, and I won't hear you say otherwise," Regan said, standing up to him with fire still burning in her eyes.

"A good friend, yes, but a wise one? Never, my girl, never! First he speaks out against Henry VIII, even to the point of defending Anne Boleyn against the king. Only a fool would do that, but your father didn't care about the consequences, just what was right. And where did it get him? The Davies were reduced to near poverty for his trouble, and me along with them."

"But Elizabeth made it up to him, giving him lands and a title and taking me on as a ward of the court," reminded William's daughter. "He didn't have such a bad end."

"Of course not, but when Anne Boleyn's daughter rewards your father for his kindness to her mother, what does his daughter do? She stupidly offends the queen by stealing the attentions of one of her gentlemen! Regan, Lord only knows what hell awaits you in Ireland, but I've a good mind to simply walk away and let you find out for yourself. I'm getting too old for royal feuds and revenge,'' he said quietly, taking a long drink of his ale and placing the tankard down on the table before moving toward the door. ''Better you find a room close by the palace somewhere and let your fancy gentleman visit you when he can sneak away.''

''Gerard, he loves me, I swear he does.''

''Oh, then in that case, he'll leave the queen and marry you, I suppose. Well, you won't want me in the way lecturing about right and wrong, so I'll leave you to your life and get on with mine.'' Stopping before her, Gerard ran a callused finger down her cheek where a tear had trailed. ''Good luck, child.''

''Don't go,'' cried Regan, clutching his arm. While she couldn't admit he might be right about Dudley using her, she also couldn't survive without someone who cared about her. And Gerard did care—perhaps too much, but he cared. ''I don't want to let Elizabeth win by shipping me out of the country, but I can't fool myself into believing Dudley would marry me to prevent it. He didn't even stop dancing long enough to say farewell,'' she acknowledged sadly. ''Anyway, if I'm to have any satisfaction out of this situation, I'll need your assistance, Gerard. Please don't fail me. Help me make the damned plantation a success so that I can come home to England and spit in Elizabeth's face.''

''Then we'd both end up in the Tower,'' he chuckled, running his hand over her weary shoulders. ''All right, Regan, I'll stay, but you must promise to heed what I say, especially in the wilds of Ireland. I hear things aren't at all what we're used to over there.''

''I promise,'' said Regan with a half smile, already anticipating the new world she would conquer, with Gerard's trusty advice. Elizabeth would rue the day she sent Regan Davies out of her life.

Chapter Two

The shadowy image of mount and rider burst into the clearing and came to a sudden halt. From his quick and graceful movements the man astride the huge beast appeared to be as spirited and energetic as his prancing steed, the wildness of the night winds through which he'd been riding clinging to him even as he dismounted and handed the reins to a waiting boy.

Bathed in the silvery light shed by the slice of moon hanging in the blackened Irish sky, and partially hidden in the shadows cast by the surrounding trees, it was easy to believe the tales the old crofters still whispered about this man's family. At the very least there was a touch of Gypsy about him; it was there in the curly shock of ebony hair that framed his handsome, aristocratic features, and in the unbridled glint illuminating the depths of his intense blue eyes.

But when Connor O'Carroll stood as he did now, in the moonlit forest with wisps of fog swirling at his feet, the worst of the rumors was easily believable. His face, strained by exhaustion and frustration, and darkened by the night, lent support to the theory that the *sid,* the fairy folk, had left a changeling in the birthing chamber of some ancestral grandmother. And that sly feat had marked all subsequent generations of O'Carrolls with their dark hair, roguish charm and sparkling eyes. At this instant, however, those deep blue eyes had lost their natural good humor and glistened dangerously as a brooding Connor O'Carroll surveyed his camp. What was it, after all, but a small fire beside a stream, hidden in the forests of the Slieve Bloom Mountains? The site boasted little more than nature had provided, other than a few sacks of oats cradling the heads of some of his men.

There was no sense of permanence here, yet this spot had been home since his own had been wrested away from him by the British months ago. Moving toward the fire to find warmth, he cursed himself yet again for his lack of foresight in leaving his keep so lightly guarded when he had ridden north with the bulk of his men in answer to erroneous reports that a distant portion of his land was under siege.

He had thought his peace made with the English queen. In fact he had fairly charmed her, or so he had believed. Who could have prophesied that she would steal his lands and give them to a foreigner when he, himself, had done nothing to provoke her? At least, nothing that she could have known about. Yet here he was, spending the night upon the damp ground while a fat English backside warmed the bed in his chamber at Geata Neamhai, or as the foreigners translated it, Heaven's Gate.

Looking at his men sprawled around him, and listening to an occasional snore or sleepy grunt, Connor knew that his followers were more complacent than he about their present circumstances. True, they were fighting men, used to uncomfortable conditions, but the realization that they had accepted their surroundings rather readily, deepened his scowl. Though all slept with drawn swords or dirks beside them, few had stirred at the sound of his stallion's hoofbeats when he had ridden into camp at hell-bent speed. They had grown used to the sounds of Connor's nocturnal wanderings and the noise of raiding parties returning in the black of night.

Raiding! Connor glowered at the very word, dropping from his broad shoulder the rabbits he had snared. As if availing himself of his own game and cattle constituted thievery! And they *were* his, the Irishman swore, his brilliant blue eyes narrowing with fierce determination. No matter what the English Crown might say, or who was presently in possession of his keep, Geata Neamhai belonged to the O'Carrolls, and as the present earl, he would win it back... or die trying.

In the flickering shadows of the camp fire, an eerie orange glow highlighted his taut features as he began to skin the rabbits. At that moment, Connor O'Carroll looked very much like the devil the English had proclaimed him to be. But those few who were awake and viewing him now were his followers. They saw less than a demon and more than a man standing in the middle of the clearing that provided shelter for them all. They saw a hero with a price on his head, whose usual ready laughter and warm heart had been eclipsed by the bitter shadow of pain and loss he carried within his soul.

One of these men stepped forward, not only to aid his friend and lord in the task of skinning the rabbits, but to ease other burdens, as well.

At thirty-six, Hugh Cassidy was a giant of a man. Though the lord of Geata Neamhai was almost six feet tall, Hugh's chin easily cleared his crown. And while Connor's strong frame tapered elegantly from broad shoulders to narrow hips and down long, lean legs, Hugh was twice his width and as straight and sturdy as a tree trunk.

A deep laugh rumbling in the cavern of his chest, Hugh knelt beside Connor, playfully nudging him aside in order to finish dressing the rabbits. When Connor's mouth tightened in irritation, Hugh only laughed again. It was no matter to him that the man beside him had become the Earl of Kilcaid. This was still the little lad who had trailed along after him when a sixteen-year-old gangling Hugh had begun his own training as a gallowglass in the service of Connor's father. Others may have been circumspect around the old lord's only child, but Hugh, with a slew of younger brothers of his own, had thought nothing of teasingly yanking the childhood locks of the future earl, or roughhousing with him on the muddy fields surrounding the keep. Hugh's attention and easy manner had earned Connor's adoration, and a bond had formed between them that neither class nor Connor's years in England could conquer.

Even now, when Connor could easily quell other men with a sharp look or snarled command, Hugh paid his lord's temper little heed. And a devil of a temper it was, though Connor's roaring usually abated as quickly as it arose. But what was one to expect from an Irishman of Connor O'Carroll's sort, a man who lived and fought hard, a man whose passions ran close to the surface yet were deeply felt?

Finishing with one rabbit and reaching for another, Hugh eyed his young master, ten years his junior, and a smile formed about his pleasant, wide mouth.

"Well, my lord," he began irreverently, "I see you've brought me my meal, but what are the others to do? From the results, I'd suggest you leave the hunting to your men, and content yourself with something more profitable."

"My purpose in leaving camp was not to forage for food. The game was simply an afterthought, though I've no doubt I could have brought back an entire herd of sheep and it wouldn't be enough to fill your belly, Hugh," Connor replied, repressing the grudging smile struggling for release at the corners of his mouth. "As it stands, perhaps if I'd had a better teacher at the hunt when I was a stripling, my present efforts would produce enough reward to meet your exacting standards."

"There wasn't a better man to be had than the one who taught you," Hugh muttered, his pride wounded. "It was those years following the English gentry's pursuit at hawking that ruined your talents."

"Perhaps you're right," Connor replied with a tired smile. "But now it would seem I am the quarry the English are circling, and Henry Sidney means to have his men run me to ground."

"Sidney's forces aren't hunters," Hugh grunted as he finished cleaning the game. "We've been out here these two months, and they've yet to find us. No, they're more like weasels, the way they squirmed their way into the keep to secure it for the new tenant's arrival when the hawk had flown. Geata Neamhai may be nigh impregnable, but we'll find a way to roust them yet, Con, you can be sure of that."

"Aye, though I won't see O'Carroll lands or the keep destroyed in the process. But that isn't the only problem we face. Once I succeed in regaining what is mine, I must make Elizabeth content to see this hawk back in his nest."

"Go on with you. I may see you as a hawk, but I warrant *she* thinks of you more as a peacock than a bird of prey, and I can't say as I blame her," Hugh replied with a hearty chuckle. "If I live to see my grandchildren's offspring, I'll never forget the sight you made when you came home from the English court, dressed in embroidered velvets with the looks of a poet. Imagine a fighting man dressed like a courtier! *I'd* never wear anything of that sort."

"You'd never find a tailor willing to undertake stitching you so fine a doublet," Connor said, his eyes gleaming with amusement. "The very size of you would overwhelm anyone who makes his living plying a needle. But I'll have you know that what I was wearing was extremely fashionable in London. In fact, the she-devil who reigns there now was quite taken with my fine clothes . . . and, I might add, with me."

"The only thing taken was your land, boy. Not even your charm could protect Geata Neamhai from the queen's greedy grasp."

"No, she fairly doted on me. I'm sure of it."

"Then it's a good thing she didn't hate you, or only the saints above know where we would be now," Hugh grunted as he placed the rabbits on the spit and adjusted them over the low flame of the fire. "As it is, she's placed a bounty on your head, and a measly fifty sovereigns at that—an amount to make it worth some poor bastard's while to capture you, but paltry enough to make it an insult. Is this your idea of a female who dotes on you? Didn't I teach you anything about women . . . or common sense for that matter?"

"I know what I'm about, Hugh," Connor said, his deep voice ripe with warning and his blue eyes sparking dangerously. "If I can regain my lands and then reach the queen's ear, I'll turn things around."

"What makes you think so?" Hugh asked, already licking his lips in anticipation of the tasty breakfast the rabbits would make.

"I told you, she finds me irresistible," Connor said, his mood considerably lighter as he viewed the scowl forming his friend's response.

"If that's the case, then you must have made a powerful enemy at court."

"Yes, and I know exactly who to blame," Connor said, compressing his full lips into a thin line. "It's Robert Dudley, the queen's favorite, and he'll do anything to see that he remains such, no matter whom it destroys."

"But that was years ago. All of this because you were a boy playing at a man's game?"

"I certainly didn't seek to curry Elizabeth's favor. It was she who sought me out. Perhaps she had intended to call me back to London."

"I told your father no good would come of your going to the English court," Hugh said, his voice edged with exasperation.

"You might be right, Hugh, but remember it was Mary's court to which I was sent, Catholic Mary and her Spanish husband."

"Aye, but it was the redheaded witch succeeding her who wouldn't grant you leave to return home, the one who has now stripped you of all that is rightfully yours."

"And the one who will give it all back to me when she comes to her senses."

"And if she doesn't?"

"Then I'll take it," Connor whispered in a tone of such deadly calm that it made his words seem more an oath than a simple rejoinder.

"Spoken like a true O'Carroll," Hugh said, clapping his friend heartily on the back, "and I'm not ashamed to admit that such spirit is the reason the Cassidys have been content to serve your family for generations."

"Oh, is that the reason?" Connor asked in amusement. "Not because O'Carroll land is home to the prettiest maids in all of Ireland?"

"Well, if truth be known, that might have something to do with it," Hugh admitted good-naturedly. "But come and join me in a drink of whiskey before the others are awake. It's been a rare while since we've shared banter along with serious talk, and God Himself knows we've had little enough joy these past few weeks."

"Whiskey? Where the devil did you get it?" Connor asked. "You haven't been out pilfering from the tenants? I've told you I'll have none of that, no matter how dry your throat becomes."

"Calm yourself, my lord. It was a gift from a grateful lady who has been a wee bit lonely since her husband rode off to join the O'Neill."

"You're trying to tell me she gave you a jug of her husband's best in payment for your company? Come, Hugh," Connor said, raising a skeptical eyebrow shaped like a raven's wing, "you don't expect me to believe that do you?"

"No, I don't," Hugh responded with a sly smile. "Surely you know I'm worth two jugs at least, and that is just what she gave me. I've done one in already, but I'm willing to share the other with you. Now what do you say?''

"I say aye.''

Though it was close to dawn, the two men seated themselves on a fallen log as though they hadn't a care.

A scarce hour later, Connor found himself close to being intoxicated, not by the powerful drink, but as a result of a lighter heart and shared laughter. His joy came to a jolting end, however, when a short whistle in the darkness announced someone's approach. Though the two high-pitched notes signaled a friend, the men, nonetheless, were instantly on their feet and readying their weapons. Hugh wrapped his large hands around his pike while Connor drew his sword, their fierce appearance enough to give any enemy second thoughts.

But, as the branches at the edge of the clearing parted, they saw it was not a foe, no, not even a man. It was Sheila Dempsey armed with the only weapon she ever carried, her sharp tongue. Not that she needed anything else to protect her, Connor thought wryly as he replaced his sword in its sheath. No tenant on O'Carroll lands would dare to cross Sheila. But few knew as Connor did that the woman's crusty manner was only a habit she had acquired to conceal her soft heart.

As if the force of the north wind were at her back, the older woman hurried across the compound, stopping in front of the Earl of Kilcaid and his companion. Taking the time to remove the shawl covering her faded red hair, she placed one hand on a bony hip and stood eyeing the pair of men before her as though they were children in for a scolding. It was hardly the proper attitude for a castelain to take with her lord, yet Connor seemed not at all bothered by it.

"Ach, I've slipped from Geata Neamhai and dragged myself out to find you so that I could be back before I'm missed and what is it that greets me but two men in their cups? To be sure, I've never seen a sorrier sight!''

"Now, now, Sheila," Connor soothed indulgently, barely hiding a smile at the motherly figure fixing him with so hard a stare, "lifting a mug or two doesn't mean that we've lost our wits. What is it that brings you out at such an hour?"

"I must speak with you, my lord, but I'd as lief know you're sober enough to understand my words before I give them to you," the woman said with a disdainful sniff, her sharp gaze shifting to the jug Hugh now cradled protectively in his arms.

"Then speak, Sheila" Connor commanded softly. "My head is clear, and surely a woman as wise as yourself wouldn't begrudge a lonely man something to keep him warm until sunrise. I've heard it said that your Michael was known to take a drop or two."

"It was my poor departed husband's only flaw."

"No, Sheila Dempsey, Michael's one flaw was leaving so handsome a woman as you a widow," Connor teased, enjoying the slight flush coloring her cheeks.

"Get on with you! Now I know you're drunk," the woman retorted gruffly. "I've seen two and fifty winters, enough to make me aware of fading looks. And at my age, I've not time to waste here listening to your prattle. I must return before the English invaders awake and find me gone. We don't want them suspecting you've still eyes and ears within the keep's thick walls."

"You're a valuable and loyal friend," Connor said simply, taking the woman's hand, "and I bless the day my father made you castelain of Geata Neamhai. I don't know what I would have done without you, especially in light of recent events."

"Connor O'Carroll, you know full well that my actions don't speak of bravery, or loyalty for that matter. I shouldn't have been in that castle when the English took your home," Sheila protested, embarrassed by the young man's warm compliment as she drew her hand away from his while she tried to make light of her devotion to him. "But there I was, still in your service, working past my prime, and all because you've yet to take a wife."

"I'd been thinking to become a priest like your Patrick," the earl pronounced, his pious tones at odds with the spark of devilment twinkling in his eyes.

"I'd rather you be more like my Dennis," Sheila replied flippantly. "Though he rides with the O'Neill, he's managed to father ten young ones through his marriage to Aileen."

"And I'd wager a score of others besides," Hugh interjected with a deep laugh that halted abruptly when Sheila pierced his humor with a dark look.

"This is what you would wish for me, madam?" Connor asked solemnly in spite of the amusement playing across his well-drawn features. "I'd say your son is overly given to the appetites of the flesh. And to me it's quite apparent he takes after his mother."

"Aye, and the very thought is enough to make a man's blood run hot, even in this damp cold," Hugh said impishly as he sidled up to the austere Sheila. "Come put me out of my misery, sweet lady, with a kiss."

"To the devil with ye, you young pups!" Sheila retorted, brushing the huge man aside as though he were a fly, yet blushing with pleasure all the same. "Since you seem to want to do no more than laugh and make merry at my expense, I'd best be off, and not bother you with details about the imminent arrival of the man to whom the English queen has given Geata Neamhai."

When the castelain turned as if to depart, Connor's hand reached out and closed atop Sheila's thin shoulder. Spinning her around, the look on his face was as ominous as any summer thundercloud. "Why didn't you tell me right away?" he accused fiercely as he towered over the older woman.

"I tried," Sheila said defiantly, not at all cowed by the man whose cradle she had rocked over twenty-five years before. "But it would appear, my Lord Kilcaid, that you're more of a mind to plague an old widow than to listen to what she has to say."

"All right woman, out with it before I send you to live with your daughter-in-law...and her ten brats," Connor threatened.

"Sidney sent word to his men late last night that the Davies party has landed in Ireland. They are traveling by carriage and should be at the keep in two or three days."

"So William Davies has come, has he? 'Tis a pity he shall never reach Geata Neamhai alive," murmured Connor, his cool, calm voice contradicting the glimmer of hatred aflame in his blue eyes. For a moment his keen mind evaluated possible plans, and then returned to the conversation he had had with Hugh a short while before.

"Sheila, can you manage to smuggle out my English finery and get it to me through one of the shepherds?" the earl asked.

"Aye, but what are you doing, Connor, dressing up to make him welcome?"

"Never mind what I'm doing. Hugh, gather the men. There are plans to be made and work to be done."

"Aye, Connor," the large man replied with determination. "Will you take him along the forest road?"

"I think it best. The trees will provide cover for a small force to ambush Davies while the bulk of the men can wait to retake my keep when Sidney's forces ride out to Davies' rescue."

"And not a day too soon," Sheila complained. "Those Englishmen have been stuffing themselves with your provisions as though they'd never seen food and drink before. If they stay much longer, you'll be lucky to find anything left at all."

"Don't worry, Sheila Dempsey. The rightful lord will be back in your castle soon. Then you'll have someone to scold and mother once more, and all will be right again."

"Not all. There's still the matter of obtaining a lady for the lord of Geata Neamhai," Sheila rejoined in a sassy tone. "And as I see it, getting rid of the English may be a far easier feat."

"Run along with you, Sheila," Connor said, laughing at her audacity. "And mind your tongue about a wife. There's men's work to be done at the moment, and no place in my thoughts for any woman."

Chapter Three

As the carriage hit yet another rut in the apparently endless road to her new home, Regan flinched at the jostling her already weary body received. Despite her full skirts and the blanket folded beneath her, the constant bouncing of the seat left her most uncomfortable. They had been traveling almost a fortnight, and the young Englishwoman found the strictures imposed by her temporary guardian quite disagreeable, from the supposed need to always comport herself as a dignified lady of the realm to his unconscionable insistence on this horse-drawn prison, no matter how innovative it was. Even the sweet scent of her nosegay couldn't revive her flagging spirits in the wet gray mist of late afternoon. Impatient with the whole situation, she gave in to her distress and rewarded her companion with yet another statement of her dissatisfaction.

"Gerard, I still don't understand why you insist on my riding in this modern vehicle of torture. Just because the queen enjoys this novel means of transport doesn't mean I have to. At least when I rode sidesaddle I could avoid the worst of the discomfort."

"When I allowed you to ride horseback, young lady, we were still in England, safely under the jurisdiction and protection of Her Majesty Elizabeth. On these heathen shores of Ireland, I will not expose you to the untested dangers which might lie outside the coach." Gerard Langston's voice was firm, his authority immutable; after all, the sovereign had given him the responsibility of delivering the Countess of Westfield to her new home, and he was not one to shirk his duty, especially given his loyalty to the girl's father.

Besides, he had had plenty of experience with Regan and her impetuous desires. She might promise to stay close to the guard riding with them, but let her catch sight of a child playing or a rare herb or flower in the field, and she'd be off the road and in the brambles after it, no matter what she'd promised. In England such behavior, while annoying, hadn't been dangerous; here, such was not the case; better the Lady Regan stay confined, despite her protests. "Anyway, I agreed to keep you company in the coach today for the purpose of pleasant conversation, not to suffer your complaints. A lady greets adversity in silence, though I imagine," he added dryly, "that a true lady would never have been sent from court for distracting the queen's favorite courtier."

"And I'm quite certain that a true gentleman wouldn't constantly harp on the subject. Dudley is as much to blame as I am. After all, he is the one who pursued me," retorted the comely blonde. "Besides, with Father's dying after he'd received the title to the Irish estates, the queen had no choice but to send me to Ireland. From the talk at court, Sir Henry Sidney's not having an easy time keeping English settlers over here. Do you suppose conditions are as bad as they say?"

"Like most things, I venture, they're better than some reports state and worse than others."

"But the towns are so small and even the cities are not bigger than the tiniest hamlet in the Cotswolds—a few cottages, not even shops or a church. I've yet to see a native woman in any fashionable dress: they seem to prefer shapeless rags to kirtles and proper skirts. And the inns—" Regan hesitated at the memory of the lodging they'd shared

wo nights past: a humble inn where straw pallets were
scattered before the hearth in the same room where men sat
drinking and gaming, with no facilities for a hot meal or
washing up. Even as she and her maid had tried to rest while
Gerard stood watch, a knife fight had broken out over the
outcome of a card game, and the loser had fallen dead before her horrified eyes. Her maid, Beatrice, had collapsed
in hysteria and refused to travel a foot further, insisting that
she be allowed to return to England. Finally, Gerard had
reluctantly dispatched two of their men to see the girl home,
though it meant his charge was now without female com-
panionship. Hopefully that would change once they reached
Heaven's Gate; there had to be at least one reliable woman
here.

"Now, child, don't be thinking on the killing again. To be
sure, such things happen in England, as well," he offered,
stroking her hand gently.

"Gerard, what kind of people can live like animals, answering only to the demands of nature, as coarse and vio-
ent as they may be?"

"Mayhap a people who have no choice, but live and die
as best they can," the older man answered, having seen
more unhappy souls in his life than his charge would ever
know. Even when the Davies suffered royal disgrace, they
had been far from starvation or the despair of watching a
child die for lack of warmth or shelter. "Not everyone has
the education or means to improve his lot, Regan, despite
the pretty words the priests offer up."

"But to die for the turn of a card... The innkeeper said
he had a wife and four babes in arms," whispered the young
countess, her voice revealing her confusion at what she had
witnessed as her hands crushed the sweet-smelling flowers
she held. "Why weren't those men home with their families
instead of off seeking amusement?"

"A man has to flee his yoke now and then to find the
strength to shoulder it again, child, especially when the

burden is a heavy one," advised Gerard gently. The girl was apt to see much worse in this land before it accepted her, he thought, best she understood its ways.

"I fear no one has a happy life over here," said Regan sadly, "and we probably won't be any different."

"Come now, have you forgotten the lovely home of Sir Henry Sidney and his family? And he said Heaven's Gate is just as nice. You must admit, the queen's governor of Ireland showed us gracious hospitality and a very pleasant evening."

"In a building surrounded by guards where all the servants were English and even the furnishings were imported from home."

"And on your father's estate, aren't the servants English, and the furnishings?"

"But that's to be expected in England," disputed Regan. "Maybe the English would get on better over here if they worked with the natives instead of trying to replace them with more Englishmen."

"I thought you believed the Irish totally uncivilized?" questioned Gerard, pleased that the girl's thinking had broadened. Though he'd insisted on bringing a party of soldiers for protection, nothing would please him more than turning their weapons into ornaments and the men into happy tenants of Heaven's Gate.

"As you said before, maybe they've never had the chance to be otherwise. I'm going to offer them one," stated the Countess of Westfield. "No Irishman or woman willing to work will be forced to leave my estates, no matter what the other English do."

"I think that's a very wise decision, Regan, one your father might have made," pronounced the Davies' retainer, giving her a proud smile as the carriage suddenly stopped short and the driver began to curse. "Now what? We've been damned fortunate not to run into trouble before. I hope our luck hasn't run out."

"Could we have arrived?" asked the girl, shifting her bulky skirt so she could move closer to the window and peer out. "I don't see a castle anywhere. There are only trees."

"I doubt this is our destination, Regan, but you stay here while I go and find out what's wrong. No matter what happens, don't leave the coach—and hold on to this, you may need it." Handing his charge a small knife, Gerard looked sternly at her, trying to instill some fear in the usually rambunctious female. "This isn't a game we're playing. It could mean our lives," he cautioned as he opened the door and stepped down.

"William, what's the problem?" he called.

"From the looks of it, there's a disabled carriage blocking the road up ahead, sir, and there's no run to go around," yelled the driver. "I barely stopped the horses before they ran into it as we turned the bend."

"Philip, have six of the guards surround our carriage to protect Lady Regan, and have the others come with me. Do you suppose this might be a trap to ambush our party? It's all too lonesome in these woods."

"No, sir, and if I may say so, no band of ruffians would have a carriage like that one," the guard replied, stepping out of Regan's earshot as he and Gerard advanced toward the unmoving vehicle.

Well, if anything were wrong, they would surely have been attacked by now, decided Regan, edging closer to the door so she could watch, even if she couldn't hear. Unfortunately, her view was obscured, and only by sticking her head out of the window could she catch a glimpse of Gerard and Philip. But who was that with them?

An Englishman, by the look of his finery, though like all the fashion in this country, his was sadly out-of-date. Clearly, Gerard did not seem threatened by the other's words as he extended his hand to the stranger and motioned the guards toward the stranded carriage. Dark ebony hair, somewhat longer than common, framed a handsome, aristocratic face, while a firm chin and broad shoulders gave the man definite interest, in Regan's mind. Even standing beside Gerard, who was no small figure of a man, the fellow presented a royal image; perhaps he was one of Elizabeth's tenants as well, she hypothesized. But why wasn't Gerard bringing him over to the coach to introduce to her?

"Lady Regan, you shouldn't be hanging out of the window like that," objected one of her guards. "It's much too dangerous!"

"Oh, don't be silly. That gentleman isn't about to attack anyone. Can't you tell he's a member of nobility? But, you're right, there's no point in leaning out a window. I'm going to meet the man. He looks quite safe, and you will protect me, I'm sure."

Without another word, Regan opened the carriage door and held out her hand, waiting for a guard to assist her down. As usual, they obeyed her dictates. Holding her skirts slightly aloft to avoid the muddy ground, Regan advanced to meet her destiny.

Intent as he was upon winning the trust of the chief guard who had come forward, Connor didn't immediately see the inquisitive maid alighting from the carriage. While the retainer had given no indication as to the identity of his employer, Connor was certain that William Davies sat within the enclosed coach not fifty paces away, and the handsome Irish lord could think of little else other than the death blow he would deliver to the usurper of his lands and title. But approaching the thief was proving more difficult than he had imagined.

Though the steel-haired commander stood eyeing him suspiciously, Connor's composure didn't waiver. He knew he hadn't given the Englishman cause to suspect he was other than he purported to be. Dressed in English finery, emerging from the crest-adorned carriage stolen early that morning from the nearby estate of the English plantation owner, Sir Thomas Watkins, Connor O'Carroll looked every inch a loyal subject of the English queen. He had gone so far as to introduce himself as Watkins, and there was nothing to make anyone doubt him.

Alone as he appeared to be, his men well hidden by the trees along the road, even a fretful nursemaid would have been hard put to worry that he posed any sort of threat. Indeed, the very words he uttered, spoken in the flat, drawn-out cadence he had learned to mimic during his years in the English court, proclaimed that he and this guard were countrymen. Yet the man was reluctant to allow him to approach William Davies' carriage, acting for all the world like some anxious father protecting a virginal daughter from an invading army.

Hiding his growing impatience to be done with the deed behind a smile of increasing charm, Connor thought to sidestep the graybeard. If his Celtic dagger did not find its mark soon, the small force concealed behind the natural screen provided by the trees would become restless and uneasy. Still, the Earl of Kilcaid adhered to the rules of his dangerous game, taking his time and playing his role as he explained the plight in which his broken carriage was supposed to have left him. Desperate as he was to regain his home, Connor would not be hurried, knowing he might never again have an opportunity such as this.

Finally he moved forward, only to find that the Englishman did not give way but continued to block him, even though the man's manner and tone was respectful and polite. Damn the bastard! To strike him down would give Davies' soldiers time to react before the carriage could be reached. Not that Connor was afraid of hand-to-hand combat with any man. He merely wanted to take no chances with William Davies' death.

Struggling once more to contain his Irish temper, Connor looked past the man's shoulder toward his goal and his plans were irrevocably altered. There, approaching him from the coach, was a lone, lovely female. Her dress was English, but her skin was the hue of fresh Kinnity cream and her hair the color of pale Irish moonbeams shimmering upon some darkened glen.

Though she was not exceptionally small, an illusion of feminine fragility clung to her. It made Connor want to protect her, not shatter her world by murdering the man who was in all probability her husband, brother or father.

Yet even as sympathy plucked at his traitorous heart, Connor sensed something was wrong. While the woman walked gracefully toward them, no masculine voice called her back. No man's face appeared at the window to monitor her progress. And when she opened her mouth to speak in melodic tones, the words she used were her own and not a hollow repetition of orders delivered for her lord. Mother of God! How many blasted coaches were there in Ireland? Had he halted the wrong vehicle? If that were the case, he had to get this innocent out of here, before she was hurt or his own plans to kill the usurper of Geata Neamhai went awry.

But first, there could be no doubts. He couldn't allow the woman to go on unless he knew with certainty that William Davies was not in that coach. In spite of his quandary, Connor's fine, handsome features betrayed none of his inner turmoil. Studying the woman before him as he rose from a courtly bow, Connor smiled boldly and allowed her officer to relate the fabrication he had been told.

"My Lady Regan," the older man began respectfully, though disapproval exhibited itself in the thin set of the fellow's lips, "there was no need to leave the carriage. I was just coming to advise you of the situation."

"Then I have saved you steps, Gerard," the blond maiden said, dismissing his obvious vexation. The impish smile which played about the corners of her mouth amused Connor and led him to believe that this was not the first time she had taxed her escort's patience. The girl was apparently a handful, though in truth Connor judged she would make a fair armful for any man.

Not at all shy, she spoke in a clear voice as she asked, "Now tell me, what is the reason for our delay, and who is this stranger?"

"Ah, my lady, but I think it is you who is the stranger to these lands, a cultivated English rose transported from home to these barbaric shores," Connor interrupted with calculated gallantry which, he realized with surprise, would have been sincere had the situation been less desperate. His mouth slipped into an easy grin, designed to act as a lodestone and attract the woman's acceptance and goodwill, if his pretty speech had not already done so. Perhaps then he could find out with whom she journeyed.

"My lady, this is Sir Thomas Watkins, owner of a nearby estate," Gerard said hastily before Regan could return this audacious fellow's flirtation. It had been that nettlesome tendency of hers which had landed them in this predicament in the first place, the beleaguered Englishman fumed, and he was not about to allow her to get them into any further trouble with her smoky green eyes, profusion of curling blond hair, and promising smile. "Sir Thomas has lost a wheel of his coach, which now sits in the exact middle of this cursed road, so that our own vehicle cannot pass around it."

"I am surprised to see another carriage in the wilds of this uncivilized territory," Regan commented sweetly, ignoring Gerard and addressing the possessing stranger. "After all, they are only starting to come into use in London now that everyone is rushing to imitate the queen."

"Ah, but there are those who, even though they reside in this remote outpost, try to maintain the civility and novelty of dear London," Connor responded, thinking of the pompous Thomas Watkins and the hubris that had prompted the idiot to import such an expensive contraption as the coach.

For his part, the Earl of Kilcaid despised the infernal thing, feeling that if a man wanted to travel by means other than his own two feet, he should experience good, solid horseflesh beneath him and the wind at his back. Sitting in the carriage was confining, and Connor O'Carroll was not a man to accept restraint of any sort graciously.

But for all of his distaste for the gilded box which now sat on three wheels, and despite his impatience concerning the whereabouts of William Davies, Connor managed to bestow another smile on the Lady Regan, a dazzling, devastating smile that had always charmed every woman who had ever been its recipient, even the august Elizabeth Tudor. But when answering dimples appeared as reward, he discovered that he felt a satisfaction which had nothing to do with his reason for being on the forest road.

Noticing the effect this presumptuous fellow was having on the young woman in his charge, and all too aware of the brazen glint shining in the gentleman's eyes, Gerard intruded once more.

"By your leave, my lady," he said. "I will have our men move Sir Thomas's coach to the side so that we may continue our journey."

Looking speculatively at her new neighbor, Regan suddenly wondered if a hot bath and warm fire could not wait. Though she had managed to convince herself that she would spend her entire exile in Ireland nobly pining for Robert Dudley, despite the fact that the rogue didn't deserve it, the beautiful Regan saw at once that acquiring Sir Thomas Watkins's friendship might make her banishment more bearable.

This man was devilishly handsome, much better looking than any gentleman of Elizabeth's court...except of course for Robert, she amended quickly in an attempt to defend, even to herself, the one mistake she had made while in the queen's household.

But it was not as if Sir Thomas's well-formed countenance had anything at all to do with her temptation to offer him aid, Regan persuaded herself. He might have the deepest, bluest eyes she had ever seen, but that certainly didn't temper her impulse to help him. No, the root of her generosity was merely charity. After all, how could anyone leave a gentleman of quality stranded on a deserted road in a hostile land? While Gerard would undoubtedly reject any delay of their journey, she *could* require her men to assist him. With that thought in mind, Regan spoke before she could falter in her determination.

"Surely if the wheel is not damaged, it can be reattached before we are on our way," Regan said, halting Gerard as he was about to turn and bark the order to move the disabled vehicle.

"Lady Regan, who knows how long that will take?" the older man protested, exasperated that this slip of a girl would not allow herself to be guided by him in this matter.

"It makes no difference. Have the men see to it," Regan directed, refusing to be swayed by Gerard's objections.

All too aware of the nobleman's masculine beauty, the romantic young woman fantasized about what it would be like to be courted by such a man. She would not, of course, allow herself to rush headlong into repeating the mistake she had made with Robert Dudley, but still, Regan thought, studying the roguish attitude of the long, lean form before her, capitulation wasn't necessary with as splendid a man as this. The pursuit itself would bring pleasure enough.

"But my lady..." William Davies' trusted retainer groused as he regarded Regan's dreamy expression and wondered if the girl had been born without any common sense at all.

"It's best you tend to this immediately, Gerard," she cut him off in gentle reprimand, coming slowly back to reality.

"While I appreciate your concern, dear lady, don't you think you should inform your lord of the situation, and await his decision?" Connor interjected, nodding toward Regan's own coach. Now would be the moment of truth. Was William Davies in the blasted vehicle or not?

"I haven't any lord," Regan answered demurely, pleased at the pointed question. It meant the handsome Sir Thomas was curious about her possible ties to another. Well, now he knew. She was under no man's protection...at least, no man living in Ireland.

"Do you mean to tell me you're traveling alone?" Connor pressed, as though concerned for her safety.

"I have no companions other than my guards," Regan stated, treating him to a pretty display of even white teeth while avoiding Gerard's fierce glower of censure for disclosing such information to this stranger, noble though he might be.

"Then you mustn't consider tarrying here," Connor said, anxious now to send the seductive vixen on her way. He turned to address the steel-haired guard who stood at his lady's side so protectively in spite of his obvious vexation with her.

"Have your men ease my coach over to the side of the road. That should give you space enough to continue," Connor ordered, authority over all around him coming easily.

"Right then, your lordship," Gerard agreed, eager to remove Regan from the danger of not only these wild surroundings with their threat of roving brigands, but from this handsome and courtly peacock, as well. "It will take only a few moments."

"Wait, Gerard. That is not the order I issued," Regan said, put out that her man would scurry to obey the commands of another. Did being female mean that she was continually expected to surrender her sovereignty to any male present? She thought not! She was her own mistress now, and Gerard had better come to realize it.

"We cannot leave Sir Thomas to further difficulty, Gerard. I would like the carriage fixed. Please see to it now."

"Lady Regan, I—"

"Now," she said stubbornly, and watched him stalk off to do her bidding, his ramrod-stiff back the only visible sign of his disapproval.

"There is no need to inconvenience yourself," the false Sir Thomas assured in honeyed tones, determined to sooth ruffled feathers in order to get the girl away before William Davies appeared and all was ruined. "I have already sent my driver for assistance. My men should be here soon. I suggest you continue your journey."

"But it is no inconvenience, I assure you," Regan protested sweetly, though her girlish daydreams of a few minutes before were fast fading in the face of this man's refusal to accept her aid *and* her company. His flirtatious manner had seemed to indicate that he would have been amenable to a bit more time with her. Yet now the opposite appeared true, despite the fact that she had just bestowed her most bewitching smile.

"See here, madam," Connor said gently but firmly, prodded by his desire to see the lady depart, comely as she might be. "While your intentions are charitable your soldiers might well be clumsy in their attempts at the task to which you have set them, and I've no wish to see my new possession damaged further. It's best to let things be until experienced help arrives."

"It is but a temporary measure they take. They will do no harm," Regan responded in a soft voice, appalled by the man's sudden lack of manners. "I could not go off and leave you in distress."

"My dear madam, you are not rescuing me from distress, you are causing it, so why not give way to my wishes and be gone?" Connor continued, becoming so increasingly disturbed by the woman's headstrong insistence on interfering in his plans that overtones of exasperation and building temper crept into his speech. He couldn't remember when he had last been this harried. Was it the urgency of the moment or this woman's presence that made him act this way? He couldn't truthfully say, and he became all the more irked at the situation in which he found himself.

Immediately Regan was affronted by the insolence of the man she knew as Sir Thomas Watkins. Here he was, rudely dismissing her after blatantly offering, with all his pretty words and good looks, the temptation to dally awhile. Well, the devil take him then! Let him sit in the middle of this muddy patch of ground that passed for a road in this godforsaken land until doomsday!

"If I have offended, sir, then I am sorry. I was merely trying to help," Regan said in tones edged with haughtiness as she attempted to salvage her pride. Quickly, before she could disgrace herself, she turned toward her coach, where she could dispatch a messenger to inform Gerard that he would simply be moving the obstruction to the side of the road after all.

Upset as she was, Regan was unaware of what a fetching picture she made as she struggled to maintain her dignity. Nor did she know the degree to which her unhappy state tugged at Connor's heart.

"Wait," he called impulsively, cursing himself for his foolishness even as he closed the gap between them. Reaching Regan, he noted the sheer film of unshed tears which bathed her sea-green eyes and found himself completely undone. "A pox on my carriage! It's your well-being that has me concerned. I simply didn't know how else to send you on your way. You do not appear to be the most pliant of women," he added with an endearingly boyish grin, trying for some unknown reason to make amends. Though he knew he shouldn't care how she felt, he discovered that he did. Truly Englishwomen were the most vexing creatures, and this one in particular!

"I don't care about your intent," Regan said hotly, though she nevertheless weighed the possibility that he had indeed been driven by a need to safeguard a woman on her own. 'Twas, after all, a common enough masculine tendency. But her days at court and expulsion to Ireland had caused Regan to grow wary of the protection men promised and then denied. This one was no different from the rest. Despite her earlier dreamy suppositions to the contrary, he was mortal after all. Angered at having been once again taken in by a handsome face, she added for good measure, "You've no call to worry about me."

"I know," Connor admitted softly with more truth than Regan could guess. "But don't you realize Ireland is a perilous place for the English?"

"Don't worry yourself on my behalf. I'm not afraid of anyone," Regan retorted spiritedly. Still smarting from his discourteous treatment and his attitude of male primacy, she stared at her presumptuous, would-be champion with fire blazing in her eyes.

But her blistering tone failed to provoke Connor as she had hoped. Rather, it evoked a response that bewitched him as the heat of her words signified that her womanly passion would be enough to warm any man's bed, if not ignite his very soul. In an attempt to forget his illogical ardor, Connor concentrated on trying to make this headstrong vixen understand the danger in which she had placed herself in more ways than one.

"You can't stay here," he fairly growled. "Don't you realize you are near O'Carroll lands, a dangerous place indeed?"

"I know full well where I am, but the lands no longer belong to O'Carroll."

"Oh?" Connor asked, his blue eyes darkening. "And are you also aware that since his estate was taken from him, the

O'Carroll and a band of bloodthirsty followers rove this property? Think of the delight they would feel to find such a dainty morsel as you here, protected by only a handful of guards."

"How fainthearted you perceive me to be, Sir Thomas. I've no fear of the former Earl of Kilcaid," Regan said, her mouth curving into a secretive smile.

"You should. He is a troublesome villain and his behavior the last few months is all the more reason for you to pass through these lands quickly," Connor pressed, irked at the woman's stubbornness, yet admiring her mettle in spite of himself.

"I'm afraid that is not to be, sir. You see, *I* am the new owner of Geata Neamhai, though of course I shall call it Heaven's Gate."

"What are you saying?" Connor asked aghast, his carefully crafted English accent almost slipping away. Surely this fair creature could not be the enemy! "That's not possible. We'd heard the property was deeded to William Davies."

"William Davies was my father, may he rest in peace," Regan said, crossing herself. "After he died a short while ago, her majesty transferred the properties and title to me. I am the new Countess of Kilcaid," she concluded, perversely enjoying the disbelief and horror that flitted across the well-drawn features of the man beside her.

"A woman?" Connor sputtered, forgetting his role as a loyal subject of Elizabeth Tudor. "She's sent a bloody woman?"

"That's right, she has," Regan cooed. Repaying this knave for his arrogant behavior tasted sweet. Indeed it was the first thing she had savored since coming to this isolated country.

Connor stood in turbulent silence, staring moodily at the flaxen-haired maiden. This fine bit of woman was his enemy? Dear God, how could he kill a creature who so artfully combined the fragility of a flower with the heat of a firebrand? Yet if he wanted to regain Geata Neamhai how could he not?

As he continued to stare at Regan Davies while she gave orders to have his carriage moved, Connor's dagger lay hot against his thigh. It was tempting to consider carrying out his plan, yet as much as he desired to flout the English decree that had turned his home over to foreigners, he knew he was damned. She was naught but a female, alone and unarmed. He couldn't kill this woman who was little more than a girl. O'Carrolls didn't murder the helpless. There was nothing he could do but bow to the honor of his race and allow the Englishwoman to live.

"I understand, Sir Thomas, that our lands border each other," Regan said, intruding upon his thoughts. "Please be assured that I shall uphold the peace on my estate. I would appreciate you doing the same on yours."

"You don't know what trouble it is you're facing," Connor said, his voice a mere whisper and his face ashen.

"Don't feel compelled to advise me in my affairs or think to watch over me just because I am female," Regan said, her pride getting the better of her. "I am quite capable of fending for myself. However, I don't want to be encumbered by any incompetence on your part along our common boundary. You see, I intend to be the best ruler Heaven's Gate has ever had."

"Oh, do you?" Connor asked hoarsely. "Well, let me assure you that *I* intend to do *everything* in my power to see to it that Heaven's Gate, as you call it, remains in the hands of its rightful owner."

"I have only just told you that I won't need your assistance," Regan replied haughtily, the measure of irony in her companion's words completely lost on her. "But I have no time to argue the matter now. I see my man signaling that the road is clear," she said, climbing into her carriage and leaning out the window. "And so, sir, I take my leave. Driver, go on."

As he stood watching her go, Connor felt the heat of the dagger against his leg once more. It seared his flesh with its accusations of cowardice so that he let out a muffled oath at its impudence, though most of his anger was directed at his own inability to act.

When the carriage had finally disappeared down the forest road, Connor cursed the cruel joke Providence had played. A woman coming to take his keep from him! Elizabeth had gone beyond the beyond, he thought hotly. But fate would be damned, and Regan Davies along with it. Though he could not bring himself to deliver the wench to death's keeping, he vowed to find a solution that would rid his home of her presence yet. There were ways to make a woman hie back to England posthaste, he concluded thoughtfully, and he was, if nothing else, resourceful.

Chapter Four

Regan sat stiffly against the seat of the coach, her uncomfortably perfect posture giving evidence to the outrage she felt. The small rosebud mouth, usually so expressive, pouted at the thought of her abrupt dismissal by the insufferable Watkins. Well, she'd certainly had the satisfaction of startling him with both her name and her purpose in being in Ireland!

But that offer of his... as if she'd ever go running to him for help! She'd sooner meet the devil O'Carroll when she was alone and unarmed than face that pompous peacock's condescending attitude again. He should have molted long ago; his clothes and demeanor were years out of date, and his ideas, as well. No matter what he thought, being a woman did not make her his inferior, and she would succeed managing the O'Carroll estates or die trying.

The driver halted the carriage momentarily for Gerard to enter, and Regan pointedly turned her face away from her advisor. She waited until he was seated before speaking.

"Gerard, I am fully aware that you have undoubtedly prepared a blistering lecture regarding my overly familiar conversation with Sir Thomas. However, you needn't bother to deliver it. I promise you I will not be seeking any further contact with the man. As a matter of fact, I shall consider it a great favor if you'd instruct the guards that he is not welcome at Heaven's Gate."

"Not welcome? What did the man say to you, child? I'll turn back at once and call him out!" sputtered Gerard, his face growing red at the thought of Regan's suffering insults, even if she had brought them on herself. "No matter how tempting the opportunity might be, a true gentleman does not take untoward liberties with a woman of noble breeding, even in Ireland."

"No, it was nothing specific he said, only that he believes me in dire need of a man's protection," Regan admitted ruefully.

"Isn't every woman?" questioned her guardian.

"Certainly not our sovereign—"

"Aye, but she has tens of thousands of men ready to defend her at a moment's notice. I fear the same isn't true of you," stated her father's most trusted servant. "You've only me."

"But I don't need thousands, Gerard, as long as I have one loyal friend like you," soothed the young countess, sorry now she'd distressed the older man with her anger. "But, look, do you suppose those are the towers of Heaven's Gate ahead?"

In the distance on a rise in the plain, a square keep appeared, four imposing pinnacles of hewn rock surrounded by a high stone wall. Though Regan couldn't see a moat from her vantage point, she could tell the drawbridge was up.

"Indeed I would think so," exclaimed Gerard, unable to hide the excitement that crept into his voice. Despite his initial misgivings, he'd discovered this trip to Ireland better than a spring tonic for his spirits, giving him the energy and determination of a man half his age. Leaning out of the window, he gave instructions to the driver. "William, sound the trumpet and let the English know Lady Regan has arrived and expects a proper welcome. It wouldn't do to be ambushed so close to our destination."

"Don't be such an old maid, Gerard. No matter what happens to us now, we're assured of entering either through Heaven's Gate on earth," laughed the young woman, "or up above."

Within the O'Carroll stronghold, Sheila Dempsey was angrily calling down curses on her lord and master, lambasting his foolhardy plan, one that obviously hadn't succeeded. "Sure and I knew he was getting too big for his britches," she fumed, "refusing to listen to me last night and thinking he knew best. Well, the devil take him and Hugh. They deserve it!"

Fortunately the English soldiers in residence disdained the Gaelic tongue and paid her no heed as she moved through the keep, sending servants on the run to air the master bedchamber and see to the fires in the Great Hall. She didn't want to be dismissed upon the English usurper's arrival. What good would that do Connor?

"Oh, you had a plan all right, milord Connor O'Carroll, but could it be you were too filled with whiskey to remember it when the sun came up? You stupid lout, if I had you in arm's reach, you'd know my wrath, but just you wait and see if I don't get my chance. Damn you and your golden-tongued promises! Foolish like a blushing maid I was to believe you could stop Davies from claiming Geata Neamhai. Pray Lord, he didn't kill you, though seeing the estate settled by English tenants might do that yet," fumed the old housekeeper as she hastened maids about their tasks.

"Girl, stop your gawking and clear the rushes from the Great Hall. I know we changed them two days ago, but the new master is arriving and we can't greet him in a slovenly fashion."

"Aye, but I was just now finishing clearing the plates from the soldiers' dinner. They leave such a mess, they do," complained the serving maid. "It seems all we do now is clean up after them."

"Mayhap we shouldn't work at it so hard after all," mused Sheila, an inspirational plot forming. Let the new English master see the chaos the soldiers were causing. If Connor couldn't prevent Davies from arriving, maybe she could spur his departing. "Brigid, never mind the Great Hall, but help Annie with the master's bedchamber," she instructed, not wanting Davies to question either her abilities or her loyalty.

The sound of the drawbridge being lowered wiped all else from her mind. While the thought of appearing cooperative and welcoming galled her, Sheila was wise enough to recognize that she was O'Carroll's only chance to work from within the keep. Solemnly she wiped her hands on her apron and prepared to meet the new master, temporary though he might be.

"Well, Connor, she's in," announced Hugh in disgust as he viewed the Davies carriage disappear behind the gates of Geata Neamhai. While the earl had ordered his men back into the safety of the hills, he and Hugh remained where they could watch the front gates of his family estate, almost perversely needing to witness its violation. "I still say we should have reclaimed the keep the first night Wolf's men took possession. They would never have expected us to come popping out of the walls at them, and there's no way they would have known about the tunnel."

"Few do," said Connor quietly. "But I've told you more than once, Hugh, I won't risk the lives of my people. Lord of the manor or not, I can not justify spilling their blood when it's avoidable."

"Even today, we could have taken the keep if we charged her while the coach was approaching the bridge. Everyone was watching the grand arrival and we could have regained control before they knew what happened."

"And if we didn't succeed, we would have alerted *her* and the English guard to our purpose," disputed the O'Carroll. "This way, she believes me a harmless, if boorish, neighbor, and she'll have those greedy, squatting soldiers out of there by daybreak. Little Mistress Regan is too stubborn a filly for admitting weakness to anyone—or accepting help unless she's forced to. With the official guard gone and only her retainers in place, our job will be much easier."

"But is she really that foolish? Surely the English Wolf won't want to part with your food and drink quite so readily just because the lady tells him to be gone. The man will exaggerate the danger you pose..."

"Mark my words, Hugh, the lady won't hear a thing he says. I'll even wager a bottle of whiskey on it—English or not—that one has a fire in her that's almost Celtic. She does exactly what she wants, be it wise or not."

As the carriage crossed the drawbridge into the courtyard, Regan refastened her head covering, smoothing her blond tresses into place, preparing to assume her role as the rightful mistress of Heaven's Gate. It was no matter that she'd previously scorned the property and even the notion of life in Ireland. Now was her chance to be worthy of her father's name, as well as her sovereign's dictates—and to prove Watkins wrong about her abilities to manage and defend her lands.

Waiting for Gerard to alight and help her from the coach, the young Englishwoman looked about curiously. There was a large contingent of soldiers standing at attention on the steps to the main keep, accompanied by a small red-haired woman. The courtyard itself was far larger than she'd imagined from outside the walls; apparently it sheltered not only the keep itself but a smithy, a stable and even a small garden, as well as numerous undefined sheds. It would seem O'Carroll had owned a prosperous estate indeed.

"Lady Regan, may I present Sir Henry Sidney's deputy Captain Wolf, and Sheila, the manor's housekeeper?" Gerard said. At his words, the soldier bowed stiffly from the waist while the woman beside him curtsied.

"Captain, this is the new owner of these lands, Lady Regan, Countess of Westfield and Kilcaid," proclaimed Gerard. "Here are the deeds duly signed by her majesty and validated by Sir Henry."

The officer's reply was lost in Sheila's sudden protest.

"Lady Regan? But what of Sir William Davies? We had been told he would be the new master," the woman questioned without thinking. A female was taking over Geata Neamhai? Had Connor's Irish blood run so hot at the sight of her that he abandoned his thoughts of revenge? What else could explain her arrival unharmed?

"My father had a date with the Almighty he could not postpone," said Regan coldly, amazed at the servant's interruption. Were all the Irish so free-spoken? "However, quite frankly, I fail to see how his passing affects you."

"No, mistress, though I give you my sympathies, of course. Begging your pardon, I was just astounded by your traveling all this way, a woman alone and all," extemporized the housekeeper. "Didn't O'Carroll try to scare you off on the road?"

"Woman, are you totally daft? He'd never try to attack with my men in the area," blustered the military officer. "Believe me, Lady Regan, despite his noisy threats of retaliation, my men have kept this property intact for you—"

"Except for the contents of the wine cellar, the kitchen stores, and the game they poached," muttered Sheila so that only Regan heard her.

Looking at the O'Carroll housekeeper, Regan weighed her loyalty. Obviously the woman had no patience with Wolf, but if he'd misused the estate, wasn't that appropriate? Nevertheless, the housekeeper was Irish and Regan couldn't help but wonder if Sheila's feelings for her former lord overrode her love for the land itself.

"Milady, I assure you we've searched the area for that scoundrel day and night in all types of weather for weeks—"

"Except when they were drinking the tenants' mead, bedding the maids, or riding to the hounds," his critic rejoined quietly.

"And we haven't seen hide nor hair of him. I guarantee the man is miles away by now. That spawn of Satan's loins knows he doesn't stand a prayer against her majesty's loyal servants," concluded Captain Wolf.

"Aye, but then what honest soul does?" asked Sheila rhetorically. Raising her voice so the others would hear her, she continued, "Milady, I've had the captain's belongings removed from the master's chamber upstairs. Perhaps you'd like to retire there and refresh yourself?"

"Thank you, Sheila, I will shortly, and I will speak with you after dinner regarding your duties here. Captain, her majesty appreciates your efforts on her behalf and you have my thanks as well. However, I'm certain you and your men would like to return to your post with Sidney, so I won't detain you further."

"But, Lady Regan, O'Carroll—"

"You said yourself, Captain, that he's probably miles away by now. Besides, the rest of my men will arrive within a few days. There is no need to trouble you anymore," said the countess firmly. If there were no danger, she thought, why continue to permit these soldiers to deplete her stores. "I should like you and your men to accept my dominion over Heaven's Gate and depart. Until you do, I fear the servants and tenants will not respect my authority."

"Very well, I will send half of my men home on the morrow, Lady Regan, but I must remain with the others until your contingent gets here. In all good conscience, I can do no less," stated the captain in a transparent effort to prevent this easy assignment from disappearing before his eyes.

"I appreciate your concern, sir, but that is not what I wish," protested Regan, already tired of this military sycophant. Before she could continue, an authoritative Gerard spoke up.

"Captain, you will leave in the morning with all but a dozen of your men," he commanded in his old regimental voice. "As the Countess of Kilcaid's majordomo I will assume the obligation to protect her and her household. Should you doubt my provenance, you may contact Sir Henry Sidney on your return to the city."

"Very well," Wolf replied reluctantly. "If that is what Lady Regan really wants—"

"It is," confirmed the young Englishwoman, "and now, Sheila, if you will direct me toward my rooms, I can find my own way, and you can see to your other chores."

"Yes, milady," the servant agreed, leading her mistress inside to the south-tower stairs. "Right at the top of these steps, and you'll find the earl's apartments, I mean, your ladyship's quarters."

Regan nodded and began to climb the curving staircase, but a slight touch on her arm made her hesitate.

"May I say, your ladyship, you handled the Wolf right smartly, you did. Geata Neamhai will be a far sight richer with that predator gone from underfoot," said Sheila, toadying to the estate's new overlord though she realized there was a grain of truth in her words, as well. As much as she'd expected to hate the new English master, she found herself oddly respecting the spirit of this young woman, despite her enemy bloodlines.

"I gathered from your remarks in the courtyard, Sheila, that the guards were more plunderers than defenders, but from this day on, my lands are to be called Heaven's Gate. They belong to the English now and I want everyone to clearly understand that fact," instructed Regan, not missing the slight scowl that crossed the servant's face. "Now, please see to settling the rest of my party."

"Of course, milady." Sheila's voice was as respectful as before, but there was a cold edge to her words as she regretted her momentary softening. She should have known better, the old woman reflected bitterly as she went back to the courtyard. No English man or woman could have a decent soul; hadn't King Henry proved that?

For her part, Regan climbed the steps of the tower slowly. She'd had enough unsettlement in the past few hours and would welcome a bit of quiet solitude—and the chance to explore the master bedchamber unaccompanied. Nothing told as much about a man as his quarters, and when a man had a reputation such as O'Carroll, she couldn't help but wonder about its reality.

Yet Regan found O'Carroll's apartments somewhat disappointing; perhaps his essence had dissipated in his absence. The rooms themselves were neither as bad as she'd feared nor as good as they would have been in an English castle. The windows were small as always when the keep was also a fortress, barely admitting the sun's entry, but the late afternoon rays made a valiant attempt, and there was a healthy fire burning in the large fireplace of the main room.

Though the tapestries on the walls were desperately in need of an airing, the colors and detailed work in the woven hunting scenes evidenced considerable talent. The oversized four-poster bed was an especially welcome sight with its linens turned back, though the draperies hanging around it were badly faded and in need of a major repair. Someone, presumably Sheila, had even supplied a basin, lavender and water for washing, she discovered appreciatively. Despite the absence of her maid, Regan was undressed, washed and beneath the heavy sheets within minutes... and asleep seconds after that.

* * *

After Regan was settled in her chambers, Gerard stalked throughout the keep with purposeful strides. The past few weeks had been hard on her, and he determined he would see to it that the days ahead were easier. The sooner everyone within the walls of Heaven's Gate recognized him as the voice of authority for the castle's new mistress, the smoother things would progress for his lady. It was not that Regan couldn't be commanding when she so chose, but he knew full well that her path would be less difficult if the inhabitants of this fortress learned that the Lady Regan's word would be upheld by his blade and those of his men. His position in the newly established hierarchy of the keep would assure hers.

And what better place to begin making his authority known than with that impudent hag who had met them upon arrival? Though the Dempsey woman may have run things in the past, she was about to discover that her superiors had, in fact, arrived, and that he, himself, was one of them. This thought replaced the frown Gerard had worn with a smile of sorts, and he unconsciously hastened his stride as he went in search of Sheila Dempsey.

The Englishman soon discovered, however, that Heaven's Gate was a larger place than it seemed at first glance. And Sheila Dempsey proved to be elusive. Wherever he went, he observed people busily working at tasks the woman had assigned them, but she was nowhere to be seen. Up one staircase, down another, Sheila Dempsey had been there before him and already departed. In an effort to conserve his labored breath, Gerard barely muttered that the Irish wench had to have wings to be all over the environs so easily while he was finding it increasingly difficult to continue. He consoled himself with the fact that his present weariness was the result of being cramped up for so many hours in that infernal carriage, easily overlooking his all-too-rapid advance into middle age.

After a tour of three of the towers, a cellar, innumerable sheds, the barns and a vegetable patch, Gerard's thirst had grown along with his anger. By now, it had become a point of honor to confront the Dempsey woman before everyone met in the Great Hall for the evening meal. But being a practical man, Gerard decided to quench his parched throat before continuing with the quest that was beginning to rival, at least in difficulty, the ancient search for the Grail.

Making his way into the Great Hall, Gerard bellowed for a serving maid. To his surprise, however, no one answered his summons. A quick search of the area showed that there wasn't a soul about, and an enraged Gerard stormed off in the direction of the kitchens and a servant who could fetch him something to drink.

Spying the chimneys of one small building across the courtyard, the Englishman wasted no time in approaching his destination. His heavy tread crushed the gravel beneath his feet as he determinedly made his way toward the doorway of the building, his demeanor that of an attacking soldier ready to rout out and destroy his foe.

Advancing into the room as though he were assailing it, Gerard was caught up short at the sight of the very woman who had led him such a merry chase for a greater part of the afternoon.

Interrupted in the act of instructing a cook, Sheila Dempsey stood regarding him with cool arrogance, as though questioning his intrusion into her domain. Gerard was only too aware that he, himself, appeared a wild man in comparison. Without doubt, this was not the sort of encounter he had envisioned when he had decided to teach this Irish witch her place. The realization compounded his anger and frustration, so that his speech was gruffer than any he had ever employed when addressing a female.

"Woman," he roared, "there was no one in the hall to serve me. What must a man do in this ill-run keep when he is thirsty?"

"What does a man do?" Sheila echoed in a soft voice that was belied by the hands which flew to her hips, a gesture that cautioned the cook to retreat to a safer portion of the room. "I will tell you what he does, Englishman. He goes to the well in the courtyard and hauls himself up a bucket of water. That's what he does!"

"That may have been how it was, but I'm here to tell you that things are changed. See to it that there are attendants in the Great Hall at all times."

"Aye, and should I see to it, too, that they fetch and carry for Sidney's men upon request, no matter how that hungry hoard depletes your lady's stores of food and drink? If you thought about it before you started giving orders, you'd see that there was a reason for making it difficult to come by refreshment."

"All right, woman, all right," Gerard conceded reluctantly. "Leave things as they are until Sidney's men depart. But after that, standards will be met. This is no longer the home of an Irish outlaw, but the residence of a fine English lady."

"Is that so?" Sheila asked, her voice gaining in volume. "And I'll have you know there was not a finer or more gracious hall in all of Christendom than Geata Neamhaí when the O'Carroll was its lord."

"You will find, Sheila Dempsey, that what suited your former master may not find favor with the Lady Regan. If you cannot reconcile yourself to having a new mistress, then perhaps it would be best for you to leave Heaven's Gate immediately."

"That won't be necessary, sir," Sheila murmured, looking down at the floor so that this pompous stranger wouldn't see the fire burning in her eyes. Biting her tongue, she admonished herself to bide her time, promising that the unreasonable enemy before her would get what he deserved. Though she hoped Connor didn't slay this gray fox right away, the Widow Dempsey's motives were far from charitable. She rather relished the thought of Gerard Langston's captivity. In order to get her through the present moment of forced humility, she conjured up images of setting him to emptying chamber pots.

"Right then," Gerard blustered, disappointed that he found his first victory at Heaven's Gate to be a hollow one. "Just remember, my good woman, that you are the Countess of Kilcaid's castelain and the property you guard is hers. For now, just see to it that a proper dinner is prepared for her."

"Are you daring to assert your authority in my kitchens as well?" Sheila blurted before she could catch herself.

"Aye, woman, that I am. Your new mistress's rule reaches to every corner of this miserable keep, and in many instances I will be her voice. Now see to it that the dinner you order prepared is fitting for a great lady who is doubtless weary from travel. I would think that sustenance is what she needs—good mutton and beef and fowl," Gerard said, unconsciously licking at his lips.

"Given the circumstances, I know exactly what the lady requires," Sheila replied demurely, the sly look gleaming in her eye escaping the soldier's notice. Damn his impudence! She'd show this proud rooster who ruled the kitchens of Geata Neamhai, and she'd ruin his evening meal besides. There was only one greater revenge a woman could wreak upon a man other than spoil his supper, and that was an appetite the soldier's silver mane made questionable anyway. Aye, let him salivate until the dishes were uncovered, and then let him see how much he would eat.

"Leave it to me, sir," Sheila called out as Gerard left the room. "As you ordered, I'll see to it that the Lady Regan is well taken care of."

"Milady, mistress, Lady Regan, oh, madam, wake up," cried the serving girl urgently. When she still got no response from her repeated urgings, she finally dared to touch the woman sleeping in the master chamber. "Milady, please wake up. Sheila won't serve supper until you've come downstairs, and the men are all drinking overly much, but she says it's not fitting to sup without the mistress. Won't you please open your eyes?"

Slowly, ever so slowly, the situation penetrated Regan's drowsy state of mind till she understood sufficiently to leap up from the bed with a speed that had the maid scurrying to a spot just inside the door, but far removed from the bed and its unpredictable occupant.

"Don't be frightened, child. I won't scold you or beat you. In fact, I'm quite pleased you had the good sense to persevere. Come now, help me dress and tell me your name," suggested Regan.

"Annie, milady, Annie Barone," confided the girl softly as she hastened to brush the gown her mistress handed her.

"Now then, Annie, tell me how you come to speak English so well. I understood that not all the Irish had mastered our tongue."

"Oh, that's the O'Carroll's doing, mistress. He spent time in the English court as a lad and when he came home to Geata, ah, Heaven's Gate, he made us all learn English."

"But, whatever for? Few English landlords expect their servants to speak their own language properly, let alone a foreign tongue," pressed the countess as the young girl assisted her into her gown.

"His lordship always said it's a damn sight better to understand what your enemy is saying about you than to fight him unaware," confided Annie before she realized the import of her words.

"And do you think I'm your enemy, Annie?" questioned Regan softly.

"Oh, no, milady, not you, no, please don't think that because I said what I did that I'm not trustworthy...I never—"

"Of course, I won't think that. I just wanted you to realize that not all English are your enemy...though they may be foe to O'Carroll. Come now, lead me to the delicious supper that awaits," instructed Regan.

Upon entering the Great Hall, Regan was astonished at the number of men apparently in her service, or Wolf's. She looked more closely at those seated at the trestle tables and noticed that at least three-quarters of them had weapons at hand. Prepared to fight they might be, but she, or Heaven's Gate, was still responsible for feeding them, at least seventy at rough count! No wonder Sheila had complained about their appetites.

"Lady Regan, at last," called Captain Wolf from the head table where he and Gerard sat alone. "I was afraid you weren't going to join us."

"And miss the first sumptuous repast in my new home?" countered Regan as she seated herself between Wolf and her advisor. Though things were apparently peaceful enough between them now, she couldn't be sure their earlier argumentativeness wouldn't recur, and she would not have the English appear divided in front of her Irish staff. "Certainly not, though it smells as though you two gentlemen have drunk enough ale to thoroughly destroy your appreciation of our evening meal."

"All we've seen for the last hour and a half was bread and ale," complained Wolf. "What's a man to do but eat what's before him?"

"In England many a poor soul would be grateful for such fare, but I suppose a fighting man of such vigorous activity as yourself craves a meatier diet," said the countess, her voice quivering with indignation at the soldier's presumption.

"Well, naturally. I mean you would not give a wolf-hound a meal of corn mash and expect it to bring down a buck, would you?" snorted the English captain.

"But *you* have not even seen the buck, let alone brought him down," growled Gerard, "and all along I venture you've been eating like a king."

"Since Sheila and the serving women are here now, gentlemen, let us end the discussion," said Regan firmly.

"Begging your pardon, milady, but I just didn't think it fitting to serve before you were in the hall, your first night and all," explained Sheila, her eyes suspiciously downcast as if she feared meeting Regan's glance.

"That's all right, but have the maids skip serving the soup and start on the main course at once," suggested the new mistress as she saw the large pots the women were carrying. "I fear the men have partaken of too much liquid sustenance already."

"I'm frightfully sorry, milady, but the kitchen didn't prepare any roasts or vegetables tonight, Lady Regan. Supper is warm porridge and fresh-gathered honey with brown bread."

"Po-porridge?" sputtered Gerard, barely able to get a word out. "Woman, did I or did I not specifically tell you to fix a good and proper meal for her ladyship after her long trip?"

"Aye, that you did, sir, and so I did. A simple healthy cereal for a weary body after such a long journey, that be the porridge, with the honey for a sweetening touch," defended Sheila. "Surely Lady Regan understands it's not wise to overtax the body with rich food after such an ordeal as your journey from England."

"And what of *my* body, woman?" exclaimed Captain Wolf.

"You and your men, sir, will be traveling tomorrow so your stomachs should be rested tonight. Besides, sir, you ate a half side of pork at dinner," retorted Sheila as she started to serve the porridge.

Struggling to contain her amusement, Regan spoke before either of the men could continue their complaints.

"Gentlemen, you will simply have to avail yourselves of additional bread if the porridge does not suit you. What is done is done and I will not see food go to waste. Sheila, I will speak with you in my chambers immediately after dinner."

"Of course, milady," acknowledged the housekeeper, signaling the maids to begin serving the soldiers.

After the meager supper was finished, Regan retired to her quarters, determined to explore the enigma that was Sheila. While awaiting her arrival, the young countess opened the writing desk in the solar, a small room between the corridor and the main chamber, and found not only ink and paper but a basket of letters written in a very stylish hand, though her Latin was too poor to fully comprehend their intent. Was O'Carroll that learned a man that he wrote his missives in such a formal tongue, or did he wish to avoid nosey servants?

"Lady Regan, I am at your service," announced Sheila with a small curtsy. "What was it you wanted?"

"First and foremost to know your purpose, Sheila," replied the Englishwoman. "I am not foolish enough to believe you as simple as you would like me to think, but neither do I perceive you as malicious. Tell me how you come to be housekeeper here."

"Here? Oh, milady, I've never known anyplace else. My mother and father, indeed my grandfolk before them have always served at Geata Neamhai, and so should I, you being willing, until death claims me," said the redheaded servant. "I'd not like to learn a new trade now."

"And your own children, what of them and your husband?"

"I only had females, I did, milady, and they've all gone off with their men, all about Ireland and a few to England, but it's not meet for a woman to live off her son-in-law's bounty. No good would ever come if it, I venture," answered the housekeeper, untruthfully. "As for my husband, I had three, I did, and buried them all. So if you be looking to find another home for me, I fear there be none too ready to have me."

"I simply wonder at your willingness to serve an English household when you yourself are Irish. I certainly appreciate your information regarding Wolf and his greed, and will overlook the poor excuse for a meal in consideration of the porridge's speeding the troops on their way. However, can you truly be loyal to me when I have benefited from the O'Carroll's misfortune? That is what concerns me, Sheila. If you can, you and all the other servants are more than welcome to stay at Heaven's Gate, but—"

"Oh, Lord, no, your ladyship, it's not at all like that in Ireland. We learn from a young age that politics mean little to the little folk. Our loyalty is to the land on which we were born and no more. Geata Neamhai, er, Heaven's Gate is my home and I'd like to stay here, no matter whose hand is on the helm, though I might add yours is a might prettier than O'Carroll's ever was."

"In that case, Sheila, welcome home," Regan replied dryly, not entirely taken in by the older woman's smooth tongue. "And now, shall we plan tomorrow's meals so my men do not decide to leave with Captain Wolf? I take it there is sufficient food in the kitchen stores?"

"Aye, milady, and there be a healthy garden, running streams and forests full of game for the taking, should we run shy," replied the housekeeper, apparently compliant, even as she planned what she would tell Connor later that night.

Chapter Five

Regan purposely avoided breaking her fast in the Great Hall the next morning, preferring a solitary cup of broth and bread in her quarters to sitting on a raised platform in full sight of the household before she was fully awake. Nonetheless, she received a full report from Gerard on the morning meal's acceptability.

"Whatever you said to that Irish crone last night certainly was well put," he complimented his mistress. "Rashers of thick bacon, eggs aplenty, hot bread and fresh-churned butter, enough so not a man went hungry, even Dillon, who ate a dozen eggs by himself. Of course, Captain Wolf and his men left at sunup as you ordered, so they missed the feast, but that left more for us."

"What of the soldiers he left behind?"

"They ate like birds compared to Dillon, but Sheila put most of them to work turning over some land south of the wall for another garden. Though they complained, I insisted the orders be followed. The others are standing watch. Would you believe it, Regan, that after I supported her, that woman actually wanted to use our fellows for house chores, too? But I let her know they are fighting men, not field hands," snorted Gerard. "I wish you would reconsider your decision to keep her around, girl. She's a far sight too big for her britches, no matter how tiny she is. I daresay if she could, she'd have us mucking out the stables next."

"In truth, Gerard, the men *will* do that and anything else necessary to make Heaven's Gate a successful plantation—"

"You're still wanting to prove the queen wrong—or is it love for Dudley that spurs you on?" groaned her major-domo, envisioning the struggles that lay ahead.

"You may not believe this, but neither of those is my reason," said Regan with a small smile, thinking of the joy she would have making Watkins eat his words about needing *his* help. "I have just decided to be a good neighbor. Now, look at this—if I am reading the maps and deeds correctly, Heaven's Gate extends twelve miles north and south, and six miles east and west, with the main keep about three and a half miles from the village."

"Aye, the east-west border is a small tributary, but why this sudden interest in boundaries? You said yesterday when we arrived that you'd seen enough rolling hills and stench-ridden peat bogs to last you a lifetime."

"Now, Gerard, would that be any way for a landowner to speak? I think it only suitable for me to see to my property and inspect its limitations like a good general anticipates his army's victories by knowing his men."

"Ah, the truth emerges, I should have guessed! Despite your angry words yesterday, you want an excuse to ride your borders searching for a glimpse of your pretty neighbor, Sir Thomas."

"Hogwash! I do not care if I ever see that primping pea-cock again, let alone speak with him," scoffed Regan. "I merely want to investigate my holdings."

"Then you won't mind if I accompany you?"

"I certainly would mind. How can I freely visit the tenants and see the state of things for myself with an armed escort? You would scare the inhabitants into hiding with that ferocious scowl of yours."

"And what better way for O'Carroll to reclaim his land than by taking you prisoner? You've heard the tales of cattle raids in this part of the country. What makes you think he would hesitate to abduct a lone woman riding without an escort if he could? I absolutely forbid it!" pronounced Gerard sternly.

"All right then, I will take a few men, three or four as guards and one of the stable boys as a guide," agreed the young woman reluctantly. Still the compromise was better than she had expected. "While I am gone, however, I want you to inspect the keep itself with an eye to its defensive strengths and weaknesses should we have to endure a siege. When the rest of our people arrive, I want everything in readiness for them."

"And you do get what you want, Lady Regan, don't you?" asked Gerard with a grimace. Yet as much as he hated to acknowledge it, his young mistress did seem well organized and capable of command. All the same, he'd warn the men going with her to be on the lookout for trouble, just in case O'Carroll was still roaming the vicinity.

"Yes, Gerard, I usually do," Regan agreed readily. "And, when I do not, it is not for lack of trying, I assure you."

In spite of her best efforts to appear comfortable and countrylike, the young Englishwoman looked every bit a countess when she descended to the courtyard. The only riding clothes she had were of royal-blue velvet with silver embroidery on the sleeves and bodice, which set off her coloring but did little for her role as the authority of the manor. She would speak to Sheila about a seamstress for some simpler things; until then, this would have to do.

"Don't you want a cloak, milady?" suggested Sheila as she watched the new mistress mount the horse Gerard had chosen. "The rain springs up terrible fast sometimes, and the O'Carroll holdings are widespread."

"The Davies lands," said Regan. "But thank you for your concern. I think the sun will hold."

"Yes, your ladyship. Now, Tommy, have the mistress here in time for dinner, you hear? No losing the way in order to skip your evening chores or you'll have to answer to me," threatened the housekeeper, the thin line of her mouth giving no doubt as to her annoyance.

"Aye, ma'am. Not to worry, I'll take care of her right well," answered the lad, full of youthful assurance.

Then the drawbridge was down and Regan could taste her freedom. Instructing the guards to follow her and Tommy to stay beside her, Regan set off across the fields with a song in her heart. She was responsible to no one but herself for the first time in months; there was no sovereign to question her, no Gerard to criticize, no other women-in-waiting to carp.

As she rode, feverishly at first, the hills seemed to unfold, one upon the next, unending meadows lush with wildflowers and the sounds of singing birds, until Regan's mood softened and she began to notice the small beauties of the scenery. Every once in a while, her party startled a rabbit or quail from its hedgerow, but no one interrupted the young countess in the gradual easing of her tension, both physical and mental. It was as though she were awakening from an uneasy sleep to find the world had become perfect in her absence, even if it was Ireland.

Indeed, an unexpected paradise opened itself to Regan's explorations, from the small village church, picturesque in its very lack of pretense, to the lea where honeybees buzzed happily about, making their sweet nectar. Was it beautiful because she had anticipated much less from this stormy land, or did she find it enchanting because it was actually so? The unending variations of green that engulfed the landscape as far as the eye could see filled her senses.

She suddenly threw back her head and laughed aloud, acknowledging with surprise that she, the English Countess of Westfield, was glad to be in Ireland, so glad in fact that she almost uttered a prayer for Elizabeth before she caught herself; no use being too sentimental. Turning to the boy who had kept pace with her, patiently answering her occasional questions while her own men fell farther and farther behind, Regan addressed him.

"Tommy, as much as I hate the afternoon to end, I think we had best start back."

"Aye, milady, but I could come with you again tomorrow if you like," offered the boy. Without waiting for a reply, he turned the horses southward, obviously quite at home on his mount.

"Thank you, Tommy. I would like that. Tell me, have you always lived at Heaven's Gate?"

"Yes, ma'am. My father's been the O'Carroll blacksmith for ages and ages, only I guess he's yours now. I help him out and look after the horses. That's one of my favorites you're riding now; I helped birth her."

"You must have been awfully young for a chore like that."

"No, milady," Tommy laughed. "She's only three. Besides, Master Connor says a man is never too young to pitch in when a job needs doing. He lets me help out plenty on the place, between the sheep and the cattle he has, and all—" The boy hesitated, suddenly embarrassed at his confidences and uncertain how his new mistress would respond.

"That's all right, Tommy. It will take a while to get used to my being here, but there is no reason a lad such as you cannot remember O'Carroll kindly even though Queen Elizabeth considers him a renegade."

"But, don't you?" asked the youngster in surprise.

"Me? Heavens, no, I've never even met the man," confessed Regan. "My sovereign told me to travel to Ireland to take over his property and I did as she ordered. I have nothing against Connor O'Carroll personally."

"But do you think that's right? Just moving in like that when the owner isn't even in residence, just because some old English lady told you to?" spouted Tommy, his youth evident in his passionate question. To hide his distress, he jumped down from his horse and led it and Regan's to a nearby stream, still talking as he went. "I mean, taking over somebody else's land doesn't seem real fair after they worked so hard to make it special. Would you like that to happen to you?"

"No, but..."

For a moment Regan hesitated, wondering how to ex-plain the vagaries of court politics to this child, unschooled in any book sense, but apparently well versed in the golden rule.

"Things are not always as clear-cut as they may appear, Tommy. In England, all nobles swear fealty to the Crown and promise to obey the sovereign's dictates. If they dis-obey her wishes, they could forfeit their lives and those of their families."

"I hear tell that when you take an Irishman's lands, it's tantamount to taking his life," said an annoyingly familiar voice from across the stream. "Or so the Irish around here believe, those foolish enough to voice their opinions to *this Englishman,* that is." With a flicker of his wrist, the man Regan knew as Watkins tossed a coin to the wide-eyed Tommy, who quickly caught it and dared not look up from the treasure he held in his hand. "There, lad, that's for guiding your mistress safely around the property and back home without trouble. You haven't seen any sign of O'Car-roll, eh?"

"No, no, sir, not me, and Captain Wolf left with most of his men this morning, so I guess he figures it to be safe around here, too," gushed the boy, his face reddening ap-parently from pleasure at his unexpected reward.

"Well then, Lady Regan, I wish you good day though I'd suggest you travel with a larger party in the future. One never knows what devils you might encounter in this heathen land," said her audacious neighbor, still inappropriately garbed in outdated styles. When *was* the last time he'd been back at court?

"Yet *you* ride unaccompanied," challenged Regan, her emerald-green eyes sparking at the man's unfailing arrogance.

"*I* am not a helpless female dressed for a royal audience," the nobleman called over his shoulder as he cantered off, singularly unconcerned about giving Regan an opportunity to retort. As her guards joined them at the stream moments later, Regan was still sputtering angrily.

"That pompous pile of outdated manners, if he thinks he had the last word, he has another think or two coming from me. I swear I will make him eat his words, helpless female, indeed. Just wait, Sir Thomas Watkins, I am going to make Heaven's Gate outshine your old plantation before you can look twice, or I am not Regan Elizabeth Davies."

"If you say so, milady, but we'd better hurry back now or Sheila will have my hide, for sure," answered the boy quietly, his earlier enthusiasm oddly vanished. Remounting quickly, he set a pace back to the keep which discouraged further conversation, but Regan was too irritated with Watkins's manner to take notice.

"I suppose there was some reasonable purpose to your letting the woman alone, even when you came upon her with just Tommy for company," snorted Hugh, expertly skinning a rabbit while leaving no doubt whose skin he'd prefer to be peeling. Connor had just returned to their camp and told his friend about the encounter with Regan. "For the life of me, I don't understand why you just didn't grab the bloody female and send that old fop of hers a message that her hide could be bought for the price of Geata Neamhai. You know Tommy wouldn't have betrayed you."

"No, but I had no way of knowing if there were others in her party, and as it turns out, four guards arrived just as I left," defended Connor, though in truth the thought of kidnapping the girl hadn't occurred to him. Even now, it somehow seemed cowardly to reclaim what was his by taking what wasn't.

"Since when can Connor O'Carroll not hold his own against four fellows?" scoffed Connor's second in command.

"There will be other chances to abduct her if we decide it necessary," replied Connor calmly, finding that he had strangely enjoyed the brief encounter with Regan Davies, although he certainly couldn't admit that to Hugh. Indeed, perhaps it was the chance to aggravate her that he truly relished. Her bright eyes seemed to catch fire when she was angry, and the heightened pink in her cheeks made her fair complexion even more spectacular than he'd remembered. For a titled Englishwoman she had more spunk than he would have expected; with the exception of Elizabeth, those females he'd met in England hid behind handkerchiefs and fans to protect their delicate sensitivities, or so they claimed.

"Remember," he continued to Hugh, "our men are set to start escalating our efforts to relieve Ireland of the Lady Regan. Until then, let the wench believe herself happily ensconced in her new home. Soon enough we'll show her the error of her ways."

"Aye, Connor, but I hope you're not being taken in by soft eyes and a simpering face," drawled Hugh. "It's been a while since you—"

"Don't fear for my welfare, friend. It hasn't been that long. Besides, I was right about her forcing that fool Wolf to depart with his men, and I'll be just as unfailing in my anticipation of her response to our scheduled devilment. Just you watch."

"You don't leave me much choice," complained Hugh, only half in jest. This inactivity was sorely trying his patience, but his loyalty to Connor demanded his compliance. Certainly though, a few words of advice now and then might be shared without appearing traitorous. Connor said all would work out and it would, he imagined, one way or another.

Peace reigned at Heaven's Gate when Regan's party returned. Even Sheila and Gerard seemed to have struck a tenuous truce whereby his men were helping to arrange the furniture in the Great Hall under her supervision. Near the hearth, a small alcove had been fashioned so Regan and her guests could dine without being constantly under public scrutiny by the assembled soldiers and servants.

"Thank you, Sheila, this is much more to my liking. A lady enjoys her privacy more than a man, I do believe," explained the Countess of Westfield and Kilcaid. "I suppose it will take me some time to become accustomed to being mistress of so large a household."

"If you say so, milady," replied the housekeeper. "We are here to please you. Did you enjoy your ride?"

"More to the point," intruded Gerard brusquely. "I noticed you led your guards on your return though I gave them strict orders to ride with you, not behind you."

"Oh, Gerard, sometimes you are such a mother hen. I arrived back safely, didn't I? Tommy was an excellent guide. He showed me all over the northern extent of Heaven's Gate and we had no problems whatsoever. We did see Sir Thomas Watkins on the opposite bank of a stream, but—"

"Ah, I knew it! Let you out of my sight and..."

"It was still a lovely day with no untoward occurrences. Nothing else need be said," Regan remarked emphatically. "Sheila, as soon as I refresh myself, you may serve dinner."

"Yes, milady, and believe me, you will not be disappointed," assured the housekeeper.

Indeed, her word was gospel. Never had Regan tasted a sweeter, more succulent roast, cooked and seasoned to perfection, and served beautifully. Even Gerard was pleased, though he wouldn't admit it. Perhaps the fresh air and the private dining area had heightened her appetite, but when Regan laid her head upon her pillow that night she fell asleep instantly, dreaming that she had truly passed beyond heaven's gate.

That placid sensation did not linger, however, for within a day, it seemed all the demons of hell had set their sights on her holdings in which to do mischief.

First three men sent to gather firewood disappeared without a trace, though both the remainder of Wolf's men and Regan's own searched the area for them. Then, she received word from the coast that with the exception of her soldiers, the rest of her household and those tenants she had sponsored for emigration to Heaven's Gate had been further delayed by storms. While not a major crisis, it meant Regan had to tolerate Wolf's extra men and Sheila's complaints about them that much longer.

That selfsame afternoon, the milkmaids returned from the cow pasture with the news that there was no milk. The cows had already been milked dry despite the fact they were known to be O'Carroll stock. Sheila put the trouble off to the spirits of Geata Neamhai unhappy that the English had taken up residence, while Gerard scoffed and said every animal had an off day once in a while and their udders would be twice as full in the morning.

However, he proved wrong when the maids returned with empty pails and the news that two of the cows had apparently been stolen, since they were no longer with the herd. At this news, Gerard began to curse loudly, denouncing the Irish Gypsies who were undoubtedly at fault. Sending a guard of a half-dozen men to the field where the cows were kept, he instructed them to watch the animals carefully and milk them when the time came. But under no conditions were the men to return to the keep without full pails of the nourishing nectar so much a part of the Irish diet. Once supper had been served and the men had still not come back, Regan insisted on riding out to find out what happened.

"Honestly, milady, we saw no one and yet the cows are dry, they've not a drop of milk," exclaimed one of the guards.

"Very well. Gerard, you stay with the men tonight. Light torches if need be, but find the culprits who are stealing our milk," ordered the young Englishwoman.

"But, Regan, the cold damp ground—you know I'm rheumatic," protested the older man.

"I'll send someone out with blankets. After all, Gerard, you are the one who blames O'Carroll for this. Let's see if you can catch him," baited his mistress as she headed back to her own bed in the tower.

The next morning, not only Regan, but Sheila and the milkmaids as well, rode out to the cow pasture at dawn, only to find the gray-haired advisor and his hand-chosen men still feeling the effects of an abundant supply of Irish whiskey.

"Gerard, how could you do such a thing?"

"Not so loud, child, I haven't the head for your prattle," he pleaded weakly.

"But you—you were the one I trusted," berated the girl. "You were supposed to set a proper example for the men, not lead the debauchery."

"Milady, the serving women who brought the jugs said you sent them, that the contents would provide us with more warmth than the blankets you'd sent earlier, and it was cold."

"Which women? Do you know their names?"

"No, I thought you sent them. Besides, we really didn't look at their faces, just the gifts they were offering," admitted her man sheepishly. "I don't suppose there's any milk?"

"Not a drop," confirmed the milkmaids.

"Can we take them back to the keep?" suggested Gerard.

"And stable cattle in my courtyard? Not in my life time," sneered Sheila. "It's bad enough with the horses about."

"That won't solve our problem. I'll spend the day in the pasture, and I won't drink my warmth, I'll enjoy the sun," decided the mistress of Heaven's Gate.

But even Regan's vigilance proved fruitless as the sun started to set and not a single cow was producing milk. Sheila muttered anxiously about the wiles of the fairy folk even as she started to ration the butter and soft cheese she'd stored previously.

"Me ma used to tell of the spells they'd weave, you know. They have the powers, milady," she counseled Regan. "I've heard tell how they stopped the moon from shining on a bright night with not a single cloud in the sky, and every one knows about the babes they've stolen in the dead o night and replaced with changelings. With that kind o power, what's it to drying up a few dozen milk cows? I wager even a single spirit could handle that chore."

"What did you say?" questioned Regan suddenly.

"That drying up a few dozen—"

"That's it! Don't you see? It's not necessarily that some one's constantly stealing the milk, but that the cows aren't giving their usual quantity," said the Englishwoman as the truth dawned on her. "And if that be the case, I can reverse it, I'm certain."

"But how, milady? You're no herdsman's daughter." Sheila was clearly distraught, but whether from her mistress's sanity or chagrin that she herself hadn't recognized the problem Regan couldn't decide.

"Surely you know of the different properties of the plant and herbs that grow in this area?"

"Of course, milady, who doesn't? Chamomile soothes the stomach and peppermint the nerves—"

"And purple lettuce encourages the flow in a newly delivered mother whose milk has not arrived. I imagine it will do the same for the cows, but first I suggest we move them from the field they've been in. They must have been frightened or upset or possibly fed something to stop their milk. Once we move them and give them some curatives, I warrant the milk will flow again."

When Regan's prophesy proved correct, the servants and soldiers took it as a sign of good fortune and were inclined to credit their new mistress with great powers. In turn, the English relaxed a bit, content that their mistress would solve any problem that arose, a state that Connor used to his advantage.

Under the cover of darkness, he sent his men to harvest the vegetables in the garden near the keep while Sheila raided the inner crops. Fully matured plants and the just-sprouting alike were uprooted and spirited away so that when morning arrived, only bare earth remained. Amid the general consternation, and Sheila's show of vehement anger, Regan appeared surprisingly calm.

"Sheila, you told me we had sufficient foodstuffs to withstand a siege if need be."

"Aye, milady, but I counted on a ready stock of fresh greens and potatoes for gravies and soups," protested the housekeeper.

"If necessary, you may purchase what produce you require from the tenants outside the walls. Gerard will give you the coins needed. If our mischief-makers are O'Carroll and his men, and not the wee folk as you previously supposed, they are obviously not as well provisioned as we are, since they resort to thievery. I'd hardly expect you to begrudge your former master a few heads of cabbage and some potatoes, Sheila."

"Well, of course, I don't, I suppose, milady," admitte[d]
the older woman hesitantly, taken completely by surprise [at]
Regan's attitude. If the new mistress continued to be th[at]
difficult to rattle, Connor had best intensify his attacks!

"Good, then if there's nothing else, Tommy and I will [be]
visiting the western lands this morning. I want to check th[e]
cattle again and we may venture into the village."

"Do you think that's wise, ma'am? I hear tell many of th[e]
townsfolk miss the O'Carroll and blame you for his goin[g]
off. Captain Wolf found them quite unhelpful."

"Actually, Sheila, I doubt the earl's gone too far off, an[d]
they might be more willing to talk to me than Captain Wol[f]
particularly if he were as ill-mannered in Kinnity as he w[as]
here."

"As you wish, milady," replied the housekeeper, shak[-]
ing her head at the stubbornness of the girl; there were time[s]
when her obstinacy approached magnificence.

Kinnity was a pleasant enough little village, suppose[d]
Regan later that afternoon, or at least it would have be[en]
had anyone even acknowledged her existence. The Irish ha[d]
turned their backs on her and gone about their business. T[he]
affront was so obvious that Tommy felt obligated to try [to]
make excuses as they headed back to Heaven's Gate.

"Milady, don't feel bad. Most folks in Kinnity don't co[t-]
ton to the English. Like you said about Master Connor, it[']
not personal. It just is. I'd wager some of them you tried [to]
question didn't even understand what you were saying, yo[u]
not talking native and all," said the lad.

"Do you think they'd accept me better if I did know the[ir]
language?"

"I can't rightly promise, ma'am, but I don't see as how [it]
could hurt, and I could even teach you some."

"All right, Tommy, but not a word to Sheila or Gerar[d.]
Tell me how to say *good morning*."

"*Mora duit* and *goodbye* is *slán*."

"*Mora duit . . . mora duit . . . slán.* Why is it easier to say farewell than to greet someone?" she asked rhetorically. "*Mora duit . . . slán.* What about *thank you?*"

"*Go raibh maithagat.*"

"*Go raibh maithagat* . . . that trips the tongue, Tommy. I fear I'd have to be thankful to even remember that. *Go raibh maithagat* for your trouble."

"*Ta failte,* milady," replied the boy with a wide grin. "That means *you're welcome.*"

"Wait! What was that?"

"*Ta failte,* it means you're welcome," he translated again.

"No, not you, Tommy, listen a space. It sounds as though an animal is hurt."

Reining in their horses, the pair sat quietly, waiting for the sound to recur. When it did, Tommy recognized it at once.

"It's a lost sheep, milady. Them animals are so dumb, they'll get stuck in a bramble bush or a ditch and never try to get out, but just sit and cry."

"Well then, we'd better see to it. If the poor thing is on Heaven's Gate lands, it's my responsibility, dumb animal or not."

"Yes, milady." Slipping from his saddle, he handed Regan his reins and moved into the bushes toward the desperate cry. A moment later he emerged from the brambles with a small, scrawny creature cuddled in his arms.

"But, Tommy, that can't be a sheep, it has no wool," she protested.

"It's a young lamb, not a full-grown sheep, milady, but someone has shorn it, out of season though it is. That's probably why it's so frightened."

"Then why would anyone take its wool now?"

"I think it's a message for you, milady," said Tommy softly, turning the animal in his arms so Regan could see the brand burned into its rump . . . the O'Carroll mark she'd witnessed on the cattle of Heaven's Gate.

"Branding ruins the regrowth of wool. What would make him do such a thing? Oh, I suppose it's because I'll get the wool if he doesn't take it now," realized the English mistress of the Irish estate. "All right, let's take this little fellow back to the keep until we find the rest of his mates. Give him to me and I'll wrap him in my cloak. When we get back, I'll send Gerard and the guards out to check on the rest of the flock. Maybe this poor lamb is the only naked messenger O'Carroll sent."

Unhappily, Regan's hope was a futile one. When Gerard and the men checked the sheep pastures, they found the shepherds missing and every single sheep shorn. Not very professionally either, complained Gerard.

"I warrant the wool won't even be usable," he observed.

"Still, he didn't butcher the animals, and they will regrow their wool. Things could be worse," said Regan, determined not to abandon her efforts to remain calm in the face of dilemmas. "This just means we have to be more careful with the guards in the outer fields. He's struck at the cattle and the sheep. There's not much more he can do."

Regan's imagination, however, was inferior to her enemy's. The next morning, the cistern, which had been full of clean water only a week earlier suddenly ran foul, filling the pumps with smelly, brackish water that no one could drink. When Gerard sent men up to explore the problem, they discovered a pair of dead goats rotting in the storage tank. Outraged by this obvious act of sabotage, Regan dispatched a rider to inform Sir Henry of the situation, but not only did the governor not reply, the rider did not return.

In the meantime, Sheila set the kitchen help to boiling and straining the water, even adding herbs, but nothing seemed to cleanse it sufficiently. As unhappy as she was with the decision, Regan finally ordered the cistern emptied. A massive pail and bucket brigade was formed and every hand was pressed into service; yet, it was still three days before the reservoir was empty and another before Regan was satisfied with its cleanliness. Then the only remaining problem was refilling it, and the weather proved uncooperative; for the first time in months, there was no rain for ten consecutive days!

Since the only other available water source was a rapidly running stream a half mile away, the soldiers were again utilized as jugs, kettles, barrels, all manner and shape containers were transported to the stream, filled and lugged back to the main keep. With over fifty people still in residence, however, the water was ever being exhausted before it seemed possible. Again Sheila and the maids mumbled about the fairy folk and their games, but this time, Regan could offer no natural solution.

One morning, thoroughly dispirited and weary from the growing discomfort of rationed water, and mounting complaints from the tenants, Gerard, and her own soldiers, the young Englishwoman could stand no more. Telling the housekeeper that she was off for her morning ride, Regan dressed simply, took soap and toweling along, and rode only as far as the stream. There, she posted Tommy as a guard and went the last few feet to the water alone, anticipating a refreshing, if chilly, wash. Only—the stream wasn't there anymore. Dry rocks and moist gravel confronted her where once gurgled a delightful gushing abundance of water.

"Tommy, Tommy, hurry, come here quickly," she cried in angry frustration.

"What's wrong, milady? Are you hurt?" The boy arrived on the run, anxious for Regan's welfare. "Oh, it's all right then. I thought something happened to you."

"Aye, I'm all right, but what's happened to our stream? It was here yesterday."

"Sometimes, in the heat of the summer, the water dries up for miles around, milady," offered the lad.

"But it doesn't happen overnight, Tommy. That devil made this happen and I won't stand for it. We're going to make it unhappen, I swear," announced Regan in a determined voice. "Get the horses and bring them here. We'll follow the stream back to its source and see what caused this."

"Yes, milady."

It wasn't far, probably less than a mile, before she found the problem: a felled tree, aided by heavy boulders and branches piled deep on either side of it, had diverted the normal path of the water. While a deep pool was forming above the barricade, and a new stream was meandering slowly westward, barely a trickle of moisture escaped the carefully constructed trap. Clearly the dam was man-made, realized Regan, and just as clearly, it could be unmade.

"Tommy, ride back to the keep and get Gerard and the men. Tell them to bring along some rope and extra horses so we can move those boulders. I'll wait here and start getting rid of some of the smaller branches."

"No, milady, you can't. Your captain would flay me alive if I left you out here in the woods alone. You know he doesn't even like you riding with only me," protested the youth.

"What could happen to me here? It's already daylight and clearly that despicable lout O'Carroll has taken off for the hills. He apparently is not the type to meet adversity head-on, but prefers to hide behind his craven deeds," judged the blonde, already unfastening her undergown and tying up her skirts, glad she had dressed for bathing. "Now, go on with you, while I start dislodging some of the mess."

"Lady Regan, I cannot leave you here," exclaimed Tommy, his voice cracking in agitation.

"Well, I certainly can't find my way back without you and one of us has to make sure no further damage is done to this stream. For all we know, that blackguard might try to poison this water next," said Regan in a worried voice. "Could the horses get back to the keep alone?"

"Yes, milady, of course."

"Very well then, go tie my wrapper on the one saddle and my cloak on the other and send them on their way. Surely the sight of riderless horses will bring Gerard on the run with as many men as he can muster."

"Right away, ma'am," agreed the lad, relieved at the solution Regan had created. "I'll be right back."

Already wading into the artificially made pond, his mistress just nodded and started to pull at the nearest tree limb. She met with no success and decided to move closer to the center of the blockade and try there. Now though she put herself even more off balance, standing as she was on an uneven, newly watered bottom, while shoving an immovable mass. Not willing to acknowledge the futility of her small weight against the interwoven branch-and-boulder dam, Regan persisted in pushing and pulling at the limbs she could reach. Finally in a moment of great delight, she felt a part of the tree give way, coming free in her hands...and landing her soundly on her bottom, beneath the now muddy water.

Sputtering angrily even as she tried to remind herself that she had wanted a swim, Regan regained her feet only to hear obnoxious laughter from her right. Almost afraid to look in that direction, she attempted to brush her now-sodden hair from her face and smile before turning to greet the unwelcome observer.

"Ah, good morning, Sir Thomas. Out for a ride, are you?" she asked demurely, determined not to reveal her true state of mind. Though she'd like nothing better than to drown the grinning idiot, she'd act the role of a lady. "Personally, I favor a dip in the water on warmer days like today."

"Oh, then you're responsible for the new swimming hole that's sprung up here?" Connor replied, as if seeing a half-clad female, thoroughly drenched and displaying all her curves, was a normal occurrence. He did have to hand it to her, he thought to himself, the girl didn't scare easily.

"Actually, you can't thank me. Someone, O'Carroll probably, plugged up the stream with this pile of stones and branches, and I'm trying to open it up while I wait for the rest of my men," explained Regan, moving to dry land and stepping out of the water. "I'm tired of letting that spawn of Lucifer wreak complete havoc on my property—"

"*Your* property?" The words almost choked Connor as he said them. How dare she lay claim to the Geata Neamhai so casually? While the woman's dampened attire did provoke his physical interest, Connor O'Carroll's fury eclipsed any attraction he might have felt. "Woman, as I understand it, until O'Carroll concedes defeat, this property is *his*. At least that's what the townsfolk are saying."

"Be that as it may, Sir Thomas, Heaven's Gate is mine, and I don't need the Kinnity folk—or you—to approve. Now, if you'll be on your way, I have work to do here."

With a graceful toss of her head, Regan plunged back into the chilly water just as she heard Gerard's voice.

"Regan? Where are you? Regan—"

"Over here, Gerard, and don't fuss so, I'm fine," she called, noticing that her neighbor had already disappeared. He evidently was not one who relished hard work, let alone physical challenge, despite his rather athletic build. Well, she had other matters to concern herself with, not the least of which was pacifying an irate self-appointed guardian.

"Fine? Fine, you say? Damn it all, girl, I find Tommy with a twisted ankle and you half-naked, knee-high in water and you say you're fine? What in hell's name did you send the horses back for then? You frightened me half to death and now I find you playing around in a bloody pond? I've a good mind to turn you over my knee here and now," blustered the gray-haired man, angry at the scare the riderless horse had given him but thankful that Regan was apparently unharmed.

"Oh, Gerard, you know you only say that when you are worried about me. Really I am fine, but the stream, as you can see, is not. Tell the men to remove this outrageous dam, and I will tell you all about it on the way back to the keep,'' suggested his ward as she left the water and gave him a hug.

''Ugh, girl, you're soaking wet—''

''Better that than hurt, though I don't suppose O'Carroll feels that way. Gerard, we have got to do something. I am afraid he will destroy Heaven's Gate before he lets me enjoy it.''

Damned right I will, agreed Connor as he slipped from his hiding place amid the trees to return to camp.

''*Her* property, hah! Till now, I've been gentle,'' he muttered angrily, recounting the events of the morning to Hugh. ''From here on, we show no mercy whatsoever. She may have been a bit uncomfortable without milk and water, but let us see how she likes soot-filled rooms caused by clogged chimneys, a rapidly shrinking staff, and disappearing foodstuffs. Gather the men together and get a message to Sheila that I want two or three of our people to leave every day. Let them be sent on errands outside the walls and not return like her messenger to the good Sidney. Enough is enough,'' complained the Irish lord. ''As of this moment, we wage war.''

Chapter Six

The next day began with a brilliant morning. From her bedchamber window, Regan was pleased to note Wolf's few remaining soldiers gathering to leave now that the rest of her own forces had arrived a few hours earlier. But this fact alone did not account for her fine mood.

The sun was warm and friendly overhead as the mist burned off the meadows, so that the contrast of the clear azure sky against the hazy green of the fields and the deep brown of the distant mountains painted a romantic landscape indeed. Surveying the lands below her, Regan was struck by the almost mystical beauty of Heaven's Gate. The place was weaving a spell on her, she was certain, casting an enchantment that made her almost content to be there, instead of wishing herself back in England.

As she remained gazing at the abundance of natural loveliness below, Regan luxuriated in the sweetness of the air. It was such a tranquil scene beneath her chamber window, that the new Countess of Kilcaid dared to hope all of her recent misfortunes were behind her, and that peace, if not happiness, would govern her new life in this place that was so different from anything she had ever known.

"'Tis a foolish thought, indeed," Regan chided herself with a toss of her hair as she moved toward the door. It wouldn't do to be overly confident, not with O'Carroll still at large. Yet as she descended the long, stone stairway that led to the Great Hall, Regan's practical nature found itself vanquished by her newfound buoyant spirits.

Humming the melody of a bawdy drinking song, which would have made Gerard blush, Regan smiled at her servants as they curtsied and bowed at her passing. Their outward show of respect caused the new mistress of Heaven's Gate to wonder if her optimistic feelings of a few moments before were really as illusionary as she had decided.

After all, she told herself, her self-assurance climbing, she had handled every annoying problem since her arrival. Not any one of them, not even their sum total, had caused her to pack her trunks and desert the destiny the queen had decreed for her. She was, after all, a Davies and English. What need she fear from these Irish who were tenants on her land? They could come to accept her, couldn't they? As long as they had food in their bellies and roofs over their heads, they wouldn't care who owned the lands. Hadn't Sheila Dempsey herself corroborated that fact?

As for the O'Carroll, she was safe enough from him within the thick walls of this fortress, and he couldn't have caused all of the problems that had plagued her these past few days, could he? Surely troubles such as she had experienced were to be expected when one ran an estate of this size, especially one which had been so haphazardly managed for as long as Heaven's Gate appeared to have been. Well, now the estate would bloom and blossom under her care, Regan decided. Even Connor O'Carroll himself would be hard put to find criticism with the improvements she would make.

As Regan entered the courtyard, intent upon reaching the stables, her progress was halted by the rapid approach of a near breathless man, who threw himself before her, trying to find the strength to deliver his news.

"Your ladyship," he wheezed, "please, but I must have a word."

"What is it?" Regan questioned, her recent high spirits plummeting as she feared the imminent disclosure of some new calamity.

"It's the tenant house, my lady. One of the ones outside the walls of the keep," the man gasped, continuing to struggle.

"Which tenant house exactly?" Regan asked slowly, though she suspected she already knew.

"'Tis the first of those you were readying for your English farmers, lady, and it's sorry I am to be telling you this, but it has been destroyed."

"How?" Regan demanded curtly, the storm clouds gathering in her eyes quite efficiently eclipsing the sunshine of the morning for anyone who was the recipient of her gaze.

"It burned, mistress, aye, it went aflame though there was no one near. It can only be the devil's own work, that's what the men are saying, and not a one of them brave enough to take on the demon and attempt to put out the blaze. They just stood by and watched it burn, so that all that's left is just a heap of charred wood and smoldering stone."

"And does the devil usually start fires in Ireland?" Regan asked, her eyes narrowing. "I can assure you he does not do so in England."

"It may not have been the prince of hell, himself," the man mumbled.

"No, it probably was not, so why didn't you men work to save my property?"

"Well, there was no proof that it was the devil, but then again there was no proof it was not," the man replied, avoiding Regan's stare. "In this country, Lady Regan, you'll find that we give the demon his due, and proceed with caution in such matters."

"With superstition you mean," Regan reproved, her tone icy.

"Call it what you will, mistress, but the fact remains, you'll find no man willing to fight blazes that set themselves, and after this morning, very few to guard against it happening again."

"My people will do as I tell them," Regan commanded, "or they will find themselves looking for another home."

"Be that as it may, there's not a man among us who will take on either fairies or the spirits of hell in your name."

"But they would do so for Connor O'Carroll, wouldn't they?" Regan asked in annoyance.

"There would be no need," the man said diplomatically, with a soft laugh. "'Tis rumored that the O'Carroll is demon enough that the Prince of Darkness himself is afraid of him. As to your subjects, though my opinion is a humble one, I do not think you will find it to your advantage to rout these folks from their homes. It will take a while to find English settlers willing to come to Ireland. In the meantime, who will do your planting and tend your crops, guard your borders and watch your sheep?"

"Yes, the men do such a commendable job of guarding my sheep," Regan responded dryly.

"Besides, your ladyship, your Irish tenants mean you no harm. It's just their way to avoid the otherworldly whenever possible. There's nothing for it but to hope that the incident doesn't happen again."

"Perhaps there is more to be done," Regan muttered thoughtfully as a scowl marred her pretty features. Be damned, she didn't want to do this, but what choice did she have? She turned to regard the man before her once more. "Go to the stable and order horses saddled for the both of us. You will accompany me to the site of this recent disaster."

As Regan watched the man scurry to do her bidding, she wrestled once more with her unpalatable options. First she'd talk with her own people. But should she find little success in managing them, the only recourse was to turn to her ir-

ritating neighbor and his less superstitious English tenants
for help in building up her lands.

Mounting her horse, Regan failed to notify Gerard of either this latest turn of events or her own planned course of
action. She told herself that this decision was based upon a
natural concern for her faithful follower. Surely, Regan
persuaded herself, Gerard would still be abed at such an
early hour, exhausted from overseeing the destruction of the
dam until well into the night and then tending to the proper
quartering of the men who had arrived before dawn.

Simple consideration for the man demanded she not disturb him over such a trifle, Regan thought. Yet no matter
what she told herself, the comely noblewoman knew the real
reason she did not inform Gerard of what she was about to
do. If her efforts with her own men failed, she did not want
Gerard to witness her as a supplicant to Thomas Watkins,
the man against whom she had so loudly and vehemently
railed.

Connor remained at the edge of the field, among the
dense trees that lined its perimeter and formed a canopy over
his head. Hidden in the shadows of the forest, he looked
every bit the darkling prince as he sat easily astride a worthy mount. His clothes, fashioned of the richest velvet in the
deepest ebony, were trimmed sparingly with silver threads
and cloth. Though London hadn't seen the cut of his garments for a few seasons, the Earl of Kilcaid managed to appear noble indeed, the man enhancing the work of his tailor
rather than the other way around.

As the shadows played over his handsome features, a
roguish gleam lit Connor's deep blue eyes when he spotted
the Lady Regan emerge from the keep, the straight set of her
back attesting to her anger.

The O'Carroll's soft chuckle both alerted and rankled
Hugh, who was sitting beside him atop his own horse.
Hugh's plain garments, hurriedly donned in the predawn

hours, placed him in sharp contrast to Connor and made his body look more like a tree trunk than ever. He blended into the mottled light of the forest and seemed a part of it, although his emotions did not match the tranquility of nature's cool stand of trees.

"I still say you should have lured the Englishwoman into the cottage and then set it afire," the hulking Irishman complained as he and Connor watched Regan Davies ride across the fields of Geata Neamhai on her way to view the site of the most recent disaster.

"It's not necessary to kill her," Connor reminded him calmly while his gaze followed the crimson-cloaked Regan on her journey. "After all, she's only a woman. Slaying her would be akin to using a sword to rid us of a troublesome fly, when all we need do is shoo it away."

"Yes, but best you remember that flies are pesky creatures, my Lord Kilcaid, and this one appears determined to hover where she is not wanted. Nothing we have done has routed her. What makes you think the destruction of this cottage will be any different?"

"You must have patience, friend, though it is the one attribute I fear you lack," Connor replied firmly, annoyed at being distracted from the distant figure that claimed his attention.

"Why do I need patience? You have more than enough for the both of us," Hugh grumbled, casting his earl a disgruntled look. "And as if that woman wasn't enough, there's the sight of you dressed as an English gallant. Such finery has no place on these lands in these times."

"How often must I remind you that it is easier to monitor the intruder if she regards me as a meddlesome neighbor?" the nobleman asked, fast losing all traces of the patience his friend had accused him of having. "It is all part of the game, Hugh."

"Pray you recall that Geata Neamhai is the wager you're gambling, Connor, and gaming can be a dangerous enterprise."

Connor released a sigh of exasperation too long pent up as he tried to remind himself of the times Hugh had coddled him as a child while trying to teach him something of importance. However, it had not been uncharacteristic of Hugh to pound sense into his young charge, as well, and Connor was becoming sorely tempted to resort to the same tactic in order to stop his companion's constant complaints in the matter of Regan Davies. Instead, he decided to attempt some humor with the quick-tempered giant whose sharp criticism was exceeded only by his loyalty.

"Have you grown too old to enjoy a challenge?" Connor teased, the corners of his mouth giving way to a smile rather than a scowl. He edged his horse closer to the one upon which Hugh sat, and lowered his head as if to share a confidence. "When I regain my home perhaps it would be best for me to pension you off, reserving a spot for you in front of the hearth. Then you and Sheila can pass the time weaving a blanket to warm your ancient bones."

"I'm not so old that I couldn't unseat you from your mount with one blow, lord or no lord," Hugh growled as Connor skillfully guided his horse just out of range. "The day I stopped knocking sense into your head was a sorry one indeed. All of these elaborate shenanigans to rid us of a mere lass..."

"That's right, she's only a girl so cease your grumbling. Though it is my bed she warms at night while I sleep beneath the stars, I am not immune to the humor in the situations we have created for her. I vow we have plagued my Lady Regan beyond any torment she has known before."

"Aye, we probably have at that," Hugh conceded as he moved alongside his lord. "But, then, you've always been one to raise as much hell as any twelve demons. The thought of it is almost enough to make me feel sorry for the English wench.''

''Hugh, as comely as the maid may be, she's still the enemy. When you bed down on the damp ground tonight, see if her plight moves you to sympathy,'' Connor replied, merriment shining in his eyes at his friend's indignant snort. ''For now, come and let's make our way along the edge of the woods to see how the Lady Regan enjoys our scorching devilment.''

A scarce thirty minutes later, Regan haughtily drew herself up to her full height, her manner as aristocratic as she could manage. Though she struggled to hide the utter rage she felt, her usually lovely lips were pursed in scorn. These peasant louts were thickheaded beyond belief. No amount of reasoning could convince them that dark magic of some sort was not taking place on the lands of Heaven's Gate, and no command, however curt, could persuade them to follow her instructions for the rebuilding of the charred cottage or the construction of others like it.

While Regan thought it possible that the men's protestations of fairy magic were due to their ignorance, the possibility also crossed her mind that such tales were only a ruse to mask their support of the rebel, O'Carroll. No degree of bowing and scraping, no display of hushed, anxious voices on their part could expunge such a suspicion. After all, despite Sheila's assurances, Regan was all too aware that these Irishmen had no feelings of allegiance to her. She was not one of them.

But no matter how she studied it, the fact remained that their motives made no difference. They were crafty enough to know that right now, she needed them as much as they needed her, and as a result, the men were neither going to refurbish this cottage nor erect others. Yet without buildings to house them, she would never be able to keep English tenants to help her resettle her newly acquired lands.

How Elizabeth would laugh at her failure, Regan brooded, her fists clenched tightly in the folds of her skirt as her simmering temper threatened to boil over. Doubtless, she'd be forever banished from England, condemned to spend a lifetime in this land with years of lonely nights in that huge, cold bed, with no true lover to cherish her. Well, she'd be damned if she would accept such a fate so easily. There were still options. There were always options if one looked carefully enough. But the only plan open to her was a distasteful one indeed: Thomas Watkins. Actually it wouldn't be Watkins himself who assisted her, it would be his men, Regan amended, trying to find some degree of consolation in her present plight.

She would have to ask Watkins to lend her some laborers until the bulk of her own forces arrived. After all, the rogue had English tenants living on his property, men who had neither been born in this land shrouded with the mist of superstition, nor weaned on tales of fairy folk. They could be persuaded to complete the task she would set them even if her own men could not.

Though her pride continued to chafe at the solution to her dilemma, Regan was wise enough to be practical. While her brow furrowed at the decision she had made, she mounted her horse, nonetheless, and addressed her guard, issuing an order she would have thought impossible but a few days before. Then, she and her men were off. Riding swiftly toward Watkins's plantation, the new mistress of Heaven's Gate was ignorant of the piercing blue eyes that narrowed as they noted the direction she took.

As her horse traveled fleetly across the fields, Regan began formulating an approach she might use when she made her request of Thomas Watkins. Yet the closer she drew to the border that separated her lands from his, the more difficult she found it to concentrate on the matter at hand. Unbidden memories of raven hair and restless blue eyes surfaced to tumble amid her more somber thoughts, scattering them in all directions.

In spite of his arrogant behavior, Regan couldn't help but admit that the man's dark good looks were striking. His clean jawline and handsomely sculpted nose had surely been created for the purpose of dooming any woman who set eyes on him.

But a man needed more than looks to commend him, Regan reminded herself, and she knew nothing more of Watkins other than what the eye could see. The man himself was an enigma. At their initial meeting, his serious flirtation had oddly changed to arrogant dismissal within a matter of moments. And yet, whenever she had seen the handsome devil since, she had sensed an intense interest in her. At all subsequent sightings, the man's playful smile had been belied by the fire burning in those incredibly blue eyes of his. The very thought of it made Regan shiver, though the morning had turned quite warm indeed.

Soon after traversing her border, inquiries made of some peasants tilling the soil had Regan and her party proceeding in the direction of Wren's Nest, Thomas Watkins's keep. Though the land around her appeared prosperous and neatly kept, English order imposed upon Irish countryside, Regan noticed very little of it. Her thoughts continued to center upon Thomas Watkins and the reception she would receive at his hands.

When Wren's Nest finally came into view, Regan's musings became more tumultuous than ever. As she scanned the walls of the fortress for some sign of its master, a telltale crimson stained her cheeks, until she recalled that the man in question had a penchant for intolerable rudeness, which quite overrode his passing good looks.

"Lower the bridge for the Lady Regan, Countess of Kilcaid," one of her guards called, and a few moments later Regan and her escort were within the thick walls of Wren's Nest.

The courtyard of the keep was a hive of industriousness. All around her, the common folk were busy and obviously subservient. There was no sound of laughter, no easy talk from the men who went soberly about their work. As for the women and children, it was apparent that they dared not lift their eyes as they scurried to complete the tasks assigned them. The observation filled Regan with surprise and then with anger, which helped to still the foolish flutters that had been besetting her heart.

What kind of master was Thomas Watkins that he held his people within such a constant grip of fear? No matter what her troubles at Heaven's Gate, Regan far preferred her own sassy serving maids and charmingly indolent men. The realization helped the lovely Countess of Kilcaid to completely cast aside her unsought girlish fancies regarding the man who had so intrigued her on the day she had come to Heaven's Gate.

It was an aloof Regan, therefore, who dismounted and demanded of a brown-clad English toady to be taken to Sir Thomas Watkins.

My purpose here is only that of a business transaction, Regan reminded herself as she swept regally up the broad steps in the shadow of the Englishman who had greeted her. I will ask for the man's assistance and pledge him an equal number of days' labor from the inhabitants of Heaven's Gate once I have established order there. In fact, I will propose that Watkins receive three days work for every two his men give me. There! she concluded, that makes the transaction profitable for both of us, and relieves me of any obligation to my neighbor.

Still, as Regan paced within the Great Hall, her men standing just outside its door, she found herself experiencing a case of jitters all the same.

"But not because the man has any hold over me," Regan swore to herself as images of the doleful inhabitants of Wren's Nest came all too easily to mind. "It's merely that I have never initiated business with the landed gentry before. Everyone is nervous when embarking on a new experience.''

Her skittishness explained to her satisfaction, the Countess of Kilcaid nevertheless continued to stalk the confines of the hall, a few moments of waiting for Thomas Watkins stretching into many. In an attempt to find some measure of calm, Regan began to study her surroundings rather than her folded hands, and was surprised to note that the peacock had furnished himself with quite a sparse nest.

Though the few tables and benches were undoubtedly English in origin, they were country plain and not the sort of thing one would see at court. The cavernous walls were almost barren except for one tapestry and that was of undistinguished needlework done in dull threads.

Perhaps the lord and master wishes to shine all the brighter against such a plain background, Regan mused, though she was hard put to quash the rebellious thought that a man such as he would stand out no matter what his situation. The unsummoned admission irritated the cool English beauty, and she resumed her pacing once more.

Not a patient woman to begin with, Regan continued to chafe at waiting as she wondered if all this were some ploy designed to humble her, or even worse, if Thomas Watkins did not mean to appear at all. She was becoming more waspish by the moment, so that she snapped an uncharacteristic response at a servant who came forward to offer her refreshment. God's blood but Gerard was right, her impulsive temper was a dangerous trait, and if Watkins kept her waiting too much longer, he'd find out just how dangerous.

Regan's murderous thoughts were interrupted by a smooth, cultured voice addressing her from the far end of the hall. Swirling about quickly, she found herself facing a little man not quite into middle age, but certainly courting it most ardently. Though dressed in richer clothing than the servant who had shown her into this room, his garments were of the same nondescript brown hue. His features, however, were quite distinctive. A bulbous nose and receding hairline framed small gray eyes, but their effect was lost immediately when the man smiled in an effort to be charming, and displayed a gap-toothed grin.

"I was told, my dear, that you wish to see the lord of Wren's Nest," the man said in a manner Regan found all too dignified and familiar for a servant addressing a lady.

"Yes," she replied tersely, "I have come to see Sir Thomas Watkins."

The man stood regarding her for a moment. He liked what he saw. The woman before him was young, beautiful and apparently not given overmuch to conversation as some females were. But most important of all, her lands adjoined his, and if rumor were to be believed, she was neither wed nor promised to any man. In short, she was ripe for the taking.

"For what purpose?" he asked, his voice much smoother than the coarse grain of the fabric he wore.

"I think that better discussed with the lord of Wren's Nest," Regan said coolly. "When may I see him?"

"But my dear countess, I thought you understood," the man said, his smile patronizing. "I am Sir Thomas Watkins."

Regan stood speechless while possibilities whirred in her mind. Without doubt she knew that there were no two men by the same name living in the vicinity. Which then was the imposter? Could this possibly be a servant the handsome stranger of the forest road had sent in his stead in order to toy with her or else to avoid her altogether? Gathering her thoughts quickly, she stammered a reply.

"You . . . you are Sir . . . Sir Thomas?" she asked softly.

"But of course!" he replied, capturing her hand and bending low to implant a damp kiss atop her fingertips.

Who else would greet you in the main hall of Wren's
Nest?''

Who else indeed, Regan wondered, withdrawing her hand
from his. But as the unsettling Englishman snapped his fingers to signal for wine, the promptness with which his summons was answered and the look of guarded dislike on the
servant's face left Regan with no doubt that this was indeed
her true and rightful neighbor.

"You must forgive me, my lord," Regan began, muster-
ing as much composure and dignity as the situation allowed. For all the world, she would not appear the helpless
female in front of such a weasel of a man. Should he think
her weak or in any way foolish, Regan knew with innate
certainty that she would have nothing but trouble, of one
sort or another, with the lord of Wren's Nest. Under the
circumstances she would not, she could not, confess how she
had been duped into believing that another was her actual
neighbor.

Pushing the mystery of that handsome devil aside to be
dealt with later, Regan attempted to take charge of the
matter at hand.

"You see, Sir Thomas, I heard no one announce your
arrival in the hall, as befits a man of your degree," Regan
said, a tinge of imperiousness in her voice implying that her
failure to know his identity was a fault that lay with the
running of the household rather than with her.

"Ah, my pretty countess," Watkins responded, not at all
put off by Regan's grand manner when the matter of ad-
joining lands still dangled before him, "you will find that
although we struggle to maintain English standards in this
godforsaken country, we are, nevertheless, a bit more in-
formal here than at home. I suppose it is because we must
rely so heavily upon the Irish population to form the bulk
of our servantry. They are, you will learn, almost untrain-
able."

"I see. Thank you for your counsel, my lord," Regan re plied dryly.

"But enough about servants, Lady Regan. How may I b of service?"

"Laborers are what I wished to discuss with you," Re gan stated. The enigma of the roguish imposter was con suming her. However, no matter how hotly her blood ran the moment, she forced herself to proceed with the origina purpose of her visit even though all she really wanted to d was retire to Heaven's Gate and mull over this latest strang turn of events.

In order to bring her present ordeal to a close, Rega hurriedly placed her proposal before her posturing neigh bor. Her newfound insight into her situation helped shap her words. She stressed only her desire to ready her lands quickly as possible for proper English tenants and quite ig nored recounting her recent problems. There was no talk c charms or black magic or fairy folk working mischief on he new home. Instead, she simply intimated that she consid ered English workers far superior to any laborers Irelan might have bred. She spoke as though this were an irrefu able fact, and Watkins readily agreed to both her premis and her proposition, as she knew he would.

"I am delighted to know, Lady Regan, that you are intelligent as you are beautiful," Watkins said at the con clusion of their bargain, laying the foundation for the su he intended to press in the near future. To emphasize h desirability, he paused and bestowed what he considered t be his most charming smile before proceeding. "You wi come to find, my dear lady, that in times of need you ma always come to me. I fear I must confess that no matte what you asked, I would be quite unable to deny so lovely woman her request."

"Thank you, my lord, I will bear that in mind, though do not think there *will be* further need," Regan responded her voice clipped and brusque.

"Ah, but you are still as yet unfamiliar with this wild land," Watkins replied, hastening to voice his concern for the newly arrived Englishwoman in the belief that all females found a protective male quite attractive. "I am certain you will come to discover that while the mere Irish are of very little use in serving us, they are quite practiced in helping themselves to all that belongs to us English... cattle, foodstuffs, anything of value," he added bitterly.

"While I have had no problems yet," Regan lied as she rose and made ready to depart, "I will heed your advice."

"Please do," Watkins said, his hand upon her arm staying her for a moment. "Otherwise, those raiding thieves will carry off all you own. Why, just last week, one of the rebels had the audacity to steal my carriage, a costly possession as you no doubt know...."

"Your carriage?" Regan asked, her heart beating quickly. Then the flirtatious imposter had not even been an Englishman! "Why, what would an Irishman want with a carriage?"

"Only the Lord in heaven knows," Thomas Watkins replied, elements of dark rage creeping into his voice. "Who can determine how the Irish mind works?"

"Was the vehicle recovered?" Regan found herself asking, unable to suppress her curiosity even to escape this odious individual.

"Yes, *with* a broken wheel," Watkins replied, his wrath growing more apparent until he remembered the lady in his presence and the sickly smile slipped once more into place. "However, there is no need to worry your pretty head. The carriage is even now undergoing repair and shall soon be as good as new."

"And did you ultimately catch the culprit?" Regan asked quietly, unable to stop herself from doing so as she counted the number of days it had been since she had last seen the mysterious impersonator.

"No, but when I do, the knave will die a slow and painful death, I assure you," Watkins said with confident finality.

"Then you know who it is?" Regan asked, her breath stopping for an instant while her pulse skipped furiously.

"Oh, I've no doubt who was behind it," Watkins said, relishing his role as an authority on Irish behavior. It was, after all, another opportunity to impress his beautiful guest. "The thief was O'Carroll."

"O'Carroll?" Regan echoed, taking pains to hide her shock at the fool she had been.

"Yes, no one other than that black devil would have the audacity to do such a thing," Watkins confirmed. "So you see, dear lady, the man is still in the vicinity. You had better take a care since you are the owner of the lands he once possessed. In fact, now that I think on it, perhaps it would be best for you to accept my protection for the time being, until he has been captured and executed."

"Really, you are too kind, but there is no need. I have men enough to see to my safety," Regan protested automatically while images of the Irish rebel swirled round in her head. He had played with her, toyed with her, caused her untold trouble, all with the intention of sending her scampering. And always he had been there, in the background, waving and smiling... laughing at her! Not only had he trespassed on her lands, he had even invaded her unguarded thoughts and, at times, her dreams. That bastard!

We will see to whom Heaven's Gate belongs, Regan vowed obstinately, even as she bid the lord of Wren's Nest a composed and haughty goodbye.

Mounting her horse, Regan set out for Heaven's Gate, surrounded by her men. As she rode, she digested what she knew. Everything made sense now. Everything fell into place... all the trouble, all the mysterious events plaguing her. O'Carroll was trying to regain his former lands! Well, the devil take him! When next she saw him she'd scratch his eyes out! When next she saw him . . . and then there he was!

He sat atop a hillside, not fifty yards away. Gone were the outdated clothes of the English court. He was garbed instead in the dress of an Irish chieftain. Bare, muscular thighs showed beneath his tunic, powerfully gripping the sides of his horse. A saffron cloak, attached by means of a large silver brooch, fluttered behind his shoulders, its deep yellow color making his hair appear more black than ever. This was no pompous peacock to be trifled with.

Gone, too, was the infuriating, roguish smile with which he had always greeted her. He was everything that was masculine, warlike and regal as he sat regarding her, silently and solemnly.

Regan understood, now, the fire that had burned in his deep-set eyes with bright, blue flame whenever he had looked at her. It was the look of a proprietary male, all right. But it was the land he had been coveting, Heaven's Gate he wanted to possess, not her.

While they stared at each other and Regan's guards closed ranks around her, O'Carroll's men appeared at the crest of the hill in lines stretching out on either side of him. They were numerous, raw and rough. Though they carried weapons that the rest of Europe hadn't seen in battle in almost a hundred years, their ferocity was nonetheless all too obvious. But what was most frightening was that Regan recognized some of the faces that stood alongside O'Carroll. A few of them had been seen within the walls of her keep as recently as yesterday. God help her! She was being besieged from within as well as without! There was no one to trust in this savage country, no one other than the people she had brought with her from England. But were they strong enough to withstand an onslaught from this murderous-looking man?

Grasping the reins of her mare tightly, a fearful Regan managed a defiant glare in O'Carroll's direction. If he were going to slay her now, she would not give him the joy of seeing her grovel at his feet and beg for mercy.

And yet, the rebel earl did not stir. Nothing broke the ominous silence as he continued to hold her with his powerful gaze, refusing to release her.

In that moment, Regan experienced an epiphany. This mighty show was meant to do less than kill her but more than strike terror into her heart. This was a declaration of war! There would be no more game playing, no more trifling and laughing at her expense. The gravity of the O'Carroll and his desperate-looking men told her that.

Regan was more frightened than she had ever been, but she would not surrender to the wishes of the man who had feigned to be her countryman. She would not leave Ireland, though but a few days before, the thought of doing so had influenced her every action. Wrapping her cloak more tightly about her, she cast Connor O'Carroll one last contemptuous look and set off swiftly with her men toward Heaven's Gate, praying that the rebel meant no more at present than to make himself and his enmity known.

As her foot pressed still harder into the side of her mare, Regan heard no hoofbeats or angry mob in pursuit. Neither did she hear derisive laughter at her flight, as the O'Carroll and his men preserved the formal, ritualistic silence of their sudden appearance. Her supposition, then, had been true! War had been declared. The next time she saw the man, blood would be spilled. Regan knew it with a certainty.

Her horse was flecked with foam when Regan rode into the courtyard of Heaven's Gate. Slipping from the saddle, she tossed the reins to a servant and turned to survey her home. She was glad to see the evidence of the rest of her troops settling in; their arrival would make what she had in mind much easier. Her sharp eyes noted that there were fewer men than usual within her walls, and tonight, she determined, there would be fewer still. The shepherds, the plowmen, and all others who had left her gates that morning would find no welcome in her home that evening. That would leave her with a small enough number of men, the ancient among them, to be watched carefully.

As for the women and children, Regan was no longer so naive that she did not know they would have to be monitored as well. However, she was not about to turn them out. The idea of doing such a thing was distasteful. Besides, wouldn't their presence within her walls help guarantee the safety of the keep? She thought ruefully of young Tommy and his huge eyes when the O'Carroll had approached them. And she had been fool enough to attribute the apple-cheeked lad's speechlessness to the coin the rebel had thrown in the boy's direction! The fact that such a child had been drawn into the strife between English and Irish saddened Regan. But it was a harsh world, she reminded herself, one that was apt to become much harsher now that Connor O'Carroll's animosity was out in the open.

Like a general planning the next battle's strategy, Regan assessed possible tactics as she strode off in search of Gerard. In no mood for one of his lectures on her impulsiveness, she decided she would apprise him of only what was necessary at the moment. She had been to see her neighbor, contracted for a number of English laborers and found out that Connor O'Carroll was indeed roving the countryside. That in fact it was he, in all likelihood, who had been afflicting them with each vexation they had experienced since their arrival.

As for the man's identity as the spurious Watkins, well, that could wait until another day, Regan determined mulishly. She had enough things to think about without absorbing Gerard's chiding words, as well.

Connor rode hard and fast, his usually full lips set in a grim line, as he vowed that tonight the Lady Regan's men would feel his sting. Damn the woman! His show of force had not driven the wench off as he had hoped it might. Instead, she had closed her gates to many of the men whose rightful home was Geata Neamhai, displacing them while keeping their women and children hostage.

Bile rose in Connor's throat as he thought of the way in which his people were being treated. And the most vile thing of all was that some of the guilt was his. He could have rid these lands of the woman easily and he had not. But even now, angered as he was...treacherous as she was...Connor could not picture his dagger marring Regan's marble-white skin. A haunting vision of eyes as green as the Irish hillsides in spring rode before him so that he could only do away with it by concentrating on images of venom and hatred.

Pressing on, a look of bitter determination lit Connor's face once more when he recalled what other strategies his seductive enemy had employed. Parties of her men rode the estate by day, familiarizing themselves with all of Geata Neamhai's features. At night the Englishmen put their newfound knowledge to use, roaming the terrain and seeking those they considered to be intruders, those who were Irish. Their tenacity hampered Connor's movements, making food and other necessities hard to come by though it was his game, his crops that were being kept from him.

For days his forces had stayed just out of English reach, studying them, taunting them, defying them. But now, by God, they would feel his wrath! They would learn what it meant to engage the Irish in battle. Suddenly in the darkness of the night, Connor heard a familiar voice at his shoulder.

"It warms my heart to see so murderous an expression on your face, me lad," Hugh's booming voice sounded over thundering hoofbeats as he pulled his mount beside Connor's. "'Tis the Earl of Kilcaid I am beholding now, and not some mooning adolescent caught in the spell of a comely

English witch. I don't mind repeating, Connor, that your behavior had me worried."

"Aye, well, you've repeated it often enough in these last days, Hugh Cassidy. And to be truthful, I grow weary of your rebukes," Connor fairly growled, unwilling to admit that his actions of late had mystified him, also. Oh, notions of honor were all well and fine, but Connor knew his response to Regan Davies went beyond that. Perhaps he *had* been bewitched, but the spell had had nothing to do with sorcery. Rather it was the result of a shapely female form, a profusion of gloriously blond hair, and a pair of heavily fringed green eyes. No, it hadn't been honor at all, he chided himself in disgust. But lust was behind him now. The Englishwoman's recent actions had quite broken the charm.

Melting into the shadowy darkness cast by a copse of trees, Connor threw off thoughts of the beautiful thief who had stolen his home, and scanned the landscape bathed in the pale light cast by the stars and moon. There were more important things to occupy his mind, he told himself as he signaled his men to halt and be silent, and that included finding the area where the English would be patrolling this night. Damn! but there was no trace of them, the earl swore silently. Fiery natured to begin with, his patience strained these past few weeks beyond bearing, Connor sat like a savage beast watching hungrily for some sign of his prey.

Then, he saw movement on a distant ridge. A group of horsemen were silhouetted by the silvery glow of the moon. The moment of reckoning was at hand. Connor's narrowed blue eyes glinted dangerously as he directed the attention of his men to what he had seen. Without hesitation the order was given, and half the men of Geata Neamhai followed their lord into battle. The rest were placed in Hugh's command so that the attack could be mounted from both sides. There was no doubt in any of their minds that the land would exact a blood price that night.

* * *

"Throw open the gate," yelled the captain of the guard.
"I've wounded here who need attention."

The sentry ascertained the identity of the caller and then
ordered the drawbridge lowered, while the men stationed
along the walls focused their attention on the party below.
From the looks of it, a confrontation had occurred at last,
and the Englishmen were anxious to learn how their com-
rades had fared.

The rhythm of the hoofbeats tapping across the wooden
planks was slow, an indication that the animals had run hard
and long. But for what purpose had the horses exhausted
themselves—chasing the enemy or retreating to safety? The
shadowy figures moving across the bridge did little to satisfy the curiosity of those who watched their progress. Those
who returned slumped in their saddles might be merely
weary rather than wounded, and those slung across the
backs of the beasts that carried them might be hurt rather
than dead.

The patrol party was met in the courtyard by Gerard, who
listened gravely to the captain's report. Noting the condition of those of Regan's men who had made it back, the
iron-haired veteran knew that the skirmish had commanded too high a toll. Examining one or two of the
wounded, he issued a summons for the acting captain of the
guard, and one for his mistress, as well, to inform them of
the dire situation. Then he turned to his task once more only
to be surprised by the burden held by one of the horses. This
was no soldier of his, but an Irishman, and one who was
half-dead by the look of him. At least he was dressed as an
Irishman, Gerard noted with growing alarm when a sick-
ening feeling of familiarity took hold of him as he recognized the dark curly locks and handsome profile of the man
he had met on the forest road. Thomas Watkins had been
wounded! Exactly what in heaven's name had gone on tonight?

Chapter Seven

Even as the stranger's blood dripped onto the newly laid rushes in the Great Hall, Regan found herself relishing the sight of the dark-haired demon laid low. In the past few weeks he had caused her enough grief to more than earn the ugly wound on his thigh. Yet, tempting as the prospect might be, could she do nothing while the man bled to death?

"Regan, for pity's sake, I didn't awaken you to stand around and gawk at the poor fellow, no matter how oddly he's garbed," reprimanded Gerard. "Do something for him!"

"Aye, I'd like to do something all right," muttered Regan, moving closer to the unconscious figure of her enemy. "Annie, light more tapers, then fetch me water, clean cloths and my medicines—"

A loud wail of distress interrupted the countess's instructions as Sheila entered the hall and rushed forward to kneel by the stricken man.

"My Lord," she cried, looking angrily at Gerard. "Have you killed him? He meant you no harm."

"Hold your tongue, woman, or get away from here. Our neighbor's not dead yet, but he might be if you don't let your mistress care for him," cautioned Gerard. "Though why you should be so concerned about an English landowner, I can't imagine."

"Never mind her, Gerard," snapped Regan quickly as she threw a warning glance at the housekeeper. "I want you to clear the soldiers and servants from the hall at once. I certainly don't need the distractions of an audience and I fear moving the poor man until I can examine his cut more thoroughly. Sheila will help me tend our unexpected visitor, but in his current condition, even you would agree this fellow isn't going to present any danger."

"No, but you might represent death to him," mumbled Sheila, taking the requested supplies from Annie.

"And Gerard, stand a guard at the door," added Regan as though the woman hadn't spoken, "so Sheila and I are not disturbed. We have much to do—and much to discuss."

"Yes, milady," answered her man, obediently escorting the curious onlookers from the hall. For the middle of the night, quite a few had arisen to investigate the excitement, but his mistress was right; they couldn't remain. Besides, in the semidarkness, with Regan and Sheila hovering over the man, there was not much to be seen anyway.

Once the last of the stragglers had gone and Gerard had pulled the heavy door shut behind him, Regan tore open the remainder of her patient's leggings, exposing the gaping wound. Apparently the sword had cut clean and quite deeply. Looking sternly at Sheila as she tried to stanch the bleeding, Regan issued directions in the same hard voice with which she questioned the servant's motives.

"Move your hands higher up. Press down with all your weight to slow the flow a bit 'til I can prepare the comfrey poultice. In the meantime, tell me all you know about this man."

"Gerard said it earlier, milady. He's your neighbor," evaded the housekeeper, obviously concerned for their patient but uncertain how far she could trust Regan. Connor was, after all, a fugitive of the court with a price on his head. Would this Englishwoman allow him to die, or would she save him merely to turn him over to the English authorities?

"My 'neighbor' maybe, but *not* Sir Thomas Watkins, however. This villain is O'Carroll, who haunts the fields and streams of Heaven's Gate when he's not stealing my milk or shearing my sheep."

"They were his before they belonged to you," disputed Sheila, brushing a stray lock of hair from the man's forehead while she continued to apply the required pressure to his wound.

A low moan escaped his parched lips, and for a moment, his breathing became more labored as he suddenly tried to fight off the woman attending him. Then he shuddered violently and fell back to his quiet state though his breathing sounded easier.

"Milady, you must help him," insisted the red-haired servant. "It matters not who he is. He is a wounded man and he was attacked on your land."

"A wanted man," pronounced her mistress sharply.

"I cannot deny it, Lady Regan, yet he's had many the chance to kill you and he has refrained from bloodshed. That very first time he met your carriage, before you even arrived, he had forty men hidden in the woods, each of them prepared to fight to the death for Geata Neamhai, but he never gave them the signal."

"And just why was he so kindhearted?" demanded the young countess, more out of curiosity than anything else. She had already made up her mind that she had no choice but to save O'Carroll, much as it might gall her to do so.

"You were a woman, and, by his code of honor, Connor couldn't take your life then or later in the woods—or at the stream—or in the pasture near Kinnity where you found the wee lamb. Don't you see, milady, much as he wanted Geata Neamhai, he is a good man. This land may have made him your enemy, but it's not worth your life . . . or his."

It crossed Regan's mind that while this might honestly be Sheila's opinion, there was no guarantee O'Carroll felt the same. Obviously he was dearly attached to the O'Carroll properties or he wouldn't still be in these parts, orchestrating the misfortunes that had beset her. However, she reflected as she kneaded the comfrey-and-herb poultice, the devil had had many opportunities to kill her or even kidnap her. From the breadth of his shoulders and the muscles evident in his legs as he sat a horse, the Irishman was not one to lose any physical contest, no matter what his opposition. Like as not the keep's own men would have gladly given him leave to take her.

Staring at his strong chin and long frame while the housekeeper continued to plead his case, Regan found herself wondering what he would be like as a lover. If he were so passionate over mere acreage while refusing to harm a woman, what glories could he bring her to were she to win his heart?

"Ridiculous," the young blonde exclaimed, taking up a fresh cloth and wetting it, turning her body and mind over to the task at hand. Briskly she moved Sheila aside and began to clean the wound.

"All right, while the comfrey sits, I'll sew the leg first."

"Sew it? Milady—"

"Sheila, either you trust me to treat O'Carroll as I deem fit or you can cart him back to the woods as he is. At this moment, I'm not really certain which I'd prefer—but, I assure you, his chances are far better in my hands. However, you must not reveal to Gerard who he really is and caution the others to be careful, as well," ordered the Countess of Kilcaid as she threaded a needle. "I fear he would kill O'Carroll without hesitation."

"Aye, that would be likely, but why aren't you doing so?"

"A few moments ago you begged me to care for him—now, you question my purpose?" snapped Regan imperiously. "I do not want his blood on my hands. Let that be enough."

Realizing how arrogant she sounded, the young woman weakened and reached out to pat Sheila's hand.

"Whatever the reason, I will treat him properly, even though he does not deserve it."

"But he does, your ladyship, he does," whispered the red-haired woman softly.

"Time alone will tell. For now, let us see to the patient," instructed Regan brusquely. "You hold him down while I stitch the wound closed. Then we'll apply the poultice and see what happens."

"You'll not regret helping him. God will smile on ye—"

"As long as Connor O'Carroll's men don't frown, I'll be thankful," the English noblewoman said dryly.

But the next hour was harder than Regan ever imagined possible; for, as her fingers pulled the fiber through Connor's tender skin, her mind marveled at the muscular formation of his body and she found herself comparing his presence to Dudley's. What she had once seen as noble in Elizabeth's courtier now seemed weak and pretentious by comparison to this rugged Irishman. Even unconscious and half-clothed, Connor exuded a masculine strength that made her feel weak. Could the tenants' tales of the devil and his darkling prince have any truth to them? It seemed foolish, yet why else should she have such irrational thoughts?

Pressing the poultice into place as Sheila bound the cloth around his thigh, Regan found her eyes straying to the fabric covering his manhood, and she blushed. Speaking rapidly in an attempt to obscure her embarrassment, she addressed the older woman.

"There now. We have done all we can for him. He needs warmth and rest in a peaceful corner of the keep where no one will give him away or disturb him."

"I will have the soldiers take him to the master's quarters," offered the housekeeper without thinking. "Oh— I'm sorry, milady."

"That's all right, Sheila, I understand. Actually, my rooms might be the best place for him—quiet and private and I will be nearby if his condition worsens."

"But that should be my place, not yours, milady."

"Think on the matter again, Sheila. Remember, this is supposedly my English neighbor, Sir Thomas Watkins. I hardly think he would tolerate an Irish nurse—nor would Gerard expect him to. O'Carroll's life may depend on our remembering his position here."

"Aye, mistress. I'll call the men," agreed Sheila. "And, Lady Regan . . . thank you."

A short while later, despite Gerard's protestations of impropriety, Connor was settled in Regan's bed, while she, alert for the first sign of consciousness, rested on a nearby pallet, softened with extra blankets.

Muttering about "some people's children," Gerard set a heavy guard outside the solar, instructing them to enter at even the slightest sound. As for himself, he retired with a large cup of whiskey, shaking his head at the problem he'd inherited upon William Davies' death.

As dawn approached without Connor's return to the camp outside Kinnity, his men had all they could do to restrain Hugh from breaching the keep single-handedly.

"Are ye daft, man? We don't know for certain that he's even been taken prisoner," argued one of the few brave enough to challenge Connor's second. "If you go in there now, what will it gain? Sheila would send a message if anything were wrong."

"Aye, if they haven't locked her up for assisting Connor," brooded Hugh. "You know I'm not one for standing by and he's already much too late in returning. If it were one of you missing, I'd say you found a soft skirt to dally with, but not our Connor. The only reason he's not back is because they caught him . . . or killed him, and we have to do something about it either way."

"Now is not the time for impetuous actions," cautioned an older man in the group. He had only arrived at camp that day, being one of the most recent deserters from Heaven's Gate, but that gave him a certain authority for knowing the ways of the new mistress. "Lady Regan wouldn't allow him to be executed, even if he were somehow taken. For all her spit and fire, she's a soft lass who couldn't bring herself to dismiss us though she knew full well we could have saved her cabin, and chose to let it burn instead."

A shrill whistle echoed through the woods and all fell silent till the pattern was repeated twice more. Sheila was coming herself, and for her to risk leaving the keep suggested trouble. As the men realized this, they began to mutter among themselves in small groups awaiting the housekeeper's appearance.

"You stupid lout," she exclaimed angrily as she entered the clearing and headed straight for Hugh on the run. Barely reaching the huge man's chest, the slight female started verbally and physically abusing him at once, pounding futilely against his broad chest with her small fists. "How could you let him go off without you when you knew the danger? He's always been too confident of his own abilities, but I trusted you to keep him in check!"

When Hugh showed no distress at her barrage, the feisty nurse changed strategies and began aiming swift kicks at his legs till he simply picked her up and held her high in the air at arm's length so she presented no immediate danger to anyone.

"If you're going to buzz like an angry hornet, you might as well fly," he announced calmly, years of experience in dealing with Sheila giving him the knowledge that soon enough she'd calm down and be rational. Until then, he'd

suspend her above the ground, her feet and tongue flailing
wildly until she accepted the ineffectiveness of her fury.

"All right then, set me down nicely. I'm over my ha-
rangue," she announced at last, "but I still blame your ir-
responsibility for what's happened to that poor lad."

Hugh nodded and released the old nurse.

"Well, what has happened, old woman? What have those
devils done to him?" he demanded anxiously as the others
crowded around to hear.

"I don't know all the details, but the English guards
brought him back to Geata Neamhai with a bad cut to his
thigh, almost bad enough to take the leg off, I daresay,"
began Sheila.

"Those bastards, they'll pay, I swear it! And the she-devil
that sits in Geata Neamhai will pay the highest price of all."

"But she has patched him up right well—"

"Aye, to make him fit for hanging, I suppose, as soon as
he's healed? Well, we won't wait for that to happen," vowed
Hugh. "Brian, get our men together. Sheila, when you go
back, be certain the tunnel entrance is unbarred and we'll
slip in without giving—"

"Not so fast with your haste for vengeance. There's still
too many of them for you to attack and win, even with the
element of surprise," argued the housekeeper. "Besides,
he's lost too much blood to be in any condition to travel.
And, don't you think Sidney would have every damn English guard on your trail as soon as he heard...? Much as I
know you won't believe me, the girl is caring for him right
properly, washing him herself, using the best herbs for the
poultice, mixing them herself, even giving up her bed for
him—"

"She merely wants a healthy prisoner for the English
governor to hang," disputed Hugh. "That doesn't make her
an angel of mercy. I don't trust her or her ways."

"You didn't see her working on him, sewing him up like
he was one of her own people, every stitch costing her as

much pain as him. She's even got the old gray fox believing Connor is Watkins, so Langston wouldn't just let him die. I don't know her game, Hugh, and I can't pretend to guess, but for now, until he can travel without bleeding to death, the healthiest place for Connor O'Carroll is right in his own bedchamber."

"Sheila makes sense, man," agreed one of the others, starting a growing chorus of approval.

"Aye, she speaks sound, son. Give her leave to do as she sees fit," urged the older man. "Sheila can contact us right quick if we're wanted and then we can go in with all our forces. For now, let the lad recuperate in comfort."

"And besides, think how much more he can bedevil her with what he learns about her staying in the keep," added the red-haired housekeeper. "Once he's well enough, he'll have more strategies devised to drive her mad with frustration. Then he'll be back in the keep for good."

"Very well, but, Sheila, I want a report every morning and night, even if it's just to say that nothing has changed and I want that tunnel kept available, as well," instructed Hugh begrudgingly, uncomfortable with the concession he'd made and hoping it was the right move. If he failed Connor now, who would save the O'Carroll?

Regan shifted uncomfortably under the blankets on the pallet at the side of her bed. The devil who'd tried to destroy her and her property was sleeping in her place while she was on the hard stone floor, she fumed. Where was the justice in that? her English heart demanded.

Still, she recalled uneasily, as simple as it might have been to employ a poisonous herb instead of the healing comfrey in her poultice, she hadn't been able to do so. Did any man deserve to have his life taken from him without knowing the manner or cause? Though Gerard would have undoubtedly said *yes* if the demon in question were O'Carroll, Regan kept remembering Sheila's eloquent defense of him and her insistence that the Earl of Kilcaid had quite deliberately refrained from harming the new mistress of Heaven's Gate. Yet, Regan couldn't help but wonder if, for all the hell he'd caused her, he didn't deserve to suffer.

In order to distract herself from such nagging questions of conscience, the young countess thrust off her covers and stood up, a slim white silhouette in the shadowy darkness of the master chamber intent upon checking her patient's condition. Her nightclothes were inappropriate wear for nursing and for sleeping as well, mussed as they were from his care, but Gerard hadn't waited for her to dress before dragging her off to the Great Hall to treat their "neighbor." By the time she returned to the chambers with the unconscious man, there hadn't seemed any point in getting dressed again. As she picked up one of the tapers Sheila had left burning and moved to the head of the bed, O'Carroll groaned loudly and tried to roll over onto his injured side.

"No, no, you mustn't dislodge the poultice, or the bleeding will start again. Here, lie still and I'll bathe your brow," she instructed anxiously, wondering if she shouldn't have dosed the dressings with whiskey before applying them to ease his pain. It was too late now; but, if his restlessness continued, she might send a guard for some liquor. In the meantime, Regan placed the candle on the floor and dipped a cloth into the waiting basin of lilac water; hopefully, its coolness would ease his distress. The floral aroma was well reputed for its calming effect on anxious patients. Yet, O'Carroll continued to stir restlessly until Regan resorted to a song one of the ladies-in-waiting had often used to soothe the irascible Elizabeth.

Heaven, he must have died from his wounds and gone to heaven, decided a barely conscious Connor. What else could explain his being in his own bed with a sweet-voiced angel petting his brow and singing hymns to him? And she was definitely a glorious creature, well curved in body, with long untamed blond hair curling wildly around her shoulders and probably down her back. Wanting to see more of her, the drowsy Irishman shifted on the bed but was quickly overwhelmed by the excruciating pain in his thigh.

Hell, not heaven at all, he cursed to himself; I'm condemned to a hell with a beauty as perfect as this one within reach, but unable to move closer. Groaning at the inexplicable fate he'd drawn, he slumped farther down on the bed, again sending waves of throbbing heat coursing through his leg.

"Shh—relax, O'Carroll, I'm here to help you, but if you don't stay still, you'll tear out the careful needlework that's keeping your leg in one piece," cautioned Regan, sitting beside him and pushing him back on the pillows. "Just lie back."

"I can feel your touch," he said in wonderment. Angels weren't supposed to be incarnate.

"Of course, you can. You are wounded, yes, but you still have all your faculties intact. You are not dead, for pity's sake." Her voice held a note of amusement, but as long as she continued to wipe his brow with that cooling cloth, he could tolerate her laughter at his expense.

"Not dead? Then what am I doing in my bed?"

"*My* bed, I will thank you to remember, sir," corrected his nurse.

"We could share it, you know, it's plenty large for two," proposed Connor with a lopsided wink. Maybe this situation had possibilities after all, he thought saucily as he tried once again to sit up. "Ohh—"

"I told you to be still, but you will not listen, will you, you stupid-headed Irishman?" snapped a weary Regan, seeing all her healing arts in danger of being wasted. "Do you think I worked on you for hours, even lying about your identity to Gerard so you could come to and die because of your pigheadedness? Damn you, Connor O'Carroll, it is just like you to refuse to listen to me because I took over your bloody lands! Well, I tell you, it's for your own good!"

"What? Your taking over my land is for *my* benefit?" shouted Connor in disbelief. "Woman, you are completely mad."

"I am talking about my medical advice," she shot back, "but my owning Heaven's Gate is probably for the best as well. At least, my tenants will have decent housing—"

"If the devil doesn't return to burn them out—" he taunted.

"That was your work—you—you—bastard!" cried Regan, her fury at his insolence overcoming her concern for his wound. All at once, without conscious thought, she drew back her right fist and delivered an angry blow to his grinning face, a blow that connected with enough force to knock him backward on the bed, even as the door to the room opened. In the second before Regan turned to find two of her guards standing there with daggers drawn, she was oddly pleased to see O'Carroll lying ashen faced on the bed, with a trickle of blood dribbling from his lower lip. This wound, minor though it was, was her doing, and she damned well wouldn't treat it.

"Lady Regan, are you all right? We heard some muffled shouts and Gerard told us to keep alert," explained one of the men as they stopped at the foot of the bed. Confronted by the odd sight of his mistress, clad only in rumpled nightclothes, kneeling almost on the patient's chest, while Watkins nursed a bloody lip, the guard wasn't quite certain what his next move should be. "Should we call for Gerard?"

"No, no, I am fine, really," assured Regan, getting to her feet. "I fear Sir Thomas, however—"

"Who the hell is that?" protested Connor loudly, determined not to let this blond vixen have full control of the situation, though his leg hurt like Hades.

"That Sir Thomas may have torn open the stitches in his leg during his spell of delirium," Regan continued. "I believe I have calmed him now, but I want you to hold this taper while I get the covers out of the way and check his wound."

"No! You and your people have done me enough damage already," sputtered her patient, fiercely clutching the blanket she wished to remove. "I'll be damned if I let any female disrobe me in front of servants."

"I have no doubt about your eternal reward, sir," the mistress of Heaven's Gate replied icily, even as she yanked the woolen covering from his grip, "but, I will not be having your death on my conscience because the stitches became infected."

"No! I tell you, I won't permit it," protested Connor, as he moved his leg to avoid her determined hands but only succeeded in generating new waves of excruciating pain. "Oh—"

"Shall I instruct my men to hold you down, sir?" asked a no-longer-patient Regan. "I assure you they will do my bidding if need be. If you are ashamed of your wares, I must tell you, I have seen them and they are not that inadequate."

An angry snarl was her only response as Connor lay back on the bed, turning his eyes away from the humiliation of her ministrations and the men who stood watching. An eternity later, she was through.

"The bandage appears to have kept the stitches intact, and there seems to be no new bleeding. Andrew, fetch Sir Thomas a flagon of whiskey, please. I'll feel better if he enjoys a quiet, though drugged, few hours of sleep," admitted the mistress of Heaven's Gate. "I am quite weary myself."

"Is your stomach too weak to watch me die, Lady Regan?" mocked Connor as the guards left and she rearranged the blankets. "I told you once that to take an Irishman's land is tantamount to killing him—and you have done that to me already."

"Not by choice," confessed the tired woman as the guard returned with Connor's whiskey and departed once again. "It was only by royal decree that I came to Ireland. What Elizabeth ordains, no man, let alone woman, dares defy. Here, drink this."

"Why not just return to your family in England?" asked Connor. Much as he was attuned to hating the woman, she wasn't without redeeming qualities. If what she said about patching him up was true... well, it was more than most enemies would do for their victims. Of course, he'd been careless when he'd confronted her men at arms, but that was neither here nor there. He'd been wounded often enough to know he'd heal, and more quickly than she'd anticipate, a fact he might be able to use to his advantage. For now, however, he wanted information.

"Surely your people would protect you from Elizabeth's wrath. Besides, as furious as her anger may be, it can dissipate just as quickly. Of course, you couldn't be received at court, but there's nothing wrong with a small cottage on some relative's estate in the country."

"Oh? And that's why you've accepted my ownership of Heaven's Gate so readily? Because you don't mind a small cottage yourself?" laughed Regan as she took the empty flagon from his hand. She should be furious with his manner yet there were those devilishly blue eyes that caught her own and seemed to delve deep into her soul. It was as though his spirit called out to hers, seeking a kinship, longing to be one though their minds were worlds apart.

"Geata Neamhai if you please," he corrected drowsily, "and I am the rightful owner of my family's heritage, not some noble English squatter seeking to improve her status with the queen. What of your family? With your father gone to his reward, what ties have you?"

"I have none, so forget your foolish dreams of my abandoning this place and leaving you in peace," suggested Regan, drawing the blankets up over her patient's broad chest, her hands lingering perhaps a second too long. "O'Carroll, I am here at Heaven's Gate to stay."

"We'll see about that," murmured Connor as the whiskey called him to sleep. "We'll see . . ."

"Aye, that we will, sir, that we will," echoed Regan, more than ready to sink down onto her pallet for some much-needed rest. This time, there was no hesitation before her eyes closed and her mind quieted its thoughts.

Chapter Eight

Considering the long night Regan had spent, it was well past midmorning before Sheila had the heart to awaken her mistress. When the noblewoman turned her first conscious glance toward the bed that had quartered her patient, and found it empty, however, she was far from pleased at the housekeeper's thoughtfulness.

"Sheila! What happened to O'Carroll? Did Gerard discover his real identity or did his condition worsen?" she demanded anxiously, jumping from her pallet. Though she was not entirely certain that her own life wouldn't be easier if the Irishman were gone, whether to a stockade or another life, it shouldn't have happened without her knowledge. "Why didn't you awaken me?"

"He's fine, milady," assured Sheila.

"Aye, that I am, thanks to you," came a masculine brogue from the other side of the room, Connor now having given up all pretense at an English accent. "Indeed, I wish my friends were half as concerned about my welfare as my enemies."

Wheeling around quickly, Regan was astounded to see the invalid of last night sitting before the open desk, his leg propped on a chair, as he apparently explored her correspondence. Immediately she was beside him, grabbing the papers he held.

"How dare you have the impertinence to read my letters? You forget yourself, O'Carroll—"

"No, but you do. I am Sir Thomas Watkins of Wren's Nest, at least for the duration of my stay," he replied with an easy grin, clearly taking no offense at her manner. "That's what Sheila said this morning and I believe you did, as well."

"Be it Watkins or O'Carroll, you still have no business delving into my personal papers," snapped Regan, angry spots of pink appearing in her creamy cheeks. "You are certainly no gentleman."

"That is one claim which I have never made, dear woman. What is more, if Watkins is any measure of the type of man you'd welcome into your bedroom, I'd never attempt to imitate the English noble state," he commented dryly, momentarily entranced by the combination of her blond hair, disarrayed by her slumber, and her angry eyes sparking while she searched for a reply. When it came, he wasn't disappointed; the girl had spirit.

"I suppose, sir, that some things are so far beyond the reach of an Irishman that it's better not to even try," she said haughtily, refusing to acknowledge the distaste that she herself felt for Watkins. "Nevertheless, as a guest—"

"Guest or prisoner?" he asked sharply.

"Guest, of course. You may leave the keep at any time you choose, O'Carroll. I fear at present though that your leg may not support you for too far a distance," she cautioned. "Some wounds take a long time to heal."

"Exactly," concurred her patient. "Why then are you willing to nurse me back to health and even hide my identity from your men? The differences between the Irish and English don't ordinarily encourage such charitable actions."

"Why must everything be on a national scale? Can't we just be two people, one assisting the other in time of need?

Does politics always have to control our destinies?'' she protested.

"When the English sovereign can force me from my estates and make me a renegade, it's rather difficult to put politics aside,'' he responded curtly, surprised by the sudden welling of tears in her eyes. Could she really be so naive as to expect him to abandon his legal right to Geata Neamhai because she'd treated him with kindness?

Watching her as she stood beside him, still clad only in her white linen nightclothes, he sensed a small nugget of concern for her growing within him. Losing her father so abruptly, being sent from Court to attend to the old man's holdings in a land where her kind was hated…she couldn't be more than eighteen or twenty, yet she had handled his attacks on the keep quite admirably. For a moment, Connor's eyes crinkled as he recalled the visions of her he'd witnessed: dripping wet in the pool his men had created, on horseback carrying the shorn lamb back to the fold, even marching stiff backed through Kinnity, without showing her distress at the residents' disdain.

"I apologize if my forthright manner perturbs you, Lady Regan, but you will find I rarely disguise my opinions—"

"Or your identity?'' she challenged, as she remembered her first encounter with Connor O'Carroll.

"Well, not to my own people at any rate,'' he muttered, having the decency to recognize his own arrogance. Deciding to turn the conversation to safer topics, he nodded at the papers she held. "You will find those pages are not yours at all, but notes I've written to tell my men I am safe and they are not to attempt to free me. I'd hate for anyone else to be hurt, let alone die, on my account. If you permit it, I'd like to send a messenger to my camp.''

"And will this one return?'' questioned the young woman.

''That is up to your ladyship, I should think,'' answered Connor, fully aware that her order now barred the gate to his messengers.

Glancing at the paper she held, Regan shrugged. For all she knew of Gaelic, this might be detailed instructions of how and when to stage an attack on the keep just as easily as the message he described.

''Well?'' he prodded, smiling at the knowledge that not only could she not read his words, but that he had already read her private journals before she awoke. ''If you're not certain I've told you the truth, have Sheila translate the note for you.''

''Considering her past duplicity—''

''Loyalty,'' corrected the Irishman.

''I am quite certain my housekeeper would say exactly what you told her to say and not a syllable more,'' continued Regan. Yet, what else could she do but send the message? If she didn't and they were attacked... ''Very well, Sheila will see your letter is dispatched, but make no mistake, O'Carroll. If there is any siege on Heaven's Gate, Gerard has instructed the guards to kill without question, but I will reserve the pleasure of killing you for myself.''

Connor's raucous laugh couldn't be held back as he imagined this gracious female actually raising a dagger and shedding any blood, his at that. He chuckled till tears rolled down his cheeks and he began to cough. Finally he contained himself sufficiently to speak.

''You might take pleasure in the thought, milady, but I verily doubt you could stomach the deed,'' he said, looking around in surprise for Regan.

''Now then, did I not teach you better manners than to mock a fine lady?'' Sheila chided in annoyance. ''Come along, back to bed with you before you push yourself too far. Lean on me.''

''Haven't I always?'' teased Connor with a wink, his good humor still evident as he tried to support as much of his weight as he could bear so as not to burden the older woman.

"Ah, get on with you," said the servant, blushing all the same as she helped him back to the bed.

"Where did she go?"

"Her ladyship is dressing since the noonday meal will be served shortly and her man will find it peculiar if she doesn't appear. But you mark my words, Connor O'Carroll, you had best make peace with that woman. She's not the muddleheaded sort you're used to, all curves but no substance. English or not, she has fixed you up right proper."

"I know, Sheila, I know, and her hiding me here as well involves risking Sidney's wrath," admitted the Irishman, "but this is quite awkward for me too, you know. Here I am, an invalid in my own keep, secreted away from even the servants like some illicit lover—"

"Don't get your hopes up, O'Carroll, I'd never be that desperate," said Regan, reentering the room. Garbed in a deep emerald-green gown and soft white kirtle with a lace-and-pearl embroidered collar, her long hair caught in golden netting that seemed to deepen its own vibrant hues, she looked every inch the lady of the manor. "I would say you were more like the black sheep the family keeps under lock and key."

"And yet you, milady, saved my life. For what it is worth, I do appreciate your efforts, Lady Regan, but understand, I cannot let that stop me from one day reclaiming Geata Neamhai as my own." Before she could protest, he continued. "Until I am safely healed, however, I would be amenable to a truce of sorts."

"A truce?" Regan repeated slowly, her vibrant green eyes carefully searching his features for some clue to his meaning. Was he going to laugh at her again or did he mean it? A distinct twinkle in his eye and a lazy grin made her hesitate.

"Yes, my men will cease their mischief as long as I remain in your care, but when I return to my camp, I will resume my claim on these lands," explained the Earl of Kilcaid.

"Very well, I admit I could use a respite from your pranks. A week of peace then, presuming you heal properly," agreed Regan, moving to take Connor's hand in contract. "No shenanigans for seven days and by then, who knows, you may have come to enjoy being a guest rather than the lord of the manor."

"That I doubt," refuted Connor quickly, though he had to acknowledge to himself that the prospect of eyeing such a lovely lady as Regan for a week might be quite enjoyable, especially if he healed quickly.

Once she made her pact with Connor, the hours seemed to pass quickly for Regan. The chores of the morning had been done by others, but she still rode out to see the new tenant houses. Watkins's men were hard at work, and she made a note to stand a heavy guard at the site that night. Though Connor had promised no more mischief, she was not certain his men would comply.

Her only immediate problem seemed to be Gerard, who demanded to know how "Watkins" had come to be riding with Irish renegades, sporting their colors the night before.

"In his delirium he shouted something about being kidnapped while he was swimming in a lake. Apparently the rebels gave him some of their rags to cover his nakedness," Regan fabricated quickly. "He was in their custody when he spied our patrol and broke away, trying to reach the safety of armed Englishmen. Riding rapidly behind him, the Irish pursued him, and our men, not knowing he was one of us, mistook him for an enemy as the Irish engaged them in battle."

"Are you certain that is what took place?" her advisor asked, not fully convinced in the matter.

"I'm not certain of anything. I wasn't there," Regan snapped, exasperated that he continued to question what she considered a brilliantly plausible explanation. "Sir Thomas hasn't spoken of the matter since he has regained consciousness. If you are so concerned, why not ask him yourself? That is, if you want to remind him it was one of my men who wounded him."

"Do you think that if we don't discuss it, he will forget that fact? That would be for the best. We wouldn't want him considering us unneighborly," Gerard said, a note of anxiety in his deep voice. "Still, perhaps we should..."

"Fine, fine, whatever you decide," offered his mistress, in a final ploy to allay Gerard's suspicions long enough for her to relate to O'Carroll the falsehood she had told. Her nerves were taut from the necessity of sustaining such a lie to the only real family she had. Yet, she knew in her heart that if she told Gerard the truth, he would insist on notifying the English governor of O'Carroll's whereabouts and the Irishman would hang in short order. That she couldn't allow, especially since, somehow, his being declared a criminal seemed her father's fault. Oh, why had Elizabeth ever deeded the land to the Davies anyway?

"Gerard, I find I am still rather weary with the events of last night. I believe I will dine with our neighbor in my chambers, so please instruct Sheila to have two trays sent up."

"I will, indeed, but wouldn't it be more appropriate if I joined you?" suggested her second in command. "As I recall, Sir Thomas had a rather improper manner and quite a flirtatious eye."

"For heaven's sake, Gerard, you are speaking of a seriously injured man," chided Regan. "He's in no condition to require a watchdog. Besides, I need you to keep order in the Great Hall. I have noticed that the men tend to become overly rowdy with their drinking contests unless they are supervised."

"Very well, milady." Gerard frowned. "I'll do as you say, but I will post a guard outside the door nonetheless."

"Thank you," said his mistress, already moving to the staircase to her tower, oddly excited at the thought of seeing O'Carroll again. It's only because you fear for his welfare, she told herself. He is much too stubborn a man to remain quiet and he may have ripped open the stitches. But when she reached her chambers, Regan discovered her fears were for naught. Her patient was abed and his wound already beginning to heal.

The evening passed easily between them since the issue of ownership of Geata Neamhaí, Heaven's Gate, was not a matter of debate. Indeed, Regan reflected as she prepared for bed, Connor was quite an accomplished conversationalist, sharing tales of Irish folklore and anecdotes of life at the keep, even a few stories of his days at Elizabeth's court. If only he weren't Irish . . .

The debate in the woods outside Kinnity was a great deal less harmonious.

"Sure and 'tis Connor's hand, but who is to tell me they didn't torment him until he wrote the words?" demanded Hugh. "I say we storm the keep and get him back."

"You said that all last night as well until Sheila finally brought word he was alive and being cared for," reminded Padraic. "Now, we have his own letter and you are still talking raid."

"Hugh, 'tis a full moon tonight and we'd have to travel almost a mile across open fields before we'd even get to the keep. It's just not a good idea, lad," said one of the older men.

"Aye, if we hadn't gotten his orders—"

"Damn it all, I still say he would not have written those orders willingly. After weeks of wearing the woman down, he tells us to stop all activities against her. It makes not a whit of sense—unless he's out of his mind with pain,'' declared Hugh.

"Or in love," offered a man in the back of the group, much to the laughter of the others.

"Not bloody likely," snapped Hugh. "But, all right, if you are all against me, I'll abide with the lot of you, at least for a bit."

In the morning, Regan awakened to find Connor rolled to the edge of the bed, lying so he could watch her. Quickly she felt for the covers, but she was still adequately clothed; there was nothing amiss there. A slow grin crept over his rugged features and his eyes twinkled as he greeted her.

"A good morning to thee, fair maiden."

"And the same to thee, O'Carroll, though I suppose I should say Watkins." It was so difficult to remember to call the Irishman by her neighbor's name since the very thought of that horrendous toad of Wren's Nest repulsed her. "Did you sleep well, sir?"

"Aye, quite well, indeed, though it would have been better I'm certain had you slept up here beside me. Believe me or not, Lady Regan, but I am not the kind of man who appreciates a woman sleeping at his feet. After all," he said with a saucy grin, "where is the pleasure in that?"

"Sir! I hardly think such conversation is appropriate—"

"And what about our relationship is appropriate?" he challenged with a grin. "Besides, you told me yourself, I'm too ill to be concerned with any appetite but that for food. When do we break our fast?"

"Oh, you are a beguiling scoundrel, all right," said Regan, unable to hide a smile. "Sheila told me you were a rogue, but I never imagined—"

"Imagined what?"

"Nothing." Nothing she could possibly admit to him, anyway, she amended silently. Once a man knew a woman found him attractive, he merely toyed with her, or so it had been with Dudley, and she was not about to have that happen again. "After I wash and dress, I will ask the guard to fetch our morning meal. Can you wait that long?" she asked teasingly.

"Aye, especially if I can watch you wash and dress," Connor promised. Seeing her furious blush, he relented and eased her embarrassment. "Sorry. I just could not resist teasing you, Regan. Of course, I respect your privacy too much to peep, though I have seen you in that nightdress, you know."

Shaking her head at his familiar attitude, Regan slipped behind her screen to commence her morning ritual. Today she hadn't planned any excursions. Indeed, she would remain at Heaven's Gate and keep her patient company during the long day. Perhaps, if the stitches were holding, she might even encourage him to exercise a bit.

And so, the day passed in a friendly camaraderie. Throughout their games of chess, contests of wit, storytelling and songs, Regan found herself growing more and more comfortable in Connor's company. When Gerard arrived at her quarters to render "Watkins" his thanks for the new workers and to offer his best wishes for a speedy recovery, Regan actually resented the insistence of her self-appointed guardian that she dine in the Great Hall that evening.

"Your household misses you, Regan. That is a compliment. At least a dozen men and women asked if you would be supping with us. I do think it is your place," he chided gently. "I am certain Sir Thomas will understand your obligation."

"Of course, Lady Regan. Please see to your duties. I only regret that I have kept you from them," apologized Connor. "Indeed, you should have a good night's rest, as well. Why don't you have your housekeeper prepare other quarters for you tonight?"

"Thank you for your concern, Sir Thomas, but since this is my bedchamber, I prefer to remain in it," the countess replied, her eyes snapping their annoyance at his presumption. "However, I will join the household in the Great Hall for dinner. As a matter of fact, since nothing more has been heard of the O'Carroll since my men routed him the other night, I believe a special evening of celebration is in order. It is too bad you can not join us in delighting in Heaven's Gate's good fortune," Regan said, tossing her head back with exactly the right haughty gesture common to the English royal court. "Good night, Sir Thomas. I trust I won't awaken you later."

It was almost midnight when the door to the chamber opened again and Connor lifted himself on one elbow to welcome Regan back, not that he was waiting for her, but he hadn't been able to sleep. To his immense shock, the body filling the doorway was far from feminine.

"Hugh?" he called. "Sweet Mother of God, what are you doing here?"

"I came to take you home, boyo."

"What? Didn't you receive my message? I assured you I was fine," said Connor in amazement. What had gone wrong?

"Sure and I got something, but the Connor I know wouldn't have written instructions that cowardly. 'Leave the girl alone, she's caring for me'? For all you know about medicine, she might just as well be poisoning you! And what about your men? You think we wouldn't take proper care of you?" snapped Hugh, already spoiling for a fight. Getting in had been too easy with the guards busily drinking the extra whiskey Regan had ordered, and he was ready to butt heads.

"Sheila's been overseeing her nursing efforts, but, Hugh, Regan is not the evil woman you think her. She is as much a pawn of Elizabeth's as I am," began Connor.

"Whatever she is, you are leaving with me, now."

"But my leg—"

"I'll carry you if need be, but you'll not spend another night in the clutches of that English witch," declared Connor's closest friend.

"And if I want to?" questioned the Earl of Kilcaid, still not realizing Hugh's distrust of Regan.

But the only answer he received was a hard right to his chin, followed by a swift left hook for good measure. Then he was bundled into a blanket and tossed over Hugh's broad shoulders.

With any luck at all, Hugh thought, we'll be through the tunnel and back in camp before the English ever miss you, lad. If not, I'll wallop a few more heads, but I'm taking you with me now.

And he did.

Chapter Nine

Sweet Jesus, but his head hurt. Connor clenched his eyes shut. Had the enchanting English witch drugged his wine just as her attentions had won a bit of his confidence? And his bed! He was no longer in his own bed at Geata Neamhai; in fact he was in no bed at all. Instead, he had been cast upon the dark, dank ground. Yet his surroundings did not carry the odors of a dungeon, but the sweet scent of the outdoors. Where in perdition was he, and what had happened to bring him there?

The struggle to sit up caused Connor no little amount of pain. While he waited for his vision to come into focus in the darkness, the thought of too much whiskey crossed his numbed consciousness, yet he discarded such a notion. He had been but a stripling when the potent drink had last had such an effect upon him. Besides, he couldn't remember imbibing it in any quantity since fate had delivered him to Regan Davies' care. Or had he ever really been there at all, he considered, recognizing the fact that he was now in his makeshift camp with a canopy of stars over him. Could it have all been some dream visited upon him by the fairy folk?

He started to rest his head in his open hands in order to give his mind some further opportunity to clear, when the slight pressure of his palms against his jaw brought a fierce throbbing. All at once he remembered with crystal clarity what had happened, and his rage was boundless. Instantly he was on his feet, his anger sweeping away whatever cobwebs had remained in his brain, and giving his bruised body a surge of strength that made it impervious to pain.

"Hugh!" he roared, his eyes searching for the hulking form of his second in command. "Hugh Cassidy!"

"Yes, Connor, what is it?" came a deep rumbling from behind.

The young Irish lord turned with demon speed and saw the bemused, self-satisfied expression, which not even the darkness could hide, on his old friend's broad face. For Connor, it was instantly eclipsed by a vision of Regan Davies when she found her patient gone and supposed that her kindness had been repaid with treachery.

"You stinking mongrel whelp!" Connor said, his voice dangerous in its softness and his fists closing into menacing weapons. "How dare you presume to disobey my orders?"

"Now, Connor, don't make me hurt you," Hugh began, a trace of supplication in his voice, "when all I've done is save you."

"Save me! Save me from what, you great oaf? From the clutches of a mere English girl? I'd made her feel guilty she had taken my home. We were well on the road to making peace with each other, a peace which could have led to her abandoning my property."

"You young fool! Listen to what you're saying. Do you think you could have charmed the girl into giving up so rich a prize as Geata Neamhai? If I didn't save you from Regan Davies, then I have certainly saved you from yourself!"

Connor took a determined step forward with the intention of throttling this meddling giant, but the movement brought a searing pain to his thigh, and he remembered the wound he had sustained during battle.

Devil take him, but he was in no condition to fight Hugh at present! Enraged, Connor stood taking the measure of the man before him, the temptation to brawl still quite strong. Realizing, however, that it was no real option, his quick mind sought some avenue of revenge, one that would teach this overprotective dolt his place. Suddenly, a gleam of inspiration shining is his deep blue eyes, Connor knew what he would do. There were other ways to remind Hugh Cassidy who was lord! In fact, he thought, quite pleased with himself, he had found a solution that might solve all of his problems.

The moment Gerard had left her chamber and shut the door behind him, Regan began pacing the confines of the room, silently railing at herself for having been a fool, for having placed any trust at all in a man of Connor O'Carroll's caliber. She had given the rebel his life in return for not having taken hers that day on the forest road. And what had the swine done? He'd vanished into the night without so much as a thank-you or a by-your-leave. How long would it be before he broke the tenuous truce between them? Regan wondered. It was a foolish question, she quickly chided herself. The man had broken their fragile peace already.

"You are still an idiot when it comes to trusting a man, Regan Davies," the raging beauty whispered to herself as she continued her pacing. "Will you never learn? What made you think the Irishman wouldn't flee at first opportunity? And it was shame at your own stupidity which coerced you into protecting him yet again, even after you had found out he'd escaped. Why couldn't you just have told Gerard the truth rather than saying that Thomas Watkins was well enough to travel and had returned home? You proud fool, what will you do now?"

Regan's quiet berating of herself was interrupted by a rapping at her chamber door.

"Enter," she commanded, regaining control of her emotions and drawing herself up to her full height, so that she presented a creditable appearance of authority.

Slowly the heavy wooden door pushed inward, and Sheila ntered, looking anxiously about.

"Is it true, then, milady? He was well enough to travel ind you let him go?"

"You should know what happened, Sheila," Regan re-orted. "You were part of it, weren't you?"

"By all the saints, your ladyship, I've no idea what you're alking about."

"Don't you?" Regan asked with scorn. "How did you nanage to spirit him out, Sheila?"

"I swear, milady, I had naught to do with it! I thought in our kindness you had decided to free him rather than see iim at the end of hangman's noose."

"I didn't want his death. Why would I save a man's life inly to hand him over to his executioner? But, neither did I xpect to be betrayed. And that, Sheila, is exactly what your O'Carroll has done. At the first opportunity, why even be-ore he should be walking on that leg, he slipped back into he forests so that he can wreak more havoc on Heaven's Gate. I should have let him bleed to death, I should have..."

Regan stopped her tirade, trying to conceal the quiver that iad crept into her voice. But Sheila was not to be fooled. So hat was what was at the core of the matter, she thought. The girl had feelings for the Earl of Kilcaid. Oh, she might ant and rave and try to deny them, even to herself, but they vere there all right. Sheila had not lived this long without gaining some perception about the mysterious workings of he human heart.

Crusty and gruff as she might sometimes be, loyal to Connor though she was, the older woman could not help out feel some pity for the young Englishwoman before her. Women, no matter how keen witted, were too often at the mercy of their emotions; hadn't she, herself, been in just such a predicament with her own Michael? Without stop-ping to think why, Sheila's empathy drove her to comfort her mistress, and she took the young hand within her own scrawny grasp.

"You knew in your heart, lass, that he is not some domestic beast to be gentled and kept by your side, happy to sit up at your command and do your bidding. He's the O'Carroll, and all of the O'Carroll men are strong-minded and domineering. Their bravery has been the subject of many a tale told by the seneschal, the clan poet. To be sure, they're proud, honorable males, as well. And Connor is the finest of the lot. He couldn't have given up his fight with you even if he had wanted to."

"I don't know what you're talking about," Regan protested, withdrawing her hand from Sheila's. "O'Carroll certainly didn't display any bravery when he ran from this keep. As for me, I am not such a babe that I thought a few stitches in a rebel's leg would mend the gash inflicted on this land. Nor did I think it would heal the animosity between us. I am simply angry—no furious, that I was feeble-minded enough to allow myself to be betrayed. I will never make that mistake again."

"Betrayed by Connor? No, Lady Regan, you've just said that you didn't expect his sojourn here to put things to rights between you," Sheila said. "I'm of the feeling that if you've been betrayed at all, it was by your own heart."

"You forget yourself, old woman. Besides, your conjectures are completely wrong," Regan said, turning around and walking to the window in an effort to hide the truth not only from Sheila but also from herself. It wasn't that she was hurt because the handsome rogue she had been tending was gone; she was infuriated because her enemy had escaped. That was the source of her upset. It had to be.

Clutching at this possibility to keep from being ashamed of her unmanageable emotions, Regan faced Sheila Dempsey once more.

"I have admitted that I have been a fool once where O'Carroll is concerned, Sheila," Regan said brusquely.

"However, I have also told you that I will not commit such an error again. I will not be spied upon nor have my efforts to improve Heaven's Gate undermined. You had best contact your daughters. I want you gone from this household."

"Gone?" Sheila echoed. "From Geata Neamhai?"

"No, from Heaven's Gate," Regan responded, sorry for the pain she saw reflected in the old castelain's eyes yet firm in her decision. She could not, after all, place her people in more danger than was necessary.

"But, your ladyship, in truth I have no daughters. I've only two sons—one a priest and the other an itinerant soldier who roams the lands in the north. Neither of them have a place for me."

"No daughters? Well, it seems you have made lying a vocation, Sheila. You've misled me about that just as you lied about having nothing to do with O'Carroll's escape," Regan said.

"But I swear, mistress, I knew nothing about it. I didn't help him to leave," a distraught Sheila protested.

"And would you have if he had asked?" Regan questioned gently, dismayed by the raw emotions playing across the older woman's face.

There was no hesitation before Sheila raised her head and answered.

"Aye, I would have," she said in a whisper holding no hint of contrition.

"Ah, the truth at last," Regan commented. "Why then, Sheila, should I give you a roof over your head and food in your trencher, when your loyalty is given to O'Carroll rather than to Heaven's Gate and to me? When you would take the part of a man who stole away like a thief in the night over that of your rightful mistress?"

"Connor O'Carroll is no thief," Sheila answered defiantly. "'Twas not he who stole this land from anyone. And as for my staying on in this keep, it is my right. It is my home, not yours.''

"Do you think I actually wanted to come to Ireland?" Regan asked, incredulous at the liberties this woman had taken in her speech. "A keep a hundred times richer than this would not have tempted me. I am here only because the queen commands it. I wish to God I had never set eyes on the wretched place, but I will do as Elizabeth bids me, and stay here until the land is settled to her satisfaction. Though I would rather not, I will remove every Irish inhabitant of Heaven's Gate if need be in order to follow her majesty's dictates.''

"Listen to yourself, when the O'Carroll tried to regain what was his, were you hurt in any way? Did any of us harm you? If you send these people off these lands, you are sending most of them to their deaths. They will surely starve.''

"And you, Sheila, shall I keep you also?"

"I am an old woman, what happens to me doesn't matter when compared to the fate of the others," Sheila stated. "If you wish me gone, I'll go now though it will break my heart to do so.''

"What happens to the others means more to you than your own welfare?" Regan questioned slowly.

"Aye.''

"Then with that in mind, I will tell you what I will do," the Countess of Kilcaid said with newfound wisdom. "You will train someone of my choosing to take your place. When that task is accomplished, you will be given a snug, little cottage in the village and a pension. You will not starve, Sheila Dempsey, but neither will you play me false. If, at any time during the remainder of your stay here I feel that you are working to restore the O'Carroll to Heaven's Gate, I will turn out not only you, but every Irishman living within my gates or on my land. If you think I haven't the manpower to do so, know that the real Thomas Watkins will be only too happy to help me. Have I made myself clear?''

"All too clear, milady," Sheila grumbled, though in truth she wondered at this Englishwoman's soft heart. Had she been mistress here instead of Regan Davies, there would be no second chances for the inhabitants of Geata Neamhai. But then, she supposed, that was the difference between being brought up under desperate circumstances and enjoying a comfortable life at the English court.

Many weary hours later, having finally spent her energy in restless tossing and turning, Regan drifted off to a fitful sleep. Every time she had closed her eyes, she had found disturbing visions of Connor O'Carroll rather than comforting slumber. She saw him cocky and confident on the forest road; laughing at her as she rode her borders; sitting boldly astride his horse, dressed in the manner of an Irish chieftain; lying easily in her bed with the coverlets slipped down from around his powerful, masculine chest. The images stirred yearnings in her that she fought to deny. To give in to such irrational feelings would be to relinquish all hopes, all desires, of ever returning to England.

In an attempt to expunge images of Connor, Regan concentrated instead on thinking about those who shared her new home. Her Englishmen posed few problems, but the tenants and servants who were Irish were another question altogether, and Regan wondered what she would eventually decide concerning their fate. Deep within her heart, she did not wish to dispossess anyone, not even Sheila. The young Englishwoman remembered all too vividly what it had been like growing up listening to her father's complaints that Henry had stripped him of his rightful title and lands. In those days, Regan had understood her father's bitterness and had agreed with him, just as the Irish undoubtedly concurred with their former lord.

She recalled hating those who had taken her birthright from her. Now she understood that in reality they hadn't taken anything at all. They had only received what the king had given them. How then could she dismiss the feelings of the Irish and live among them knowing that she would be forever the interloper, the outsider, yes, the thief who had stolen O'Carroll lands?

O'Carroll, Regan thought with a groan. There was that name again, and there, too, were images of those deep blue eyes that twinkled so seductively whenever they looked at her. Instinctively Regan knew that focusing on the dark-haired earl anew meant it would be several more hours before she found sleep. Yet she could blame him no more for that than she could blame him for wanting Heaven's Gate. This was a sentiment, however, that Regan would admit to no one, certainly not to Sheila, and not to Gerard, either, for that matter. He would only reprove her for being overly softhearted and blame it on the fact that she was a mere woman.

But, Regan mused, she was not the only one to have a soft heart. O'Carroll had demonstrated one, as well, as Sheila had been quick to point out. It was true that on several occasions, the man could have killed her, and yet he had never touched her. Instead, he had patiently tried to drive her out by becoming a damnable nuisance rather than an actual threat. Only a man assured of his power could risk such gentle behavior, especially if O'Carroll felt about his property as her father had felt about his.

But perhaps such restraint was at an end, Regan speculated. It might be that Connor would now openly attack the keep. Then she could think of him as a true foe and come to hate him as she should. The thought, however, gave her less solace than she had supposed, and when she finally drifted off to sleep, it was with thoughts of O'Carroll's next move foremost in her mind.

"Regan! Regan!" Gerard shouted as he stormed through her solar and knocked upon her bedroom door even as he opened it.

"Whatever is it?" the young woman asked, looking up while her maid finished dressing her.

"I've received reports that there is a large army of men riding hard toward Heaven's Gate. It might very well be that we shall find ourselves under attack momentarily. I want you below in the Great Hall with the other women."

"So it has begun," Regan muttered as she followed Gerard out to the corridor. But instead of going below, she continued out onto the battlements of her keep.

Standing at the wall, Regan scoured the lands below for a sign of the approaching horsemen while Gerard yelled at her to return inside as he walked up and down, issuing orders to the soldiers. Ignoring him, the countess continued to strain for a glimpse of the danger that had spurred her men into action. Finally she was able to make out figures near the horizon, though who they were or what they wanted she could only guess. All at once she was aware of another presence at her elbow. It was Sheila.

"Milady, I neither signaled the riders nor knew anything of this," the older woman hastened to inform her. "Please, don't carry out your threat to punish the others. I swear I had nothing to do with it."

"Are you so sure it is O'Carroll, then?" Regan asked, though she knew the answer without having to ask.

"Aye, I'd know him anywhere," the Irish servant replied, anxious for her lord as he rode onward to face English arrows and cannon fire. "Didn't I care for him since he was naught but an infant? And won't I mourn him as though he were my own son if he is cut down? But you must believe me, I would never have aided him in a direct assault on the keep. 'Tis madness, and can end in nothing but his destruction!"

Regan could feel the tension around her grow as Connor's forces drew closer. She heard Gerard shouting commands to those ready to defend her walls with crossbows and cannons. Yet her awareness of the activity surrounding her existed only on the periphery of her consciousness, so strong was her concentration on the Irishman leading his band at a fast clip toward Heaven's Gate.

Even as she followed his approach, Regan couldn't help but think of the wounded man with the roguish smile she had tended but a few days before. How incongruous that such a pleasant, witty companion could be the treacherous enemy who now made ready to assault her keep. Didn't the fool know he would open his wound once he engaged in combat?

Fighting the regret she felt at such a turn of events, Regan continued to watch Connor O'Carroll ride boldly in the direction of her gates. Near enough now to be distinguished from those around him, the rebel Earl of Kilcaid presented a magnificent picture of a man. Regan's breath caught in her throat as she beheld his broad shoulders, fine features and dark, curling hair. She had little time, however, to lose herself in reverie as Gerard's deep voice boomed beside her.

"By the grace of God, that looks like Watkins!" he yelled.

"No. 'Tis Connor O'Carroll," Regan replied, steeling herself for the eruption sure to follow.

"O'Carroll!" Gerard thundered. "What do you mean, O'Carroll? Is that not the man we met on the forest road, the man you bargained with at Wren's Nest, the very man whose wound you nursed in your own chambers?"

"It is the stranger we met when we came to Heaven's Gate, and the very same whose gash I tended, but it is not the Englishman I encountered when I rode to Wren's Nest. He is not Thomas Watkins."

"You knew, and yet you deceived me, Regan," the silver-haired Englishman accused, "me, who cares for your welfare more than for my own life. Why did you take him in and see to him knowing that he is your enemy? How could you have lied to me to protect him?"

"Because I owed him a debt," Regan said quietly.

"Oh, and the fact that he is a fine figure of a man had nothing to do with it, I suppose," Gerard taunted.

"Perhaps it did," Regan conceded, recalling the pleasant aspects of sharing a chamber if not a bed with Connor O'Carroll. "But that is not how it began. It was a point of honor."

"And to what has your honor brought us now, milady? To a siege of your keep, that's what! Regan, dear girl, when will you learn that life does not proceed according to the whims of your soft heart?"

Gerard's wrath, her own feelings of regret and the murmured excitement of the Irish within the keep forced Regan back to the reality of the situation she now faced. She was, after all, responsible for the safety of Heaven's Gate and its inhabitants. With effort, she hardened her heart against her handsome enemy as his fighting men reined their horses just out of arrow's range, and he boldly came forward alone.

"What challenge will the man have the audacity to voice now?" an irritated but fascinated Regan asked, more to herself than to anyone else.

"Why mistress!" Sheila cried, clasping her hands in delight when she spied the wares with which Connor's horse was laden. "The O'Carroll's purpose is not to issue a challenge at all."

"Really," Regan commented dryly. "What does he want then, simply to mock my authority and flaunt his escape?"

"Saints preserve us, no, milady," the older woman said, a grin spread across her face as she silently approved the Earl of Kilcaid's cleverness. "Why anyone can see that the O'Carroll has come acourting."

"Courting?" Regan echoed in amazement. At Sheila's affirming nod, the Englishwoman's face flamed redder than any summer sunset. "How can you be certain?" she demanded.

"Look. He wears his finest clothes, and see how his men hang back while he proceeds alone bearing gifts so that he can declare his suit. Why, lass, what else can it be but that he has fallen under your spell and has come to offer you his name!"

"What else indeed!" interrupted a still-fuming Gerard. "As if the Lady Regan would be empty-headed enough to believe that outlaw—that charlatan—capable of an honorable offer. In truth, if this is what the man is about, then she knows his intent is merely to lure her into the marriage bed in order to regain his lands! Shall I give the order to the archers, milady? One hail of arrows and our troubles cease."

"I shall have the life of any man who lets an arrow fly . . . or that of any man who issues the command to fire," Regan stated in all seriousness, never taking her eyes from the ruggedly handsome man now almost directly beneath her as she contemplated her response to his outrageous gesture.

It was plain to all who watched that the Countess of Kilcaid was flattered by the O'Carroll's attention but undecided as to what she should do. There was a tension in the air that fairly crackled as the dark-haired rebel and the blond Englishwoman continued to stare at each other so openly. His gaze was one of temptation. It beckoned her to his side, arguing seductively that she abandon the differences between them and accept all he had to offer. In return, her look was receptive, all softness and femininity. Yet Regan remained unmoved until Connor sent her a devilish half smile that raged at her reserve while promising all the delights of paradise.

"Open the gate," she commanded at last.

"Op-open the gate!" Gerard sputtered. "Are you daft, lass? I'll do no such thing!"

"Then I'll have you removed from your post and issue the order myself," Regan stated in deadly earnest. "Placed under guard, unable to observe what is happening, you will have more to worry about than if you simply do as I ask. Now have the portcullis raised and the drawbridge lowered immediately."

Glowering fiercely, Gerard did as he was bid as Regan hastened to the Great Hall, where she would greet Connor O'Carroll.

"I would think you'd be used to the headstrong behavior of the young mistress by now," Sheila clucked sympathetically, "yet here you stand fussing as though she were your own daughter receiving her first suitor."

"It's true, I feel as though she is my own. But unfortunately, I have all of the aggravation of being a father with none of the authority and respect that should attend it," Gerard answered gruffly, his eyes following Regan's descent.

"Come now man," Sheila soothed, "'tis natural a maid of her beauty should attract wooing. Surely you realize that."

Gerard realized it only too well and recalled vividly the situation in which Regan's last capitulation to passion had landed them.

"What I understand, old woman, is that the Lady Regan is entertaining the possibility of a disastrous match. She should have kept her gates closed against O'Carroll," Gerard grumbled. "She is a countess twice in her own right, and she need not ally herself with a landless rebel."

"Ah, but to my way of thinking, the question of land has yet to be truly settled. An alliance between the rightful Earl of Kilcaid and the Lady Regan would do naught but put an end to all animosities and be best for the both of them. As for her being recognized nobility, well that does not protect her from the emptiness of a lonely bed or the feelings of her own heart. Love can terminate feuds no matter what one's station in life, don't you think?" Sheila asked quietly, a gentle smile softening her sharp features.

The effect caused the gray-haired soldier to momentarily forget the danger Connor O'Carroll now posed. Gerard was nothing short of completely shocked at the transformation Sheila had undergone before his very eyes. One moment he had considered her a squabbling, bothersome old crone, and the next, he saw a feminine side to her that made him nervous. Surely the woman was not suggesting that they settle the bad feelings between them in a like manner!

With a curt nod to the castelain, he turned on his heel and strode rapidly after Regan, not certain whether his departure was prompted more by his concern for his charge or fear for his own safety.

Ordering Hugh to remain outside the keep and command the men should Regan's apparent compliance mask treachery, Connor urged his horse across the lowered drawbridge. When he entered the courtyard of Geata Neamhai, he was greeted loudly and joyously by those of his people who still resided there.

Surveying his countrymen and kinsmen, Connor was quite taken once again with his own shrewdness. He had been correct in his assumption that Regan Davies was not indifferent to him. All he had to do now to save his people from foreign servitude was win the Englishwoman's promise to accept him as a husband. After that deed was accomplished, he had no doubt that he could gain the queen's approval of the match. After all, wouldn't Elizabeth see his marriage to Regan Davies as the end of his rebellion, something that would bind him ever closer to the English throne? Though it should have grated him to be considered a loyal subject, Connor didn't care what the redheaded queen thought, as long as he possessed Geata Neamhai again.

As for the reason he intended to marry Regan, Connor felt no compunction at all. Many marriages were founded upon the acquisition of lands and wealth. Sometimes the brides were aware of it, and sometimes they were not.

Though the proud and willful Regan was the sort who would have to be left in ignorance as to his motives, Connor assumed he could be successful in wooing and sweet-talking her into matrimony with no mention of lands whatsoever. The roguish Earl of Kilcaid saw nothing dishonorable in his actions. In fact, Connor thought, dismounting from his horse, his very acceptance of his usurper as his lawful wife was a magnanimous gesture on his part indeed. What more could either Regan or Elizabeth want?

Love? Connor didn't know whether he really believed in anything other than passion. The last time he had thought of love, he was a smooth-cheeked youth who had discovered that his attraction to maidens originated in his loins rather than his heart. Since then, he had never been able to reconcile the ideals of courtly love with the way he felt about females in general. After all, what man would want to worship a woman from afar when he could have her in bed beside him? If retaking control of Geata Neamhai meant that he had to sacrifice his opportunity to find the love celebrated in song by the poets, then so be it.

Satisfied with his logic and the righteousness of his plans, the Earl of Kilcaid turned to unload his horse of the trinkets brought to pave a path into Regan's heart. These included a pouch of sweet-clover honey, a coronet of fragrant meadow flowers, a small harp, his own silver goblet, a fine blue cloak and a large silver brooch, wrested after much effort from a resentful Hugh Cassidy.

Handing the reins to a servant, and depositing the gifts into Tommy's waiting arms, Connor turned to make his way into the Great Hall. His bearing was as regal as that of any prince and his stride purposeful, if somewhat slowed by the still-painful slash to his thigh.

Entering the central chamber, Connor's gaze devoured every familiar stone, each well-remembered table and tapestry. Soon, he vowed, this would all belong to him again.

And then his dark blue eyes lit on Regan, seated in the lord's chair, and he almost forgot his purpose in being here.

She was dressed in shades of deep rose and cloth of gold, the hues emphasizing her delicate coloring. For added measure, the low, square cut of her tight bodice and the high collar that ran along its sides and back drew attention to the creamy mounds peeping over the neckline's edge. Then, there was that pale blond hair, hanging freely over her shoulders as though her maid had lacked the time to dress it properly. And as always, there were her heavily fringed emerald eyes, so lovely that a man could easily become enchanted by them. That was, Connor reminded himself, unless he had more important tasks to see to.

He approached her, the soft, fine wool of his cape flowing gracefully from his shoulders. With the experience of a courtier, he swept into a formal bow and was glad to find Regan's reception warm and cordial. She called for wine and offered him the place beside her, seemingly oblivious to Langston's fierce scowl. When she smiled, the thought struck Connor that this English rose might in reality be the most precious treasure the O'Carroll clan had ever captured. Then he smiled in turn, ready to unleash every bit of charm he might possess in order to win the fair Regan . . . and Geata Neamhai, too.

Chapter Ten

Regan was in her chamber attending to her appearance before facing her suitor at the evening meal when Gerard entered her suite, his booming voice arriving before him.

"Regan!" he roared. "Where are you? I must speak with you immediately before this travesty goes one step further."

"I am right here," she replied, appearing at the entrance to her solar. "Now calm yourself if you wish to have a few words with me. I am nervous enough without your adding to my flustered state."

"And well you should be," the silver-haired Englishman berated, moving to her side and towering over her. "Have you taken leave of your senses, girl, to give that Irishman access to Heaven's Gate, and then treat him as an honored guest besides?"

"He is a lone man within my walls, his followers are without. What harm can it do?" Regan asked, seating herself before the small flame burning in the hearth.

"You've gone completely daft if you think a man as dangerous as O'Carroll can do you no harm!"

"And how much more danger would he present if left to roam my lands, angered that I would not even consider his offer of marriage?" Regan asked, an element of wisdom present in her voice that caught her advisor by surprise.

"Then you're not seriously contemplating taking him for your husband?" He sighed in relief. "Thank God!"

"I did not say that," Regan admitted in all candor. "He is a worthy adversary, might he not be an even worthier mate?"

"Oh, verily," Gerard pronounced, his tone jeering. "What could be more meet than to ally yourself with an enemy of the Crown, and cut yourself off from every loyal Englishman whose misfortune it is to live on these wretched shores? Don't you understand, girl, that devil isn't smitten with you! Marriage is simply the price he must pay to become lord of Heaven's Gate once more. And you, are you willing to relinquish your inheritance and your only opportunity to return to court in order to lay beneath that black rogue in an Irish bed?"

"There are many things to be considered, 'tis true," Regan responded, staring into the flames. "That is why I have yet to decide whether I will petition the queen for her consent to such a match."

"I'm afraid she would approve a wedding to Satan himself in order to keep you from her sight and away from Dudley, though certainly a marriage to O'Carroll wouldn't be all that far removed," Gerard grumbled.

"Don't look so troubled," Regan said softly as she reached out to pat the Englishman's scarred hand in reassurance. "I am in no haste to make a decision, though I do find the man attractive. And, in truth, I must admit he has laid claim to a piece of my heart."

"A piece of your mind, you mean."

"Still there is no need to worry yet, old friend. Though I am receptive to his wooing, I will not consent unless I am convinced that it is me he treasures and not Heaven's Gate," Regan said with a laugh, even while a warm look of speculation played across her profile.

"God have mercy on us," Gerard muttered.

"God has already been merciful," Sheila said, bustling into the room in answer to an earlier summons from Regan. "Hasn't He allowed us to witness the love match developing before us?"

"And God save me, too, from the absurdities women spout of love," Gerard scowled. Though irritated by Sheila Dempsey's declaration, he couldn't help but notice how much redder the castelain's hair appeared in the firelight, and how a few weeks' worth of good meals had made her appear slender rather than scrawny. His awareness of such trifling things caused Gerard's choler to rise so that he stormed from the room without another word, intent upon reaching the masculine haven only the company of his guards could provide.

Regan never looked more enchanting than she did that evening. Again Connor O'Carroll was accorded a place of honor at her right hand, though Gerard had insisted the privacy screen be removed from the table. The older man wanted to see *all* that went on between the two of them.

Dressed in the customary garb of Ireland, Connor did not look out of place beside the lady of the keep. His black good looks and easy charm made him appear all the more dangerous to Gerard and the other Englishmen who spent less time devouring the feast prepared under Sheila's supervision than watching the behavior of the Lady Regan and the Irish rebel.

Many times throughout the course of the meal, O'Carroll's dark head bent toward Regan's pale one, and his whispered words were answered by the Countess of Kilcaid's tinkling laughter. Observing the two together, Gerard feared he was losing his battle to save Regan Davies from the clutches of the outlaw earl. And always, there was Sheila, hovering over the two in the background, seeing to their comfort and enjoyment.

For her part, Regan was aware of neither Gerard no
Sheila. She was completely absorbed in the attentive, en
gaging man seeking to win her troth. Though there was a
air of latent wildness about him, he wore the manners of th
nobility with a natural grace. His speech was cultured, hi
words honeyed, and the melodic quality of his Irish pro
nunciation gave his deep, resonant voice a charm Rega
found enticing. The young countess felt herself falling s
swiftly under his spell that she wondered if she were th
victim of some slyly administered love potion.

It was evident that the man possessed a virile strength i
every aspect of his being, yet when he boldly reached be
neath the table to take her hand in his, Connor's touch wa
surprisingly gentle. His fingertips brushed the back of he
hand in a lazy motion until he engaged the tips of her fin
gers in a caress unlike any Regan had ever imagined. An
then, without warning, his entire hand enclosed hers in
quick, possessive squeeze. Satisfied that she hadn't shie
away, Connor removed his touch entirely and brought hi
hand to the top of the table to lift his wine goblet in a salut
to her loveliness.

Throughout the entire incident, Regan had struggled t
maintain her composure, to hide the boundless pleasure sh
felt at this small intimacy from both those watching an
from her suitor himself. Lord but his skin against her
turned her blood to fire!

Frightened by the sensations a mere touch had created
Regan longed to flee from the Great Hall. When the mea
was at last done and the singer brought forward to provid
entertainment, she quickly rose to excuse herself and retur
to her chambers. Stating her intentions, Regan saw disap
pointment mirrored in Connor's eyes. Her ensuing guilt, i
logical as it was, caused her to break her gaze away from hi
and in so doing she noticed Gerard's approving nod. On
man wanted her to stay, the other to leave. Confused an

unsettled, she turned and scampered from the room like a frightened doe eluding a hunter.

No matter that she had thought her rooms a sanctuary, Regan was unable to find any peace there. In an attempt to distract herself from her dilemma, she sat at a table, studying her accounts, struggling to reconcile a list of supplies she wished to order from England with the small amount of funds she could afford to let go from her coffers. Her lack of success might have been explained, however, by the fact that her mind was not engrossed in her task. Instead, the young woman's thoughts constantly wound their way through the columns of numbers and goods to return to the man who had come to court her.

Idly putting aside her quill, Regan speculated about what Connor O'Carroll was doing at the moment. Had he remained in the Great Hall to lift a few more cups, or had he retired to the chambers she had ordered prepared for him?

Still reeling from the tumultuous emotions which had besieged her during the evening meal, Regan was certain she would find little sleep when she crawled into her bed. How ironic, she mused. Last night she had lain awake because the man had disappeared, and tonight she'd have no rest because he was near once more. What had become of her, that the whereabouts of Connor O'Carroll should suddenly be of such importance?

Letting go a mighty sigh, Regan rose and put away her writing supplies, tidily rolling the sheets of paper and tying them with a scrap of ribbon. Still restless, she looked out at the large silver moon hanging in the black, star-studded sky. Her still-smoldering senses proclaimed that this was a night for lovers, and she regretted that she had left the central chamber of the keep in such haste.

A soft rap at the door cast such foolish notions aside, and Regan turned to find Sheila on the threshold of her rooms.

"It's begging your pardon, I am, milady," the older woman began, "but I wanted to know if aught was wrong with the meal."

"Everything was perfection," Regan declared, surprised by Sheila's doubts. The woman was usually so opinionated and self-assured.

"It's just you left so suddenly, your ladyship, that—"

"I had other matters to attend," Regan interrupted, trying to forestall any inquiries.

"More important than those taking place in the Great Hall? Though it isn't my place to advise you, a woman shouldn't run from love. Surely it exists in England, too."

"Yes it does, but I have never felt its pull so powerfully as I have since I arrived in Ireland. Perchance it is the result of your summer moon, or green hills, or..."

"Or of becoming acquainted with Connor O'Carroll," Sheila stated simply. "Was it he you were escaping?"

"No, of course not!" Regan protested.

"It's a good thing that's the case, because if it weren't you'd have no place else to run. The O'Carroll is even now outside your solar, and craves the opportunity to speak with you."

"In my rooms? At this hour?" Regan asked in disbelief.

"Aye, 'tis still early enough. The hall below offers no privacy at all, you'll agree, and he wishes to have a word with you alone. Shall I usher him in, or are you afraid?"

"Afraid? I've nothing to be afraid of," Regan blustered. "Send him in, there's no reason for me not to see him."

"Very good, milady," Sheila said, punctuating her words with one of her infrequent curtsies, a sign that she approved Regan's decision. "I'll send him in directly."

Regan's eyes darted quickly around the solar. Sheila had spoken the truth. There was nowhere to hide with the exception of her bedchamber, and Regan had no doubts but that it would delight Connor O'Carroll to seek her there. Shutting the door to the room she had so recently shared with him, she hurriedly lit another taper and then sought a chair.

Suddenly he was in her doorway and, with a few long strides, in the center of the room itself. The chamber, which had seemed so large and empty a moment before, was filled with his presence.

"Milady," he said, bowing and bringing her hand to his lips.

Regan merely nodded her head in greeting, not ready to trust her voice with words of welcome.

"You know why I've come," he stated, the velvet smoothness of his sonorous voice echoing in her heart as it did within the confines of her solar.

Again she nodded.

"Then what say you?" Connor inquired, his deep blue eyes watching her intently.

"I can say nothing until you've asked, O'Carroll," Regan managed to whisper.

"My name is Connor. Say it, Regan," he commanded gently but forcibly all the same.

"Connor," she repeated, his name sounding like a lover's song upon her lips.

"Regan Davies," he said, taking her dainty hand in his two strong ones, "I have come to Geata Neamhai—"

"Heaven's Gate," she mumbled.

"I have come here," Connor continued, superbly hiding his annoyance at her interruption, "because I couldn't stay away from you." So saying, he knelt beside her chair and placed a tender kiss on her cheek.

Regan thought her face had burst into flame when his lips touched her. And still, she did not shift away, but waited to see what this man would do next . . . and how she would react.

"No one has ever accused me of being dull witted, and yet against all logic, in spite of all danger, I have come to woo you, to make you my own," he murmured, his questing mouth finding the softness of her graceful neck.

"Reclaiming Heaven's Gate through me is not the action of a dunce, Connor," Regan interjected to distract them both from the fires their contact had ignited.

"I wish it were only the land that was at stake, Regan," Connor whispered in her ear, "because then I'd not be as anxious as I am now. It's you I want to possess."

"And why do you feel this way about me?" Regan asked breathily while he nuzzled at a sensitive spot near her shoulder.

"Why?" Connor asked, so astounded at her question that he had to search for an answer. In all of his memory, no woman had ever pondered the reason for his attraction before, and certainly they had never thought about such things during his foreplay. They had simply accepted his sweet compliments as their due.

"God help me, my beautiful English witch. I don't know why, but I want you more than I've ever wanted any woman," Connor replied. As he reveled in the sight of her, he found no hardship in feigning these words. They rolled off his tongue so readily that he was hard put to remember that it was his birthright he was pursuing and not actually Regan Davies. "I think," he concluded softly, "that you've cast a spell upon me for which there is no release save one."

"And that is?" Regan asked, allowing him the liberty of placing his lips lightly upon her own.

"I am asking you to be my true and legal wife," he said, lifting his mouth ever so slightly from hers.

"The lawful wife of an outlaw. My but you do things strangely in Ireland."

"Not strangely, Regan, but wonderfully," Connor persisted, tracing a path from the hollow of her throat to the beginning of her breasts with the feathery touch of his thumb. "What say you? Surely you feel something magical between us. Will you plight me your troth?"

"How could I say aye?" Regan demurred. "I do not know you all that well."

"I have in mind a way to become very well acquainted," Connor replied, allowing his hand to brush against the straining tip of Regan's breast. Then his mouth once again covered hers, his tongue finding a course to her own.

After a glorious moment of surrender, Regan gathered her senses about her and turned her head from his. Another glimpse of those darkly fringed blue eyes and she knew she would be lost.

"Don't be shy, lass," he coaxed, entreating her to abandon her qualms. "You'll find that here in Ireland there's nothing thought of two lovers coupling without benefit of clergy. It's a practice more common and open than in England where the term virgin holds many a well-kept secret. Yet if you insist, I'll yield to you in this and allow you to set the pace. I would not offend your maidenly innocence," Connor acceded gallantly, though his voice was thick with desire.

Regan blushed, only too mindful that virgin and innocence were not terms she could claim as her own. Connor, however, mistook the cause for the heightened color that inflamed Regan's cheeks. He respectfully moved apart from her, although it cost him considerable effort to do so. Had he not known better, he would have accused this shy minx of seducing him, obliquely but effectively.

"Well then, Regan," he said, his voice little more than a ragged whisper, "since you cannot answer me until we become better known to each other, give me leave to stay a while and court you properly. A few days spent together should settle any doubts you harbor, one way or another."

At Regan's affirmative reply, he crossed to the table and poured them each a measure of brandy, which he placed on the chess board.

"Can I interest you in a more innocent game?" he asked with a grin.

Consenting, Regan joined him, and they settled to their play, each concentrating pointedly upon the board to avoid the temptation beckoning them.

For the next few days, Regan and Connor spent almost all their waking time together. Connor watched with growing admiration as Regan went about the day-to-day task of managing the keep. It pleased him that she joined in any work that had to be done, and in order to impress her, he allowed himself to be pressed into service, as well. Occasionally he would leave her side for the purpose of riding out to see to his men, but he was never gone for long.

In the private moments of the late evening, he would join Regan in her solar. There were other games of chess, and one of dice where Regan forfeited a kiss or two. Sometimes Connor sang to her, ballads of love and yearning, or told her stories about the keep's previous owners, and his own boyhood there. The result was that Regan found her days and nights in this foreign land to be happy ones, so content was she in Connor's company.

On the fifth evening of his sojourn in his own home, Connor surprised Regan in the corridor outside her rooms and led her into a darkened corner. Here he embraced her and bent his head to hers, showering her with all the passion a man could show a woman short of taking her to his bed.

Regan allowed his attention, swayed by her attraction to her handsome suitor, and with each kiss, every caress, felt her resolve to put Connor off slipping rapidly.

Holding her against the wall so tightly that she was aware of the length of his manhood through her heavy skirts, Connor pressed for her decision.

"What say you, Regan Davies?" he asked, so carried away by the part he had chosen to play that he forgot he was acting, and his voice became little more than a murmured groan. "Will you take me as your husband?"

Regan moved beneath him as she cast about for yet another delay that would save her from giving Connor his answer and yet keep him by her side.

"What of the queen's permission? We've still to obtain that," a fairly breathless Regan reminded him.

"Don't worry about Bess. Once we're married I'll gain her forgiveness and her blessing for both of us. Just put yourself in my care, sweeting, and I'll see to the queen. But to be honest, I'd rather see to you at the moment. I willingly admit that my longing for you drives me to distraction. Have pity, lovely Regan. Come to my chamber and I'll teach you what pleasure a man can give a woman," Connor pleaded more in earnest than he cared to admit as he tried to steer Regan to his room.

But for Regan, the sweet, mindless spell of loving had been broken. Far from reassuring her, Connor's vow to protect her from the queen's wrath, followed by his urgings that she give herself to him, was too reminiscent of Dudley's promises, spoken shortly before she had been banished from her homeland. Nervously she pulled away from his grasp.

"I am sorely tempted, Connor O'Carroll," she said by way of apology as she fabricated an excuse to retire to her own bed alone, "but the night finds me too exhausted and worn out from labor to indulge in pleasure, be it mine or yours."

"Tired?" a stunned Connor asked, completely taken aback. The fragrant smell of her, the sight of her, the velvety touch of her skin and the sweet taste of her mouth swept away any thoughts of slumber he might have had. Why hadn't he had the same effect upon Regan?

"Yes, of course, I'm tired," Regan said, persisting in her lie. "It's a monumental chore to keep Heaven's Gate running, especially since so many of its former inhabitants have left not only their homes, but their work as well. Things have to be done. You haven't seen me lounge away my time, have you?''

"No, I haven't, and if you are truly fatigued then, of course, you must rest," Connor said with more understanding than he felt. His lips smoothed the anxious furrows of her brow and then he escorted her to the door of the master chamber. "But next time, you will not escape so easily," he promised with a roguish smile.

Regan refuted his seductive threat with laughter, and with a flick of her skirts she was through her door, which was shut and bolted firmly behind her.

"Tired!" Connor muttered as he stalked away down the corridor. Never had a woman put him off with such an excuse, but neither had any other woman seen to the running of an estate the size of Geata Neamhai. Still, it was an evasion Regan would not use again, Connor vowed as he descended the stairs from the upper rooms two at a time. He had a plan, and since he was bound to have a restless night anyway, he decided to put it into action immediately.

When Regan woke the next morning, the keep was a beehive of activity. The old rushes had already been swept from the floor and new ones were being strewn in their places. Tables had been scoured and tapestries taken down for washing. Walking into the courtyard, Regan saw that the stable was in the process of being cleaned, and she heard the blacksmith's anvil ring out.

"Well, will you tell me you are weary this evening?" asked a deep voice, rich in both resonance and amusement.

Spinning around, Regan saw Connor, an indulgent expression lighting his handsome features.

"This is all quite enterprising," Regan said with an appreciative smile, "but with these folk so busy within the keep itself, it will be my lot to work in the fields this morning."

"Come here," Connor commanded, catching her hand and pulling her behind him, up the steps to the battlements. "Look! Do you think there will be anything left for you to accomplish outside or inside these walls today?"

Below her the countryside was alive with industrious labor. There were Connor's own men plowing her fields, tending her sheep, felling trees on the horizon.

"He said you ordered this," came Gerard's sullen voice at her elbow. "Tell me he has lied so that I can have him imprisoned."

"He did what I desired," Regan said, pleased that she had to resort to no more than a half-truth to forestall an unpleasant scene. Gerard appeared about to argue when he saw Sheila approaching to speak with her mistress, and he chose, instead, to leave without another word.

Dealing with the Irishwoman quickly, Regan then turned her attention to the bedeviling Connor O'Carroll, not certain whether she should be pleased or annoyed with him.

"Now see here, O'Carroll..."

"Connor," he corrected with a smile.

"It's O'Carroll in this matter. Who gave you leave to issue orders in my keep?" Regan asked, hard put not to answer Connor's unabashedly charming smile with one of her own. "Did you enjoy playing lord of the manor once more?"

"Darling Regan, if I have done something to displease you, let me know what it is. I simply put all that I have, all that I am at your disposal to alleviate your weariness."

"*All* at my disposal?" she asked with an impudent grin.

"All," he repeated, the solemnity of his voice at odds with the sparkle dancing in his eyes.

"Fine. I can use the extra labor with which you have so thoughtfully provided me, and I'd be a fool not to take advantage of it. Meet with me in my solar within the hour and I'll have a list of tasks your men can undertake on my behalf."

"And me? Surely you will have something I can do for you?" he asked, a boyish look making him appear like a youngster expecting a reward.

"Aye. I'll think of something to keep you busy, too," she replied, fighting to keep her amusement at bay.

"A well! You want me to help dig a new well?" Connor exclaimed in disbelief a short while later.

"You did ask me to find you a task," Regan said with a wide-eyed look of innocence. "But if you feel it is too strenuous with your wound still not properly mended, then I suppose..."

"It's not too strenuous at all," Connor fairly glowered before recalling his purpose in returning to Geata Neamhai. Calming himself considerably, he proceeded. "If that is what you wish, then that is what I shall do. I seek only to please you. It is just that I thought, out of gratitude, you might have something else in mind."

"Oh, but I am grateful, Connor! And there is always tonight," Regan said, her demeanor full of promise.

But when a filthy Connor returned that evening, it was he who was fatigued. After bathing, he sat on the edge of his bed, intending to dress and seek out Regan. However, the next thing he knew, it was morning and a servant was knocking upon his door to summon him to Regan's presence.

The Irishman's temper was raging as he stormed to her rooms, but the moment he saw her, his ill humor dissipated like fog burned off by the golden rays of the sun.

"All right, mistress, you've had your jest," he said good-naturedly, "and perhaps I did deserve it. What is it you demand of me today? Perhaps you would like the moat filled in, or the southern wall of the keep moved northward?"

"Connor, your wit is endearing as always," Regan responded, her smile illuminating her face with a glow her companion found provocative in spite of his still-weary muscles. "Actually, all I want is your help in planning the work to be done at Heaven's Gate these next few days. There are so many improvements to be made."

"Improvements! What's wrong with things as they stand?" he demanded, his temper beginning to simmer anew at this insult to his home. Damn women, he thought, all they ever want to do is change things.

"What's wrong is that they won't continue to stand unless repairs are made," Regan said simply. "Everywhere I look there are things to be done. The ceiling beam in the kitchen must be reinforced, it's starting to sag. The stables could use a new roof. Replacement chains should be forged for the drawbridge. The far pasture needs clearing of bramble. There are some fields which can be plowed, and others made more productive if an irrigation ditch is built. Of course, if you are to help, you must stay away from the tenant houses until I can dismiss Watkins's men. I don't want him to know you are here."

"Regan," Connor protested, amused at her enthusiasm. "What you propose as tasks for the next few days will take much longer than that to complete."

"Aye, that they might, milord," she said coquettishly, her reply ripe with promise.

"You sly wench," he said, laughter filling his deep voice. "I concede. We'll at least begin these things together."

For the next two weeks Connor pushed his men hard, even the highly resentful Hugh. But he drove himself harder than anyone else. The outlaw earl approached his work with all the passion he would have demonstrated to Regan had she allowed him into her bed. Yet labor was not the physical release he sought, and his longing for her did not abate.

There were times he became frustrated with his situation. After all, he was a fighting man, a noble and a courtier, and here he was doing menial chores at the direction of a mere bit of a woman. He told himself that he undertook the tasks

assigned him only because he would benefit from his ef
forts when Geata Neamhai was his again. What he quit
overlooked was the fact that beneath it all, he really did see
to win the approval of the beautiful Regan.

There were days when Connor's labors took him afiel
and he did not return to the keep that night. On such days
Regan rode her lands, inspecting the work being done an
making suggestions. It gladdened her heart to see her me
and Connor's peacefully toiling side by side, and could sh
have persuaded herself that the world around them woul
leave them alone to continue in this manner, she would hav
taken the comely Connor as her husband posthaste.

On those mornings when she did not wake to find him a
her table, she missed him with surprising force. There wa
no one to tease her and make her blush, to indulge he
whims or amiably reprove her when her concern for Heav
en's Gate made her overly demanding. She ached for th
sight of his engaging smile, and the devilish sparkle of hi
dark blue eyes. The keep was decidedly empty without hi
vital presence and so, Regan discovered, was her heart.

Waking for a third morning to find herself without Con
nor's company, Regan resolved to meet with him tha
afternoon. Much against Gerard's advice, she ordered pro
visions packed, and departed with her guard for the north
ern pasture where Connor and his men were constructing ar
irrigation ditch.

Setting out across the brilliant green fields, a gentle breez
at her face, and looking forward to the prospect of sharing
a meal with the handsome Irishman at her journey's end
Regan felt elated. Everywhere she looked, Heaven's Gate
was prospering. Her people had shelter, food on their ta
bles, and the promise of an abundant harvest in the fall. Bu
more important, now that Watkins's men had returned to
their homes, there was tranquillity here of a sort that the
young countess had never known.

After a lengthy ride, Regan spied the work site. She had no trouble distinguishing Connor, even from a distance. His broad shoulders and dark head made it an easy feat to accomplish.

As she approached, he stood beside the ditch clad only in crude leather breeches, his bare, bronzed chest glistening as the result of his exertions. At the sight of her, his flashing smile illuminated their surroundings, transforming a mere field into an enchanted glen. This was not a man, Regan told herself, who loved the land more than he did her.

Standing beside her horse, he reached up to span her tiny waist with his hands. He lifted her off the saddle with ease to settle her on the ground in front of him, so close that there was scarcely any space between them.

"Ah, I see my staying away has made you long for me as I had hoped it would," Connor said, his mellifluous voice hanging in the air like a gentle morning mist.

"Fie, sir!" Regan laughed, allowing him to raise her hand and press her fingertips to his mouth. "'Tis merely that I deemed such industriousness should be rewarded."

"And so it should," Connor replied, a seductive glint lighting his heavily fringed eyes.

"What I had in mind, milord," Regan said, stepping back to put some distance between them, "was a proper midday meal for you and your men."

"But your appearance, sweeting, has unleashed appetites of a different sort."

"Then you'd best restrain them. Merciful Lord, but I had no idea you Irish were such a lusty lot," Regan retorted playfully.

"That we are," he proclaimed, catching her mood. "You English might spend your time writing melancholy sonnets, but our poetry is on our tongues, and in our..."

"Connor!" she protested, pretending to be offended.

"Hearts. I was about to say hearts."

"You don't fool me, you rogue. That was not the though
you had at all," she said adamantly. "And do away wit
that boyish expression of being so ill used. Don't think
don't know what a magnificent actor you are."

Though her jovial barb was only banter, it contained
kernel of truth, reminding Connor of all of the pretendin
he had done since he had begun to court her. The realiza
tion made him feel guilty and uneasy, so that he quickl
chose another topic.

"But what are we doing standing here?" he asked
"Come and see the irrigation ditch and meet my men."

"You mean those who used to be my men?" she in
quired wryly.

"Those who could be again if you would but plight you
troth to me," he rejoined, stooping to kiss the skin at th
base of her neck.

"Connor, this is not the place for lovemaking," Rega
protested weakly. His nearness, his touch, made her word
quite difficult to utter, and she did so only after great strug
gle.

"I told you before, we are much more complacent abou
this sort of thing in the countryside of Ireland," he said
seeming to respect her qualms but persevering in his pur
suit of her all the same as his lips left her tender skin and hi
hand crept round her waist.

"And is this the sort of husband you would be?" sh
asked, "Always trying to get your hands on me even afte
you had gotten them on Heaven's Gate?"

He stopped his playfulness then, staring at her so fixedl
that Regan feared she had either offended him or stumble
upon the truth. But influenced by his near nakedness as sh
was, the young foreigner knew she was incapable, at th
moment, of discerning which it was.

"'Tis but a jest, Connor," she said in an effort to recap
ture the lighthearted humor she had destroyed. "Come an
present the others to me."

Boldly taking Connor's hand in hers, she led him to a cluster of men. Some of the faces she saw were familiar, though many were not. For the most part, the Irishmen accepted her since she stood at Connor's side, her fingers entwined in his. Soon there were genial gibes aimed at the Earl of Kilcaid concerning rows of cradles filled with wee ones. The cheerfulness around them was contagious, and as Connor joined the others in mirth, Regan felt comfortable with him once more.

When it was time to eat, he was courtly and considerate as ever as he spread a blanket beneath an oak for her comfort. Here the young countess distributed the food and drink she had brought along, making certain each man who approached had his fill. Her generosity and personal attention made high spirits soar further, and Connor was proud of her popularity.

Finally the men returned to their digging, giving Regan and Connor some privacy. The pair remained beneath the oak, the earl's raven head resting in Regan's accommodating lap. Now that the distraction of the meal had subsided, Regan could take more notice of the people around her. They seemed a decent lot, she thought, until she noticed a man the size of Goliath. He had not come forward to greet her or to share in her feast, but periodically took a respite from his labors to deliver a deadly glare.

"Connor, who is that mountain of a man staring so fiercely in our direction?"

"You could only mean Hugh Cassidy," Connor responded, not bothering to look, drowsy now that his belly was full and Regan such a comfortable pillow. "He was a soldier during my father's time. Now he is my chief at arms and my closest friend."

"How could you befriend such a bear?" Regan asked, her sentiments on her lips before she could stop them.

"Bear!" Connor exclaimed, his mouth forming a lazy grin. "Why Hugh is more like a lamb."

"Connor! Connor O'Carroll!" the subject of their conversation suddenly bellowed.

"I've never known a lamb to roar."

"Well, it's common in Ireland," Connor replied. "I've been known to do so myself on occasion."

"You're more of a randy goat than a lamb," Regan said with a laugh as he raised his head to steal a kiss.

"Connor!" Hugh Cassidy yelled once more, glowering at Regan rather than at his lord.

"Hadn't you ought to see what's amiss?" the young woman asked, dangling a wildflower so that it barely skimmed Connor's well-formed chin.

"I know what's wrong," Connor replied, stifling a yawn. "He's annoyed because I'm spending this time with you."

"Do you mean he thinks you should be digging alongside him?"

"No, my pretty one, I mean that Hugh disapproves of a match between us as much as your Gerard does. We really should arrange for them to meet. I'm certain they would get along famously."

"Perhaps you should join him, Connor."

"It makes no difference whether I do or not," he said, rolling to his side and raising himself on an elbow so he could look at his lovely companion and turn his back on his overbearing mentor at the same time. "He'll be vexed no matter what I do. But as for you, I think it best you be on your way back if you do not want to see me in the same ill humor. It is a long ride home, and I do not want you abroad after dusk. This ditch won't be finished until after nightfall, and I won't return until the morning. Though I know it will be difficult, try and sleep well without me," he said with an endearing grin, easily brushing aside the flower Regan threw in his direction.

Walking to her horse with Connor by her side, Regan sought a retort with which she could repay this swaggering Irishman for his last brazen remark. Noting the progress the men had made with the ditch, which now almost reached the lake that would feed it, she was inspired.

"You know that I think you have done an admirable job, milord," Regan began bubbling with amusement, "but now that I see it, I think perhaps the water should flow into the field from the other side—"

"Regan, the ditch is fine where it is!" Connor roared, fighting the urge to smack her bottom. Instead, he swept a giggling Regan into his arms and walked to the edge of the lake, threatening to deposit her soundly on its muddy bed.

At Regan's screams and laughter, Connor's men leaned on their shovels and grinned as they watched the pair. It was a joy to see the Earl of Kilcaid so light of heart after so many months of hardship. Even Hugh found his mouth forming a smile at the sight of Connor's tomfoolery, though in truth, he hoped his lord would actually make good his promise and drop the English witch into the chilly water. But Connor and Regan were aware of neither his men nor her guards as she squirmed against his bare, muscular chest.

"I yield, sir, I yield!" Regan protested, nearly breathless with laughter.

"So be it," Connor responded, backing away from the lake and carrying Regan to her horse. He placed a kiss atop her nose before settling her securely in the saddle. Then he addressed her in mock severity. "Just see to it, wench, that you remember those very words when I return to the keep tomorrow."

Chapter Eleven

By the time she and Sheila descended from the storage rooms in the east tower, Regan was weary, exasperated and distinctly uncomfortable. Once again unable to sleep, she'd risen early to distract herself with work. But the remedy had worked too well. Even wearing one of her simple new cotton gowns without the accompanying weight of underskirts and overskirts that were so much a part of her London wardrobe, the Englishwoman felt bedraggled and overdressed, certainly in no mood for romance.

Headed for the pump in the courtyard to fetch a cool drink, she was annoyed to hear Connor calling her name. Despite her interest in his overtures to affection, she was in no mood just now for such a diversion. Where had he been last night? her heart demanded.

"Regan, are you busy?" he asked, coming to stand beside her. Though he'd intended to return early this morning, the irrigation finally completed last night, work at the cottages needed some last-minute supervision, and it had taken longer than he'd expected.

"Yes, and I've *been* busy most of the morning and a good part of this afternoon, too, as you would know had you arrived as scheduled. Why is it that men simply can't be found when there are chores to be done?" she asked quizzically, brushing an irritating strand of loose hair off her forehead and leaving a grimy streak in its place. Knowing full well that he'd probably been completing the tasks out in the fields, she couldn't help but sound out of sorts. She craved his touch so much that she grew more and more afraid of its repercussions daily. How long could she be true to the commands of her conscience while betraying those of her heart?

"It's a sixth sense that comes along with our gender," chuckled the Earl of Kilcaid as he carefully wetted his handkerchief and wiped her face with it, encouraged that she allowed such an intimate gesture. "In this case, however, my men and I were busy finishing the ditch you commanded dug and seeing to one or two other improvements I hope will please her ladyship. Tell me, though, what labors were you and Sheila performing so industriously on this warm afternoon?"

"We were taking inventory of the many chests of linens and woolens in the storerooms. I wish to equip each arriving family with some useful goods rather than just giving them a ceremonial welcoming speech," explained Regan with a certain degree of pride. She'd been trying to think of ways to show the new tenants that she supported their emigration and what better method than to lessen their discomfort on unexpectedly cool nights? Waiting for Connor's praise for her practical nature, she was somewhat surprised at his lack of enthusiasm. After all, the new residents would eventually serve the purpose of enriching the estate, even if they were English.

"You were taking count of *my* linens so you could distribute them to your needy countrymen?" Connor's voice was brusque as he tried to contain his temper. He'd been slaving in the field for her and she intended to scatter his wealth to the wind! Regan's impertinent generosity caught him so off guard he forgot his personal determination to be gentle toward the lady this day. "Regan, those goods were given to the O'Carrolls over the years by our Irish tenants and their parents and grandparents before them. You cannot just dole them out like shiny coins to the poor—''

Astounded at the absurd attitude Connor was taking, Regan looked closely at the man she had begun to admire over the past weeks. Tall and commanding as ever in his Irish tunic, his broad shoulders were stiff with annoyance and his brows drawn together in displeasure. Surely he didn't expect her to act merely as a caretaker of his property with no voice in its operation? Even if they were to wed, Heaven's Gate would be as much hers as his, and he must accept that fact, no matter how unpleasant it might be.

"May I remind you, my dear Connor, that by order of the queen, what was once yours is now mine, to do with as I see fit—''

"Ah, I've something I'd like to make yours," muttered a randy Connor under his breath, still not abandoning his hopes for the evening. Surely the week's work, mental and physical, was not to be in vain?

"I should think that even you would prefer the blankets to be used for warmth rather than allowing them to grow damp or be chewed upon by moths, which is what's happening now," chided Regan, measuring his reaction to her words.

"Is there sufficient for the Irish as well?" he asked softly after a moment, gently extracting a broken cobweb from her fine golden hair. Then, with an easy familiarity, he rested his hands on her shoulders and began to knead away her stiffness as he waited her response.

"Aye, there's sufficient for half the county, I should think," she confirmed, sighing in contentment as her sore muscles went slack under his careful manipulations. "I don't know quite what you're doing to me, Connor O'Carroll, but the magic in those Irish paws of yours is making me feel quite well."

"A bit less tired, then?" he asked hopefully.

"Absolutely, milord, thanks to you."

"Good, then you'll hear what I have to say with an open mind?" At her curious look and nod, he continued. "First, if you wish to distribute the materials from Geata Neamhai's storerooms, I promise not to interfere, but only if you agree to put some of the goods aside for future emergencies that might arise, and if you allot the Irish families camped in the woods equal shares with the newly arriving English. It was, after all, Irish toil and sweat that produced those linens and English law that's preventing my tenants from enjoying their homes within the keep."

"It is not English law, it is their own unquestioning loyalty to you," argued Regan, stepping away from Connor's comforting hands. Though she'd already made up her mind that his request was only reasonable and she would certainly accede to his suggestions, it wouldn't do to surrender her will too easily.

"If they came to you tomorrow and said they wanted to return to their positions in the keep, would you permit it?" he challenged, hands on hips, eyes flashing. When there was no answer to his question, he replied for her. "You know damnably well it would be a foolhardy decision on your part, and one Gerard would never countenance. But, that does not mean your attitude is the proper one," he argued, his own patience with the young woman amazing himself.

"Very well, equal shares for English and Irish alike," consented the countess, pleased at the genuine concern Connor had for his people. "I'll have Sheila see to it. Now, what else did you want?"

"What else?" Unprepared for her swift acquiescence, Connor wasn't ready to leave the topic so fast.

"Yes, you distinctly said that first there was the issue of the linens," she reminded the oddly tongue-tied Irishman, bewildered at his sudden forgetfulness. "That implies there is a second matter at hand."

"Oh, yes. Well, actually, I was wondering if you'd care for a short ride to check on your tenant houses," he said

tentatively. Remembering her open enjoyment of his close-
ness in the fields the day before, he had planned this next
effort very carefully. If he could get her outside the walls, on
neutral ground rather than in the keep, which symbolized
their struggle for authority...

"Now? It's nearly the hour for the evening meal, and I
want to wash this ancient dust from my face and don a clean
gown," Regan said in surprise. "Besides, I have been trying very hard not to make your stay here any more difficult
for Gerard than it has to be. I can't see him calmly bidding
me adieu so that you and I could go riding alone. You saw
the number of guards I rode with yesterday."

"I wager he wouldn't but if you sup first and claim to be
retiring to your chambers early, he needn't know," pressed
her dark-haired suitor.

"But why—"

"Trust me, Regan, I promise you won't be disappointed," urged Connor, offering a silent prayer he
wouldn't be, either, as he squeezed her hand gently. "You
surely know by now that I wouldn't harm you," the beguiling Irishman coaxed. "You really must see what we've accomplished. I think you'll be pleased, honestly."

"Can't it wait till morning?" While the prospect of a
covert rendezvous in the moonlight was oddly appealing,
Regan's good sense still controlled her will.

"But the men have worked so very hard to please
you—"

"And you, I imagine," said the young Englishwoman,
continuing to wrestle with her conscience. The evening
promised to be a mild one and she hadn't seen the work that
Watkins's men had completed, let alone what Connor's
fellows might have done after the English had returned to
Wren's Nest.

On the point of accepting his invitation, she suddenly recalled the unexplained fire that destroyed one of the cottages barely a fortnight ago, and she hesitated again. Yet, as

much as Gerard distrusted O'Carroll, she had never had occasion to doubt Connor's veracity, at least not since they'd made their truce.

"Very well, O'Carroll, but this had better not be a ruse or you'll regret it," she warned saucily. "And, I plan to tell Sheila where we're going."

"I already have," said Connor with a wide grin, recalling that he'd also cautioned the housekeeper that they might not return until morning.

"All right then, I'll see you right here in two hours," agreed Regan, at once thrilled and nervous at the prospect.

Waiting in the shadows of the courtyard near the entrance to the secret tunnel, Connor found himself wondering if Regan would indeed arrive as she'd promised. If she didn't, what of it? Connor asked himself. It wasn't as though he couldn't get any Kinnity lass he wanted, and they had no qualms about openly sharing the pleasures of their bodies. The question of Geata Neamhai aside, why he was so attracted to this English wench? Perhaps, he considered, it was just the apparent impossibility of the challenge that motivated him.

Yet, when she laughed, the world was a brighter place. Her smile seemed to envelop every feature: her lips would part ever so slightly and curl upward as her green eyes opened wide. Her cheeks turned rosy and the gentle tinkle of her laughter was as musical as a madrigal. Heavens, he was beginning to sound as though he cared for the woman. How totally absurd.

"Connor?"

"Right over here, your ladyship," he answered quickly, determined to put such disturbing thoughts aside. He was pleased to note she'd worn the soft hooded cloak he'd given her. While he could guarantee they would leave the keep undetected, he'd prefer not to have the guards on watch at the top of the walls notice their fair-haired mistress cantering off toward the woods when they hadn't opened the drawbridge for her.

"But where are the horses?" the lovely blonde asked in confusion.

"Tommy's holding them outside the walls, at the end of this corridor," he explained, taking her hand and leading her behind the rarely used storage shed and into the ancient passageway beneath the dry trench of the moat. Showing her this hidden entrance could only win Regan's confidence and thus help him accomplish his goal to be her husband. Besides, now that he was made welcome here, he no longer needed secret access. It was not, after all, as though so narrow a passageway could be used to move his men in to assail the keep. "Watch yourself, there isn't much room."

"I didn't know this tunnel was here!" Regan exclaimed.

"You weren't supposed to, but it is something I wanted to share with you, to demonstrate how much I trust you. Think of it as another gift tendered by an anxious suitor," the Irishman replied. "Only the owners of Geata Neamhai know all its secrets."

"Oh, then you've accepted my right to Heaven's Gate? What a nice way of telling me," said Regan in surprise. She stopped in her tracks and when Connor turned back to see why, she leaned toward him in the cramped corridor, the two of them slightly off balance. Pulling his head down to hers, she planted a sweet kiss on his startled lips.

Unable to resist such a tender repast, the dark-haired rogue caught her to him and lengthened their gentle exchange, enjoying it every bit as much as she. Regan felt soft and pliant in his arms, yet she was so fiery in nature, it wasn't long before he realized her tongue was gently licking at his, teasing and inviting in its questioning darts. About to encourage her efforts, it suddenly dawned on him that they were still in the underground tunnel. Mother of Mercy, he groaned in annoyance, this was not what he'd planned at all!

"Regan, if you wish to see the tenant houses before the light is gone, I think we'd best be going," he said awkwardly, pulling away from her embrace. Having never in his life played the reluctant swain, Connor found it ironic that he should be forced to do so now, but this wasn't the time or place.

"All right," she agreed, taking a deep breath, smoothing her dampened palms on her cloak and turning from him. "I merely wanted to thank you for the trust you've shown in me, and let you know how much I appreciate it."

"Believe me, the feeling is mutual. Not every woman would go riding off into the forest with a wanted renegade," he said lightly, capturing her hand and leading her forward. "But I really didn't mean . . ." How could he tell her he wasn't abandoning the quest for his lands, and still keep her in a loving mood? "That is, Geata Neamhai has many secrets to which its owners are privy. This is just one."

"Yet, you are confident enough of me to share it," marveled Regan. "How can you be certain I won't post guards here to prevent you from entering and leaving at will?"

"You haven't turned me in to the authorities yet, dear lady, though I suppose there's always that possibility."

"Connor, I'm serious, how could you take such a chance on my knowing your secret?" she pressed.

"Actually this is the first time I've consciously used the route since you've been in residence," he stated simply as they slipped out into the summer twilight, preferring not to explain his earlier exit with Hugh. His first strategy of the evening had proved successful; she was thoroughly delighted with his show of trust, and he was confident that, after tonight, he'd never need the tunnel again.

"But, why? You could have easily snuck into the keep and caused harm," declared Regan in mystification. As Connor helped her onto her favorite horse and mounted his, signaling Tommy to return to the keep, she puzzled over the many facets of the Irishman's code of behavior.

"Because what I do is done openly," he said quietly, if not honestly. Turning the horses away from the keep, he was amazed at the discomfort he felt in lying to the woman beside him. "Besides, how many of my men would have had to die, how much of this land would have been destroyed if I had done so? No, don't worry about it, Regan. I'll regain Geata Neamhai soon enough, and if you but say yes, legitimately, too."

"In a strange way, I almost wish I had royal approval for such a match," confessed the Englishwoman, "though I fear our queen wouldn't be very pleased."

"I suspect very little pleases the Virgin Queen," said Connor dryly. "But, here, tell me, what do you think?" He'd stopped the horses on a small hill overlooking a settlement of sturdy-looking cottages, each with a newly thatched roof. With a cry of enthusiasm, Regan nudged her steed and rode down to the new community.

Turning to look at the spot where ashes had smoldered a bare fortnight ago, Regan was astounded to see a quaint stone lodge now standing in its place.

"Connor, did you and your men do all this?" she asked in amazement.

"Aye, the thatching and outfitting the places with a bit of rough furniture, too. Nothing grand, mind you, but they certainly improved the dull wooden huts Watkins's men erected."

"And what about this one of stone? It looks special." Sliding down from her horse, Regan was at the door, ready to explore the interior. Her attentive guide hurried to tether the animals and join her.

"Well, I thought that once the true ownership of Geata Neamhai is decided, the loser might want a place of his own," said Connor, unable to restrain the laughter in his voice.

"Oh, then you've had it built for yourself?" questioned Regan with a broad smile, amused at his explanation for the overseer's cottage. "Somehow, after the spaciousness of the keep, I hardly think a small place, no matter how charming, would satisfy you."

"Ah, but you haven't seen the interior," chuckled Connor, throwing open the door and carrying Regan across the threshold.

"What in heaven's name are you doing?" she asked, though not struggling in his arms.

"This way, milady. I'm merely practicing the arts of an attentive bridegroom," explained the canny rogue, setting her down in the main room of the lodge. Obviously intended as the center of the family's life together, it contained a wide hearth, a large wooden bed, and a table with chairs placed around it. Outfitted completely with candles, a few plates and mugs, fresh rushes on the floor, even a washbasin and urn, the house was clearly ready to become a home for some lucky souls, acknowledged the Countess of Kilcaid wistfully. For a brief moment, she envisioned the laughter and joy that would someday fill these quarters and felt sad. Why couldn't she have such a future?

Then she heard the striking of a flint and turned to find Connor on his knees lighting the kindling beneath the waiting logs. She should protest, she knew, but what harm would there be in watching a fire with him? Sheila had been informed where the two of them were and would send assistance if they were away too long—or would she? Before Regan could weigh the matter of the housekeeper's loyalties, Connor was beside her again, removing her cloak and urging her to a bench before the dancing flames.

"I can't believe your men did all this in so little time," she marveled. "They seem to have thought of everything."

"Including a jug of mead," announced her host, delighting in her nod of agreement as he withdrew the cork and poured the sweet nectar into two waiting goblets. In a moment he was seated beside her.

"Shall we drink to the devil who destroyed the first house and made way for this?" he suggested, handing her one.

"I would rather toast the angel who had this lodge built of stone so it could withstand unexpected flames," answered Regan softly, her eyes holding his as she raised the glass to her lips ever so slowly. She had made up her mind; tonight she would be his.

"Aye, I'll drink to him," agreed Connor, his deep blue eyes reflecting the fire in the hearth.

The slight clink of their glasses seemed magnified in the quiet shadows of the cottage. There were no tapestries on the walls, no fine carvings or elegant furnishing to entice the soul, yet as Regan sipped the honeyed wine, she knew contentment and realized that tonight she craved the roguish Irishman as hers, regardless of the consequences tomorrow might bring. This time, she wouldn't refuse his advances, she would encourage them.

Reaching up to touch his face with her slender hand as he sat quietly watching the dancing flames, she drew her soft palm across his rough cheek and jaw before sending her fingers to trace his barely parted lips in as provocative a gesture as she dared, her wordless caress a clearer invitation than any spoken language could have provided.

By way of an answer, Connor dipped his fingers into the mead and trailed them over her mouth, permitting her to lick the droplets as they fell. Then he wet his fingers again and renewed his motion, this time depositing small beads of nectar on her chin and graceful neck. But before she could object to his teasing game, the Irishman was drinking the magic elixir from her skin, his mouth capturing the golden liquid and the rapidly warming flesh beneath it, sending shivers of delicious anticipation up and down her spine.

Could it be just the wine that was making her feel so heady or was it Connor? Without even consciously framing the question, Regan knew the answer as she leaned closer to his foraging lips, eager to be devoured. Breathing became an effort as she seemed to need every ounce of air to just murmur her pleasure in response to his ravaging mouth. And then, all at once, the coarse, lapping sensation that had seemed so strange at first, but so natural now, ceased, and Regan felt bereft.

Opening her eyes in search of him, she saw Connor laying a blanket over the rushes on the floor before the fire, and her soft woolen cloak over that. Needing no further encouragement, she joined him on their impromptu pallet, reaching out for him even as he pulled her into his embrace. There was no hesitation as their mouths sought and found each other, each eagerly sensing the other's need. This was no tentative exchange of appreciation as had occurred in the tunnel; this was the ready exploration of a man and woman discovering their differences even as they explored their passions.

As if in slow motion, their tongues danced in time, twisting and intertwining as Connor relished the responsive female Regan was revealing herself to be. When his mouth left hers to trail kisses down to the tender throbbing pulse in her neck, her deep throaty moan aroused him further. Trying to release her nipples from their fabric, he found himself as clumsy as a green lad until she willingly assisted his efforts. In a moment, her gown was pushed to her shoulders, and he'd opened the ribbons that had held her bodice closed, but Regan made no protest.

Whether he was devil or angel, Regan had no clue, but Connor O'Carroll made her feel alive as no other man had ever done. Sighing in delight, she did not say a word as her gown slid to the floor.

There was a sudden rush of cool air on her feverish skin, but then Connor was kissing her again, her lips, her throat, even her bosom. Quickly the chill turned to heat as he drew one nipple into his mouth and washed it exquisitely with his darting tongue. Nearly overcome by his loving attentions, Regan couldn't believe it when next he dribbled mead on her breasts and slowly, oh so slowly, savored each extravagant mouthful.

"Connor," she whispered huskily when his lips began a return to hers. "No one ever...I mean, I thought they were there to suckle babes—"

"And anxious suitors," he added hoarsely, cherishing her inexperience as much as her instinctive reaction to his attentions. The lodge had been a wise decision, he prided himself. No one would disturb them or interfere with the inevitable ecstasy soon to be theirs. Of course, he'd have to be gentle the first time, but from the enraptured look on Regan's face, he doubted their first joining would be their last of the night. Gently feathering the nape of her neck with kisses as he drew her up to rest against him, he reached for the mead, but before he could grasp the jug, she had taken hold of it.

"No," she said firmly, moving slightly away from him and holding the liquor out of his reach.

"No?" Connor couldn't believe his ears. She was refusing him? Try as he might to hold his temper, his voice was a barely restrained roar of outrage when he next spoke. "No? You mean you honestly can lie there and tell me you want to go back to the keep now?"

"No," Regan said with a happy smile, delighted at having caught Connor off guard. "I don't mean that at all. It's just that now it's my turn to pleasure you."

Before the Irishman quite knew how it happened, she'd removed his tunic.

"Connor," she exclaimed when the task was accomplished, "I didn't know that under your garment you wore—"

He stopped her cry of surprise with another kiss, reminding Regan of her purpose even as she pushed him back onto the pallet to be ministered to willingly, as she had accepted his attentions.

Unable to resist her, Connor reached out for the pins that constrained her glorious blond tresses and extracted them one by one as she trickled the mead over his body and proceeded to lick him clean. All he could see was her long golden mane, shielding her face as her flickering tongue held him enthralled, but he certainly wasn't about to complain. If her medicine had healed his wounded thigh, what could she do for the rest of him?

When her playful teeth caught the hair on his chest along with his nipple, and teasingly tugged, he was hard put to stop from ravishing the maiden right then. But, his conscience cautioned him, let her move at her own pace; the reward will be all the sweeter. And he listened to his own advice, allowing her to massage him and caress his muscles, her hands traveling lower and lower until the exquisite torment he felt bordered on pain. Then, there was no postponing the inevitable. Capturing her playful hands in his larger ones, he drew her up to him and kissed her nose, demanding her attention.

"That's one toy, little one, that you'll have to leave alone a bit longer, or it won't be ready to play when you are," he cautioned, sitting up and drawing her onto his lap as he set his finger to gently rubbing the tender area of her feminine core.

"But, what—" she protested, trying to escape his stroking hand. It wasn't that it was unpleasant, but no one had ever touched her in such a way.

"Haven't I made you feel wonderful so far?" he pressed, feeling the signs that her body was nearly ready for him. When she nodded hesitantly, he explained further. "I want the whole night to be memorable for both of us, and the more your body is prepared for me, the less discomfort you'll feel the first time. It's only natural," he reassured her as she started to speak. "No, kiss me now and let me love you. Questions are for later."

Relaxing in his embrace, Regan wanted nothing more than to please Connor; there would be time enough later to tell him this wasn't her first experience. All that mattered at the moment was tonight and the two of them in this special place. She raised her face to his and welcomed the touch of his lips.

Lifting Regan off his lap, he laid her down on the finely woven cloth and reclined beside her. With one hand, he continued to stroke her as the other pulled her head to his and his insatiable mouth captured hers. Rapidly their breathing turned to panting as each craved possession of the other. A desperate sense of madness drove them on, and she wrapped her arms around him, pulling his body closer to hers, signaling the splendid release her body craved and could no longer postpone.

Tentatively Connor readied himself to enter her and as he thrust upward, he sent his tongue to more feverishly exploring hers, intending to distract her from the pain that had to follow. But, surprisingly, there was no physical barrier to obstruct him, and Connor's mind balked at the fact. But his body pressed onward, already too overcome with unquenchable desire to interrupt its inevitable course. Positioning himself for Regan's comfort, he pushed the mystery aside and began to move, urging her to join him in the rhythmic motion older than civilization itself.

Clearly not distressed, Regan matched his every thrust and escalated the pace till there was no higher plane to explore and they became one, sharing the essence of their bodies and souls in an explosive crescendo of passionate release that left them spent, collapsed in each other's arms.

While exhausted and physically sated, Connor felt emotionally betrayed. Here she had put him off for weeks, protecting her chastity, and she wasn't pure! Should he denounce her as a liar and expose her fraudulent claim to innocence or would more be learned if he remained silent? True, she had satisfied him well enough, but so could many others. Puzzled and angry at her deception, he rolled aside and feigned sleep to give the matter more thought.

Her arm resting possessively on Connor's well-muscled chest, Regan allowed her fingers to gently toy with its curling hairs. Though she had just lived through it, the Englishwoman could not believe this miracle of rapture she'd experienced was the same activity that she'd shared with Dudley. How different that had been, she mused sleepily: a quick grappling in the dark of the gardens, worried that someone might see and tell the queen, offering only a temporary sense of belonging, and certainly not granting her fulfillment as this had. This dark-haired Irishman, renegade or not, was twice the man that noble courtier could ever be; that was obvious in Connor's concern for her, and she had to acknowledge it.

"Connor—I—I don't know what to say," she whispered softly, not quite ready to accept his troth but needing to verbalize her pleasure. "I've never felt so alive, so much a part of the heavens as with you here tonight. *Go raibh maithagat.*"

For a moment, Connor's angry thoughts tumbled one upon the other in disarray as he heard her attempt a Gaelic thank you. Did she care that much for him to learn his language? Then, his heart closed and he surrendered to the hot fury coursing through his veins, the ire that demanded he hurt her as much as her deceit had wounded him.

"Good, then you'll give up your claim to Geata Neamhai?" he asked brusquely. The furthest thing from his mind was the resolution of his estates, yet she'd played him for the fool, refusing to sleep with him, allegedly guarding her innocence. He couldn't excuse her deceit that easily and so, he'd said the first hurtful thing that came to mind.

"What?" Regan couldn't believe her ears. This gentle, caring man who'd just introduced her to true intimacy, the man she'd believed herself ready to love, was now negotiating for the return of his property? What kind of a fiend

was he? "Connor O'Carroll, you're a filthy, no-good swine
who deserves to be hanged. Indeed, I should have let you die
when they brought me your ugly hide. I don't know why I
didn't—"

"Probably because you missed your English lover and
decided I'd make a handy replacement, at least partly noble and relatively attractive, even if I am Irish," sneered
Connor as he rose from their makeshift pallet and drew on
his clothing. "Lady Regan, you've a few things to learn
about the Irish. They don't forgive easily."

"Aye, and they're as stubborn as jackasses and not a whit
more logical if you truly thought the reward for bedding me
would be Heaven's Gate. Did you honestly expect me to
deed the property to you in gratitude for services ren-
dered?" asked the Countess of Westfield and Kilcaid, her
voice suddenly extremely cultured and proper, making her
words even more astounding. "Well, my dear sir, let me tell
you true. As poor as Heaven's Gate may be, it is still worth
a thousand times your pitiful performance here tonight.
Despite my insincere flattery and your colossal arrogance,
another, a better man, has pleased me more than you ever
could."

"Aye, he pleased you mightily all right. That was obvious in your startled response to my touch," Connor
mocked, unable to restrain his ungentlemanly comments. As
he stood over her slender form, he fought to contain his
temper, wondering at its unexpected eruption. He certainly
didn't love the woman; by all that was holy, he didn't even
really care for her. Why in blazes should her having known
another matter to him in the least? She was only, after all, a
means to an end, a plan that hadn't proved the success he
had hoped, though there had been a few satisfying moments along the way, whether she admitted it or not. "So
who is this superior lover of yours, milady? The one to
whom I compare so unfavorably, I mean?"

"No one with whom you would have an acquaintance," Regan taunted. "He is a gentleman in service to the queen."

"And her willing ladies, apparently," Connor retorted. "With or without her majesty's leave?"

"That is none of your business," said the blonde angrily, her blush giving her away. "Besides, you told me repeatedly that chastity was an overvalued virtue at best. Why should it make any difference who he was?"

Noting Regan's use of the past tense, Connor grinned. So that was it, a few awkward groping encounters, probably extremely unsatisfactory, but the innocent maiden had fancied herself in love, undoubtedly embarrassing herself and the entire court. For, he'd discovered, that while English nobility might be extremely practiced at infidelity, they had little use for those who were discovered in their perfidy.

"Having spent time at court myself," he reminded her, "it well may be that I know this paragon of passion. Indeed, I may have taught him a trick or two."

"Hah, I doubt the Earl of Leicester had any use for the likes of you," scoffed Regan before she realized what she was saying.

"Dudley? That pompous jackanape? Good lord, woman, you are a ninny! No wonder Elizabeth packed you off here!" Torn by the desire to throttle the stupid wench for having fallen for Dudley's advances, and the need to punish her for giving Elizabeth the means to displace the O'Carrolls from Geata Neamhai, Connor threw Regan her gown and turned his back on her.

Striding to the hearth, he kicked dirt on the waning flames, trying to push away the knowledge that Dudley had not only been the one to falsely betray him to the English sovereign, but had also arranged for his "used goods" to be packed off to Ireland. The man's brother-in-law, Sir Henry Sidney, needed no excuse to hound the Irish other than their existence, Connor scowled in disgust, yet Dudley's involvement made the situation personal. Lord, but that English devil had a long reach; yet, Connor O'Carroll would be damned before he'd surrender his family estates to that bastard—or his abandoned doxy.

"Are you ready to leave?" he snarled at the silent Regan.

"I have nothing more to say to you, if that's what you mean."

"Fine." Extinguishing the small candle on the table, he led Regan from the lodge, helped her astride her horse and set a fast pace back to the keep; the sooner he was rid of her, the better he'd like it. Much as he hated to admit it, and he never would to his friend, Hugh had been right about her all along.

For Regan, the ride back to Heaven's Gate was the most desolate experience since losing her father. Here, she'd felt precious and cherished such a short time before, and now angry words had been spoken that would never be forgiven. Why was life so uncertain? When finally she slid from her saddle at the entrance to the tunnel, Connor claimed the reins to her mount and nodded stiffly.

"Our truce has come to an end, Lady Regan. Geata Neamhai will remain yours only as long as you can hold on to it," he announced solemnly. Then he disappeared into the darkness of the night, leaving Regan to enter Heaven's Gate feeling as she had the first time, alone and unsure of what was to come.

Chapter Twelve

By the time she reached the courtyard, however, Regan's hesitation had disappeared in the face of her growing anger and resentment at the way O'Carroll had treated her, using her for his pleasure and then discarding her when she wouldn't meet his price. Though she was still confused by his actions, one thing was certain: she would not abandon her inheritance, not without a struggle, and never for a scoundrel like Connor O'Carroll.

The first thing that need be done even before she retired, was to post a guard on his secret tunnel. If she were truly at war with that blackguard, she couldn't afford a single misstep. That evil-hearted renegade would take advantage of every weakness in her defense, of that she had no doubt. Hadn't he proved so tonight?

Stopping briefly in her quarters only to wash and repair her appearance, she headed immediately to the one loyal friend she had, Gerard. Once the young woman had roused him from his sleep, she issued orders to double the watch on the walls and informed him of the tunnel.

"A hidden tunnel into the keep?" demanded the gray-haired retainer suspiciously.

"I couldn't sleep and decided to take a walk. By chance, I happened on the entrance to the tunnel. I only noticed it because someone had left its door ajar and I decided to explore."

"By chance is it now?" bellowed the Englishman, irritated at this rude awakening at so late an hour, but even more angry at the guilt he felt, believing himself somehow remiss in not knowing of the passageway. "You go stealing off after dark without letting anyone know your whereabouts and now you come back in a dither, spouting the need for more security? Regan Elizabeth Davies, what part of the story aren't you telling me?" As bleary-eyed as he was, Gerard could not help but notice a reticence, a change in his charge's usual demeanor, and he was not about to let it go unchallenged. "Well, what have you to say for yourself?"

Forcing herself to meet Gerard's piercing stare without flinching, Regan reiterated her earlier story, stressing her concern for the safety of the keep.

"I told you. I was restless. Nothing untoward happened, but anything might have with an unguarded entryway like that. Who knows how often O'Carroll or his men may have wandered about without our knowledge? We could have all been murdered in our beds, while he played the part of suitor." Though she didn't believe such a possibility for a moment, Regan convincingly directed Gerard's attention from her escapade back to concern for Heaven's Gate.

"Damn it, woman, I told you weeks ago not to permit that Irish devil of a fugitive within these walls. He probably dug the tunnel himself. But, you wouldn't listen to me, you knew better—"

"Aye, that I did," snapped his mistress, swiftly losing the remnants of her already strained patience. "And, if nothing else, my actions earned us enough time to finish the tenant houses in peace—"

"Aye, with the necessary help of your English neighbor, I might remind you."

"And the so-called Irish devil," added Sheila sarcastically as she arrived to learn the source of the loud commotion, heard throughout the keep. "Let's not be forgetting the O'Carroll's efforts on your behalf, milady."

"I fear his efforts were purely for his own sake," disputed Regan, "but if that deceitful renegade thinks I'll ever surrender Heaven's Gate willingly, he knows nothing about me or women in general. Gerard, see to stationing the guard. I am going to bed now, but we will speak again in the morning."

"That we will, Regan. You can rest assured of it," muttered her commander as she headed for the tower stairs.

"Poor lamb," sympathized Sheila, shaking her head at Regan's abrupt departure, "but then, the course of true love is never smooth, especially when land is an issue."

"True love?" choked Gerard, staring at the red-haired housekeeper in disbelief. "My heavens, woman, don't you understand English? She's ordered me to double the guard to keep him out. She wants nothing to do with O'Carroll. In fact, I suspect, she's ready to have him drawn and quartered or, at the very least, boiled in oil, and you still dream of weddings? You're as daft as a moon-sick calf."

"That's simply because she hasn't gotten her way," said Sheila softly. "Pride is a heavy burden and I fear the two of them carry a might weighty portion of it, but you'll see, old man, one day soon, you'll see." Smiling sweetly, the Irishwoman gathered up her skirts and headed off toward the kitchen to fetch a soothing potion for her mistress, but not without a backward glance.

"If this is Irish love, saints preserve me," Gerard grumbled, storming out to the courtyard. He hadn't expected total harmony in these heathen outlands, but neither had he expected such madness in the females. He hoped it wasn't catching.

* * *

By the time Sheila finished in the kitchen and reached Regan's chamber, the young woman had already undressed and slipped beneath the bed coverings in an attempt to forestall conversation. While she could fob off Gerard's questions, Regan realized the housekeeper suspected, if not knew for certain, Connor's purpose in enticing her to leave the keep, and that was an experience she had no wish to discuss.

"I brought you some warm milk with a wee touch of brandy, milady. It will warm you up right and proper and send you off to sleep," the older woman explained.

"And why wouldn't I drift right off?" asked Regan, accepting the drink if not the accompanying solicitude. Truth be told, it tasted quite soothing...perhaps her nerves were spent.

"Oh, I expect you and the O'Carroll had a tiff of sorts or you wouldn't be doubling the guard against him, milady. I know whenever I quarreled with my Michael, I always felt cold and our bed seemed peculiarly empty."

"O'Carroll and I have never shared a bed," retorted the Englishwoman, finding solace in half-truths. "Why would you even think to compare us to you and your husband, unless you hated your Michael as much as I detest that scoundrel of an Irishman who craves Heaven's Gate more than..."

"More than what?" asked Sheila softly, noticing the sudden filling of the girl's eyes. Love was surely the issue, the housekeeper decided, and the poor little thing feared he loved his land more than her. Oh, the pain of being young.

"More than anything else in the world, apparently," cried the blonde, throwing off the covers and jumping up from the bed. "He's called off his truce, Sheila, and declared war, challenging me to keep Heaven's Gate, if I can."

"Oh, your ladyship, it's just the Irish way, spouting off in anger, not meaning a word of it. He'll not do anything to harm you or his people," assured the housekeeper soothingly.

"I think he meant what he said, and if that be the case, I want everything of his out of here by evening. If need be, I'll give him the contents, but never the keep."

"Begging your pardon, mistress, but I don't understand."

"Anything within these walls that was reserved for Connor O'Carroll's exclusive use is to be removed from Heaven's Gate before the next sunset. That should be plain enough," snapped Regan. Opening the wooden desk that belonged to the lord or lady of the manor, she gathered his journals and a heavy silver inkstand engraved with the O'Carroll coat of arms. Carrying them to the narrow window in the tower wall, Regan held the items suspended in space outside and suddenly let them drop from her grasp, turning back to a startled Sheila with a satisfied look on her face. Now she had started to fight back. No matter how insignificant the gesture, it made her feel better. "From his clothing to his chess pieces and furniture, if it was made to his specifications, I want it all out of here!"

"But—"

"If you choose not to obey my orders, you will be out as well," pronounced Regan coldly, too weary for further argument. "You do recall our earlier agreement?"

"Yes, milady, but what shall be done with the goods?"

"Just dump them outside the walls as I did. I am certain that his people will find a way to retrieve anything valuable."

"Aye," agreed the housekeeper quietly. She knew the girl was making a terrible mistake, but nothing she could say would dissuade her; it was better to be still.

"But, the gifts, Sheila, my woolen cloak, the brooch, his silver cup, anything he brought me, gather that separately in the courtyard," instructed Regan as she remembered the dancing fingers of flame he had kindled for her just hours ago. Unknowingly he had provided her with fuel for another blaze this evening, she decided, returning to the master bed. "That is all. You may go now."

When the other woman turned and left without a word, Regan wondered if she were being too capricious in her desire to see Heaven's Gate purged of O'Carroll's presence.

No, screamed her soul in its fury. He has declared war; you are only answering his battle cry.

Yet, hours later, as she lay unsleeping in her lonely bed, unbidden sensations of the night before haunted her existence. No matter how she twisted and turned amid the linens, seeking an escape from her torment, she could still feel his mead-flavored kisses. Persistent memories of passion's fulfillment underscored her current emptiness and seemed to emphasize his unwarranted cruelty. So, she had been with Dudley first, so what? Connor O'Carroll had wanted her for weeks, teasing, enticing, arousing till finally she had succumbed to his desires. But what had it earned her? cursed Regan. A few moments of undeniable delight—and the promise of a war she could not win.

When sleep continued to elude her, the weary female arose from the bed, washed herself and began to dress. If there was no escape in slumber, perhaps she could find some in being busy.

Just as her maid helped her complete her toilette, a persistent knocking at the door signaled Gerard's impatience for her presence. "Regan, the rest of your tenants have arrived," he announced breathlessly. "Finally, things are going along as they should."

"What?" She felt as completely miserable as she had ever been in her entire life, O'Carroll was about to put the keep under siege, and Gerard was jubilant because more Englishmen had arrived, more people her men would have to defend.

"I've set Sheila to ordering a welcoming feast for this evening and I'm ready to take the families down to see their new homes. I thought that since you are the lady of the manor and the one really responsible for those cottages, you might like to accompany me."

"No. I mean, I don't think it's a good idea to rush their relocation. After all, they've been traveling for a long stretch," she reminded him slowly. "Let the tenants stay with us in the keep to get oriented. In a week or two, then they can move into the houses."

"My Lord, girl, what has gotten into you? You hounded Watkins and even O'Carroll for extra men to ready the places and now you want to let them sit idle? You are not making sense," chided her guardian, mystified and concerned at Regan's uncharacteristic behavior. First, her peculiar explanation of discovering that tunnel last night, then her demand that O'Carroll's personal goods be discarded, and now this hesitancy to see Heaven's Gate properly tenanted. What was wrong with her? "Regan, what really happened when you found that passageway? Obviously, a good deal more than you told me last night."

Well, there it was, her opportunity to explain to Gerard how she had insulted O'Carroll's manhood and put all their lives at stake with her uncontrollable temper. But she couldn't do it; she couldn't disappoint the dear man any more than she already had. He'd thought her a fool for the mistake she'd made with Dudley; he'd never forgive her for O'Carroll. A lie was the only answer.

"I—I didn't want to upset you, but when I went down into the courtyard to take a walk, O'Carroll was waiting."

"So? He's been in and out of the keep for weeks, over my strenuous objections I might add. What makes last night any different?"

"He wanted—that is, he tried to kidnap me," Regan said hesitantly, unsure of how Gerard would react. "He grabbed me and tried to take me through the tunnel, but I managed to get away from him. Anyway, he said he was tired of waiting and our truce was over. If I wanted to keep Heaven's Gate, I would have to wage a war for it. That's why I made you double the guard. He could attack us at any time.''

Gerard was silent, filling in the missing pieces of the story that his young charge had obviously omitted: a bit of kissing, a stolen caress or two, the enticement that got her into the hidden passageway in the first place. Had the attempt to take her been in the open courtyard, his men would have heard and come to her aid, so she had to have entered the tunnel willingly, only to discover later that its hidden promise was not a healthy one.

"How does that explain discarding his personal wares?" he asked, deciding not to press her for further details of her rendezvous. "Would it not make more sense to keep whatever we have of O'Carroll's? After all, if he truly loves his home, he is not going to want to see it destroyed.''

"But he burned down the tenant house, he admitted it.''

"That was yours, not his," replied Gerard. "I agree it wouldn't be wise to send your tenants outside the walls to live at this time, but I also think you should change your mind about his possessions. He will find it much easier to decimate the keep if there's nothing here he wants," the older man concluded, wondering if indeed Sheila might have been right. More and more this dispute resembled a lovers' spat more than a war. Had he been O'Carroll and serious about it, the attack would have occurred last night before Regan could have had the time to sound the alarm ... *if* he had wanted to fight in the first place.

"All right, I will speak to Sheila about putting O'Carroll's goods in one of the storerooms," conceded the Countess of Kilcaid, "but our tenants will stay in the keep.''

"Aye, we'll find space for them somewhere, though there won't be much room.''

"If we feed them enough Irish whiskey, they won't care where they sleep," suggested Regan with a laugh as she recalled some of her soldiers' overindulgence with that particular liquor.

But they need not have worried about cramped quarters, discovered Regan when she entered the Great Hall that evening. Fewer than a third of the Irish retainers were still in service. The others had taken their families and disappeared since last night, another sign, she feared, that O'Carroll's threat was not an idle one.

Standing before the assembly in a gown of emerald green with soft touches of golden thread interwoven in the bodice, the young woman looked every bit the royal landowner; her stance was self-assured and her beauty undeniable, while her slight hesitancy was perceived as a soft femininity. In her heart, Regan Elizabeth Davies was Countess of Kilcaid and, no matter what the personal cost, she could not, and would not, disappoint her dependents.

"Welcome to Heaven's Gate, my friends. I wish you might have joined us last week when harmony reigned over these beauteous lands and the sun's warmth held the promise of joy unending," she began, her eyes taking the measure of those newly arrived.

Few seemed the emotional sort, but clearly they were relieved to reach their destination and anxious to start their new lives. Most had abandoned whatever their holdings in England to come this far, and Regan knew she must encourage their dreams of happy homes. Yet, the truth was, they had undoubtedly sensed problems in this unfamiliar land, and it was her chore to explain the situation without intimidating them.

"Unhappily, however, the O'Carroll, the Irish lord from whom Elizabeth confiscated these lands, has not fully relinquished his claim to them. There is every possibility that within the next few days, he will challenge my right to ownership of Heaven's Gate and all it entails. Therefore, I must ask you to accept your lodgings here within the keep for as long as is necessary to protect you and your loved ones. For now, let us thank God for your safe arrival and partake of this sumptuous feast the kitchen has prepared.''

At Regan's signal, the maids entered, bearing overflowing trenchers of roasted meats, fresh vegetables and hot bread. Shouts of approval greeted her. Whether they indicated appreciation of her position or the plenteous food, she didn't care; at least her listeners were temporarily satisfied. For her part, the very smell of the heavy, hearty fare made her lose her appetite and, after visiting briefly with her guests, she left the hall for the cool air on the battlements.

Nodding to the men on duty, Regan found herself pacing the narrow walkway, looking off into the distance where Connor had appeared just a fortnight ago. That day, too, they had expected war and he had outfoxed them, arriving instead with words of seductive compromise. Was it foolish to expect another reprieve from that blue-eyed spawn of Satan who'd bewitched her so?

What explanation could there be for her emotional response to the temptation he presented, other than witchcraft, she asked herself, as the moon began its quiet ascent. Certainly she was no green girl, completely unfamiliar with the ways of men; Elizabeth's court had accustomed her to the games of flirtation, if not all of the ways passion came to fruition.

Connor O'Carroll was her enemy, but, knowing that, she had still been unable to keep her body from betraying her. A wayward memory of his broad shoulders and powerfully muscled legs made her feel faint even now, despite his mistreatment of her. A pox on him, Regan cursed, why weren't a woman's feelings more controllable?

As much as she wanted to hate the devil, thoughts of his twinkling eyes and roguish smile made her grow warm in the cool evening air. What was wrong with her, she fussed impatiently; she should be thankful the renegade was gone from her life and they'd sealed the keep against his treachery. So why didn't her heart recognize that gratitude?

Maybe a cup of chamomile would soothe her nerves, otherwise, she feared, this would be a long night indeed.

"Adams, the Lady Regan is missing. I want a search party equipped with torches and weapons ready to leave in five minutes," came an anxious voice from the courtyard below.

"Gerard, I'm here, it's all right. I'll come right down," she called, hurrying to the foot of the stairs to intercept her worried guardian. "I just needed a breath of air—"

But he was in no mood for explanations; grabbing her by the shoulders, the older man proceeded to shake his mistress, his earlier concern for Regan fading rapidly into anger at her abominable lack of consideration.

"Damn you, child, I thought you'd been spirited away somehow, right from under our noses. You weren't in the hall or your chambers, you'd said nothing to Sheila or anyone else. What was I to think, but the worst?" he bellowed, his fury clearly evident. "I swear if you ever, ever frighten me like that again, I'll—I'll send you off into the woods alone for O'Carroll to find. Nothing worse could befall you in reality than what I've already feared in my heart!"

Gulping at the air to calm his raging temper, the man suddenly pulled his charge into his arms and embraced her tightly.

"At my age I've too few days left to waste them worrying about you," he said gruffly, his callused hand stroking her cheek.

"Oh, Gerard, I'm sorry, really I am, but I never imagined... I mean, O'Carroll can't have any interest in me anymore."

"You said he had an abundance of it last night."

"Aye, but we exchanged harsh words—"

"All the more reason he'll be seeking revenge then. Come inside, and from now on, you are to inform Sheila or me of your whereabouts, at all times. Is that understood?"

"Yes, Gerard, I promise," she said meekly; the thought of O'Carroll avenging himself on her personally was one she hadn't considered. Wasn't the man too honorable to punish all the inhabitants of Heaven's Gate for the perceived insult she alone had delivered?

Even chamomile wouldn't be enough to soothe her now, she feared as she followed Gerard into what was rapidly becoming her prison. Mayhap brandy with a touch of chamomile would do the trick.

"Who gave the order to return to camp?" demanded Connor that same night as he confronted Hugh by the fire. "I leave you alone for a half an hour so I can track the English scouting party and I return to find you've dismissed the men despite my instructions that they were to work on sword and mace exercises? What kind of a lieutenant are you?"

"One with a heart for your men, Connor, even if you've lost yours. You've had them working all day long, practicing with their bows, drilling silently, tracking through the woods on foot and horseback, even fighting hand to hand with each other," retorted Hugh, the only one man enough to question the O'Carroll's commands.

"I want them suitably prepared to storm the keep. If there are English losses, that's one thing, but I am responsible for my own, and they've been getting fat and lazy, living off her ladyship's bounty. Well, she'll not be so giving anymore, that I promise you," snarled the Irish renegade as he watched his men and their families feasting on a side of beef, one of Regan's final gestures of goodwill.

"Then shouldn't they enjoy a good meal and a sound night's rest?" reasoned his deputy calmly. "I mean, if we're to mount a siege tomorrow—"

"And who in bloody hell put you in charge of my battle strategy?" demanded Connor angrily. "I was under the impression, mistaken though I may be, that *I* am the leader here. Are you challenging my authority?"

By now all of those in the camp had fallen silent, food forgotten in their amazement at the O'Carroll's irrational fury. While not one to suffer a fool's blunders quietly, neither had their liege ever mistakenly placed blame before. To a man, the soldiers realized that Hugh was not questioning the O'Carroll's authority, but defending his humanity.

"Of course not, sire. You are the Earl of Kilcaid, Connor O'Carroll and, if I've offended you, it certainly wasn't done intentionally," said the big man quietly. Though his voice could echo like the thunder when he wished, Hugh understood that his friend needed gentling, not antagonism, despite his clear wish to brawl. "Why don't we share some whiskey to ease the bitter taste of our misunderstanding, and you can tell me your plans?"

"Damn you, Cassidy! When I am ready to let you blab my strategies across the countryside with that flapping big mouth of yours, I'll tell you," growled the Irish lord as he grabbed the jug and headed off alone. "Until that time, just leave me be."

Watching the distressed O'Carroll depart, Hugh shook his head in disgust. Obviously that English wench had affected Connor more than he was willing to admit. The hulking soldier only prayed that O'Carroll hadn't lost his heart, or they'd all be finished.

By the following afternoon, Gerard was hard put not to toss Regan from the ramparts or, at the very least, bind and gag her. She was everywhere and into everything, challenging the schedule he'd posted for the guards, questioning the accommodations he'd allotted the new tenants, even suggesting the herdsmen and shepherds bring the sheep and cattle back to the Great Hall for safety. This last notion was what finally confounded Sheila and brought her to appeal to Gerard.

"You have got to do something with that woman, Langston, or I may just strangle her and feed her to the chickens," the housekeeper threatened. "She's been in my kitchen five times already today, changing the menu, reorganizing the root cellar, complaining about the quality of my soft cheese and butter. She may be the lady of the manor, but I am telling you right now, if those sheep spend the night inside the walls of the central tower, *I* will not."

"Oh, Sheila," sighed Gerard helplessly, "and you thought what ailed her was something as simple as love. I only wish it were so. At this moment, I think she and that Irish outlaw of yours deserve each other. Maybe we should let her go riding alone, outside the walls...."

"Come now, old man, you don't really mean that?" asked the woman. If Gerard truly wouldn't oppose a match between Regan and Connor, there still might be a way.

"No, but perhaps if she rode with an armed escort, she could ease her tension and ours, as well," continued Gerard, already forgetting his whimsical words of matchmaking.

"Nay, I fear it wouldn't be wise," said Sheila sadly, realizing Gerard hadn't been serious. "If the O'Carroll's men were to take her, you'd never forgive yourself."

"I suppose you're right," agreed Gerard in surprise. Did Sheila really have Regan's best interests at heart after all? Or was his agitation with that particular young woman making all other females seem kindly? "At any rate, if we can't banish her from the keep, what say we hide for a bit in the root cellar?"

"Ah, get along with ye," laughed the Irishwoman heartily. "You know she'd only find us quick enough. Best if we be available for her next crisis, though those animals are not sleeping in my kitchen if that's what her ladyship wants next."

* * *

At the edge of the forest, Connor sat alone, watching the occasional movement on the wall of his former home, the hint of flickering candlelight in the tower rooms. What was wrong with him? He'd never been as cross and out of sorts as these two days, but he'd never been belittled by a woman before, either. How could that blasted female compare his loving to Dudley's . . . let alone unfavorably so?

For the hundredth time since he'd left her at the tunnel, he determined to wage the war he'd promised, and then, for the hundredth time, he decided against the shedding of blood. Who was he to risk the lives of his men merely to assuage his pride?

But you'd also regain your home, echoed a recurring thought.

"Somehow, I doubt she'd surrender Geata Neamhai without dying for it first," he said softly. "And who could know better such a commitment than Connor O'Carroll? Damnation, I couldn't kill her before I knew her, just because she was a woman, and now, knowing the woman, the deed is even less appealing," he fumed. Where was Hugh's supply of whiskey, anyway? Of late that was the only thing that didn't answer him back.

Chapter Thirteen

As his coach crossed the border onto the neighboring property the next morning, Thomas Watkins called out a warning to the guards accompanying his vehicle.

"Now, look sharply there, I want no misunderstanding. Connor O'Carroll and his lot are known fugitives of the Crown. If the advance party hasn't routed the recreants and they should appear, you are to kill without hesitation. Not only will no one question your defense of me, but the queen will see to your reward," assured the master of Wren's Nest, not very truthfully. Though a third cousin to Elizabeth, he wasn't at all sure that she would care if anyone saved him, but he certainly wasn't about to admit that to his men.

Since he had never been overly courageous himself, he wanted his soldiers ready to undertake any risk necessary to protect their master. Indeed, if it hadn't been for the Davies woman's failure to call on him again, he would never have ventured forth from the safety of his plantation while that devil was on the loose. It had been more than a fortnight since Lady Regan had come to request his assistance and, though his men had completed the tasks she'd set, she hadn't reappeared in his life, either with words of gratitude or a request for further aid. The situation was disquieting to say the least.

Running a gnarled hand through his thinning hair, the noble wondered what could possibly have kept her away. Certainly he'd been most agreeable in nature the day they'd met, he recalled with a grin, remembering the alluringly slender young countess. In his day, Thomas Watkins had set his sights on many a wealthy widow but found, to his utter amazement, that they were not appreciative of his attentions. So much more the reason for exploring the venue of Regan Davies, he'd decided. Her land, her beauty, his wisdom and management—though not ordinarily given to amusement, he chuckled on speculating their match could be made in heaven . . . or Heaven's Gate. Oh, how could she resist his wit?

The first inkling Regan had of Watkins's visit was the ominous cry of warning from the battlements.

"Armed party approaching. Stand ready for attack."

As her men scurried to their appointed positions, Regan attempted to mount the steps to the wall, only to be halted by an adamant Gerard.

"If this is an attack, Regan, the last place I want you is in the front line of our defense. Wait with the other women in the Great Hall."

"*If* we are under siege, I will comply with your wishes, Gerard. Until such time as we know the situation, however, I shall see what is happening for myself," the countess announced, slipping past her commander and climbing upward, leaving him to follow, shaking his head in annoyance. A moment later he heard uproarious laughter and rushed to her side.

Coming toward the keep was an armed party of two dozen men, encircling a closed coach, hardly a comical sight.

"Regan Elizabeth Davies, any moment lives may be lost, undoubtedly blood will be spilled, and you laugh? What can you find so amusing, young woman?'' he demanded with a scowl.

"That is Thomas Watkins's coach," Regan tittered. "Can you honestly believe that little man can be of any danger to us, especially imprisoned as he is, in that carriage?"

"While I admit it is unlikely we have anything to fear from our English neighbor, might I remind you that the last time we saw that particular vehicle, Connor O'Carroll was the man riding in it?" remarked Gerard. "This may just be another of his tricks to gain entry to the keep."

"If only it were," murmured Regan to herself before discrediting Gerard's supposition. "I hardly think so, however, since the men are outfitted with English weapons and Watkins's colors."

A few moments later when the carriage approached the drawbridge and Watkins stuck his head from the window to request admittance to Heaven's Gate, Gerard nodded his agreement with a small sigh of relief.

"Well, at least Sir Thomas will provide you with a happy diversion for the afternoon," he offered, turning to guide his mistress to the Great Hall.

"Aye, an experience not to be missed," said Regan drolly, already wondering how long she'd have to be polite to the repugnant toad. "But then, you haven't had the pleasure of meeting Sir Thomas. Won't you join me in greeting our guest?"

"Of course," agreed her guardian, pleased that finally something other than O'Carroll had caught his young charge's attention. Maybe the visit heralded better days ahead.

"What do you mean you've demanded a higher price on O'Carroll's head?" sputtered Regan moments later as Watkins presented his news in hopes of pleasing her. She'd begun the interview seated in the ceremonial chair for the mistress of Heaven's Gate, but the topic at hand unnerved her so, she was suddenly pacing the floor like a panicked tigress, her protective attitude toward O'Carroll surprising her.

"You must realize that the figure of fifty sovereigns offered temptation to no one. So, given my familiar relationship to the queen," said the master of Wren's Nest proudly, misunderstanding the reason he had Regan's complete attention, "I felt I should inform her of the depth of that devil's evil nature. With O'Carroll still at large after more than three months, we English must band together against the ignorant hooligans—"

"Connor O'Carroll can't be too ignorant if he's managed to elude Wolf's men and all the other patrols for that length of time," Gerard commented wryly. The irony that he'd looked to this fellow to turn the conversation from O'Carroll did not escape his notice, but Gerard Langston was too much a gentleman not to defend the former earl against such a pompous idiot. No wonder Regan had laughed at the sight of his coach.

"At any rate, I believe once O'Carroll is worth sufficient a reward, his own clansmen will turn him in and the area will be safe for Elizabeth's loyal subjects," promised Sir Thomas with an air of pride as he scurried to stay in step with Regan, his short legs unable to keep pace with her lengthy stride.

"But he is not hurting anyone," protested his hostess.

"Not hurting anyone? My Lord, woman, are ye touched?" exclaimed her visitor, stopping dead in his tracks and forgetting any romantic intentions he'd harbored. The unexpectedly mild reaction of the countess astounded him; could she truly be mad? That was the only conceivable explanation he could fathom as to why she hadn't fallen all over him in her gratitude for his efforts, even for the risk he'd taken in coming here today. "Milady, I regret speaking out of turn, but the countryside is not safe for honest citizens as long as that man rides free."

"Yes, we noticed your guards," said Gerard with a smile.

"Aye—and you've a full contingent on duty at the walls, I saw. You can't be too careful with one like him around. Surely, Lady Regan, you understand that once this renegade is taken, we can all dispense with such precautions and sleep easier at night? Believe me, if O'Carroll is not stopped, his devilment will know no bounds. The Irishman has no conscience whatsoever—"

"Why not leave the man in peace, Sir Thomas?" said Regan quietly, moving to confront her neighbor head-on. He was so small and unimposing, it was hard to believe he could possibly create such a dangerous threat to Connor. Yet, if, in truth, he did have Elizabeth's ear... "He's already forfeited his estate and all its holdings."

"Has he? Or is he still attempting to reclaim them?" questioned the little man in brown, his bulbous nose seeming all the longer as his righteous indignation grew. When neither Regan nor Gerard responded, he decided to pursue the issue. After all, he couldn't rightly court the lady until she understood exactly what he'd done on her behalf. Of course, the original missive to the queen had been sent long before he knew the Lady Regan, but she need never know his own cowardice had been the spur.

"Your ladyship, I have heard tell from my servants that not only did O'Carroll torch your tenant house, but he also was responsible for poisoning your cistern, bewitching the cattle, shearing your sheep, diverting your water supply and snatching your servants from their chores. I venture to say only God knows all he actually stole from you."

"And that is *my* business, not yours," observed Regan quickly, a slight blush coloring her cheeks as she recalled the Irishman's passionate kisses, which she'd returned in kind. "Really, sir, I do appreciate your concern, but I seek no redress against the former owner of my home."

"Certainly you can't be so softhearted as to believe that demon should go unpunished?" raged her neighbor in amazement. If she were touched in the head, she really wasn't suitable for his matchmaking intent, he decided, abruptly preparing to take his leave.

"As Englishmen residing in an Irish countryside, I venture to say our wishes are not the issue," remarked Gerard calmly. "I daresay his own people will determine his fate."

"Lady Regan?" pressed Watkins, curious now for her response.

"I—I believe the man was under a terrible temptation to reclaim his ancestral home and perhaps behaved somewhat emotionally," she said softly. "Since he hasn't been seen or heard from of late, and since there has been no further mischief on Heaven's Gate for weeks—"

"Mischief? I'd use stronger language than that, milady," refuted Watkins in disbelief.

"I suspect he's left the area altogether," continued Regan with a warning glance at Gerard. "In fact, some of the servants say that he's gone north to join the O'Neill."

"Another renegade."

"Be that as it may, why pursue a man who's lost everything already? Certainly he's too insignificant for a man of your stature to be concerned with?" flattered the young woman, trying another tactic.

"I must say I find your compassion refreshing, my child. However, your safety is of great concern to me," said her neighbor, capturing one of her hands and bringing it to his pursed lips. Perhaps the possibility of a union was not totally out of the question after all. Besides, who cared if Regan Davies was mad? He knew he could easily confine her to a tower and still enjoy the lands. "Actually, the matter is out of my hands at this point. I sent word to her majesty nearly a month ago and should receive her reply any day now."

"You will return and tell me her response?" invited the Countess of Kilcaid, a note of urgency apparent in her voice.

"Aye, your ladyship, it will be my pleasure to call upon you again, whatever the excuse," he said happily, executing an elaborate bow. "And, may I say, you shouldn't worry yourself with thoughts of that devil. Some of my men and those from other English estates hunt him day and night in anticipation of a hefty reward. But, if he's truly gone from the area, what matter is the bounty on his head? It might even be seen as a source of pride by the uneducated, I venture."

"Or the unfeeling," muttered Regan beneath her breath. Crossing her fingers, she forced her lips into a semblance of a smile and continued graciously. "Then, I shall look forward to your next visit, Sir Thomas. Have a safe journey home."

Once he'd left the Hall, Regan turned to Gerard anxiously.

"Fetch Sheila. I must send word to Connor—"

"I am here, your ladyship," came the housekeeper's distinctive brogue as she came forward from a shadowed corner of the hall. "Begging your pardon, but I wanted to hear what lies that English snake had to impart. As soon as he arrived, he evicted every Irishman from his property with not even a fare-thee-well. I was afeared he might try to convince you to do the same. He's the most hated landlord in the area, he is."

"That doesn't surprise me," confirmed Regan. "But now, Sheila, we must get word to Connor to stay well hidden and not take any chances. Given Watkins's enthusiastic pursuit of this matter, Connor's life may well depend on his stealth."

"Aye, when I think of the risks he took in coming here so often, with all the villains searching for him," murmured the older woman softly as she watched Regan's blush. 'Twas good the girl felt guilt for sending the poor lad away. "I will leave at once, milady. Annie can serve the evening meal."

"You're not going to send her off alone?" questioned Gerard in surprise. "How do you know you can trust her? She may not come back at all, or she may bring the Irish forces with her. Better she tell me where to go, and I will deliver the message."

"You? And how do I know *you're* trustworthy?" mocked Sheila. "Besides, Hugh Cassidy would as soon as cut you as not for what your men did to Connor. You'd never reach the O'Carroll alive."

"I fear she speaks true, Gerard," reasoned the mistress of Heaven's Gate. "I appreciate your skepticism, but—"

"What if one of the English patrols encounter her, a lone Irishwoman at this late hour of the afternoon, what would her chances be then?" challenged the gray-haired commander. If he could just get to the outlaw's camp and speak with him alone, perhaps the misunderstanding between O'Carroll and Regan could be sorted out, Gerard reasoned, still not fully convinced of the "kidnapping" story. Certainly she'd be much happier, and the keep could return to some semblance of order with the tenants properly housed outside the walls.

Should it be apparent that battle was unavoidable, he'd at least have some notion of the number of men O'Carroll commanded, and where their camp was situated. This was an opportunity that could not be missed. "Regan, I must insist on accompanying Sheila. It's the only practical solution. She can vouch for me with the Irish and I can do the same for her to the English."

"I don't know, milady," hesitated Connor's earliest nurse. "What if his intent is not what he speaks?"

"And what else might it be, old woman?" demanded Gerard, a niggling doubt in his own mind that he might possibly be concerned for this unlikely female's welfare making him more brusque than usual. "My allegiance is to Lady Regan and her good, none other."

"He speaks the truth, Sheila. Take him with you and hurry to warn Connor. Godspeed, you both," said Regan fervently, already dreading the hours she would have to endure till they returned.

"Don't fear, milady, we'll be fine...and so will he," promised the housekeeper with a wide grin. "He's blessed by the little people, so it's whispered."

"May that save him, and us," muttered Gerard, wondering just what he'd gotten himself into, as he followed her from the hall.

To the commander's considerable displeasure, Sheila adamantly refused to travel by horseback. It had been years, however, since he'd been a foot soldier, and he didn't want to return to that role now.

"Woman, time may be of the greatest essence, here. Be reasonable, horses would save us hours."

"Aye, if I knew how to travel by horse—"

"What?" he nearly roared.

"Look here, old man, I'm too aged now to be learning a new skill just to make you happy," she stated firmly, her stubborn jaw thrust forward in determination. "I've not sat on a four-legged beast in all of my years, and I'm not about to start now. Either you come with me on foot or you stay behind. It's of no matter to me."

"Oh now, get along with you. I cannot believe a woman of your character has enough spirit to challenge my mistress on occasion and the O'Carroll before her, yet you have not enough spunk for a mangy farm animal?"

"I'll not be swayed by your sweet talking either, Gerard Langston, so get thee moving or get out of my way," she announced as they neared the main exit to Heaven's Gate.

"Very well," he sighed, and motioned to the guards to raise the portcullis. "Adams, I want a double guard on duty until I return. Lady Regan's welfare will be your responsibility. No one is to enter, no one at all!"

"Yes, sir," acknowledged the soldier, passing the word to the others on the wall. Once the odd-looking pair had left the keep, he oversaw the raising of the drawbridge and the resecuring of the entryway. Whatever the two of them were up to, Regan Davies would be safe under his care, he vowed. The lady was special to him and all the retainers who'd seen her grow to womanhood; by God, no one would reach her without his knowing it.

"Sheila, I swear we've passed through this selfsame meadow a half-dozen times, and the sun is all but set. Aren't we nearly there?" Gerard demanded, stopping to mop his brow and take a drink from the meandering stream he swore he recognized.

"Actually, only twice," she admitted, squatting down beside him to quench her thirst.

"What did you say?"

"This is only the second time we've crossed this field."

"My Lord, woman, are you lost or just playing at some ridiculous child's game?" he roared suddenly, his outrage causing him to fall back on his rump in the soft grass. Here he was, weary with the exertion and the worry of the situation and she was leading him in circles? "Damn it, have you no regard for your master?"

"Aye, if by master you mean the O'Carroll and not yourself," she answered, pleased to see his face suddenly color. "I'd never go straight to his camp when there's a chance someone might be following—or you might be taking note of landmarks to return with your forces."

"You trust me that little?" he asked quietly, forgetting his earlier thoughts of measuring the enemy's strength and finding their location. Suddenly the red-haired woman's opinion of him mattered more than defeating O'Carroll. He had no doubt Regan's problem with him would work itself out eventually, but now he had to resolve this issue. "Well, what say you?"

For a moment there was only the sound of the whispering stream beside them as the housekeeper studied the tall gray-haired man lying in the grass. Certainly she could do worse, and if Connor and Regan were ever to wed . . .

"Nay, sir, I'd trust you with my life," she said with a shy smile, "but 'tain't easy to discard old hates, much as I'm trying. Come, the camp is just beyond this hill."

As the woman rose to her feet, Gerard did the same. Then, acting the gentleman, he bowed and offered her his arm for the rest of their journey.

"Sheila, saints in heavens preserve us! Why in the world did you ever bring that English graybeard here?" roared Hugh in disbelief when the guards escorted Sheila and Gerard up to the campfire. "And not even blindfolded? Are ye gone mad?"

"Stop your ranting, Hugh Cassidy, or I'll put a stop to your supply of whiskey. Then you'll have a true complaint," she snapped angrily. "Now then, give us a cup and fetch the O'Carroll. It's him I'll be explaining myself to, not you."

The huge man held her stare for over a minute before he found himself muttering angrily and doing her bidding. That wee woman had the power, he fumed, that she did. But as he watched Sheila throw back her head and down the whiskey at a gulp, he had to smile at her manner, especially when he saw Gerard imitate her actions. Mayhap the old woman wasn't so foolish after all, he speculated, refilling their cups. She might have brought them a captive worthy of ransom, rather than a spy.

On hearing that Sheila was in camp, Connor hurried to meet her, not paying attention to the rest of the message. Hence the sight that greeted him by the fire was not one he expected.

"Sheila, Gerard? What are you doing here? Is something wrong with—has something happened at Heaven's

Gate?'' he asked anxiously, not realizing his concession in using the English name of his former estate.

"Aye, that there is, lad, and Regan sent us to tell you about it," began Gerard hurriedly, somewhat surprised that his tongue was suddenly so slow moving and heavy when his mind was winging so quickly ahead of it. He had only downed two, or perhaps three, cups, not much at all.

"Well?" pressed Connor impatiently.

"Well, what?" asked Regan's man, shaking his head in mystification. Then, as understanding dawned, he leaned toward Hugh to accept another refill of his cup and turned back toward Connor, speaking loudly enough for all present to hear. "No, no, the well is fine. It's Lady Regan who's not."

"She's not?" repeated Sheila. When Connor looked to her for clarification, she could only shrug. Lord only knew what this fellow might say next; liquor had that truthful effect on some, she reflected. She'd explain the situation to Connor later anyway, away from all the curious ears now listening.

"No, she is not well, Connor O'Carroll, and you're to blame."

Him? For a moment Connor's heart stopped, but he'd only been with her once, three nights ago, now. Gerard couldn't be suggesting she was with his child? Shaking his head to clear it of such foolish thoughts, the dark-haired Irishman struggled to make sense of Langston's continuing babble.

"You see sir, she fancies herself in love with you, she does. But, then you disappear on her and she's become a very unhappy lady, a veritable scold these last few days without you around," he confided. "Lad, I pray you, if ye feel anything for her, have a heart and tell her so. Otherwise, I don't know what we'll do." As he finished speaking, Gerard looked as bewildered as the rest of them, not quite believing the words that had come from his mouth.

Then his chin dropped to his chest, his eyes closed, and a loud snore escaped him.

"What in the hell?" exclaimed Hugh, drinking deeply from his jug. "Connor, did you ever hear such absolute drivel? The man's a raving lunatic. Sheila, what's come over you bringing him here to press her ladyship's suit? I'd thought you had a better head on your shoulders."

When the others remained silent, trying to make sense out of what had just transpired, Hugh took command.

"Padraic, fetch some rope and bind him well, and the rest of you louts, leave us in peace here. Well, Connor, maybe we'll take Geata Neamhaí yet. At least now we have a prisoner to ransom, thanks to Sheila."

"No!" protested the housekeeper in dismay.

"No!" bellowed Connor.

"No?" repeated Hugh in surprise. "But I thought—"

"Whatever that witless mind of yours considered, banish it at once," snapped Sheila. "This poor man came here to do Connor a favor, not be trussed like a boar for your harebrained schemes."

"But—"

"Pay the woman some heed, Hugh," commanded the Earl of Kilcaid. "Sheila, sit beside me here and tell me what your purpose was in bringing Langston to camp. Did Regan actually send the two of you?"

"Aye, milord, she did. Watkins has fired off repeated messages to the queen, demanding she increase the price on your head and, since he's related to her somehow, he not only expects his request to be granted, but he's told half the county about it, the English half, of course."

"Yes, that's the truth," said Gerard, suddenly coming to and rejoining the conversation. "And he's after Regan's hand, too, don't be forgetting that."

"He's what?" demanded Connor, looking to the housekeeper for an explanation.

"He did make mention of the need for them to band together against you, and he's coming again to visit," admitted the woman, "but I verily doubt she'll be receptive."

"I didn't say she'd want him, I said he wanted her," scolded the Englishman emphatically. "Don't you people listen?"

"But why should the Davies woman want you warned, Connor? It makes no sense, unless she's setting a trap, maybe trying to convince you to visit Geata Neamhai with Watkins's men lying in wait," ventured Hugh, still nursing his distrust of Regan.

"Watkins's men are mounting heavy patrols in hopes of taking O'Carroll," agreed Gerard. "But Regan doesn't want him to come to the keep. We were to tell him to stay away. She's afraid for your safety, lad," he confided in Connor.

"A likely story if I ever heard one," snorted the large man as he watched his friend mull over Langston's words. "Connor, you're not accepting a bit of this, are ye? The woman wants you gone so Geata Neamhai is hers, that's what this is all about."

"Nay, Hugh, I think not," he said, looking slowly at Sheila holding Gerard's hand. Regan had given herself to him once, but he'd spurned her gift, too proud to like being second. "You say my safety worried her, old man?"

"Aye, son. She told us to make sure you knew your life might depend on your stealth. My lady wouldn't say that if she didn't care," muttered the commander, suddenly very tired again as he patted Sheila's hand. Talking seemed almost more effort than it was worth, but he had to explain to the O'Carroll.

"All right, then, I'm going to her. Hugh, saddle my horse and keep the men here," he ordered, his mind made up. She cared for him enough to worry about him; that was sufficient for now.

"But—"

"I said, fetch my horse, Hugh, and see that everyone stays in camp. If the English are patrolling, one man can get through easier than an army," O'Carroll stated firmly. "I'll accept no argument."

"Aye, milord," grumbled the unhappy soldier as he went to do Connor's bidding.

"But, Connor, she wanted you safe," stressed the small woman whose opinion he valued.

"I understand, Sheila, but don't you see? I want her. It's time she knew it."

"Good for you, lad," rooted Gerard with a chuckle. "Just give me a minute to get on my feet and I'll lead the way."

"I fear that standing may prove difficult," warned the Irishman. "Don't worry, I know the way."

"But the guards at the keep have orders to keep you out—"

"I have my own ways to get in," reminded Connor.

"The tunnel is guarded, too."

"That won't stop me—"

"What? But—" Gerard's protest was lost as he tried to stand and collapsed in an awkward heap. "Sheila—"

"Right here beside you, old man. Take my hand and I'll help you up," she instructed gruffly.

Moments later, rough as it was, he was on his feet, but O'Carroll had already departed without him, leaving a disgruntled Hugh in charge of the camp.

"Well," Gerard murmured, reaching for the whiskey, "you did say the wee folk would help him."

"And her, too," confirmed Sheila.

"Good, then help me down and let's have a drink together."

"I thought you'd never ask," she replied with a smile. "Since we've taken care of the young ones, it would be my pleasure."

Chapter Fourteen

The darkness of night fell like a mantle across Connor's broad shoulders as he hastened his horse toward Geata Neamhai. Throughout all the months of his exile, he had never longed to be in his former bedchamber as much as he did at this moment. But he discerned it wasn't the great keep that was calling him homeward, it was Regan.

Images of his beautiful English maiden guided his course more accurately than any stars in the heavens, as he galloped through the mist.

Regan! Her name tore at his throat while remorse tore at his soul. She had risked being branded a traitor, an enemy of the Crown, in order to warn him about Watkins's efforts to ensure his capture. She had loved him enough to put her life in jeopardy to save his, even though he had cast her aside after enjoying her favors.

God help him, what a fool he had been! The land was nothing to him without the delicate flower that had been transplanted there.

Self-reproach urged him onward, across rocky terrain and velvet hills, his path lit only by the moonlight as his great cape swirled behind him in the wind. And yet no matter how fleet his horse, the animal could not travel swiftly enough to suit Connor.

His emotions led the rebel earl to throw caution to the winds. He didn't care that Englishmen were nearby, attempting to hunt him down even now. Nor did he trouble himself with the lure of the higher price that had probably been placed upon his head. He only knew that he was the O'Carroll, and he was returning to his woman.

But was she indeed his, he worried as he raced onward, a dark, solitary figure riding the horizons of the Irish countryside. He could understand if she wanted nothing more to do with him. In fact, if the girl had any sense at all, she would turn him away. Such a thought was more frightening to this proven warrior than his most vivid nightmares. Not usually a religious man, Connor found himself praying fervently that Regan's heart was as forgiving as it was loving.

All he wanted, all he could hope for, given the way he had treated her, was the opportunity to hold her in his arms once more, to feather her lips with kisses, and to make her believe that he truly loved her. After that nothing mattered to him, nothing at all.

Suddenly the shadowy walls of Geata Neamhai rose up in the distance. While there had been times that Connor had praised their impregnable quality, this night they presented an irksome problem. He had no doubts that the guards would cut him down should he ride up to the gates and demand admittance. But even if Regan's men could be persuaded to inform their lady of his presence, he would not have it known that she had opened her keep to a man whom the rest of the pale was now so actively seeking. However, for all that, there was a greater problem, he recalled ruefully. There was no guarantee that she would want to receive him. Connor knew that the only way he would see Regan that night was to slip undetected into the fortress and steal his way to her rooms.

His decision made, he guided his horse to the nearby cluster of trees which had hidden him and his men on the day Regan had first come to these lands. Rubbing down his mount and tethering him to a sapling, Connor set out across the open field that would bring him home.

He bent low and used the swirling mists to cover himself as he rapidly closed the gap between the trees and the imposing keep. Proceeding as quietly as a spirit of the night, his stealthy movements transformed his appearance into that of some legendary, darkling prince.

Closer and closer he came until finally he was beside Geata Neamhai's thick walls, standing in the arid moat that could offer the keep little protection from so determined an invader.

He crouched quietly against the cold stone barrier separating him from the woman he loved. In the silence of the night, the handsome renegade studied ways to gain entrance into the fortress that he had once called home.

The stillness surrounding him was broken only by the footsteps of the guards stationed atop the battlements. From the movement he heard, Connor reckoned that more men than was customary had been posted. Scaling the walls without being discovered would be impossible. That left only the tunnel as his means of approach, and Connor cursed the arrogant confidence which had prompted him to disclose its existence to Regan. Hadn't Langston told him that, after his argument with Regan, she had set a guard at the hidden opening? But, for all the danger it presented, it was still his sole hope of entry.

Making his way slowly to the passageway's opening, he drew his sword from its scabbard. Then he eased the outer door ajar slowly, pleased at the absence of a challenge. Apparently the guards had been stationed at only the other end of the tunnel. Drawing a deep, calming breath, the earl went forward into the total darkness of the roughly hewn corridor, not daring to ignite a rush for fear of giving himself away.

An impatient Connor disciplined himself to move carefully. The only sound discernible was the soft padding of his feet as he made his way along the black length of the access, his eyes now adjusted to the unlighted oblivion within. Caution, however, stopped him before he reached the end of his path. Hardly daring to breathe, he waited for some indication of Englishmen outside. His prudence was rewarded, when through the open door, he heard a snatch of conversation between two men on duty.

Picking up a pebble, he hurled it flying through the darkness to land clattering on the other side of the courtyard, a ploy that sent one of the guards to seek out the source of the disturbance. Then, swiftly, Connor reached out to clamp a powerful hand across the mouth of the remaining man and pull him into the not-so-secret passageway. Deciding against shedding the blood of Regan's men, the outlaw nobleman brought down the hilt of his sword on the retainer's skull with considerable force, rendering him unconscious.

In the space of a few moments, Connor heard the returning Englishman softly calling for his fellow. Flattening himself against a supporting beam just inside the blackened recess of the passage, the O'Carroll answered him with a muffled groan.

Hurrying to investigate, Regan's man wielded his sword and stooped to enter, making himself an easy target for the blow the desperate Irish lord delivered. Quickly Connor bound the two with their own knitted hose, and then he gagged them, as well, heaping one upon the other so he could squeeze by into the sprawling night.

Pressing close against the wall behind him, Connor surveyed the almost-deserted courtyard, every inch and niche of which were well-known to him. Though there were other guards dispersed around its perimeter, they were set far apart, and he knew that keeping to the shadows should bring him success in making his way to Geata Neamhai's central tower.

Stealthily he began to advance from one patch of darkness to the next. Edging his way along the walls, he soon neared the kitchens. From here it would be a simple run to that part of the fortress which housed his lovely Regan.

What he hadn't counted on, however, were the dogs prowling the refuse heap for some tasty morsel. Nor had the animals expected to find a human creeping up on them in the inky blackness. Coming around the corner of the main kitchen, Connor froze at the sound of a low growl warning him to keep his distance. It emanated from a good-size hound who stood guarding the bone he had just uncovered. Not remembering the scent of the previous master of the keep, the young beast sought to contest his presence.

Retreating slowly, Connor considered what was to be done to overcome this obstacle. The rugged Irishman's quick wit and overpowering desire to reach his lady made him resourceful. Connor stepped carefully to the dairy shed where he reached in to grab a crock of yesterday's cream waiting to be clotted. Then he slowly turned his steps in the direction of the dog. Holding the cream before him as an offering, he crooned softly to the dog in Gaelic, the language it had heard as a pup. Sniffing cautiously, the salivating hound decided this was a friend, and let the human pass for the price of the crockery's contents.

Connor exhaled the breath he discovered he had been holding, and crept through the kitchen maids' entrance to the Great Hall. No one was present, and it was a simple matter to steal into the darkened hall itself. Keeping far from the two wolfhounds who dozed by the hearth, he quietly climbed the stairs to the upper chambers.

The household was asleep, as it should be, and Connor proceeded through the corridor to stand outside Regan's solar. He placed his hand upon the heavy oak door, intending to open it slowly, only to find it bolted from within. Sweet Mother of God, but did she think she had to protect herself from her own people, or was it someone else she was trying to keep out? Did she have cause to think that Watkins might return in the middle of the night and attempt to force himself on her, Connor wondered; or perhaps it was he the English beauty was trying to keep at bay.

Looking anxiously up and down the empty hallway, Connor rapped boldly on her door and, employing his best English accent, announced that a message had just been received from Gerard.

He had to knock but twice before he heard movement from within. Regan couldn't have been sleeping very soundly, if at all, to have responded so quickly to his summons.

"What is so urgent that it claims my attention at this hour?" Regan asked as she pulled at the chain to unlatch the door. "What did Gerard have to say?"

"He said you love me," came a familiar voice as Connor pushed his way into the room, hushing Regan's startled cry with a deepening kiss. Closing the door behind him, he swept the woman who had captured his heart into a fierce embrace.

"He never said any such thing!" Regan protested vehemently when Connor's mouth at last relinquished hers.

"What matter if he did?" Connor asked, still holding her close. "You had already told me when you sent that unlikely pair with a message to save my life."

"Then the more fool I!" Regan exclaimed, ripping away from his clasp, despite the fact that she longed for nothing more than to open her heart to him.

"No, Regan, it wasn't you who was the fool," Connor corrected her, his voice ripe with love as he attempted to assail her defenses. "It was I."

"You who have never been accused of being dull witted?" she retorted, circling around him, afraid that if she stood still he would take her in his powerful arms once more and she would be lost.

"Neither have I been charged with jealousy and yet I was both when I left your embrace," he said in a sincere whisper.

"I don't believe your silver tongue any longer. What have you come to do now, abduct me?" she asked, stepping back as he tried to close the distance between them.

"I have come," he said tenderly, "only to steal your heart."

"That is a theft you have already committed, but if you will recall, you considered your booty such a trifling thing that you threw it back at me. My heart is mine now, and I do not choose to return it to you."

"Then let me win your love anew," he urged, reaching out to draw her close.

"What you want to win is Geata Neamhai," Regan upbraided him, stepping just out of his range.

"Indeed, I told myself that was what I wanted," he confessed, his expression one of self-recrimination, "that all I had to do was make you want me and my home would again be mine. But I swear by all that's holy, in my scheme of love I fell into my own trap. I lost my heart to the beautiful maiden I had hoped to ensnare."

"Why should I put any faith in what you have to say?" Regan asked. Good Lord, she had acted to save him from Watkins, hadn't she? What right had he to expect more?

"Because sweetest heart," he pleaded, "I have learned that reclaiming these lands is secondary to claiming your love."

"Don't play me for a simpleton. I know how much this estate means to you," she refuted.

"Damn it, woman," he said, losing patience in his desperation to have her come to him willingly, "what must I do, what must I say to make you see that Geata Neamhai is nothing without you, that what I feel, what I want, goes far beyond Heaven's Gate?"

"It's too late for that," Regan demurred, hating her pride even as the words left her mouth, yet compelled to say them all the same.

"It's not too late! I won't have it!" Connor commanded as he towered over this woman who flinched not at all in the face of his raw fury, an emotion ironically fueled by the deep, frenzied fear he had lost her. Grabbing her by the waist, he tilted her chin upward so that she was forced to look at him as he continued his argument. "If I meant nothing to you, you would not have risked sending Sheila and Gerard to me in concern for my safety."

"'Twas no more than an impulse, a move undertaken to keep Sheila and the others from worrying about you rather than doing the work assigned to them," she lied defiantly, conquering her tremendous longing to give herself to this man again.

"You tell me an untruth, Regan," Connor reproved, his fingertip gently tracing the outline of her lips with a calm he did not feel.

"It was that and nothing more, I swear it!" Regan cried.

"I won't believe you no longer love me unless you tell me," he stated, looking like some romantic prince of myth as his eyes intently searched her face. "If that is how you truly feel then say the words, Regan," he demanded. "Say them now!"

She opened her mouth to speak but couldn't. Instead tears welled in the corners of her eyes, and she damned herself for her weakness in loving such a man.

Connor, however, knew none of her misery, jubilant as he was at her silence. In celebration of his good fortune he crushed her tighter to his chest, and his burning mouth descended upon hers, his lips searing her soul and branding her his.

Momentarily, however, he tasted the salt of her continuing tears, and he lifted his head to stare at her in concern.

"What is it, little English dove, that upsets you so? We have settled things between us. We love each other, what need is there for weeping?"

"Won't Dudley's ghost continue to come between us?" she asked, remembering Connor's fierce temper when he had learned the identity of the man who had taken her virginity.

"I told you, Regan, I was a jealous fool. I don't care that you loved him once, as long as I am the man who commands your heart now."

"Now and always," Regan promised him, joy flooding her soul as she leaned against his comforting chest. "I never did love him, you know. I was naught but a green girl newly arrived at court, and Dudley was my pretense at being queen."

"Hush," he said, stroking her hair. "We need never talk of it again. It makes no difference."

"Then you still want me to become your countess?" she asked, looking up to find him regarding her with more tenderness than she had ever seen a man offer a woman.

"You are already countess here," he said softly. "What I want is for you to be my wife. Will you finally consent, Regan Davies?"

"Yes, Connor O'Carroll, a thousand times yes!" Regan cried, lifting her head and planting a kiss along his strong jaw.

"Then what say you we seal the bargain?" he asked as he lightly ran his hand against her cheek.

"A glass of wine perhaps, milord?" Regan asked with a mischievous smile.

"I had in mind something sweeter," Connor replied, a roguish gleam in his eyes as he swooped his lady up into his arms. "Have you any mead next to your bedstead?"

"I'm afraid not, milord, you'll have to make do with the taste of me."

"It will be just as intoxicating, I'm sure," Connor replied, his voice full of promise as he carried her into the room that would henceforth be theirs. After tonight, he vowed, anticipating the passion they would share, neither one of them would ever sleep in the huge bed without the other.

The sun was just beginning to dilute the blackness of night, turning it into shades of gray. Conscious of the approaching sunrise, Regan stirred lazily, glorying in the feel of the large, masculine frame sharing her bed. Her head was pillowed by Connor's shoulder, and as she tilted her face upward and turned toward him, she could hear the beat of his heart and feel the fine hairs that fanned across his chest as they brushed against her cheek.

In the heavy shadows of the room, Connor's fine, aristocratic features were barely perceptible and his raven hair vanished completely into the soft darkness. But Regan could sense that even in repose, the Irish earl's bearing was proud. He looked like some seductive demon sent to induce a woman to succumb to temptation, or at the very least a lusty Gypsy prince, sated after his latest conquest. But as romantic as these notions were, Regan knew that in reality Connor O'Carroll was neither of these. He was something much more; he was a man who loved her so deeply that he would risk his life to make her his. He had set aside his natural animosity for all that was English, because he held her dearer than anything else in his world.

Aware of the warmth of his body against hers, and the comforting sound of his breathing, Regan knew she loved him in equal measure. They were bound to each other no matter what fate might have in store.

"The sun is coming up, Connor," Regan whispered into the stillness of the room.

"Aye, so it is, my love," he responded, his tones overflowing with contentment and laziness. "Does that hold any

ignificance for you?'' the Irishman asked, absently strok-
ng her rounded bottom.

"Only that I think it time we finally went to sleep," Regan answered, daintily stifling a yawn.

"Sleep the day away while I have you here in my arms?"

"But you didn't close your eyes at all during the night,"
Regan said, teasing a tendril of her hair along his jaw, "and
you made certain I didn't either."

"Are you complaining, milady?" Connor asked as he
rolled across the bed to gently pin her beneath him and bring
his face to hers, initiating another exchange of fiery kisses.

"No, milord, I've no complaints," she said a few minutes later, her sigh of satisfaction speaking louder than her
words.

"Then why all this talk of slumber when we've the entire
day before us?" he asked, returning to his back and bringing Regan with him, to settle her atop his warrior's frame.

"I merely thought you might want some sleep before you
have to leave," Regan mumbled, squirming so deliciously
against him that it took a moment for Connor to realize
what she had said.

"Leave!" he challenged, sitting bolt upright and sending
Regan tumbling onto the bedding beside him. "What do
you mean *leave?* Last night you agreed to be my wife, Regan. Don't think to lie to me and tell me that you've changed
your mind, because I know better than that. Your body has
betrayed you."

"Of course, I want you for my husband, Connor O'Carroll, but I do not want to make the announcement from my
bed with you beside me. You'll just have to sneak out of
here and meet me in the Great Hall where I can welcome you
properly."

"I can't envision anything you could do to surpass the
welcome you gave me last night, Mistress Davies," Connor
said, a roguish gleam in his eyes. "But if you could per-

haps hint at what you have in mind, it might make me more
willing to leave so comfortable a spot."

"Connor, be serious," Regan said, her pretty mouth setting itself into a near pout. "I can't have Gerard or Sheila
come rapping at my door to find you in my bed."

"Then you've no need to worry," Connor said smugly,
lying down and making himself at home once more. "Sheila
and Gerard probably haven't returned as yet, and they won't
for a while, I'm sure."

"They're not back?" Regan asked with a start. "Then
how did you gain admittance to Heaven's Gate?"

"The tunnel," he confessed, "and sure but it took all of
your charms to make me forget my guilt about the two men
I tied up inside its entrance. Their night was not as comfortable as mine."

"Nor as active," Regan said drolly. "But tell me, how did
you expect to escape?"

"I didn't."

"Were you so sure of me, then?" she asked with a blush.

"No, I was so desperate to hold you in my arms once
more," he admitted, tenderness creeping into his voice.

His answer filled Regan with such pleasure that she
readily forgave him for not telling her how he had managed
to penetrate Heaven's Gate during the night. After all, they
hadn't done much talking. But resting her head against his
shoulder, Regan began to comprehend what else he had just
told her.

"Connor, how do you know that Gerard and Sheila won't
be returning any moment?" she asked suspiciously.

"It would seem that Gerard had a run-in with a jug of
whiskey, and when I last saw the pair, he was all but unconscious, with Sheila refusing to leave his side."

"You didn't hit him over the head with the jug, did you?"
Regan asked in disappointment.

"No, nor did I pour its contents down his throat," Connor said with amusement. "He was doing an admirable job of that himself."

"He was in his cups! I sent him on a mission and he got drunk!" Regan exclaimed.

"Don't be hard on him when he returns," Connor requested. "If he hadn't had a wee drop, his tongue wouldn't have loosened enough to tell me how much you were pining for me."

"I was not pining!" Regan protested, aware even as she spoke how much it must have cost Gerard's pride, drunk or not, to admit to this rugged Irishman that she needed him. But her color ran high as she wondered exactly what it was Gerard had told the man by her side.

Sensing Regan's struggle with her pride, Connor kissed the tip of her nose. "No matter what Langston implied, I know that you missed me no more than I missed you. Now let us forget him and have some of that sleep you were talking about. Settle next to me, my love. I fear I'll never be able to lie in a bed again without you by my side."

Beguiled by his charming confession, Regan did as he requested. But she had no sooner closed her eyes, when there was a sharp knocking at her outer door.

"Good morning, milady," Annie called as she stood outside, awaiting permission to enter. Anxious to discharge her duties perfectly in Sheila's absence, the girl had presented herself to assist Regan in dressing earlier than was necessary in order to avoid being late. Not for the world would she have Lady Regan thinking her a sluggard.

"Annie?" Regan called out, eyeing Connor anxiously.

"Aye, milady," the girl called through the closed doorway.

"Connor, what should I do?" Regan asked in an urgent whisper.

"Let her in," he mumbled drowsily.

"I can't do that with you here," she argued.

"Then send her away," he suggested, trying to be amenable to whatever Regan wanted.

"But just how am I going to be rid of her?" Regan asked, shaking his shoulder violently when he closed his eyes once more. *He* might be nonchalant about being found in her bed, but she did not share his sentiments.

"It's very simple, tell her to leave. Go to the door, and tell her you were awake all night. You don't have to tell her why," Connor said patiently.

"Lady Regan," came Annie's strident voice.

"I can't just do that. She'll know something's not as it should be," Regan objected, displaying a streak of stubbornness Connor found bewildering.

"If you can't do it, then I will," he said, sitting up and swinging his long legs over the side of the bed.

"No, stay where you are!" Regan ordered nervously. "I don't want you discovered and my men charging in here to dispatch you before I can stay their swords."

"Lady Regan, it's Annie," sounded the servant's voice again.

"She'll have the whole keep awake soon," Regan complained, jumping up and reaching for the nightdress that had been so mindlessly discarded the night before.

"Milady, are you all right?" a masculine voice called.

The realization that one of her guards was also outside her rooms caused Regan to hasten dressing as nothing else could have.

"Why, yes, of course, I'm all right," Regan said opening the door to her solar after ascertaining that the entranceway into her still-darkened bedroom did not betray Connor's presence.

"I know you're an early riser and I'm here to help you dress, Lady Regan," the female servant said, stepping into the outer chamber.

"That's very commendable, Annie, but I never rise this early. And you, Adams, are you here to help me dress, as well?"

"Why... why no, milady. It's just that there are indications we may have had an intruder last night, and I wanted to be certain no harm had befallen you," the soldier stammered, hiding a great deal of the truth in order to avoid worrying the mistress of Heaven's Gate.

"My door has been bolted all night. I certainly haven't seen anyone," Regan stated emphatically, knowing by the man's expression that the bound guards had been found. "And if there were an intruder, I would certainly expect you to find him without disturbing me, Adams."

"Yes, Lady Regan," he said contritely. "It's just that Gerard entrusted your care to me, and ..."

"Thank you for your loyalty, the both of you," the young countess relented, her heart softening at their discomfort despite her sense of panic. "But you have not found me in the best of spirits. I'm afraid I didn't sleep at all last night. I had just closed my eyes when you came pounding on my door."

"I would never have bothered you if I had not seen your serving woman come to attend you, Lady Regan," Adams swore, glancing fiercely at the little Irish maid as though this whole thing were her fault.

"Milady, I'd no idea you had spent a sleepless night," Annie began to squawk.

"No, of course, you didn't, and neither did you," Regan said, careful to include Adams in her forgiving glance. "But I really am weary and I know, in the absence of Sheila and Gerard, I can trust the two of you to see to the proper running of my keep, while I get some much-needed rest."

"Aye, milady, you can rely on me to do me best," Annie said with a curtsy, blushing at the compliment her mistress had just paid her.

"And upon me, as well," Adams said, not to be outdone. "In fact, I shall post guards here in the solar, right outside your bedroom door, to safeguard you while you sleep."

"I'll have no men in my solar!" Regan flared indignantly. "The implication that I should be that fearful in my own home is an outrage! And if I were to feel frightened, then I should have to say that the keep has not been properly guarded in the first place."

"Well, perhaps outside the solar door, then," Adams conceded, not willing to have his mistress think he had been incompetent the night before. "But I must demand the bolt be kept off in case you need us."

"That's ridiculous!" Regan protested.

"But I'm afraid I must insist upon it, milady," the man persisted, so anxious to prove himself that he ignored Regan's icy glare. He could not help but wonder if his lady's restless night had been the result of Regan's apprehension at having Gerard gone and himself in charge. With this nagging fear in the back of his mind, he was determined to make her feel safe at all costs.

"I could not live with myself if I were lax in my duties to you. And as Countess of Kilcaid, I know that you want your men to take all necessary precautions to defend your holdings here. In my judgment this is one of them," he concluded.

"All right then, all right," Regan acquiesced, anxious not to act so obstinately in the matter that she aroused Adams's suspicions. "See to it. But mind you, I am not to be disturbed. I want no noisy oafs within my rooms, it is bad enough I have to suffer their presence without. If I am fortunate, I will fall into a deep sleep as soon as I am allowed to return to my bed. Don't bother about it if you don't see me before the midday meal. Now off with the pair of you."

The moment the door was shut, Regan whirled and ran into the bedroom.

"Did you hear what Adams said, Connor?" she demanded. "He's stationing soldiers at my door."

"That's all right, the walls are thick. No one will hear us," he commented wryly.

"Stop being such a jackanapes! With guards outside, there will be no way out for you!"

"Then I'm afraid I will be forced to spend the entire day hiding in your bed, or at least until Gerard returns. What a pity!" he mourned playfully. "But what concerns me more is that you told your man you hadn't been aware of anyone in your rooms last night. Did I impress you so little, Regan?"

"Nay, milord. You impressed me quite deeply indeed," she said with a smile, unable to resist his mischievous teasing.

"Then come here, woman. The bed is cold without you," Connor commanded, patting the sheets beside him. For once Regan had no trouble obeying an order, and she complied happily.

"Regan," the rebel earl murmured, a scarce few minutes later, as the two of them were drifting off to sleep.

"Yes, Connor?" she answered lovingly, willing to fight off drowsiness in order to hear whatever words of endearment he would croon next.

"Your guards are really a bumbling lot. Remind me to give them some lessons on soldiering once we are wed!"

Regan's indignant reply was a playful poke which her earl answered with a deep, devilish laugh.

Chapter Fifteen

Though the rising sun was not enough to disturb the O'Carroll and his countess, who were soon lost to slumber entwined in each other's arms, not all the residents of Heaven's Gate found themselves so fortunate.

As a shaft of sunlight pierced the leafy boughs overhead to fall directly on his face, Gerard Langston shifted uncomfortably and fought the thumping in his head.

Good God, he didn't remember being engaged in battle last night, yet it must have been. Here he was, sprawled on a forest floor, his head sorely wounded. He tried to rise and discovered he was all but pinned beneath a body, probably some fallen comrade in arms. Turning his head to survey the situation, he recoiled at the sight of the woman curled up half-atop him. Suddenly it all rushed back to him: Sheila, Connor's camp, the whiskey!

Lord, what had happened to Regan with him in this condition? But even as the worry entered his mind, he refused to acknowledge it; his head was painful enough without additional anxiety.

Trying to find the strength to move, Gerard could do naught but study the face of the woman who rested so peacefully against him. She looked decidedly girlish in her sleep, and Gerard had to admit that the sensation of her body partially covering his own was not all that terrible a thing.

As if she were aware she was being watched, Sheila opened her eyes and smiled up at her companion intimately, an action that caused the veteran soldier to panic.

Sweetest Lord, he thought, his mind ajumble. Could he have actually... would the drink have allowed him to...? But in his alarm, and with his thinking still clouded from all he had imbibed the night before, he found himself unable to actually complete the sentence, even to himself. It was as though finishing the thought was an incantation that would have made it so, and Gerard worked feverishly to repress the possibilities that stormed his benumbed brain, as he answered Sheila's satisfied smile with a sickly one of his own.

When she sat up to adjust her shawl, Gerard hastily disentangled himself from her and was soon on his feet. Her soft manner as she regarded him made him distinctly uneasy, a sentiment he tried to hide without much success. The red-haired woman's patent merriment at his discomfort gave her all the charm of a saucy country wench.

Adjusting his doublet self-consciously, Gerard bravely faced his giggling tormentor. Looking into her dark brown eyes, he saw the fiery nature she often wore on the surface. His fears were absurd, he determined, discounting the idea that he wouldn't remember bedding such a vixen. But as he saw open desire smolder in her eyes, he had to wonder anew. Had he or hadn't he? She peered up at him coquettishly, and Gerard was lost, vowing that if he hadn't then, by God, he would!

He took a step toward her, his intentions stamped on his distinguished features, when a booming voice halted him where he stood.

"It's about time you were up," Hugh bellowed as he strode across the now-deserted camp. "But then I never knew an Englishman who could rightly handle a wee bit of Irish brew."

Gerard bristled at the other man's remark and was sorely tempted to answer his taunt with a flying fist, until he again recalled Regan.

"I take it O'Carroll has departed for Heaven's Gate," the queen's loyal subject said, not certain he remembered Connor leaving the night before.

"Geata Neamhai, you mean," Hugh growled, handing Sheila an oatcake and a cup of water with which to break her fast. "Aye. The young fool rode off at breakneck speed. Nothing I could say would stop him."

"That's as it should be, Hugh," Sheila remonstrated mildly, generously sharing her morning meal with Gerard, and suddenly careful to keep her words of censure sweet while in his company. "Connor loves Regan and she him."

"That's what you say, though I can't fathom so absurd an attraction," Hugh said with a mighty sigh, which signaled what he thought of the irrational world around him.

"Then we have something in common," Gerard pronounced, ready to leap to Regan's defense and put this crude Irishman in his place. "I, too, feel the match is an undesirable one, but after trying in vain to dissuade the Countess of Kilcaid from her folly, I have resigned myself to abiding by her decision."

"Is that so, graybeard?" a red-faced Hugh sneered at the indignant Englishman. "I suppose that's why you were pleading the lady's case so eloquently last night, pushing Connor into riding off into the darkness and perhaps into an ambush, as well."

"I'll have no more of such nonsense, you great, witless lout! Do you think I'd be stupid enough to be used as an instrument in Connor's capture?" Sheila interjected, her tongue as sharp as her countenance. Though she'd abandoned her newfound mantle of feminine softness, Gerard was hard-pressed to find fault, impressed as he was by her fearless contradiction of the man known as Hugh Cassidy.

"Now out of my way, man. Gerard and I are going back to the keep," Sheila insisted, raising the back of her hand so that Hugh would feel its sting if he should try to stop them.

"Not without me, old woman," Hugh declared, glaring at Gerard, who met his vitriolic stare without flinching. "I want to know what has happened to the rightful Earl of Kilcaid, and God help you, Englishman, if he is not healthy when I find him. For your sake, and the sake of all your countrymen residing on O'Carroll land, he'd better be comfortably awaiting us at Geata Neamhai."

"Heaven's Gate," Gerard corrected defiantly.

"What difference what it's called, if our lad and lass have made amends and will rule the place together?" Sheila asked in a practical manner, trying to forestall the physical conflict ready to erupt at any moment.

"The difference," Hugh reminded her tartly, "is that the Pale has encroached upon these parts so that it borders three sides of O'Carroll holdings. And now I must worry that the English have invaded Connor's marriage bed, as well."

"Watch your tongue," Gerard objected hotly, his words indicative of his rapidly rising temper. "The Lady Regan does not need to ally herself with that renegade, O'Carroll. I might remind you that as of now she owns the lands...and the bed as well."

"That is only because she has stolen them, then," Hugh said, taking a step forward, and placing himself within range to easily strike Regan Davies' man.

The movement set Sheila's instincts on edge, and she planted herself between the two men, scolding them as if they were mere boys.

"With the time you are wasting, Connor and Regan will be coddling their children's offspring before we leave this camp. Hugh Cassidy," she lashed out at him harshly, "is your concern for your friend and lord of such little consequence that you will allow an argument with this Englishman to delay assuring yourself of Connor's well-being? And you, Gerard Langston," she continued, her tone growing considerably milder, "what of your duty to Lady Regan? If Connor was not able to reach her side, would you have her alone with only her guards for protection in times such as these?"

A pained expression crossed Hugh's face and a groan escaped him when he noticed the change in Sheila as she directed herself to Gerard Langston. Saints in heaven, Hugh thought crossly, was he the only one attached to Geata Neamhai who was immune to English charms? But Sheila Dempsey was right in one thing. He was squandering precious time quarreling when Connor's fate was still uncertain.

Barking the order to leave camp, Connor's second in command led his mount behind him so he could hear whatever passed between the other two, as they set off on foot.

Hugh watched Sheila drape her shawl around her as they walked in the direction of the keep. There was a sprightliness in her step that he hadn't noticed before, and it provoked him into drawing her aside for a word of reproof.

"What's the matter, old woman? Couldn't you find a man among your own kind to warm your bed?"

Sheila raised a critical eyebrow in response.

"I've done that on three previous occasions, lad, as you well know. And in each instance, I've been left on my own. This time I thought I'd try a foreigner. It could be they spring from hardier stock. Now, will you be having a problem with that, Hugh?" she challenged, her voice no more than a deadly whisper.

"Suit yourself, it's no concern of mine. But I suppose it was at your knee that Connor learned his notions of coupling with the English," the burly Irish soldier spat. "And his fate, then, will be on your head."

"No, though fate may preside over the events of the world, Hugh, each man governs his own destiny," Sheila pronounced sagely, "and you must find your own way, as

well, though it may mean choosing a path that leads you
from your home should you be unable to accept Regan
Davies as the O'Carroll's bride.''

''You talk nonsense,'' Hugh growled, taken aback by her
suggestion that there might be no place for him once Connor and the Davies wench were wed. The idea caused him to
become even more sullen, and it was a quiet group which
made its way to the ancient Irish fortress of Geata Neamhai.

When they reached the expanse of woods closest to his
former home, Hugh gladly parted company from his companions, declaring he would not enter the keep again until
it was in the O'Carroll's possession by one means or another, be it wedding or war. Just before disappearing, he
demanded Sheila send him word of Connor within the hour.
Then he set about finding a place amidst the trees that could
conceal his considerable bulk, and in so doing, discovered
Connor's horse.

The nearness of the animal and the distance of the fortress were visible reminders of Connor's unconventional
courtship, and they set an already disgruntled Hugh to
cursing beneath his breath. The business of Connor's
infatuation with the Englishwoman had done nothing but
cause upset in his own life, and most likely there were more
repercussions still to come.

Crouching in the brush, the breath of the horse fanning
the back of his neck, Hugh realized the irony of his situation. Here he was, worried about the possibility that Connor might not have safely penetrated the thick walls of
Geata Neamhai, and just as worried about the consequences if he had. Frustration building, the sturdy Irish
warrior vowed that if the English hadn't killed his friend
already, he might very well consider doing so himself.

Relieved that the troublesome Cassidy had been left behind, Gerard hailed the watch as he and Sheila approached

Regan's heavily guarded residence. At his summons, the drawbridge was lowered and the portcullis raised, but as Gerard set foot in the courtyard, Adams rushed to intercept him with such alacrity that the older man became truly alarmed for Regan's welfare and steeled himself to hear the worst.

For all his agitation, Adams had nothing to report other than finding evidence of an interloper during the night and admitting the failure of the household guard to locate such a person no matter how diligently they had searched. The revelation of their soldiers being found bound and gagged aroused little reaction in Adams's superior, who only heaved a sigh of relief that there was no indication as yet that anything had gone amiss.

Surprised by Gerard's tranquillity in the face of such information, Adams refused to step aside for him as he sought to make his way to the Great Hall.

"But don't you understand, sir, the walls were breached! Someone who doesn't belong gained entrance to the keep during the night!" the underling said, his voice rising in volume as he tried to impress the impassive Langston with the severity of the situation.

His patience already sorely tried and his head still pounding, Gerard had little desire to cosset this soldier and assuage his insecurities.

"Don't worry, Adams, it was probably just the O'Carroll," Regan's commander remarked offhandedly, anxious now to seek her out and learn what had transpired while he had been away.

"O'Carroll!" Adams burst out, shocked at the easy manner in which Gerard entertained such a possibility.

Despite Gerard's initial intentions, the man's overwrought disposition drew forth a word of comfort from his captain.

"There's no use in fretting, son. You'll find there will be many things in life you won't understand," he said, casting a sheepish look in Sheila's direction and proceeding with her to the Great Hall.

Striding into the capacious room, Gerard called for the serving maid and inquired as casually as he could concerning Regan's present whereabouts.

"I'm sure I don't know. She's not been in here this morning," the maid said, scurrying to fetch a goblet should the Englishman desire ale or wine.

"Then where has she been spending her time today?" Gerard asked sharply, his testiness halting the girl where she stood.

"How would I know such things, sir?" she replied, eyes downcast. "I am not the sort to engage in gossip."

"Of course, you're not," Sheila said, rushing forward with a knowing glance to soothe her countrywoman. "This gentleman and I know that. But we are also aware that talk among the household folk is not an unusual occurrence. Think carefully, girl. What was it you heard the others say as you went diligently about your tasks?"

"Well . . ." the young servant hesitated, "I think I might have heard some mention of the fact that the Lady Regan has kept to her rooms this morning...something about not having slept a wink last night."

"Ah, good lass," Sheila murmured, giving the girl an approving pat on the arm. "And as your reward, you may have a short respite from your labors. There is no need for you to remain here as Captain Langston will want to attend to Lady Regan immediately, reporting his return and assuring himself that it is indeed fatigue and not illness which keeps her confined to her chambers."

Ignoring Gerard's raised eyebrows, Sheila escorted the serving maid to the passageway leading to the courtyard and the kitchens beyond. Then she stood watching her go, until the confused but appreciative youngster had finally disappeared.

"Now," she said, turning to Gerard, "you must find out whether Connor is with Regan or not."

"*I* must find out!" Gerard questioned in disbelief. "Regan's refusal to leave her rooms informs me that Connor was indeed successful in seeing her last night. But I am still uncertain as to whether they have patched things up between them. The fact that she has so uncharacteristically taken to her bed could mean that Connor is with her still, or else that she is there alone, overcome with grief because of further quarreling. Truthfully, I would be hard-pressed to handle either scenario," Gerard said, gingerly raising his fingertips to his still-throbbing brow. "Don't you think that at a time like this, the girl requires a woman's touch?"

"Woman's touch indeed! How a man can be brave on the battlefield and yet frightened beyond belief when it comes to dealing with a distraught woman is incomprehensible to me," Sheila complained, throwing her hands in the air. "You brought the girl to this land. You can't abandon her now if she needs you."

"I'm not abandoning her!" Gerard objected, his pride wounded. "It's simply that I'm weary of being not only a father but a mother to Regan, as well. With things as they stand now, isn't that a job you should assume?" he asked, as his face, gray beard and all, grew boyishly hopeful.

"All right, you rapscallion," the redhead agreed, her laughter echoing in the empty hall. "I'll see to the lass...but not because of your winning ways, lad!"

"Then who was it persuaded you?" Gerard asked flirtatiously, employing all his courtly charm, assured there was but one answer.

"Hugh," Sheila responded, as Gerard's face fell.

"Hugh!" he roared. "Why, madam, there must be at least a score of years between you."

"Aye, Hugh," Sheila said, laughing once more. "You must realize that if I don't get a message to that great oaf soon, informing him that Connor is here and well, the hothead is likely to gather O'Carroll forces and besiege the keep. Now wait here until I return to you,'' Sheila commanded, still chuckling at the man's jealousy as she began climbing the tower stairs to Regan's rooms.

Seeing the guards posted outside, the castelain brushed them aside as if they were flies, telling them in the process that Gerard had ordered them to report to him in the Great Hall. Then, she opened the door of the outer room as noisily as she could and rapped at the entrance to the bedroom itself. She certainly had no wish to disturb the negotiations between the O'Carroll and Regan Davies should they be at a delicate state.

"Who is it?" she heard Regan's anxious voice call.

"'Tis only Sheila," she replied, praying that the girl was not alone in her bed.

"Then enter," ordered a familiar, masculine voice, causing Sheila to rejoice.

Sheila did not wait to be asked again. Ignoring Regan's softly uttered objections, she scurried into the chamber to find things as she hoped they would be.

"Sweet lambs," she crooned, taking in the sight of Regan's disheveled hair and Connor's self-satisfied smile. "I knew things would turn out as they should if you could but have some time together."

"Where's Gerard?" Regan asked nervously, bringing the sheets to her chin as she peered past Sheila's shoulder.

"The dear man is in the Great Hall awaiting word from me. As I think you might have an announcement to make, I suggest we go down and join him," the older woman said, all pretense at subtlety gone.

"Perhaps it would be better if he were to meet with us in the solar. I would dislike being slain by Regan's highly trained men before I reached the hall," Connor remarked, his voice full of amusement.

"Connor, they are not completely inept," Regan countered, holding fast to the sheet he was even now playfully tugging. "But still, I do think it best if we talk to Gerard away from the prying eyes of others."

"Aye, I'll summon him immediately," Sheila offered, her grin as wide as a crescent moon.

"See if you can detain him for just a bit," Connor ordered. "The countess seems to have misplaced her nightdress...again, and I'm certain she would like to be properly garbed before she sees Gerard, or rather before he sees her."

"Aye, milord. Just leave it to me. I've found new methods for managing Gerard Langston."

"What are they?" Regan inquired curiously.

"Nothing you could even imagine," Sheila replied as she slipped from the room. Now if only Gerard had already sent those guards on their way, and Tommy was nearby to be dispatched with a message to Hugh!

When she heard the outer door close, Regan looked at Connor, her large emerald eyes mirroring a sudden shyness. It was one thing to thrash about in this man's arms while caught up in the throes of passion during the black of the night, and another matter entirely to rise from her bed unclad before him in the light of day.

Subtly she adjusted a sheet around her, holding it in place as her long legs slid to the floor. Standing up, she was unsure of how she should proceed with Connor watching her so intently. "There's no need to hide your loveliness from me," the Earl of Kilcaid assured her tenderly, struggling not at all with his own modesty as he threw back the coverlet and came to join her. "I know your secrets, and am held captive by their charm."

The loving expression on his face eased Regan's feeling of discomfort, and she didn't resist as he gently took the sheet from around her and allowed it to fall at her feet. Then, with her permission, he withdrew her garments from the massive trunk at the foot of her bed, selecting a simple Irish gown of deep green, which would enhance her eyes. Bit by bit he dressed her, performing the task as gently as if she were some cherished child.

He draped a matching shawl over one shoulder and then took a moment to don his own tunic, removing his massive Celtic brooch and pinning it on Regan's garments. In his mind, she was already an O'Carroll and therefore should be dressed as one.

Next, he led her to a seat at the chamber's large desk, leaving her only as long as it took to fetch her stockings, garters and dainty shoes. Refusing to allow her to help, Connor placed them on her so seductively that Regan was ready to begin undressing again, so hotly did she desire this wondrous man.

Finally Connor produced Regan's comb and began applying it in long stroking movements to her glorious locks. While he served her, Regan had never felt so self-conscious nor so pampered. Though dressing that morning was something she would rather have done for herself, she yielded to Connor in the matter, bemused that so virile a man could play such a tender and considerate lady's maid.

Finishing, the Earl of Kilcaid kissed his lady softly and then placed the comb inside the desk. Suddenly he turned to her, full of curiosity.

"My inkstand isn't here," he informed her.

"Inkstand?" Regan asked as innocently as she could.

"Yes. It belonged to my grandsire, and I prize it highly. What did you do with it?"

"Oh . . . I moved it," she replied evasively, trying not to wince as she recalled hurling it out the window to the stone of the courtyard below. In self-defense, and with devilment in her eyes, Regan reached up to wrap her arms around Connor's neck, working to distract her beloved Irishman from his preoccupation with the things of the past, and helping him to concentrate on the future, instead.

* * *

"Woman, I can't believe you agreed that we'd join them to celebrate with a drink," muttered Gerard unhappily, his head and stomach still unsettled from the previous evening's activities. Too much had happened in the past twenty-four hours for the Englishman to be certain of anything anymore. But congratulating Connor O'Carroll after the devil had just spent the night in Regan's bed was expecting too much. "Damn it, what will I say to the man? Thank you for wedding her after you bedded her?"

"You did a fair share of speaking last night," the housekeeper murmured with a happy smile. "And, blessed be that ye did. What could be better than the two of them finally together and happy?"

"Rest for this weary body, for one thing," grumbled Regan's advisor and guardian as he followed Sheila up the tower stairs. Somehow, he realized with a groan, he was now in the position of answering to two women. Hell's everlasting fire, as much as he loved Regan, he wasn't sure he could handle this!

"Aye, the devil drink beset you, stealing away your slumber, didn't it then? I'll not be complaining," said Sheila with a wink. "Maybe you should take a nap before we retire tonight."

"I would have been off enjoying one right now, but for this foolishness of 'giving them my blessing.' I verily doubt that Connor O'Carroll waits with bated breath for that occurrence."

"In truth I suppose you gave him your consent when you said Regan loved him. Oh, isn't it grand?" rejoiced Sheila, already envisioning the babes she'd help to care for. "If the girls have her glorious hair and the boys have his frame, won't they be the most beautiful of children? Perhaps a Brendan for his father and, what was her mother's name?"

"Merciful heavens, woman, you'll be having me in my grave with all your silly dreams. They haven't even gotten the queen's permission to wed yet, and you're naming the babes?''

"That old biddy won't stop Connor from siring a tribe," began Sheila as the door to Regan's solar opened to her knock, and Connor stood there.

"Don't mind her, Gerard. This nurse of mine has always wanted to see me imitate her son Dennis and have ten young ones," drawled the Irishman lazily as the servants entered to find their mistress pouring brandy.

"Ten children?" echoed Regan in surprise.

"Aye, milady. Is there any wonder there wouldn't be room for me with him and his?" asked the housekeeper.

"I suspect the son is only as randy as his mother," said the earl with a broad grin, earning himself a playful slap from Regan.

"And what about my Patrick the priest?" questioned Sheila with a furious blush. "Don't I get any credit for my piety?"

"Piety? Is that what you call it in Ireland?" queried Gerard in a playfully innocent voice. Accepting a glass from Regan, he almost spilled it, trying so not to laugh, but Connor showed no such restraint.

In a moment the Irishman had discerned the situation and, while Regan looked on in puzzlement, Connor wagged his finger at Sheila and slapped Gerard on the back.

"That's why you came to camp, you sly dog, you. Unless Regan and I were reunited, you and Sheila would have had to remain enemies, as well," he reasoned, wrapping his arm around his lovely English countess and drawing her into his embrace.

"Well, they aren't really enemies," she qualified.

"No, definitely not," agreed Connor as the two in question reddened greatly but said nothing. "I think a more apt term is lovers."

"What?" cried Regan, looking to Gerard for confirmation. At his slight nod, she began to bubble happily. "Oh, isn't it wonderful? We both found joy here in Ireland."

"To the wonder of love, wherever and whenever in life it may be found," toasted Connor, raising his glass with a grin.

"To love," echoed his bride-to-be.

"Well, I don't know that I'd actually call it love," debated Gerard, holding his glass hesitantly in his embarrassment. "Perhaps an unexplained resurgence in the blood."

"Drink up, old man," instructed Sheila fondly. "And go take your nap. Then I'll show you love."

Before a flushed Gerard could reply, a sudden tapping at the door caused them all to fall silent.

"Yes?" said Regan questioningly as Connor slipped back into the bedchamber out of sight. "You may enter."

"I'm sorry to bother you, milady, but I wanted to inform Gerard that Thomas Watkins is at the gate seeking an audience with Lady Regan. Considering the trouble last night, the guards weren't certain you wanted any outsiders in the keep."

"Yes, ah, I've resolved that matter and will see Adams about it later," the commander explained. "As for admitting Watkins, that's up to her ladyship. He did say he'd return with any excuse, Regan."

"Yes, but he might have news from the queen." If the Englishman had new information, Regan wanted to know about it. "Annie, instruct the gatekeepers to send him in. Gerard, Sheila, if you'll make things ready, I will receive him in the Great Hall."

Nodding their agreement, the retainers followed Annie from the solar without comment, abandoning their half-empty glasses.

Perhaps a celebration had been premature, considered the Countess of Kilcaid, until she felt Connor's arms around her, enveloping her in a loving embrace. No, she decided silently, he was worth celebrating anytime.

"Don't worry, Connor," she instructed softly as he held her close. "I will be up to share what I learn as soon as I can get Watkins to leave."

"No."

"No? But, you can't think to go with me?" she protested, staring up into his deep blue eyes and knowing that was exactly what this determined man intended to do. "Connor, you can't let him see you—"

"And if you think I'll let him see you alone, you've lost more than your mind," he said, stroking her hair as he spoke. "There is no way in hell I'll permit you to meet that pompous fool while I sit and wonder what's happening."

"They say nothing is as bad as you ever imagine it will be," she cajoled, stealing a kiss. "I promise you, twenty minutes, no more, and Gerard will be there. I won't be alone."

"In that you're correct, but not because of Gerard. I won't allow this nonsense," he growled, breaking their embrace, and returning to the bedroom. A moment later he came back into the solar, buckling on his sword and slipping a dagger into his boot. "Now, either I go downstairs and hide myself out of sight before he arrives, or we keep arguing about it until Sheila comes to fetch you, and you enter the hall on my arm. I won't stay up here out of earshot like some nervous bridegroom."

"Well, I hadn't exactly intended on announcing our betrothal," she murmured, admiring the muscled strength of this man she now considered hers. Even his temper wasn't that bad when she realized he spoke from love.

"If it will keep scavengers like Watkins away," Connor ventured, "perhaps we should post notices on every tree and wall in the county. You haven't much time, Regan. Shall I be beside you openly or in the passageway leading to the kitchen behind you?"

As much as she would have delighted to shock Thomas
Watkins by entering the hall on Connor's arm, she was still
too prudent a woman to take a risk like that with the man
she loved.

"All right, the passageway, but be sure to stay out of
sight. I don't want to spend the evening binding wounds
when we have so many other delights to share," she whispered as he drew her close for one last kiss. Then he was
gone.

Chapter Sixteen

Needing a few minutes to compose herself, the Countess of Kilcaid sat quietly in her solar, reviewing with amazement the path her life had so recently taken. Where such a short time before she'd been outraged at her exile to the wilds of Ireland, at present she knew only inexpressible gratitude for the miraculous design that her days in this wondrous land had taken. Wordlessly, almost without conscious thought, she prayed that the current difficulty with Watkins would also resolve itself as being unworthy of her concern. Now that she and Connor had agreed on marriage, she wanted nothing to mar their future together, especially something as mundane as trouble with the neighbors.

With a longing glance at the bed they'd shared so happily that morning, Regan rose, smoothed her skirts and descended the stairs to the Great Hall. Forcing a tentative smile of welcome upon her unwilling lips, she prepared to meet her guest and be rid of his unwanted presence as quickly as possible. Yet her foot had only crossed the threshold of the Great Hall when her soft green eyes darkened and her cheeks brightened in fury at the sight that confronted her.

Not only was Thomas Watkins enjoying her hospitality, but so were a dozen of his armed guards, stationed at regular intervals around the room as Gerard argued with the man himself. How dare her neighbor bring men in here equipped for battle as they were?

Oh, dear Lord, could he possibly know Connor was here? Fear made her voice sharp and her anger unrelenting as she confronted the master of Wren's Nest.

"Sir Thomas! What is the meaning of this outrage? Since when do you bring soldiers and their weaponry into *my* hall?" demanded the mistress of Heaven's Gate. Hands on her slender hips, she stood mere inches from Watkins as she challenged him, praying at the same time that Connor was truly well hidden.

"Your ladyship, I mean no insult, believe me," the undersized nobleman defended, his nervous smile further infuriating his hostess.

"Then why have them inside my home? They should wait in the courtyard with your coach—unless you believe that I will attack you?" said Regan indignantly.

"Oh, heavens no, milady," gushed Watkins, grabbing her right hand and bringing it to his lips in an unwelcome gesture of obsequiousness. Though thoroughly perplexed and put off by the Irish garb she wore, it wouldn't be wise to reveal his distaste. "Not for anything in the world would I ever dream of offending you, my lovely lady. No, no, never. As I was waiting at the gate, however, I couldn't help but notice the consternation my arrival caused. Someone explained that you'd had some trouble last night—"

"It has been resolved," said Regan coldly as she reclaimed her hand from the Englishman's grasp, resisting the almost overwhelming urge to wipe it on her gown.

"In the courtyard, some of your tenants were talking about an intruder who might still be at large in the keep," continued the small man in brown. "As I was just telling Langston here, I thought perhaps you might wish my men to conduct a thorough search." Glancing furtively about the room, Watkins left no doubt as to whose safety concerned him most.

"That won't be necessary, Sir Thomas," stated Gerard, entering the conversation for the first time since Regan had arrived. "Actually, there was no stranger within our walls at all. A few of the guards enjoyed too much ale before going on duty, fell asleep, and when they awakened, mistook a cloak tossed carelessly over a barrel for a villain intent on mischief. Needless to say, they will no longer be drinking or standing guard on this estate, but you have no need to fear for your welfare while at Heaven's Gate," assured Regan's commander.

"Really, it would be no trouble for my fellows to look about, just in case," offered Watkins again. "They are here anyway."

"Absolutely not," stressed the Countess of Kilcaid and Westfield in her most regal tones. "I have full confidence in my own staff and do not need your insinuations that they are incompetent. Frankly, I would feel more at ease if these guards of yours were to wait outside. I have never countenanced armed men inside my hall, and I do not intend to start now."

Gerard gave her a warning glance and Regan feared a moment that her words had been too strong; did Watkins perhaps suspect her of concealing Connor? She couldn't very well ask.

"Of course, Lady Regan, as you please," conceded the master of Wren's Nest unhappily. He hadn't expected the presence of his men to cause such a problem, but then, the reactions of women were never easily predictable, he'd found. Still, in this case, his own safety was a factor. "With your permission, perhaps two or three might remain?"

"Oh, very well, no more than three," yielded Regan at Gerard's imperceptible nod. Already too fussed to make a further issue of the matter, she wanted Watkins to speak his piece and be gone. All this delay was beginning to unnerve her since with each passing moment she anticipated Connor's sudden angry appearance a bit more. He had promised to stay hidden, but she had little doubt that should his temper rage at something he heard, Connor O'Carroll would not be able to resist showing himself.

Quickly issuing the command to nine of his men to await him in the courtyard, Sir Thomas mopped his brow and sank onto a nearby stool, disregarding the fact that his hostess was still standing.

"Well, sir, what is this urgent topic you wished to bring before her ladyship?" asked Gerard impatiently. He too had begun to worry about Connor's reaction to this fool, and wanted the interview concluded speedily.

"A subject I would discuss with her—and her alone," said Watkins haughtily. Having surrendered in the matter of his men, he was not about to converse with underlings about what could well mean his future happiness. Regan Elizabeth Davies and her purse were the targets of his heart and he couldn't properly engage her gratitude or her appreciation, hopefully a step toward courtship, with her guardian at hand criticizing him.

"You see the need to surround yourself with armed men, but dispute my right to have my advisor present?" questioned Regan in surprise. For a little man, he possessed an amazing degree of effrontery.

"It is all right, Regan," counseled Gerard. "I will take Watkins's men to the other side of the hall and we will wait there, in clear view, should either of you want us. Certainly that would afford you the privacy you require, Sir Thomas."

"Yes, my good fellow, thank you." Abruptly realizing his hostess was still on her feet, Watkins stood and bowed ceremoniously in the direction of her chair.

"Thank you for your consideration, Sir Thomas," Regan said dryly, "but I prefer to stand, especially since I have little time. Numerous other matters require my attention this day."

"Oh, of course. I too have business to attend, but I felt it imperative to bring you my news," said the master of Wren's Nest, nodding his head at the wisdom of his decision. "Before I deliver it, however, I would like to state that being a responsible landlord is quite a heavy undertaking, especially for one so lovely as yourself. I want you to be aware that I would be more than happy to advise you, at any time."

"I wouldn't think to trouble you, sir. Gerard Langston and Sheila Dempsey have sufficient experience between them to settle most any issue," replied Regan, remembering the intimidated servants she'd seen at his estate. With this insecure weasel in charge, no wonder they were unhappy in their chores.

"But, my dear woman, they are not noble as we are, and therefore have no concept of true leadership or quality," gushed her visitor, again bestowing a widemouthed grin on Regan. "I believe, joining together, you and I might—"

"Together, Sir Thomas? I have no plans to merge Heaven's Gate with anyone else's property, and, right now, it is a matter of honor that *I* manage it as best *I* can," snapped the young Englishwoman, putting a quick end to the discussion. "Now then, tell me what word you've received from the queen."

Surprised at the young countess's dismissal of his suit, Watkins blinked rapidly a few times, trying to gather his wits about him. Perhaps . . . yes, undoubtedly, he decided, the poor thing was so nervous about O'Carroll that she couldn't think clearly enough to appreciate what he was offering her. He decided to soothe her fears. Moving to her side and once again taking her hand, he enclosed it within his two, patting and stroking it as he spoke.

"Ah, my dear child, I apologize for distracting you from my main purpose. Of course, your first concern must be that renegade, but be glad. In a very short time, I assure you, he will no longer be around to trouble you."

"He won't?" What had Elizabeth said to make Watkins so certain of himself? Distressed by his words and more so by his touch, Regan tried to extricate her fingers from his grasp by moving backward, but he merely accompanied her, continuing to clutch her hand tightly to his breast.

"No, milady, he will be long gone from here, one way or another, once the royal decree is posted," the Englishman promised with a grating chuckle.

"One way or another?"

"Aye, her majesty increased the reward for O'Carroll, all right, but she did more than that," teased Watkins, inordinately pleased at the unblinking attention Regan was awarding him. Finally it seemed she had come to appreciate his worth, and he rejoiced.

"Well, aren't you going to tell me the worst? I mean, the rest?" demanded the increasingly nervous young woman. As if the knowledge that Connor was hearing and possibly seeing this meeting weren't bad enough, she had to drag the story from Watkins. Yanking her hand back from its captor, she unconsciously brought it to her mouth and began to gnaw on her forefinger in agitation. What more could Elizabeth have done?

"You seem so perturbed, Lady Regan, perhaps I should discuss this with Langston, after all. He is more accustomed to the ugly side of life," speculated the colorless mouse before her.

"Sir Thomas, *I* am the mistress of Heaven's Gate and, unpleasant or not, I demand to know what Elizabeth has in store for the former owner of these lands!" cried Regan anxiously.

"Very well. The devil will have but two choices. There is the possibility of a pardon, but to earn it, he must surrender, renounce all claim and kinship to Ireland, and be joined in matrimony to a widowed dowager in Northumberland. Or if he chooses to remain outside the law, then once the black-hearted scoundrel is taken, and I assure you, with a price of one hundred guineas on his head, that will be soon, he is to be hanged by the neck until dead and his head mounted on a pike. That way other Irish rebels may take fair warning of the fate that awaits them for their sins," said Watkins with glee.

"What?" exclaimed Regan in horror.

So pleased was he at the gruesome punishment that was planned for O'Carroll, Watkins was totally unprepared for Regan's outburst of tears.

"Oh, oh, my dear child," he gushed, putting his arms around her and enveloping her in a clumsy embrace. Though her head towered over him, he attempted to pull it down to rest on his bony shoulder, patting her all the while and crooning softly. "There, there, Regan, I am certain you need not watch the villain's death," he assured comfortingly. "I daresay there will be plenty of other more willing witnesses."

"And I promise you there will not," said Connor loudly. Jerking the man off his feet as he yanked him away from Regan, the Irishman tossed his neighbor into a trembling heap on the stone floor. After assuring himself that concern for him was her only ailment, Connor thrust Regan behind him and turned to meet the guards who approached from the other side of the room.

"Regan, stay out of the way," he instructed curtly, taking up his keen-edged sword and preparing to do battle.

She nodded her agreement but, acting on an impulse, grabbed the dagger from his boot as he passed, knowing all the while she could never sit idly and do nothing to help him. Keeping an eye on Watkins, who had swooned at his sudden confrontation with the O'Carroll, she watched the man she loved leap onto the broad wooden planks that formed the dining table and begin simultaneously parrying thrusts with two of Watkins's men.

Across the hall, Gerard had engaged the third fellow in his own contest, years of personal combat allowing him to spar

and feint like a youth, using the other's size as a weapon
against him. Regan watched him but a moment, knowing
Gerard would easily handle the threat he faced. Then, realizing that more guards might enter at any moment, she
moved quickly to the door and barred the entrances to the
Great Hall just as shouts were heard in the corridor. Then,
holding the dagger on the still-unconscious Watkins should
he awaken, she split her attention between the unmoving
Englishman and her Connor.

The O'Carroll was a man possessed as he danced his way
down the long table, answering the challenges right and left
without hesitation till finally he knocked the sword out of
one man's grasp, jumped from the table and landed on him,
sending him hard into the floor and, with a swift stroke of
his sword, to eternal reward. Connor hesitated but an instant, momentarily favoring his weak leg. Then, noting that
Gerard had already dispatched with his opponent, the
Irishman let his eyes scan the room as he sought his other
adversary.

"Behind you, Connor, there," cried Regan as Watkins's
man sprang at her beloved. Swiveling around beneath the
carefully aimed blow, Connor came in under the soldier's
sword arm and put an end to the threat the man had posed.

By now the clamor at the door was considerable; Connor
could not delay any longer or he'd be taken prisoner for
certain. Hastily he drew Regan into a heartfelt embrace and
kissed her soundly.

"Know this, my sweeting, I will wed no woman but you,
regardless of Elizabeth's decree. You are the one who holds
my heart, and always will," he said firmly, not caring in the
least that Gerard overheard his declaration of love.

"O'Carroll, you'd best go at once," the older man urged.
"Any moment they'll be in from the north stairs."

"I'm going, too, Gerard," Regan announced quietly.
"There's little for me here without Connor."

"No," refused her dark-haired lover.

"She's right, Connor. Watkins will only charge her with harboring you and then she'll have to answer for your crimes. While Sidney might delay action, it will be difficult for a while."

"Taking her along will brand her an outlaw," Connor argued, yearning to have Regan with him but unwilling to put her in such a precarious situation.

"Not if I say she was abducted," replied Gerard. "Who's to say she wasn't? Watkins? He hasn't yet revived from his faint. His guards? They won't talk again. She'll be in less danger with you than here with me. Go ahead, lad, I couldn't live with her if you left her behind," Gerard urged, seeing the hesitancy in the Irishman's eyes.

"If you leave me behind, I'll only follow," Regan promised.

A sharp crack of the wooden door to the corridor left him no choice and, fearing for her safety more than his own life, Connor grabbed Regan's hand and hurried her down the passageway to the kitchen.

Sword drawn, eyes alert to any movement, he came to a halt just outside the main kitchen and held Regan close, listening for the sound of conversation or crockery. But all was silent. Apparently everyone was out in the courtyard or trying to break into the Great Hall.

"Now, listen carefully, I want you to act as if nothing is out of the ordinary. You are just going to your stables to order your carriage out for Watkins's inspection. Everyone knows how taken he is with the damnable things. If you're asked, two of Watkins's men insulted each other's parentage and that was the reason for the ruckus in the hall." Gently squeezing her shoulder, he planted a whisper-light kiss on her neck and urged her onward. "I'll be with you every step of the way, I promise."

"I'd never doubt you, my lord," she returned solemnly. Then, a quick smile and she was out in the bright sunshine of the courtyard.

There were women and children about, but all of the men were gathered by the stairs of the main tower, clustered together, muttering among themselves and speculating on the excitement. Watkins's coach stood abandoned, his men apparently trying to rescue him, and Regan slipped past the conveyance without incident. Then, it happened. Tommy saw her and called out so that everyone turned to look.

"Lady Regan, thank heavens you're all right. Someone said you had been attacked in the hall, but I didn't believe that, not with the O'Carroll here to protect you. Oh—" broke off the lad, suddenly aware of what he had revealed.

"Really, Tommy, what an imagination you have! The O'Carroll here? God defend us from such a plight. I'm fine and, while I do believe Gerard has everything under control inside, perhaps you'd lead the men into the Great Hall by way of the kitchen passage, just to be certain?" suggested the Countess of Kilcaid, praying no one else would notice Connor, standing in the shadows.

"Of course, milady. Everyone, this way," shouted the youth with a nod in Regan's direction. As she started to move on toward the tunnel, however, a cry came from the kitchens as Watkins's contingent spotted the man dressed as an Irish chieftain pressed against the wall. At his shout, the others turned and reentered the courtyard at full speed.

"Hurry, Regan, run like the devil," called Connor, taking her by the arm. In an instant, he had his sword drawn again, ready to fight off the English if need be to save the only thing he really treasured, his love.

But as Regan reached the door to the passageway and opened it, amazed at the absence of a guard, Adams confronted her, hand on his own drawn weapon.

"Don't worry, milady, I won't let the devil take you with him," the soldier promised as Connor slammed the door behind him and bolted it against those who followed. "It was on my watch the villain got in last night, but I swear he won't get past me now."

"No, Adams, you don't understand," protested Regan. "You've got to let him go or he'll be killed."

"That's what I said, Lady Regan. I'll kill him before I let him leave here with you," reiterated the young soldier, brandishing his sword in Connor's direction, "and nothing would give me greater pleasure."

"You're making a bad mistake," warned Connor quietly. Half-crouched in the small height of the tunnel, he balanced on the balls of his feet and circled around the Englishman, making him twist and turn to keep Connor in sight. With a small wave of his hand, Connor motioned Regan to start down the passageway, and as Adams's attention followed her, the Irishman sped forward, lifted his opponent off his feet with a single blow to the jaw and slammed him against the tunnel door. About to hit him again, he felt Regan's touch on his arm.

"He was only protecting me, Connor," she said softly. "In other circumstances, you'd reward the man."

"Aye, woman, but these aren't other circumstances," he muttered angrily, dropping his fist nonetheless. "All right then, it's time we took our leave of Heaven's Gate for a while. Move quickly or Watkins's men will be waiting for us at the other end of the tunnel," he cautioned, fully aware of just how rapidly the portcullis could be raised and the drawbridge lowered when necessary.

But time and perhaps Gerard were on their side, they discovered, when they exited the tunnel to find no welcoming party. Though shouts rang out from the walls, no arrows came in their direction. As Connor hurried Regan toward the woods where his horse was waiting, the Irishman heard Langston's voice echoing from the ramparts.

"No one let fly an arrow on pain of death! You might hit the Lady Regan, and I won't take that chance."

"Good man, Gerard," he murmured to himself. "That will assure Regan's safety a while longer."

The noise from the keep subsided somewhat as they reached the edge of the woods, but Connor wouldn't let Regan tarry. Urging her along at a quick pace, despite the twinge in his thigh, he followed behind, watching for signs of pursuit. It was only Regan's sudden gasp that turned his attention forward, his sword ready to defend her.

"Oh," she cried as Hugh stepped out of the shadows to grab her. For a moment she'd thought him one of Watkins's scouts and feared all their efforts in escaping the keep were for naught. Even when she recognized Connor's friend, however, she knew little sense of relief.

"I thought you might be needing a hand, Connor," the giant explained as he tossed Regan onto O'Carroll's horse with no outward show of effort. Holding her in place on the saddle while Connor sheathed his sword and prepared to mount, Cassidy warned her softly.

"Keep that pretty little mouth closed tight, milady. We don't need no extra noise from you yelling for help."

"But—" she began.

"Don't you understand me?" he growled harshly, covering her mouth with his huge hand. "No noise."

At her slight nod, he released her head and moved aside for Connor.

Then the former earl was seated behind her, reins in his able control, and they were off. Regan realized suddenly she was astride a horse in a gown gathered high above her knees, clasped tightly to the chest of a renegade she loved, as they tried to escape legitimate pursuit. Somehow, she acknowledged shakily, in the past twelve hours, Regan Elizabeth Davies had changed from a loyal plantation owner to the willing accomplice of a recognized enemy of the Crown, a man with a price on his head. Trembling slightly at the black picture Watkins would undoubtedly present to Elizabeth, she tried to put it from her mind, concentrating instead on regaining her breath and keeping her balance on the moving horse.

Sensing her sudden attack of nerves, the dark-haired Irishman leaned forward slightly so his lips were close to her ear, his words meant for her alone.

"I do love you, Regan. If you trust in anything, trust in that," he whispered softly, depositing a tender kiss on the nape of her neck as he repeated himself. "I love you. I have since that first day in the woods. It's a fact, one I was afraid to admit, even to myself, until last night, but a fact nonetheless."

She tried to turn to answer him, but the horses had begun crossing a rushing stream and Connor had no concentration for anything but maneuvering the animal across the slippery rocks. Content, she settled herself quietly in his comforting embrace, contemplating his sweet words.

"Since the first day in the woods," he'd said, when he had been playing at being Watkins. Indeed, were she to analyze her feelings, Regan considered, she'd been intrigued by his presence that day... and most every day since.

She wasn't certain of what love was supposed to be, the young woman reflected; she'd once thought she'd found it with Dudley, but now the truth of the matter was what she'd confessed to Connor. That episode had no more been love than she had been queen. However, she realized with total conviction that her actions this afternoon were right. Despite the unlawful appearance, she was absolutely certain that her place was beside Connor, wherever he happened to be.

As Connor and Hugh brought their horses to a halt, Regan turned around to convey her joy to Connor and was startled at the heavy hands that suddenly encircled her waist and deposited her on the ground, only to grab her upper arm in such a tight grip that it made her flinch. She didn't even have to look to know that it was Hugh, not Connor, who had hold of her.

"Master Cassidy, I would appreciate it if you would be so good as to release me," she requested politely, determined not to be a source of friction between Hugh and Connor.

"Release you, lady? Not without a pretty penny in ransom, I won't," laughed the big man, a sound beginning deep in his chest and growing heavier and broader until it escaped his mouth as thunder. "Why do you suppose Connor brought you with him? Not for pleasure, I warrant, though he might have you believing so. Do you hear this woman, old friend? Release her, indeed?"

"That I do, Hugh. Unhand her at once, she is not a prisoner here," stated the earl as he dismounted and handed the reins to one of the men who approached.

"What?" Just when he'd decided Connor had finally come to his senses about the English, the Earl of Kilcaid abruptly destroyed Hugh's bright illusion.

"I said, let Lady Regan go. She is my guest," stressed Connor, taking her hand and leading her down the path to camp.

"Guest? Aye, that's a good one, O'Carroll," roared his lieutenant, unwilling to accept Connor's words as truth. "And just how much do you think this guest of yours is worth? The price of Geata Neamhai, perchance?"

Regan stopped walking, stunned at the giant's remark; how could this man imply such a thing? After last night she knew Connor had given up any such thoughts...didn't she? Exhausted from lack of sleep and overly emotional from the events of the past two days, Regan found herself unable to reason clearly. In her weakened state, she had become vulnerable to the doubts planted by Hugh Cassidy and they beset her like tormenting demons, her mind too tired to cast them out.

"Just ignore the man, Regan. He can be rather dense at times," explained her blue-eyed Irishman, smiling down at her though his eyes flashed in exasperation at Cassidy's behavior. Quickly he moved to the man's side and began to speak quietly, shaking his head and gesturing at the giant's responses.

Try as she might to disregard them, Hugh's words had struck a nerve in Regan's heart as she recalled Connor's angry question after their first lovemaking. "Then you'll give up your claim to Geata Neamhai?" echoed anew in her mind and she felt her old doubts bubbling to the surface.

Could she have been wrong? Was this still a game to him, just a means to an end, an end whereby he owned Geata Neamhai and she was the fugitive? Suddenly her eyes filled with tears and she was unable to halt their flow, so uncertain was she of the direction in which her life was headed.

"Regan, Regan, my sweeting, what happened?" cried Connor anxiously, abandoning his talk with Hugh as he observed her distress. When she didn't reply but wept all the more, he decided the shocks of the afternoon must have unnerved her, despite her apparent strength. Gathering her slender form up in his arms, he marveled at her fragility, carrying her easily to the main camp and sending the women there scurrying for a blanket and brandy.

Moments later she was in the cool shade of a tree with Connor beside her, growing more anxious with each passing moment.

"Darling, you nursed me back to health after my wound. Now, it's my turn," he whispered softly, stroking her hair gently. "Here, drink a bit of this brandy. It'll put color back in those cheeks and give you the strength to tell me what's wrong. If I don't know, my love, I can't settle the matter."

"One question, Connor, just one," she murmured softly, her heart on fire with painful doubts.

"Of course, Regan, anything."

"How did I come to be here, in your camp, I mean?"

"Did you hit your head? Don't you remember the fight in the Great Hall?" he asked anxiously, gently running his fingers over her skull in search of a bump. When he found none, he frowned in mystification, but took her hand in his and decided to answer her query. "Afterward, you insisted that you wanted to come with me, though I believed you'd be better off at Heaven's Gate, until Gerard reminded me of the political condemnation you'd suffer."

"So, you brought me here to protect me?" she asked softly, looking up at him with tear-filled eyes. "Not as a means to capturing Heaven's Gate?"

"Perdition," he exclaimed furiously. "I brought you here, Regan Davies, because I love you, with or without that damned pile of stone and mortar. I thought we'd settled this all last night!"

"I thought so, too," she said sadly, her smile a wan imitation of pleasure. "But, Hugh—"

"Damn that jackanape. He knew I was coming to you last night, not that he approved, but that's not his place," growled Connor in an ominous voice. "What's he done now?"

"He's acting like I'm your prisoner, the way he talked about getting the keep back by ransoming me for it. I—I guess I was afraid to believe otherwise. I mean, he's so big—"

"Size doesn't guarantee either intelligence or wisdom, let alone common sense, Regan, as I am about to demonstrate. Cassidy, Hugh Cassidy," the former earl bellowed angrily. "Get your ugly hide over here, now!"

"Aye, Connor," answered the man sullenly. "What did ye want?"

"Fetch me writing paper and ink," demanded Connor without explanation.

In a moment the supplies were before him and he began to write surely and without hesitation, the words flowing easily from his quill as Regan watched in silence. When he'd finished, the raven-haired Irishman enjoined the rest of the camp to gather around them. Handing the paper to Hugh, he commanded it be read aloud while he sat back down be-

ide Regan, wrapping his arm around her shoulders and
olding her hands gently in his.

"Well, Hugh, get on with it," he prompted.

"'I, Connor O'Carroll,'—you should be reading this,
Connor, not me," protested the large man, uncomfortable
t the suspicion that Connor was about to teach him a les-
on, again.

"Read what is written there, Hugh. Everyone knows I
vrote it, but I want you to proclaim it," he demanded
arshly. "There will be no misunderstanding that way."

With a growl of dismay, Hugh frowned at the sight of
Connor and Regan so close together, but complied with the
rder.

"'I, Connor O'Carroll, of free mind and free will, do
ereby on this eighth day of July, in the year 1567, before
ny kinsmen and friends, herewith relinquish all manner of
laim and title, past, present and future to the properties
previously known as Geata Neamhai. Henceforth, it shall be
nown as Heaven's Gate, owned by Regan Elizabeth Da-
ies.'"

Suddenly his voice broke and his broad shoulders
lumped in disgust as Hugh fell silent. Every man and
voman gathered around knew the horror he felt as they
vondered what their leader was doing.

"Continue reading, Hugh," instructed O'Carroll in a
ofter voice, yet one that brooked no disobedience all the
ame. If it was the last thing he did, he would make Hugh
ealize the depth of his feelings for Regan. Looking down at
er, the small smile on her parted lips and the shiny glow of
er eyes told him she was as pleased by his gesture as Hugh
vas dismayed. Nodding at the big man, he motioned to the
vritten notice.

"'When said woman does me the honor of becoming my
vife, I hereby swear that these lands will remain hers and
ers alone until they are deeded to her sons. The only trea-
ure, I, Connor O'Carroll, desire in this world is the undy-

ing love of my bride to be. With that I will be rich enough
and desire nothing more.' "

In the complete silence that fell on the clearing as Hugh
finished, Connor repeated his proposal.

"Regan, will you share my life, not as prisoner or over
seer of my lands, but as my wife and only love?"

"Yes."

It was a small word, softly said, but it ended her tears and
her doubts, making her feel cherished and warm as she ac
cepted his commitment to her. Given the effort he'd made
to prove his love, Regan knew she could do no less.

Standing up, she walked to where Hugh stood and re
moved the paper from his hand. Holding it aloft for all to
see, the English beauty tore the page in half and gave the
pieces to Connor amid the cheers of his followers.

"My lord, I need no document to testify to your love,"
she said gently. "Whatever I have, I give to you, now and
forever."

Contending with the excited jabbering of the Irishmen
gathered around them, Connor whispered quietly in her ear

"I'll hold you to that offer a bit later when we're alone."

"Gladly, sir," Regan laughed, secure once more of her
place in his heart.

Then, all at once, everyone in camp pressed forward to
congratulate them, child and adult alike, until only Hugh
remained.

"Connor, is this truly what you want?" he asked awk
wardly, unable to meet his friend's gaze.

"Aye, Hugh, more than I've ever wanted anything,"
confessed the nobleman in a strong voice.

"Then all that remains is for me to wish you well," con
cluded Hugh gruffly. "Lady Regan, my apologies. I—
didn't know he was really serious about this love thing. I
started out as a game—"

"You don't have to regale her with boring history,"
snapped Connor, embarrassed that Regan should be re

minded of his early schemes of courtship for ulterior motives.

"It's all right, Hugh. Connor told me how he fell into his own trap of seduction," said Regan, bestowing a warm smile on the giant who cared so deeply for his friend. "I only hope that it's deep enough to keep him ensnared for life."

"I fear that it is, milady," mourned Hugh sadly to their immediate delight. As Regan and Connor chuckled heartily at his woebegone expression, the huge Irishman repeated, "I fear it is, indeed."

Chapter Seventeen

Despite his grudging resignation to Regan's permanence in Connor's life, Hugh proved his strong organizational skills when his fellows prodded him into orchestrating a celebration feast for the newly betrothed couple. Though he did not himself participate in the merriment, food and drink appeared as if by magic, while music filled the air as songs of love and youth were recalled from happier days. Amazed at the lighthearted cheer demonstrated by men, women and children alike, Regan questioned the O'Carroll as they sat apart from the others.

"Don't they resent me? I mean, it's because of my taking Heaven's Gate that they're exiled to these woods."

"It was not a personal decision on your part to dispossess me or them," he corrected gently. "We accept what happened as fate. Sometimes it's not very agreeable, but that's the way it is."

"But, certainly, it can't be a joyous experience, living in the wilds instead of a proper cottage?" Regan asked, watching a particularly intricate dance some of the youngsters were performing, their faces a study in concentration.

"Why not?" queried Connor quizzically. "They have their families with them and their friends. They're fed and given the chance to work. Yes, I suppose their immediate comforts might be greater if they were back in their own homes. However, what is comfort compared to freedom?

Would you return to the keep if it meant never being able to see me again?''

"You know I wouldn't," the blonde at his side answered quickly. "But what of the English patrols? Aren't we in danger of discovery with the noise and the music?"

"Nay, my love, remember we've been at large for nearly four months, and while times weren't often as good as now, our system of false trails and lookouts keep us almost invisible," the Irishman assured her, reclining with his head in her soft lap.

The setting sun cast its last rays, highlighting the devilment in his eyes, making them a deeper and more vibrant blue, until Regan felt she could see into his soul. A man with many cares, she reflected, lifting a dark lock from his forehead and kissing the furrow it had concealed, but few so great as his concern for his people—which brought her back to their current dilemma.

"What happens next, Connor? Not that I'm not content to be here, but—"

"Well, I am glad to hear that," said the Earl of Kilcaid, sitting up and motioning Hugh to join them. "I wouldn't want you to be unhappy while I'm gone."

"Gone?" echoed Regan as Connor's lieutenant hunkered down next to them.

"Gone where?" demanded the big man.

"The only way I'm going to clear my name and get the queen's permission to marry you is to do what I should have done months ago," explained Connor, taking her hand in his, already anticipating her objections even before he finished. "I must go to England and see Elizabeth."

"No," Regan protested immediately. "With that new reward posted for your capture, it's too dangerous for you to travel to London . . . and for what?"

"Aye, much as I hate to agree with her ladyship, such a trip isn't worth the risk," concurred Hugh. "You wanted her, so you won her, Connor. Live with her here in camp and be satisfied with that. Why do you need the English queen's permission to wed? It means nothing, whether she approves or not."

"If Elizabeth hears of our union through other sources, she could be angry enough to declare Regan a fugitive of the court, as well," said Connor, his voice deep with worry. "It's better that I see the queen first and prevent that."

"And what if you do manage to see her and she won't give her permission, Connor?" questioned Regan anxiously. "You don't expect her majesty's men to let you just walk out of court when the queen has demanded your head."

"For that matter, ye might never live long enough to get past the guards in the first place," scowled his lieutenant. "What you need is a spokesman to plead your case."

"Like me," interjected the Countess of Westfield and Kilcaid. "I'm certain I could get an audience. I've still got friends at court."

"Your friends didn't stand behind you to prevent your banishment," an exasperated Connor retorted, annoyed at the opposition he faced on both sides. "Thank you, my love, but Walter Ashcroft, third Earl of Kenwick, has long been a staunch Irish sympathizer and a good friend. I have no doubt that he'd happily arrange an audience for me and lend me his protection should I need it."

"If I were with you, you'd not need anyone else's assistance," insisted Regan. "Elizabeth did once care for me—"

"Aye, and for the O'Carroll as well, but look where that's gotten him," snapped Hugh, irritated by Connor's sudden independence. For years the two of them had struggled and fought side by side, yet, with the English witch's arrival, that bond had been severed, and Hugh Cassidy didn't like it one bit. "Damn it, Connor O'Carroll, you can't honestly mean to go off on your own and leave me to nursemaid your woman, do you?"

"I do not need a nursemaid," snapped Regan, stung by Hugh's resentment even though she rejected Connor's plan just as much as he did.

"Not only Regan, but our people need someone they can trust while I'm away," stated the O'Carroll firmly, ignoring his lady's comment. "I must know they are well cared for in my absence and, heaven forbid, should I not return, Hugh Cassidy, you're the only man among them who could keep them together."

"And if I were there at your right hand on this wild-goose chase, there'd be no question of your surviving. Between us we've been known to rout two dozen men or more at a time," thundered the mountainous Irishman, rising to his full height. "If you go to London, so do I. There's no price on my head."

"Damn it all, Hugh, am I wrong or didn't you swear fealty to do *my* will, not your own?" demanded Connor, jumping to his feet so quickly with fists clenched that Regan feared the men would come to blows any second.

"Connor, I don't believe that now is the time to settle this," she said softly, batting her eyes and placing herself between the two men. "Why don't you and I go for a walk and give Hugh time to collect himself?"

"Collect myself—" began the giant, spoiling for a fight. Connor had taught him one lesson earlier in the evening; now it was his turn to return the favor.

"Hugh," Regan addressed him in a serious tone, even as she sent a different message with a playful wink. "I think the friendship you share with Connor is too deep for the both of you to rush haphazardly into a situation which will affect so many lives. While Connor and I discuss our matters, maybe you could think of an alternative plan that would not be so danger ridden."

Why did her gentle voice and tremulous smile remind him of his mother's soft-spoken rebukes, pondered the Irishman as he exchanged startled glances with Connor. She might be right though, Hugh decided reluctantly, having had a great deal of experience with Connor's humors. Some time apart might cool them both down.

"Aye, all right then. We'll talk later," he muttered, turning on his heel and stalking away before Connor could reply. *But whether I travel with you or not*, he added to himself, *I'll not let you risk your life for an English witch. That's a fact time won't alter.*

"Saints above, woman, why did you have to interfere?" demanded Connor crossly as he strode away from Regan. "The next thing you know it'll be all over the county that I'm a henpecked male, tied to his woman's apron strings."

"Henpecked then, is it?" laughed Regan, moving toward him and standing on her toes to reach his face. *If that's what he thought*, she decided, *then she'd make it so.* Once in position, she began to rain quick darting kisses all over his cheeks, his nose, his chin, everywhere but his lips, which quickly began to twitch in amusement at her antics. "Do hens peck like this—or this?" she demanded. "Or like this?"

"The devil take the hens, you saucy little wench. I like you more like this," he whispered, his voice already hoarsened by her game playing. Pulling her close to him, he enjoyed the splendid curve of her buttocks against his palms as his lips captured hers in a ravenous demand for satisfaction. Happily, she complied.

Later, breathless and content as her successful ploy of sensual distraction enveloped her in its afterglow, Regan nuzzled against Connor on the soft grass of the secluded meadow far from camp. Alone on Mother Nature's fragrant carpet, they held on tightly and dispelled the darkness surrounding them with the shiny brightness of their love.

But no matter how much Connor wanted to ignore the world around them, he eventually felt it necessary to return to the topic of London.

"Regan, you must know how much you mean to me," he began, watching the apprehension invade her eyes as she understood his direction. "You are the earth and the stars to me. I cannot take a chance on anything happening to steal you away. It's just too dangerous for you to come to London."

"If it's too dangerous for me, then it's too dangerous for you, as well," she argued. "I'll not abide two different measures in our love."

"This isn't about measuring the depths of our feelings. I don't want to see you hurt or captured," Connor tried to explain, running his hand across her silky tresses.

"No more than I want to see anything of the sort happen to you," refuted his woman. "Besides, if we went together and presented a united front to Elizabeth, you saying you'll respect English sovereignty and me promising to keep Heaven's Gate under the Crown's dominion, what can she say?"

"She could reclaim the lands from you and award them to another English noble who'd carry out her wishes without making conditions," the Earl of Kilcaid responded. "The Virgin Queen won't take kindly to one of her subject's choosing an Irish husband, believe me, my sweet. Indeed, if she knew your purpose in seeking an audience, I warrant she'd confiscate your holdings at once."

"We could always say that you had already forced me into marriage. She couldn't take Heaven's Gate away from us then."

"I thought you feared for my safety?" asked Connor, shaking his head in amazement at the way her mind worked. "Your scheme could bring me death a thousand times on the journey. Any self-appointed moralist, English or not, would want to kill me just to bask in your thankful smile."

"Oh, Connor, don't be so absurd."

"No. I'll not hear another word about it. You are not accompanying me to court, no matter how you plead with me. Neither is Hugh."

"That's final?" asked Regan, her eyes atwinkle as she envisioned the nonverbal persuasion she might employ.

"Absolutely final," confirmed the Earl of Kilcaid. "Now then, let's get some rest since I want to be off at dawn's first light."

It was no matter they had been on dry land for days, Regan still felt the unsettling sway of the ship as she lay in her bed, until she reached out for the solid comfort of Connor beside her. Though she had longed for the excitement of London but a few months before, Regan experienced no joy in it at present. The darkness of the house leased to Walter Ashcroft summoned none of the magic and flights of fancy that had surrounded her at Heaven's Gate.

The noisy, overcrowded city was not the unspoiled habitat of fairies and other spirits. In fact, though they had never bothered her before, Regan found the heat and odors of London oppressive when she recalled the sweet coolness of her Irish bedchamber. Yet she was able to overlook these aspects of the great city and concentrate instead on her joy in having accompanied her beloved.

She heaved a small sigh as she listened to Connor's even breathing and wondered at the man's nerves that he should be able to snatch a bit of sleep on tonight of all nights.

In the morning, they would dress for an audience with Elizabeth. Though Ashcroft had informed them that their chances for forgiveness and permission to marry were not out of the question, neither were they a certainty. In fact, when the kindly Englishman had thought Regan out of earshot, he had cautioned Connor to have a care, and to keep Regan from the audience altogether.

Connor had broached the topic after Ashcroft's departure last night, but Regan had steadfastly refused to remain in hiding while he went to face the possible displeasure of the English monarch alone. Cajoling, pleading and an abundance of sweet words and promises had persuaded the dark-haired Irish rebel to compromise. He agreed to her presence at court only after he had extracted Regan's word that she would cry out and denounce him, charging him with abduction and coercion should the audience suddenly go awry.

And though Regan had readily agreed, she knew then as she knew now that she could never betray the man she loved in such a fashion. If Elizabeth denied them permission to marry, she would leave Heaven's Gate behind and live the wandering life with her Irish earl. And should the queen order his imprisonment, Regan was prepared to throw herself down in supplication, offering to exchange her freedom for his.

Disquieted by the recognition of the dangers tomorrow held, Regan sought the solace of Connor's warmth, moving herself even closer, though careful not to disturb his peace.

Softly she laid her head against his strong shoulder and fitted her body to his. Yet this nearness did little to bring her comfort and stave off her restlessness. Instead, it only increased her awareness of how very much she had to lose.

Tonight Connor had made love to her but once. His kisses were tender and unhurried, as though they were back in Ireland with no chance of tomorrow seeing them separated forever.

Though this restraint had been an act of love on his part, an assurance that they had many such nights ahead of them and need not fear the future, it was not enough to content the young countess should it indeed have been their last time together.

At the moment she hungered for him with a fierceness meant to halt the arrival of the dawn. She wanted them to transport each other to a private world where monarchs and time did not exist, a place where they could remain forever, spellbound in each other's arms. But she was not a witch, and she knew no enchantments other than the ones her body cast over her handsome lover. Should she fail in her quest, should sunrise actually occur, Regan wanted to love Connor in a way that would bind them together for all eternity, no matter what Elizabeth's decision might be.

Tentatively she reached out and ran her fingertips softly along Connor's jawline, traveling up his strong, chiseled chin and then across those lips of his that gave her so much pleasure. It was as though she were trying to absorb his features with her touch so that he would be hers forever. So that she could always carry him within her heart.

Lifting her hand from her beloved's face, the young noblewoman suddenly felt his fingers wrap around her wrist. At that moment Regan realized that he hadn't been sleeping at all, merely lying still so as not to disturb whatever rest she might find during the course of this torturous night.

"Why do you stop, Regan?" he asked, his deep, melodic voice husky with desire. "Are you seeking to please me or only tease?"

"I was but shifting the focus of my attention, milord," Regan murmured, placing her lips against the muscular cords of his neck while she moved her hand to rest atop his impressive chest. Then, palm down, fingers splayed, she began broad, sweeping motions of her hand, paying homage to each small, tight nipple and then roving down across his taut belly to play at the fringes of the triangle surrounding his manhood.

"Oh, woman," he groaned. "I've been lying here mad with desire for wanting you."

"Why didn't you tell me?" she asked softly in the stillness of the room.

"Because my need to possess you is so fierce that I feared I'd frighten you with the intensity of my lovemaking," Connor whispered urgently, turning to face her and placing his hands along the sides of her cheeks tilting her head to his. It was a wordless gesture of supplication, as though he were asking her permission to unleash his passions.

"Then show me, Connor, show me how much you want me," Regan implored.

"Aye, so be it. No matter what happens tomorrow, at least we will have had tonight."

Then Connor's mouth descended forcefully upon Regan's, demanding rather than urging her response. His broad hands swept across her breasts, kneading them with a fiery touch that bespoke insistent proprietorship.

While his tongue plunged greedily into her mouth, engaging her in a frenzied contest of parry and thrust, Connor's hand came up to brush through Regan's hair, spread in a radiant sunburst on the pillow beneath her head. Wrapping the long blond tendrils around his wrist, he bound himself to her as his fingers closed possessively around her chin, moving it upward to give the ardent earl access to deeper penetration of his woman's mouth.

Then, disentangling himself, he blazed a path of searing kisses down Regan's slender neck, and while she moaned and thrashed about, set afire by his passion, he moved ever lower until his searching mouth captured a straining nipple. Suckling vigorously at one rosy peak, he lovingly trapped the other between his rolling thumb and forefinger.

A whimpering Regan pleaded for release as she dug her fingers into Connor's flesh. Yet as much as she begged him, and cried out, she nonetheless arched her back, straining toward him, offering her loveliness for more of his merciless, sweet torture.

In their fervor, the two were like spirits possessed, and when Connor's other hand found the sweet core of her womanhood, Regan's moans became louder, and her entreaties for deliverance more incessant.

"Now, my love, now," she finally cried, the words catching in her throat as passion took her more tightly in its grasp.

"Aye, sweet Regan . . . now!" Connor ground out the words even as he thrust deeply within the woman who met his feverish lovemaking with desires as strong as his own.

Repeatedly he moved within her, his hands beneath her buttocks, raising her hips to increase the depth of their pleasure. But Regan rose to meet him with a strength and urgency that dared Connor to drive himself harder and to find new limits to his endurance.

In his wish to please her, to mark her as his, Connor was equal to the challenge Regan issued. He became the proud demon lover of myth, and his whispered words of love the incantation that would see them safe. Still, their uncertainty about everything but each other was the compulsion that spurred them onward, frantically pursuing a moment of loving so peerless that it would live in their hearts for the rest of their lives.

When the pinnacle of ecstasy came, it arrived simultaneously, crashing over Regan and Connor like powerful waves that crest and wash over a shoreline; the urgency of the mighty sensation enveloped them completely and claimed them as its own.

Regan's cry of pleasure was compatible with Connor's bellow of release, and even the music of the spheres revered by the ancients was not as mystic or harmonious.

Later, as she lay snug in Connor's possessive arms, Regan was aglow, thinking no woman had ever been so cherished, so well loved. She was content to listen to the rapid beating of her lover's heart, the evidence of his devotion.

The renegade Irish earl was sated, as well. Loving Regan so lustily had transformed him into a gentled soul who luxuriated in his beloved's softness as she molded her curves to his own hardened body.

Whatever the future granted them, nothing could erase the memory of this encounter, and they spent their remaining hours alone together, engaging in tender caresses and gentle talk.

Though Regan had not been able to hold back the sunrise, she almost thought that daylight was a small price to pay for the glories she had shared with her darkling lord under the blackness of night. The first rays of dawn, when they appeared, did not terrorize her as she had feared they would. Though still unsure of her monarch's reaction to

their petition of marriage, Regan was confident enough to
think that the love she shared with her Irish outlaw would
help them to overcome any obstructions to their happiness.

'Tis not a logical emotion, Regan told herself as she and
Connor rose from their bed. Still her euphoria remained,
and she was able to enjoy the roguish teasing to which the
Irish nobleman subjected her as they laid out the garments
they would wear when they appeared before the queen.

Since it was imperative their whereabouts remain a secret
until they arrived at court, they had complied with Ashcroft's suggestion, and made do without servants, keeping
house for each other and dividing chores as best they could.
Regan's attempts at cooking had been a source of merriment between them. Her first joint of lamb had been placed
on a spit too near the flame, and when she declared it done,
its unseasoned, charred exterior was at odds with the red
flesh found within. As much as he loved her, not even Connor could pretend that first meal was palatable, and it was
he, made self-sufficient by military campaigns and his
months of exile from his home, who then took charge of the
kitchen and provided them with nourishment.

Therefore, it was he, on that morning, who poured two
goblets of wine, cut two hunks of bread and wedges of
cheese to place before his lady. Though Regan would have
sworn she had no appetite, Connor's solicitous behavior
helped her nibble at her breakfast, his roguish wit making
the meal almost enjoyable.

But the ominous appointment awaiting them could not be
ignored indefinitely. Soon it was time to don the rich, fashionable garments Ashcroft had provided and prepare
themselves for their meeting with the Tudor queen. As they
had done for the past week, Regan served as Connor's valet
and he as her maid. The young Countess of Westfield and
Kilcaid was comfortable performing small services for her
Celtic lord, and in receiving his ministrations in return. She
had discovered she needed no riches or servants to find
contentment in a life with Connor.

As she straightened Connor's midnight-blue doublet, its dark material slashed with white, and handed him his hose, Regan wished that they had been born the offspring of simple plowmen. Had they no lands or wealth, they would have been too insignificant to garner Elizabeth's attention or to attract her wrath. But such would have meant their paths would never have crossed, she sighed, while the Earl of Kilcaid helped her into her amber kirtle and heavy dark green gown. It was best, she told herself, that she face reality and all of its attending dangers. Otherwise, she would be more hindrance than help to Connor when they stood before the court.

This was the thought in Regan's mind when Connor brushed her cheeks with his lips before he left the room to retrieve his sword. Determined to follow his example and be prepared for any eventuality, Regan picked up the dagger she had taken with her during the flight from Heaven's Gate. Intent upon sliding it into her garter, she had just hitched up her voluminous skirts, cursing the ungainliness of her farthingale all the while, when a thunderous banging on the outer door of the small house set her heart to racing.

No one but the kindly Walter Ashcroft knew their whereabouts. Or at least that was what Regan had supposed. But the royal court had its spies everywhere, and this ominous thumping on the door almost took it off its hinges. It sounded more like a battering ram than the work of a man. Had Elizabeth decided there was to be no audience after all, and sent her men to arrest them? Good God, Connor was the one with the price on his head! She had to get him out of here now, before the soldiers could take him!

"Connor! I think 'tis her majesty's forces outside. I'll see to them while you escape by the window. Hurry, my love, hurry!" Regan called desperately, her voice all but drowned out by the loud, continuous banging.

Dropping her skirts, the pretty English maiden realized she still held the dagger. Hiding the hand grasping the weapon behind her back, she quickly advanced toward the door, resolving to put an end to this disturbance one way or the other before it roused the entire neighborhood and thus made Connor's escape impossible.

"Peace, pray you," she said as she began to undo the latch. "'Twill be but a moment more."

"Regan! Stay away from there! I'll see to this," she heard Connor bark as he hurried into the room, his sword at the ready.

"Get out! Get out while you can," she pleaded, even as the door began to open, and she brought the dagger to her side. "I'll be able to engage them for a moment or two. Hurry!"

Before Connor could reach her, the thin oak door crashed against an inner wall, and Regan sprang forward, wielding her blade with a desperate will to save the life of the man she loved. Raising her dagger to strike, she found her arm stayed by a powerful grasp and heard a booming, familiar laugh.

"What's this then, Connor? Have you forgotten to fight as I taught you? Or perhaps you think the wench affords you more protection than I would have done?" asked the intruder, his large frame filling the doorway as he easily claimed her weapon and moved Regan out of the way so that he could stride into the center of the small room.

"Hugh! What are you doing here?" Connor asked, his voice a mixture of relief and annoyance.

"I told you I wouldn't allow you to go to London and face this without me by your side," Hugh replied with a smug smile, embracing the young lord roughly by the way of greeting, "though it took me a bit longer to reach you than I expected."

"And I told you to stay put in Geata Neamhai and see to the welfare of our people," Connor answered, hard-pressed to conceal his pleasure at seeing his friend once more.

"Sheila and the Englishman are keeping things as they should be. Now when are we to see Bess?"

"You're not seeing Bess at all, you churl," Connor said sternly, though a smile threatened to take control of his mouth.

"What?" Hugh questioned in obvious disappointment. "I thought once I arrived in London, you would see there was nothing to do, save accept my company."

"That is not the case," Connor stated, remaining firm in his decision.

"You young scoundrel, you're proving more obstinate than usual. We've always shared each other's fights, Connor. Has your taking this woman really changed all that?"

"Hugh Cassidy, you are still my closest friend, and the only man I would have at my back in the midst of battle," Connor said gently, to the amazement of an angry and still-shaken Regan. "But this is one fight I must undertake alone."

"Regan is with you," Hugh protested. "I should be as well. You might need the protection."

"Regan will give me all that I need," Connor teased, his melodic laugh filling the room even as he fixed his love with a reproving eye for what he considered her recent foolish behavior. "She was ready to knife you, wasn't she?"

"Aye, I have to admit the lass has more spunk than I gave her credit for," Hugh responded with a reluctant chuckle, realizing that the girl had been willing to give her life for the Earl of Kilcaid. "But in all seriousness, Connor, it is not meet that the O'Carroll stand before the English queen without his chief at arms by his side."

"Nor is it proper that my second in command tarry here when our kinsmen are without leadership in our own land. As much as I applaud your gesture of loyalty, Hugh, I must order you back to Geata Neamhaí immediately," Connor said, thankful that Regan had stayed out of the fray and allowed him to deal with his old mentor as he saw fit. "But before you go, we'll have a quick cup together, and you can tell me how you came to London and how you managed to find me."

"Finding you was the easy part, milord," Hugh replied, holding out his huge hand to take the goblet of wine Regan poured him, and nodding his thanks. "Ashcroft was the name you had given of the man who would help you. Once I contacted him, he took a bit of persuading, but soon enough I knew exactly where you were."

"And how did you manage to get from Ireland to England?" Connor asked, knowing even as he did so that he might not like the answer.

"I had some coin of my own."

"But not enough," Connor pressed, perceiving evasion in the other man's explanation.

"Well, there was the small matter of selling a tankard of gold," Hugh boasted, clearly proud of his ingenuity.

"Not my tankard!" Connor moaned. "Hugh, how could you do such a thing?"

"'Twas an easy task, there were several would-be buyers, but I haggled as much as time allowed and got a decent price."

"How much?" Connor asked morosely.

"Fifty sovereigns."

"Fifty! It was worth at least two hundred and fifty!"

"Well, I said I haggled as much as time allowed, and time didn't allow all that much," Hugh responded with a loud guffaw, his conscience clear as he recalled the silver brooch Connor had confiscated from him to give the Lady Regan.

Though she had been furious as a result of the fright she had experienced due to Hugh's sudden, boisterous appearance, Regan couldn't help but laugh at the behemoth's crowing admission. The delicate timbre of her amusement sounded all the more feminine as it burst forth in this decidedly masculine atmosphere, and earned her a grudging glimmer of approval from the rough, rugged giant who was Connor's closest ally.

As the two men renewed their camaraderie during the ritual of draining their cups, Regan thoughtfully studied

Hugh Cassidy, and sympathy for the fellow plucked at her tender heart.

His journey to London was not so much blatant disobedience as it was an act of unconstrained affection, a desperate venture to safeguard the Earl of Kilcaid from harm, and Regan was grateful her Irish earl had such a staunch supporter.

Witnessing the special bond the man shared with Connor, Regan could comprehend Hugh's anger with her. The mighty warrior apparently felt a keen sense of loss that his longtime friend, drinking companion and comrade in arms had formed attachments that did not include him. Apparently Hugh feared his days of shared adventure with Connor had come to a close. And as the older man saw it, the fault lay with Regan Davies.

But with newly gained wisdom, Regan understood that each of them loved Connor in a way the other never could, and that Connor O'Carroll had room in his heart for the both of them. Having reached such a conclusion, the pretty countess knew that she could accept Cassidy's friendship with her Celtic nobleman, and she truly hoped that one day Hugh could resign himself to her relationship with the Earl of Kilcaid, as well.

Right now, however, the time was fast approaching to send the hulking Celt on his way and to depart for court. She listened as Hugh once again insistently demanded his right to stand by Connor's side before the queen, and heard Connor's just-as-adamant refusal as he entrusted Hugh with the responsibility for all that was his during the earl's absence from his homeland.

"Now remember, I am depending upon you, Hugh Cassidy," the nobleman placated as he ushered his muscular second in command to the door, pressing a well-filled purse into his hands. "There is no other man to whom I could delegate such a duty."

"You can rely on me, Connor," Hugh replied as he tightly clasped the earl's forearm to his own.

"Aye, man, I always have," Connor said by way of thanks and farewell.

"Godspeed, Hugh Cassidy," Regan said softly as she came forward to join Connor.

With a curt nod, the huge Irishman acknowledged her good wishes, and then with an outwardly gruff goodbye to the man he had seen sprout from boyhood, Hugh was gone, the small house suddenly all the emptier for his leaving.

Regan's heart was aflutter as she stepped from the barge, despite the reassuring pressure of Connor's strong hand at her elbow. The trip along the Thames had concluded all too quickly, and as Connor escorted her up the steps leading from the sluggish river, she knew the moment of reckoning was drawing nigh.

Unsettled though she was, Regan couldn't help but be proud of the handsome figure her lover made as he walked beside her. His dark blue doublet and the white hose that matched the material beneath the slashing of his garments emphasized his dark good looks. Surely no woman would deny him anything, not even the ruler of England, Regan prayed.

As for herself, the beauteous blonde wondered at her own audacity. She had lost a contest of wills to Elizabeth when the monarch had sent her to Ireland. What made her think she would be any more successful in this instance? But a glance at the rugged profile beside her pushed aside Regan's trepidation and fired her with new determination. When Connor slipped his hand around hers, Regan realized that no matter what the odds, she had to triumph today. Too much depended upon it for the occasion to turn out otherwise.

Reaching the palace, the Irish earl and his lady were readily admitted and shown to a room where a score of other petitioners also waited. Regan hoped, when she noted the number of supplicants crowding the room, that it would be a while before she and Connor were summoned to the royal

presence. No sooner had the thought formed in her mind
however, than a richly garbed courtier perfunctorily ges
tured them forward and escorted them down the long
echoing corridors to the throne room.

Doors opened before them and the pair walked onward
passing along the path suddenly made for them through the
throng of brightly dressed nobles attending the queen.

Knees fairly shaking, Regan was aware of the curious
speculating whispers which arose as she and Connor passed
Inspired by her lover and his apparent indifference to the
danger in which they had placed themselves, Regan deter
mined to hide her own nervousness behind a mask of brav
ery and confidence.

Approaching the throne, Regan noticed that Elizabeth
was dressed even more opulently than usual. Her embroi
dered gown of gold cloth was set over the widest French
farthingale the young countess had ever seen. The tight, low
bodice was draped with numerous strands of pearls and
emeralds, and an abundance of matching gems were sewed
all over the voluminous skirt. Against the backdrop of an
elaborate, high fan-shaped collar, Elizabeth's face ap
peared very stern indeed, despite the feminine pearl ear
rings dangling from her lobes and her intricately curled red
wig. In all, she had dressed elaborately to remind them who
was monarch here, and Regan feared this boded them ill.

She was glad that the crafty Ashcroft had obtained a
much simpler gown for her own use. He had explained that
perhaps the plainness of her subject's attire would appease
Henry's daughter somewhat, causing Elizabeth to conve
niently overlook the fact that had the lovely Regan been
dressed in beggar's rags, she would still present an enticing
portrait of beauty and youth, two things all of Elizabeth's
wealth could not purchase for her.

"Ah ... the Countess of Kilcaid and the former earl. We
had not expected to see you so soon," Elizabeth said, acid
ly addressing Regan before she turned her attention to

Connor. "And, you, sir, we thought never to see again at all."

"Then, majesty, I must count myself among the most fortunate of men to once again be in your gracious presence," the Irishman replied, amusement lighting his deep blue eyes before he bowed his head and executed a courtly bow even while Regan curtsied deeply.

"Have you come to surrender?" the queen asked, not at all beguiled by his engaging manner.

"Only my pride," Connor said with a flirtatious laugh. "There is not much else left to me."

"There is your life," Elizabeth drawled as Regan visibly paled.

"That, along with every beat of my heart, every part of my being, is already dedicated to your service, most merciful queen. Surely you know how desperately I long to serve you," Connor stated boldly, flirting shamelessly with the head of state. The tone of his voice was impudently seductive, the implications it carried bordering on treason, and Regan feared that perhaps the Irish nobleman had gone too far. Regaling her with extravagant compliments was a far different matter than being so familiar with their sovereign.

"You always were an impertinent rascal, Connor O'Carroll," the queen commented as a small smile tugged at her mouth despite herself.

"But always entertaining, as well, I hope," Connor replied, exuding such charm that Elizabeth's icy demeanor disappeared altogether, and Regan's shallow breaths became less rapid until Elizabeth's attention fell upon her with full force.

"What is Mistress Davies doing here?" the ruler of England asked archly. "I understand you are worth more now than ever, O'Carroll," she continued, referring to the price on his head but her innuendo quite evident all the same. "Has she captured you and brought you before me to claim her reward?"

"In a manner of speaking," Connor replied easily. "Since I could never aspire to win the affection of the most beautiful woman in England, Lady Regan has managed to capture my heart. 'Tis a poor second best to be sure, but what else can an Irishman hope to obtain?"

"What else, indeed, you rascal?" Elizabeth asked dryly. "Tell me, is not the Lady Regan merely a means to an end? Isn't it your former lands you would like to make your own?"

Connor managed to blush as though he had been discovered in his plans, his deception flattering the monarch's opinion of her own shrewdness.

"You men are all the same," the queen pronounced with a chortle.

"By your leave, glorious queen, I am quite different from my fellows," Connor said, his voice full of audacious promise.

"That remains to be seen," the queen fairly chuckled before she turned to Regan, and her good humor dissipated as she remembered the turmoil the comely girl had cost her.

"What say you, Regan Davies? Why do you return to my court and seek permission to ally yourself to an enemy of the Crown...no matter how handsome he might be?" the older Englishwoman asked, looking pointedly at Dudley, who appeared to be concentrating on the pinking decorating his doublet.

Though she was annoyed to notice her provocative comments to Connor had roused no jealousy from Leicester, Elizabeth calmed herself with the observation that neither had Regan's presence moved him.

"Well, girl," the queen commanded, "I ask you again. How can you stand here and ask to marry a common outlaw?"

"'Tis not what I seek, your majesty," Regan replied, finding the strength to answer loudly and clearly so that all might hear. "I am requesting a pardon for this man so tha can ask your permission to wed a loyal subject of England."

"Why do you want such a thing?" Elizabeth asked when the shocked murmurs of the court had died down.

"Undoubtedly your wisdom allows you to see I act in simple obedience to your majesty's dictates that I settle Heaven's Gate to your satisfaction. Wedding this man will assure the cooperation of his people."

"You are willing to make such a sacrifice, to enter a loveless match, in order to please me?" the queen asked cunningly, her eye still upon Dudley, who, ignoring the matter at hand, had turned to engage the man next to him in quiet conversation.

"I am willing to do anything that pleases you, most gracious sovereign."

"Such loyalty should be rewarded," Elizabeth replied coldly, "without making you suffer punishment for my sake. I could show my gratitude in another fashion... perhaps betrothing you to an Englishman...my cousin Thomas Watkins comes to mind, as he petitioned me in the matter weeks ago. Furthermore, keeping O'Carroll at court with me would prohibit him from disturbing the peace and bliss your marriage will afford you."

Regan felt like swooning, sure that Connor had acted his part too well and that their cause had been lost, until she heard a masculine voice intervene.

"Your majesty, why reward this Irish renegade for his crimes by allowing him the pleasure of remaining in your presence? Send him back to his own wretched land."

"And the Lady Regan?" the queen asked her favorite courtier icily, waiting to catch him glancing in the young woman's direction. Though she was flattered by his obvious reluctance to have Connor O'Carroll as his competitor, the Earl of Leicester had yet to mention that troublesome wench.

"Bless their union and send the girl back, as well. An allegiance between the two would quell the attempts of

O'Carroll's people to reclaim his ancestral seat from th
Countess of Westfield. And, by keeping the lands in th
lady's name, we assure ourselves of another Englis
stronghold in Ireland," the courtier urged.

"Think you this is in our best interests, Robin?" th
queen asked softly, using his pet name, elated at the jealou
urgency tinging Dudley's voice and his unconcern that Re
gan would be wed to another and gone from court, unlikel
to return again.

"Aye, Bess, I do. Though they can be useful to you, thes
persons are but two of a kind. They've each broken fealt
with their people and their lands by seeking marriage to a
enemy, no matter what intentions they declare. They de
serve each other and they deserve Ireland, as well," th
courtier concluded hotly.

"As you feel so strongly about it," the queen said de
murely, "I shall take your advice. O'Carroll is pardoned an
the marriage will take place as soon as possible. But I fear
grow weary of this matter. Come, Robin, attend me."

Then she gave him her hand and allowed him the priv
lege of escorting her from the room, too caught up in he
own victory to see the conspiratorial wink Dudley sent i
Regan's direction.

Epilogue

It was hard to remember a time when this keep hadn't been at peace, Hugh Cassidy thought as he settled into his usual spot near the hearth, the place granted him so graciously by Regan on the very day she had returned as Connor's bride.

In the little more than the year and a half since the loving couple had arrived home from England, Geata Neamhai had prospered. Though the relationship between the Irish tenants and their English counterparts was delicately balanced at best, each group was too contented with their full bellies and their snug homes to quarrel with the other.

These were days of great happiness, Hugh concluded appreciatively, tending to the bundle he'd propped against his massive chest. The lord and lady of Geata Neamhai were more than content with their lot in life, and so were those who served them.

Hugh, himself, had been included in their household as an honored member. In this role, he had even been there to reassure Connor and then experience his joy when Regan had taken to her bed and been delivered of her first child. Though Hugh now shared less drinking with the Earl of Kilcaid, and no wenching at all, the large Irishman had a new purpose: he would be mentor to the infant as he had been to the father.

"Ah, there you be, Hugh Cassidy," Sheila clucked as she entered the Great Hall with Gerard at her side. Since wed-

ding her Englishman, the woman's tongue had been much
less sharp, but still Hugh didn't relish the scolding he knew
would be forthcoming.

"Must you constantly carry the babe around, never allowing the sweet lamb a moment of peace?" the castelain
asked reprovingly. "The wee tyke must have the O'Carroll
fairy blood for you to be enchanted so!"

"I'm under no charm at all. Simply put, I've much to
teach the child, and it's best to start in infancy," Hugh replied indignantly as he pulled back the coverlets and
chucked the gurgling baby under the chin. "Isn't that right,
little one? How will you learn about soldiering, fighting, the
proper handling of weapons and the ways of the hunt if
Hugh doesn't teach you?"

"But, you stubborn man, when will you get it through
your thick head that the child is a lass?" Sheila asked with
an exasperated sigh that bespoke of having had this argument several times before. "Deirdre has no need to learn any
of those things. She should be taught embroidery, and music, and other womanly skills instead. Isn't that right, Gerard?"

"Yes, of course," the Englishman replied, feeling the
safest course was to agree with his wife.

"If she grows up to be as feisty and self-willed as her
mother, it's almost certain the lass will make use of every bit
of what I teach her," Hugh retorted with a booming laugh,
which delighted his small charge.

"That had best be meant as a compliment," Regan
threatened with a smile, coming into the hall on Connor's
arm, her heart warmed by the domestic scene before her.

"As if it would be anything else, milady!" Hugh proclaimed. "I always told the O'Carroll you were the woman
he should wed, didn't I, Connor?" As close as he and Regan had become this past year, the large Irishman refused to
remember a time when he had not felt kindly toward the
gracious blond noblewoman adored by everyone within the
keep.

"Aye, I believe you did," Connor agreed, his vibrant blue eyes catching Regan's to share silent laughter. "But what are you up to now, you scoundrel? The way you dote on that child, you'll have her spoiled shortly."

"Deirdre's too good a babe to become spoiled," Hugh said in defense of the squirming bundle held in his huge arms. "Actually, I was about to take her up to the battlements and explain their significance to her."

"Saints preserve us!" Sheila protested, throwing up her hands in despair.

"Deirdre is too young to know a parapet from a battlement," Connor said in amusement.

"Aye, that's why I must teach her."

"I'm afraid you're spending such a great deal of time with this babe, that you'll be much too busy to tend to another one," Regan said all too casually. "Perhaps I shall have to entrust that one to Gerard."

The implication of what he had just heard was lost on the silver-haired Englishman, whose only reaction to Regan's words was that he had enough to do tending to Sheila without having an infant thrust on him, as well. Hugh, however, was more astute.

"What one?" he asked suspiciously.

"The one which will arrive in the spring," Connor declared, sharing his happiness with the announcement that a new child was expected.

"As if I couldn't tend to two babes," Hugh growled, much to Gerard's relief. "Together, they'll be not half as much trouble as you were, milord Kilcaid."

"Oh, congratulations, milady," Sheila enthused, her face aglow. "I'd noticed your waning appetite and I'd been hoping— I even mentioned to my Gerard, didn't I?" she asked, turning to obtain her husband's affirmation.

"Aye, that she did. But I told her it was only to be expected, what with the amount of time you and his lordship spend—" and then Gerard suddenly stopped, completely flustered as he noticed Regan's crimson cheeks and realized what he had been saying. "Surely, Regan, you realize there are no secrets here," he said, making a bad situation worse as he tried to extricate himself from such an awkward slip of the tongue.

"No, nor should there be," Connor said, coming to the embarrassed soldier's rescue. "I'd be a fool not to avail myself of so lovely a wife whenever she is willing."

"And from the looks of it, she be willing often," Sheila muttered to her husband as she prodded him toward the door and motioned to Hugh to follow so the young ones could be alone. She recognized the signs of desire when she saw them smoldering.

"Perhaps the next child will be a son," Gerard called from the doorway, in an attempt to make Regan forget his recent faux pas.

"A boy like his father or a girl like her mother, what difference does it make? It's all the same to me," Hugh declared loudly, hoping such a sentiment would earn him an even higher place in Regan's affections.

Regan shook her head fondly as she watched her peculiar household depart, Sheila shooing the men away quickly. Laughing, the mistress of the keep turned to her handsome, indulgent husband.

"Things proceed well at Geata Neamhai," Regan said, the Celtic words slipping easily from her tongue after many months of practice. Following their marriage, she had decided that if the lands were to remain with her, the name of the estate should be Connor's. She had given him that as a wedding gift . . . along with a new inkstand.

"Aye, they proceed well indeed, wife," Connor replied, his voice fast becoming hoarse with yearning and his dark blue eyes aflame with desire as he beheld the beautiful woman who carried his second child.

He opened his arms, and Regan came to him, glowing with rapture as he enfolded her in his strong embrace.

Connor bent his dark head to her pale one and murmured tenderly in Regan's ear. "When I hold you, and feel your heart beat beneath mine, I think the bond between us is heaven-sent, though Sheila swears 'tis a gift bestowed by the fairy folk.''

''Mayhap the magic originates in our own hearts, dearest husband,'' Regan responded, tilting her face toward him and enticing Connor to cover her mouth with his own. Then they shared a kiss so rich in love that both were certain what they experienced was truly a glimpse of paradise.

* * * * *

✦ Harlequin®

JANELLE TAYLOR

Valley of Fire

HARLEQUIN IS PROUD TO PRESENT *VALLEY OF FIRE* BY JANELLE TAYLOR—AUTHOR OF TWENTY-TWO BOOKS, INCLUDING SIX *NEW YORK TIMES* BESTSELLERS

VALLEY OF FIRE—the warm and passionate story of Kathy Alexander, a famous romance author, and Steven Winngate, entrepreneur and owner of the magazine that intended to expose the real Kathy "Brandy" Alexander to her fans.

Don't miss VALLEY OF FIRE, available in May.

COMING NEXT MONTH

#127 THE LADY AND THE LAIRD—Maura Seger
Forced by her grandfather's will to live in an eerie Scottish castle
for six months or lose the crumbling keep to rogue Angus Wyndham,
beautiful Katlin Sinclair discovered a tormented ghost, hidden
treasure and burning passion in the arms of the one man she could
not trust.

#128 SWEET SUSPICIONS—Julie Tetel
Intent on reentering society, Richard Worth planned to find a well-
connected wife. But he hadn't expected the murder of a stranger to revive
his scandalous past—or that his marriage of convenience to
lovely Caroline Hutton would awaken his passion and heal his
anguished soul.

#129 THE CLAIM—Lucy Elliot
A confrontation was inevitable when determined Sarah Meade and
formidable mountain man Zeke Brownell both claimed ownership of
the same land. Yet underneath their stubborn facades and cultural
differences there lay a mutual attraction neither could deny.

#130 PIRATE BRIDE—Elizabeth August
Pirate captive Kathleen James impetuously married prisoner
John Ashford to save him from certain death. But although
freedom and happiness were only a breath away, a daring escape
brought them further danger in the New World.

AVAILABLE NOW:

#123 ROGUE'S HONOR
DeLoras Scott

#124 HEAVEN'S GATE
Erin Yorke

#125 KING OF SWORDS
Lindsay McKenna

#126 THE PRISONER
Cheryl Reavis

BIG SUMMER READ

Summer Reading At Its Best

BSR